# A Different Hunger

## Lila Richards

Millwheel Press

ISBN – 978-0-473-50208-9 – softcover
978-0-473-50209-6 – Epub
978-0-473-50210-2 - mobi

In Victorian London, when an ill-advised love affair sees young Rufus de Hunte challenged to an illegal duel, his father, to avoid the scandal this would bring, banishes him to New Zealand to become a remittance man. During the voyage Rufus meets the captivating Serafina Radzinska, travelling with Anton Springer, who may or may not be her father. Despite his uncertainty, Rufus finds himself falling in love with her - even after he discovers both she and Springer are vampires. When Rufus is badly beaten by the vicious Toby Fox, and seems certain to die, Serafina, who returns his love and fears losing him, turns him into a vampire. Rufus's horror and resentment threaten their love, but when they reach New Zealand and Serafina is captured by Viviana Alexandreu, an ancient and powerful vampire seeking revenge on Springer, Rufus must acknowledge his true feelings and find a way to rescue her and to end Viviana's insane vendetta once and for all.

## DEDICATION

With special thanks to Roy for his help with editing, his invaluable comments, his humour, and, above all, for his continued faith in me and my creations.

# CHAPTER ONE

A dank fog swirled through the London streets, dimming the glare of the gaslights to a sickly glimmer, lending an air of menace to the classical grandeur of Covent Garden Market. But the Honourable Rufus de Hunte was oblivious to such intimations of foreboding. Thrusting his hands deeper into the pockets of his greatcoat, he hurried past the market's Grecian columns and the soaring glass roofs that seemed to cower behind the eddying murk. All that mattered to Rufus was reaching the lodging house at 42B Garrick Street where his beloved Charlotte would be waiting for him. For the first time since they had met (was it only three months ago?) she had invited him to visit her at night. His heart was beating so hard he could scarcely breathe, thinking of what might ensue.

Reaching Charlotte's lodgings, he raced up the stairs to the first floor, knocked on the door of her apartment, and entered without waiting for her to let him in. Whenever she was expecting him she left the door unlatched.

A puzzled frown creased his brow. The sitting room was in near darkness, the only light coming from the coals glowing in the fireplace. He could just make out Charlotte's form in the gloom. She sat by the window in a low chair, hunched over and rocking back and forth. Rufus called her name softly. He felt a prickle of unease when she failed to look up.

Moving closer, he peered into the shadows and saw she had her hands covering her face, and she was shivering although the room was quite warm. He hurried to her side and bent over her.

"Charlotte, dearest, what is it? What's wrong?"

When at last she raised her head a little, he saw that her eyes were red and swollen with weeping. He took her hands in his and uncovered her face. Even in the half-light, he could see her face was badly bruised, with dried blood congealed around a split in her lip, and more bruises on her arms. Shocked, he put his arm around her shoulder and drew her to him, stroking her hair gently.

"Charlotte, who did this to you?"

She shook her head, but said nothing.

"Only tell me who did this, darling, and I'll see that he's punished. And I'll take you somewhere safe so he can't hurt you again..."

"No!" Her voice was barely audible, and thickened by her cut and swollen mouth, but he could hear the urgency in it. "Rufus, you must leave. I'll be all right. Please, just go."

"I can't leave you like this. Let me take you to a doctor, at least."

She looked up at him with fearful, pleading eyes, and shook her head once more. "No! Please, just go, I beg you."

"But..."

"You heard the lady," came a harsh voice from across the room. "Why don't you just do as she says?"

Rufus looked up, startled, to see a black-haired man of perhaps forty years glowering at him from the bedroom doorway. His well-fitted clothes looked expensive, but his powerful build and large hands suggested a man more used to physical pursuits than theatres and *soirees*. Rufus got to his feet and faced the angry man.

"And who might you be?" he demanded, unconsciously assuming the haughty voice his father used to repress impertinence.

"I'm her husband, that's who. Joseph Winter – Mr Winter to the likes of you, *if* you don't mind. The question *I* want answered is who the devil are you? When a man goes away on business, he doesn't expect to return to find himself supplanted in his own home by—" Winter cast a scornful glance at Rufus, "—some young whippersnapper still wet behind the ears."

For a long moment, Rufus could do nothing but stare at him in disbelief. Then, his heart suddenly hammering in his breast, he turned to Charlotte. Before he could speak, she looked up at him, tears now trickling down her cheeks, the bruises livid on her ashen face.

"I'm sorry, Rufus," she whispered. "I'm so sorry."

"You see?" Her husband's voice exuded a savage satisfaction. "And don't go thinking you're the first, because you aren't, not by a long chalk."

Rufus forced himself to speak with what calm he could muster. "Is this true, Charlotte?" His voice sounded strange and disembodied.

Charlotte, cowering in her chair, whispered, "Yes. I'm sorry, Rufus, truly I am. I didn't mean to... I only wanted..."

But Rufus had already turned away from her to face her husband.

"Please accept my deepest apologies, sir." His voice was stiff with pain and embarrassment. "I had no idea, or I should never have..."

"Hah! You're not the first to say that, either."

"But—" Rufus found himself saying, "—to beat her like that? Surely..."

"A man's entitled to take measures to keep his wife in line – entitled to it by law. I should have done it long ago. Maybe then she wouldn't have taken to bestowing her favours on the likes of you the moment my back's turned." Scowling, Winter took a step forward, his beefy fists clenching and unclenching at his sides.

Rufus felt the cold stab of fear, and a shard of anger pierced his heart at the thought of Charlotte's deception. How could she betray his love with such callousness? How dared she use him so? His first instinct was to leave. Let the two of them deal with the situation between them. But in the same instant, he knew he could not just leave her to bear the brunt of her husband's fury. God alone knew what the brute might do to her, and she didn't deserve that, no matter how she had treated him.

"I'm truly sorry for what's happened," he said, "and I would never have entered the relationship had I known. But I cannot allow you to ill-treat a lady." He turned to Charlotte and took her by the arm. "Come, Charlotte, I'll take you to safety."

"Oh, no you don't," declared Winter, lunging forward and grabbing Rufus's arm in a painful grip. "You don't go playing around with my wife and slide out of it that easily, not this time. I've had my fill of cuckoos in my nest, and I won't stand for it any longer. I demand satisfaction."

Rufus whirled to face him, eyes blazing with anger. "You mean a fight? Why, certainly I'll meet you, for what good it will do. What I won't do is allow you to vent your anger on a defenceless woman."

Winter took in Rufus's slim build and air of refinement, his lip curling in an expression of contempt. "You wouldn't last two minutes with me, and where's the satisfaction in that? No, no, a duel is what I propose, pistols at dawn."

"Don't be ridiculous. Duelling's illegal."

Winter gave a derisive guffaw. "You may be a great gentleman, but you've taken liberties with what's mine, and that's a matter that touches my honour. I'll have satisfaction of you if it's the last thing I do. My second will call on you tomorrow morning. And you needn't bother to leave your card – my wife will give me the details soon enough." He flung a contemptuous glance at Charlotte, still cowering in her chair, weeping softly. "Now get out before I change my mind and give you a good beating here and now, like the dog you are."

Rufus gave a stiff bow. "Very well, then, have your second call on me."

\* \* \* \*

By the time Rufus reached his rooms, the rain had drenched him to the skin. He stripped off his clothes, tossed them into a corner to be dealt with later, then pulled on his dressing gown, wrapping the quilted brocade about him like a cloak of invisibility. He fetched a bottle of brandy and a glass from where he had left them on his desk, took them to his bedside table and poured out a large measure. It was some moments before he could master his shaking enough to drink without spilling brandy on himself. Finally, with several mouthfuls of the fiery spirit inside him, he grew calm enough to realise he was shivering as much with cold as with anger. Swallowing the rest of the brandy, he crawled into his bed and pulled the bedclothes around him before pouring another and gulping it down.

He lay down and waited for the brandy to do its work, but the turmoil in his mind made relaxation impossible. Each time he closed his eyes, he saw again Charlotte's battered face staring up at him, her husband's fists clenching and unclenching, his heavy features reddened and twisted with righteous fury. He had no doubts about the man's ability to extract his name and address from his poor wife, or his determination to pursue his chosen the path of vengeance. Rufus shuddered as he thought of the likely outcome. He was competent enough with a fowling piece, having hunted game on his father's estate since boyhood, but a pistol was a very different matter, and he'd never had reason to use one. Still, if Winter made good his threat, he must somehow manage to go through with it – there was simply no question of backing down – and for that he'd need a second.

If he went to his friends, George and Harry, they'd most likely laugh at his naivety. They'd already warned him against falling in love with Charlotte Winter, the lovely, golden-haired opera singer. Only two nights ago George had told him, in the tone of one explaining the obvious to a particularly dense child, "I know she's a beauty, Rufus, but you don't fall in love with the likes of the Covent Garden Nightingale. Take my word for it – she'll only break your heart." And knowing he'd proved right would only serve to complete his humiliation. As for his father...a shudder rippled through Rufus at the thought of the reception he'd receive from that irascible gentleman. If his mother were still alive, she'd understand him; he was tolerably certain his father would not.

Damn Charlotte Winter! Damn her to hell for deceiving him with her sweet face and her soft eyes, for making him love her, for making him believe she was free to love him. God knew, he could scarcely blame her for wanting to be shot of her brute of a husband, but why hadn't she just confided in him? She must have known he'd do anything in his power to help her. Then the thought struck him that she might not even have wanted his help. After all, hadn't her husband said it wasn't her first affair? If that were true – and she certainly hadn't denied it – she must have had previous opportunities to escape an unhappy marriage, if she'd wanted to. No, the more he thought about it, the more convinced he became that he was just the latest in a string of pawns used in her attempt to find respite from her miserable marriage. She might well have convinced herself she loved him – and however many had preceded him – but all they were, really, was a means to a rather pathetic end. What a damned fool he'd been!

Yet was it so foolish to want to love and be loved? Must he settle – as so many of his peers seemed to do – for a string of meaningless liaisons that, much as they might provide pleasure at the time, could never satisfy his longing for something deeper, until he married some lady acceptable to his father as a means to continue the family line, a sort of back-up should something unthinkable happen to his elder brother Humphrey's family? Was it so wrong, this hunger for someone to want him for who he was, and not just for his social status and his family's wealth – or, like poor Charlotte, to replace what she should have had from her husband?

Thinking of Charlotte's husband sent a new rush of fear through Rufus that banished all thought of sleep. How could he sleep with the threat of a duel hanging over him? The thought occurred to him that he could simply go to Ravenswood, the family estate in Cumberland. Winter would be unlikely to pursue him that far; he doubted the man even knew of the estate's existence, and he didn't think he'd mentioned it to Charlotte. But no, he could not run away. He'd got himself into this mess, and he had to go through with it, come what might.

Besides, whether he went or stayed, everyone he knew would soon enough be privy to the tale of his humiliation. He and Charlotte would become the subject of sniggering and gossip in the society pages, rousing her husband to even greater fury – if that were possible. Being killed in a duel with the man began to seem almost the least of the available evils. But what if he survived...? Duelling had been outlawed in England years since, so he'd inevitably face arrest, and perhaps even imprisonment, thus ensuring not only his own disgrace, but that of his family as well. The fact that Charlotte's husband would also face prison was of little consolation to him, although it might deliver Charlotte from her husband's cruelty. And if, by some fluke, he managed to kill Winter...God, that didn't bear thinking about!

Hunched, shivering, beneath the bedclothes, it seemed to Rufus that all paths seemed certain to lead to disaster. The worst of it was that, despite his anger at Charlotte's duplicity, he felt equally angry with himself for having abandoned her to her husband instead of rescuing her. Even now, she might be suffering worse violence at his hands, violence any self-respecting lover would at least have tried to prevent. Tossed in a maelstrom of anger and self-recrimination, it seemed to Rufus he would never sleep again.

Eventually, however, sheer exhaustion sent him into an uneasy slumber and dreams haunted by Charlotte's bruised, tear-stained face and her husband's threats of retribution.

# CHAPTER TWO

Rufus awoke feeling even worse than when he had fallen asleep. His throat was raw, and his tongue felt like old newspaper. With a yawn, he groped around on his bedside table for his watch. Damn! He'd forgotten to remove it from his jacket last night. He sat up, rubbing burning, gritty eyes. His head felt as though a steam train were thundering through it, and when he stood up, the room seemed to spin around him as though he were in the hall of mirrors at a carnival. Steadying himself by means of the furniture, he made his way to the pile of damp clothing in the corner and retrieved his watch. He snapped the cover open to discover it was already past eleven o'clock. With a muttered curse, he stumbled to his dressing table to find a clean shirt and underclothes.

There was, of course, no water in the jug on the washstand, so he was obliged to fetch some from the bathroom along the hall. It was only after he'd returned, and was splashing icy water on his face and torso, that he recalled Winter's threat from the night before. His heart lurched and panic gripped him so that he had to clutch at the marble washstand to steady himself. Then he remembered Winter had said his second would call on him that morning. It was nearly mid-day, and no one had called yet. Even with the amount of brandy he'd drunk, he felt sure he'd have woken if someone had knocked on his door. Perhaps Winter had changed his mind. Could he really be that lucky? Rubbing his face with his only more-or-less clean towel, Rufus decided he had no wish to test the proposition. Besides, he hadn't eaten since dinner the night before and, despite his lack of appetite, he couldn't help feeling a full stomach might help him to conjure up a solution to his problems – or at least to face the inevitable with some degree of equanimity. Deciding to kill two birds with one stone – an unfortunate metaphor, but the best he could manage in his present condition – he tugged on his clothes, applied a perfunctory brush and comb to his damp hair, dug his wallet out of the pocket of his greatcoat, and set out for the *Café Royal* in Regent Street for breakfast.

The rain had stopped overnight and the sun was making a feeble attempt to pierce a blanket of grey clouds, but the wind still had a sharp bite to it and, as Rufus threaded his way between the crowds of busy people, he found himself wishing he had thought to wear a coat. However, a roaring fire greeted him at the *Café Royal*, and he found a table close to it and ordered bacon and eggs, toast and marmalade, and a pot of coffee. The sight of the appetising food aroused his hunger, and he settled down to work his way through it.

Over an hour had elapsed by the time he emerged once more into the chill of Regent Street and, with a decent meal inside him, he began to feel more sanguine about the likelihood of a visit from Winter's second. He was tempted to stave off any potential meeting with the man by going to Hurst's Club to read the newspapers, but thought better of it; although it seemed unlikely the second would track him down to his club, the last thing he wanted was to risk such a meeting where he was so well known. Instead, he picked up a copy of *The Times* at a newsstand and set off back to his rooms. With any luck, the dreaded visitor – if he had turned up at all – would have come and gone by now.

The moment he stepped into the foyer of his lodging house, he realised someone had been there recently; he could still smell traces of pipe smoke. Still, the man who had produced it might have been visiting any one of the tenants. With a shrug, Rufus made his way up the stairs.

And ran straight into his father, who was standing on the first-floor landing, puffing on his pipe with every evidence of impatience.

"Ah, Rufus," the Earl of Ravenglass greeted him in a bear-like growl, emitting clouds of cloying tobacco smoke. "Where the devil have you been? I've been kicking my heels here for the best part of an hour."

"P-Papa," stammered Rufus, feeling every bit as foolish as he sounded. Why did his father always have that effect on him? "S-sorry I w-wasn't here sooner; I've been out for b-breakfast."

Lord Ravenglass made a point of consulting his gold pocket watch, his pursed lips showing just what he thought of young men who took their breakfast in the middle of the afternoon. "Well, are you going to leave me standing here for the rest of the day?"

"N-no, sir. Sorry." Rufus fished in his pocket for the key, and with fingers that seemed to have turned to jelly, wrestled it into the lock.

His father took in the jumbled room in one contemptuous glance, sniffing the stale air with distaste. Rufus hurried to open the window, and offered him the only chair in the room not covered with the detritus of daily life, an elderly armchair that had once belonged to his Aunt Maude Sangster.

"I think not," murmured Lord Ravenglass, flicking an imaginary speck of dust from his camelhair coat with a fastidious hand. He removed his hat and hung it on the stand near the door, then strode to the open window, from where he regarded Rufus with an air of profound disappointment. "Well, Rufus, I had rather an interesting visitor this morning."

"D-did you, sir?"

"One Jeremiah Cleave, claiming to be acting as second for a Mr Joseph Winter of Garrick Street, called on me with a tale to rival those penny dreadfuls your mother used to delight in. I don't recall any mention of a ghost or a dungeon, but the opera singer and her youthful paramour were a nice touch, I thought. I was rather hoping you could shed further light on the subject."

Rufus subsided into the chair he had offered his father, feeling suddenly faint. His father's dulcet tone did not deceive him for a moment. He gulped in a lungful of air in a fruitless effort to slow his racing heart, and stammered, "P-Papa, I..."

Lord Ravenglass interrupted him with an impatient scowl. "Oh, for God's sake, Rufus, I don't give a damn who you choose to have affairs with. I was young myself once, unlikely though you might find the notion. What I do expect, however, is that a son of mine will refrain from bringing shame on himself and his family and, let me tell you, you're proving to be a considerable disappointment on that score. When you were sent down from Oxford in disgrace, I was prepared to put it down to youthful high spirits and, after all, the university isn't the only place a man may gain an education. I was even willing to be persuaded to overlook that business with Elizabeth Fane – at least *she* wasn't the toast of London, and she wasn't married."

Rufus bit his lip. "I didn't know she was married, Papa. She didn't say..."

"Good God, boy, you might have asked. Or even used your eyes, instead of embroiling yourself in something as tawdry – and illegal, I might add – as a duel."

"I—I didn't. It was him, Mr Winter. I tried to apologise and explain to him that I didn't know Charlotte – M-Mrs Winter, that is – was married. I even offered to meet him in a fair fight if that was what he felt his honour demanded, but he insisted on c-calling me out. I'm sorry, Papa, I just didn't know. I thought she loved me as I loved her."

"Love!" Lord Ravenglass rolled his eyes heavenward. "Need I remind you, Rufus, that you're twenty-three, not seventeen?"

"Yes, sir, I mean n-no, sir." Rufus's voice was little more than a hoarse whisper. "Wh-what did you say to Mr Cleave?"

"I sent him away with a flea in his ear, of course. Told him in no uncertain terms that his Mr Winter now had me to deal with, and not just my callow fool of a son."

Rufus released a breath he had not realised he was holding. "Thank you, sir, that's very good of you. I-I'll—"

"You'll damned well listen to me," his father interrupted in a voice like a thunderclap, making Rufus jump. "This really is the last straw, Rufus. I blame your mother, you know, she was always far too lenient with you."

Rufus remained silent, thinking better of pointing out

that, since his father had sent him away to Eton at the age of eight, bare weeks after his mother's death, any influence she might have had on him was unlikely to have had a lasting effect.

"And then there's your sister," Lord Ravenglass went on. "You know Sophia is to become engaged to Lord Offord's son?" Rufus nodded. "It's a damned good match, but you know what Offord's like. The slightest hint of scandal and he'll put an immediate stop to it. And in this day and age, scandal is precisely what will follow anything so damned foolhardy as a duel, regardless of whether or not you survive it. If you die, everyone will know why. If you survive, you'll likely be sent to prison, or worse. Either way, the family name will be dragged through the mud. Then what will Sophia do? Who do you think'll have her then?"

Rufus, judging this to be a rhetorical question, remained silent as his father strove to master his rage.

At length Lord Ravenglass spoke in calmer tones. "Fortunately, I'm tolerably sure I'll be able to deal with Winter. Like most men involved in commerce, he'll no doubt be persuaded to accept money as the solution to his loss of honour. However," he went on, his voice taking on a harsh tone, "since you seem determined to spend your life in bringing shame on your family, I've decided you must henceforth be kept as far out of harm's way as I can manage to contrive."

He emphasised the word 'far' in an ominous fashion that made Rufus quake with trepidation.

"I have decided," his father continued, "that you shall join your Uncle Oliver on his estate in New Zealand. I shall book your passage today and, until you leave, you'll stay with your

Aunt Fordyce in Scotland. In the meantime I shall, of course, deny all knowledge of your whereabouts."

Rufus stared, open-mouthed, at his father. "New Zealand?" he managed to blurt out at last. "But—but that's on the other side of the world."

"Quite," said his father with a grim smile. "Whatever trouble you may bring on yourself there, it will not besmirch the family name. And now," he took his hat from the stand and placed it firmly on his head, "I'll bid you good day. I advise you to pack what you need. We leave for Edinburgh first thing tomorrow morning, and I don't expect to be kept waiting."

\* \* \* \*

Glencrae House, the home of Aunt Jane Fordyce, a bleak, grey-stone structure situated at an inconvenient distance from such diversions as Edinburgh might have offered, was damp, cold, and uncomfortable. Aunt Jane, tall and bony with skimpy grey hair dragged back into a tight bun and a voice like a crow's, had converted to the Church of Scotland following a close brush with the Grim Reaper some years earlier, and took positive pride in an austerity that would have done credit to a hermit. And if living her Spartan lifestyle were insufficient, she insisted on Rufus accompanying her on her frequent visits to nearby Saint Ninian's church.

"We must pray that the good Lord will forgive your sins," she told him, though her narrowed lips and the glint in her filmy blue eyes suggested she doubted this would prove sufficient.

Rufus had no way of telling whether a cold church, hard pews, and lumpy hassocks could assuage the guilt he still felt for his foolishness and cowardice but, if sheer misery counted for anything, he felt he must surely have earned a reprieve.

Lord Ravenglass insisted on driving Rufus to Glasgow himself, the better to supervise his safe boarding of the *Orion*, the ship that was to carry him to New Zealand . As his father's carriage drew within sight of the tall-masted ships, the shipbuilders' yards, the rows of warehouses, and all the hustle and bustle of a busy port, Rufus could not help feeling a surge of excitement.

The *Orion* itself, however, when he finally caught sight of it, proved a great disappointment. Instead of a dashing clipper, such as he had seen pictured in the pages of the *Illustrated London News*, reading with fascination of their dramatic races across the Atlantic to America, he found himself confronted by a sturdy, three-masted auxiliary ship, so-called, as his father explained at tedious length, because a steam-driven engine assisted her sail-power, so they wouldn't have to stand off-shore for days waiting for a suitable wind, or languish for weeks at a time in the doldrums. Rufus, surveying the squat, black hulk, found himself less than convinced.

Somewhat to Rufus's annoyance, as though he expected his son to abscond at the first opportunity, Lord Ravenglass also personally supervised the safe loading of his luggage. This consisted of a brassbound sea chest that carried most of his worldly possessions as well as a letter of explanation for his Uncle Oliver and a sum of money his father judged sufficient until regular remittances could be sent to him. Rufus had begged to be allowed to take his piano on board, but in vain. His father had flatly refused to undertake the extra expense of conveying it to Glasgow and paying for its passage, declaring that Rufus should count himself lucky to be having a cabin to himself.

For two nights, they stayed at a local inn while the steerage-class passengers were taken aboard and settled in their accommodations below decks. Lord Ravenglass busied himself reading the newspapers or catching up on his correspondence, but Rufus, anxious to avoid having too much time to think about his situation, made his way each day to the dockside to watch the steady stream of humanity boarding the ship via a precarious-looking gangway. They seemed to represent every aspect of life, from families, many with young babies, some with even a cat or dog in tow, or a bird in a cage, to groups of single young men or women, to quite elderly folk, alone or in twos or threes. Many were accompanied by family or friends come to bid them farewell. All carried boxes or bags containing their possessions and provisions for the journey. To Rufus, these appeared woefully inadequate for a voyage of three months or more. He decided his father was right – he was, indeed, lucky to be travelling first class, with his own cabin and meals and other amenities provided.

On a leaden day at the tail end of winter, Rufus and his father made their way to the *Orion*. The decks seethed with passengers taking tearful leave of family and friends, children running about shouting and laughing, sailors striving to avoid them as they rushed about preparing the ship to weigh anchor, and officers shouting orders and oaths at the hapless sailors. All this mingled with the cries of the chickens, pigs, cows, and sheep that would provide fresh milk and food during the voyage, and the competing strains of at least two bands playing popular and patriotic tunes from the dockside. There were even several preachers dispensing moral advice and religious tracts with equal enthusiasm.

Such was the noise and confusion that Rufus was relieved to find his cabin under the poop deck. Not much more than six feet square, with a ceiling claustrophobically low, it held a bed, a small bedside cabinet, a washstand with an enamel bowl and jug, and several wooden pegs set into the panelled walls for the hanging of clothes. His cabin trunk, lashed securely down against the rocking of the ship, stood against the wall opposite the bed. There was also a round porthole, at present closed by a polished brass cover. Despite its tiny size, and the air of gloom imparted by its dark wood panelling, the cabin did afford a modicum of privacy from the bedlam above and below decks.

At last, it was time for the visitors to return to shore. Up on deck, the Babel seemed worse than ever. The bands played louder, the sailors sang raucous shanties as they pulled and heaved on ropes and chains, and passengers and visitors alike wept for the family, friends, and lovers they might never see again. Rufus, suddenly aware of the magnitude of his venture, and of what he was leaving behind, could not help weeping along with them. Even Lord Ravenglass had to clear his throat several times as he strove to give his son a few last words of advice in a voice gruff with unaccustomed emotion.

"Rufus, my boy, I'm sorry it's come to this, but I hope

you'll look on it as an opportunity to start afresh, to make something of yourself. Many a man before you has left England under a cloud yet, through hard work and diligence has been able to make a good life for himself in the colonies. I pray you will do the same. Goodbye, my boy, and don't forget to write."

Rufus nodded, not trusting himself to speak. His father clasped his hand firmly in both of his for a moment, then strode away through the crowd. Rufus stood gazing after him until he became lost in the throng.

Finally, all the visitors were ashore. At the shrill of the boatswain piping 'all hands up anchor', the pilot boats started up their steam engines, and a great cheer went up as the *Orion* began to move away from the quay.

As Rufus felt the motion of the ship through the water, a sudden excitement seized him. Anything was now possible and, despite the friends, family, and the familiar life he was leaving behind, it seemed to him he was embarking on a great adventure. Perhaps, in his new home on the far side of the world, he could, indeed, forge a new life for himself.

# CHAPTER THREE

Rufus's initial exhilaration was soon cast down by seasickness. For what seemed an eternity, he clung miserably to his narrow bed as the ship bucked and rolled. Day and night, his unwilling ears heard the cries of the ship's officers shouting orders, the heavy tread of the sailors running to obey them, and the relentless half-hourly ringing of the bells that marked out the sailors' day. How many days he lay thus in the gloom of his airless, noisome cabin, he would have been hard pressed to say, but one morning he awoke early to a miraculously calm sea, feeling quite well again, if a little fragile.

He slid out of bed, pulled some clean clothes from his trunk and dressed as quickly as he could, then found his way to the dining salon. Unlike his tiny cabin, the spacious room would have done justice to some of the better clubs of London, boasting an ornate, gilded-plaster ceiling, extensive rosewood panelling, scarlet plush-pile carpets, and chairs upholstered in matching brocade. Rufus found a seat near one end of the table that ran almost the width of the ship. In seconds, a white-coated steward appeared at his elbow enquiring politely what he fancied for breakfast. The thought of kippers, ham, or even eggs, made him feel queasy again, so he asked for a cup of tea and some toasted bread. With a nod, the steward glided away, and Rufus began a discreet survey of his fellow passengers.

Apart from a smattering of elderly folk, most of them seemed to be families, with children ranging in age from almost adult to mere babes in arms. It was going to be a damned boring voyage, he thought gloomily, with only staid families for company. Even Captain Standish, a tall, imposing figure with greying mutton-chop side-whiskers, looked severe and humourless. Rufus saw only two young men of his own age at the table, neither of whom looked as though they'd welcome his friendship. One, a pale and sickly youth with gold-rimmed spectacles, had his nose stuck in a book, even at the dining table. The other, whose narrow face and beady eyes reminded Rufus of a ferret, responded to his polite greeting with a brief stare of undisguised irritation, then continued shovelling food into his mouth as though it were his first meal in a month, and the last he expected for some time to come. Disappointed, Rufus continued to gaze fitfully about him until the steward returned with his breakfast.

Feeling considerably restored by his light meal, Rufus ventured onto the poop deck to take the air. The morning was clear and bright, though chilly. Leaning on the rail, he gazed out over the sea. The deep blue water, its surface scarcely ruffled by the light breeze, stretched away in all directions until, at some improbably distant point, it merged with the paler sky in a thin, misty line of amethyst like the stroke of a water colourist's brush. The ship sat like a toy on a vast plate of cobalt glass. A number of the passengers he had seen at breakfast were strolling about the deck and, since he had nothing better to do, and thought it best to make at least a show of politeness to his enforced neighbours, Rufus spent his time in passing the time of day with them until the bell rang for luncheon. While he and the other passengers were eating their ham, cheese, bread and butter, and fruit, Doctor Wells, the ship's surgeon, came into the dining room and clapped his hands for attention.

"Ladies and gentlemen, if I might have a moment of your time, you are all cordially invited this evening to a dance in the room next door." He waved a hand to indicate the room's whereabouts. "A light supper will be served later in the evening."

An excited buzz of conversation arose as soon as he had left, as mothers and daughters began to discuss what they should wear, and how they should dress their hair. The niceties of women's clothing and hairstyles held little interest for Rufus, yet he found himself looking forward to an evening of dancing, even wondering which of his fashionable embroidered waistcoats he should wear.

After dinner, along with most of the other first-class passengers, Rufus made his way to the room where the dance was to take place. It was in a similar style to the dining salon, larger, with the same opulent gilding and panelling and plush scarlet carpets and upholstery. Lamps set in pairs of ornate gilt sconces along the walls furnished the room with a warm glow. At one end of the room a trio of musicians – two violinists and an accordionist, whom he recognised from the dining table – were busy tuning their instruments. They soon struck up a lively polka, and couples began to take the floor.

Rufus glanced about him, making a survey of the young ladies present. They were not, of course, of his own social standing, but he was beginning to realise he would have a very lonely voyage if he didn't make some concessions to his circumstances. Besides, one or two of them were very pretty indeed and, with no one of his own class present to pass judgement, he contrived to spend a most enjoyable evening. He even found himself engaging in lively conversation with one of them, a brunette of perhaps nineteen or twenty, called Eleanor Fox. She was not among the prettiest there, but her wit, rather unexpectedly, charmed him far more than the mere good looks of others. Perhaps, at last, he was learning to see beneath the surface of the beauty that had led him astray in the past.

\* \* \* \*

As the days passed, with little to do but walk about the decks conversing with other passengers, or, if the weather were inclement, to read from the limited repertoire of the ship's library or play cards with other passengers, Rufus began to realise the life he had led in London – gaming, drinking, riding, attending horse races and boxing matches, balls, soirees, and the theatre – had spoiled him for the simple pursuits from which the other passengers seemed to derive pleasure. At twenty-three, it seemed he was already jaded. It was a mortifying thought.

One evening at dinner, after a run of bad weather lasting for the best part of a week, Doctor Wells announced that, to cheer everyone up, there would be a concert the following night, to be held in the room where the dance had taken place. A piano and other instruments would be available, and any passengers wishing to offer entertainment were requested to present themselves to him. Rufus felt his spirits lift, and realised just how much he had missed the emotional and creative outlet of his music since leaving London. He wasted no time in introducing himself to Doctor Wells, arranging not only to play at the concert, but also to be allowed to play the piano at other times for his own pleasure.

"But of course, my boy," said the surgeon, beaming at Rufus as though he were his favourite nephew. "I'm only too happy for passengers to use it."

So the days at sea took on a new dimension for Rufus. Most afternoons would find him at the piano, frequently playing to an audience, which he would oblige for a time with a selection of popular tunes. But as soon as he was alone, he would pour out his heart and his loneliness through his favourite classical composers.

Late one afternoon, having just finished Beethoven's *Moonlight Sonata*, he decided to try out some Schumann *lieder*. He had brought the sheet music with him, hoping for the chance to learn them once he reached his destination – assuming his uncle possessed anything as sophisticated as a piano. Upon no evidence whatsoever, Rufus had formed the habit of picturing his uncle living in something like the meagre cottages that housed the workers on his father's estate, but surrounded by jungle instead of fields. A short way through the second song, he was surprised to hear a low, sweet, unmistakably feminine voice join in, singing the lyrics in what sounded to his ears like perfect German. Rufus barely managed to contain his curiosity until the song was ended, then turned quickly to the owner of the lovely voice.

Just inside the doorway stood the most remarkable-looking young woman he had ever seen. Her raven-black hair was drawn severely back into a bun at the nape of her neck, like a governess or a lady's companion, though no respectable governess would have dared to wear her elegant gown of garnet-coloured moiré silk. Her skin, as pale and translucent as alabaster, stretched like an artist's canvas over high, prominent cheekbones and a straight, rather pointed nose. Against the pallor of her skin, her wide lips were like the blood-red stroke of a painter's brush. Yet it was her eyes that dominated her singular face. Huge and dark under black brows, they seemed to invite Rufus into some sombre, secret world, which, he realised with a sense of shock, he had longed all his life to enter. Utterly unlike the girls he usually favoured, this tall, slender woman was by no means pretty, nor even feminine in the soft, pink-and-gold style that usually attracted him, yet she drew him as a flame would draw a moth. And, like a moth, he felt he would willingly risk being burnt to bask for an instant in her pale radiance.

Rufus became aware that he must have been gaping like a love-struck schoolboy. With an effort, he shook himself free of her spell, rose to his feet, and bowed with what grace he could muster. The young woman smiled, showing white, even teeth with something odd about them that he could not quite identify.

"That was beautiful!" she said, the hint of an accent in her rich voice. "I'm sure even Herr Schumann himself would agree with me."

She spoke as though she had known the composer personally, though of course this was impossible. She was far too young, certainly no more than twenty.

"Th-thank you," he said, cursing himself inwardly for the stammering that still afflicted him when he was nervous.

Having grown up with a sister and a horde of female

cousins, Rufus was not normally shy in female company, but something about this young lady had managed to disconcert him thoroughly. Or rather, it was the way she made him feel that disturbed him. Feelings whose existence he had never so much as suspected before flooded through him, making him feel alien to his own body.

The woman moved towards him with the grace of a swan on the water, and held out a long, pale hand. With a stab of unexpected joy, Rufus noticed she wore no wedding or engagement ring, although the sobering reflection that neither had Charlotte Winter counselled caution.

"May I introduce myself? I'm Serafina Radzinskaya."

"R-Rufus de Hunte, a-at your service, Miss Radzinskaya." Even his voice sounded like that of a stranger.

He took her hand. It felt smooth and cool – almost too cool, he thought, for a brief moment wondering why. But the second his fingers touched hers, a sensation like an electric shock ran through him so that he had, for the sake of politeness, to stifle an involuntary gasp.

If Miss Radzinskaya noticed, she gave no sign. "Are you a professional pianist?" she asked.

"Oh no! A mere amateur."

"A very gifted amateur, I think." She pronounced it 'sink', and it sounded delicious.

"You're very kind to say so."

"Are you familiar with the works of Mr Rachmaninov?"

"A few, yes."

"Oh, I do so like his Prelude in C Sharp Minor! It's one of my favourites. Such sweet melancholy. Do you know it?"

It was a new piece, and Rufus had only recently learned it, yet he not only played it perfectly, but found in it a depth of

27

feeling that took him by surprise. He looked up to see an expression of ineffable sadness on Serafina Radzinskaya's face, her dark eyes brimming with tears. Disconcerted once more, he leapt to his feet and hurried to her side.

"Oh, please—I'm so sorry! I didn't—I wouldn't—not for the world..." He pulled out his handkerchief – mercifully clean – and offered it to her.

She took it and dabbed at her eyes. "Please, it is nothing." Her speech had an old-fashioned, somewhat formal quality, as though she had learned her English in the classroom rather than by speaking it often. Rufus found it enchanting. "It was just—so touching. You see, it speaks to me of my—my homeland, and I..." She broke off, a wistful expression on her face. Then, seeming for a moment to be listening to something only she could hear, gave a little gasp. "I must go," she said abruptly, thrusting the handkerchief at Rufus. It fluttered to the floor between them. Instinctively, he stooped to pick it up.

When he stood up again, she had gone.

He ran to the door, but could see no sign of her in the dining salon, nor in the passageway beyond. Like a phantasm, she had simply vanished. An unaccountable sense of loss swept over him. He lifted the handkerchief and pressed it to his face. It smelled faintly of some exotic, spicy perfume. He smiled. This was no phantasm. This was a real woman and, although he hadn't seen her before during the voyage, he must, surely, meet her again soon in such cramped quarters as the ship offered. Perhaps, like himself, she'd been ill and confined to her cabin – her pallor certainly suggested the possibility of recent illness. But such an unusual woman could scarcely avoid notice for long, and he had every intention of watching out for her.

His spirits thus restored, Rufus swept up his music scores from the piano and strode back to his cabin.

* * * *

The days went by, however, and Rufus did not see Serafina Radzinskaya. A vague sense of dejection swept over him, as though she had somehow let him down and, for a couple of days, he kept morosely to his cabin, emerging only to eat. However, it was not in his nature to mope for long. By the following Saturday evening, when a ball was scheduled after dinner, he had come to the conclusion that he was not cut out for a recluse. So, completing as painstaking a toilette as his cabin's limited facilities would permit, he donned his evening dress and his most elegant waistcoat, and sallied forth in search of amusement.

In the dining salon, several young ladies greeted him with gratifying delight, their mamas also favouring him with ingratiating smiles. This could not fail to improve his spirits. He promised to dance with several of the young ladies at the ball, including Miss Fox, who was looking particularly fetching in a gown of gold silk, with a spray of matching silk roses adorning her dark curls.

The meal ended, and the steward had just collected the last of the dinner dishes, when Rufus felt his eyes drawn to the doorway.

There stood Serafina Radzinskaya.

She was dressed in a gown of black velvet. Cut low across her shoulders, it afforded him a glimpse of snowy bosom adorned with a dramatic pendant of silver and jet. Matching

29

jet earrings hung from her ears, her simple, upswept hairstyle setting them off to perfection against her white neck. In one gloved hand she carried an ebony fan trimmed with silver lace.

Rufus felt his breath catch in his throat. The other ladies in their colourful gowns seemed suddenly insipid by comparison.

Rufus looked up to find her deep gaze upon him, a faint smile hovering about her wide, red mouth. As though obeying an unspoken summons, he rose and hurried to her side.

"Miss Radzinskaya, how do you do? How delightful to see you again!"

"Why, thank you, Mr. de Hunte. How do you do?" she replied in her slightly stilted English.

She held out her hand, and Rufus took it in both of his. Once again, he felt the shock of her touch, though fainter, as though she were somehow controlling it. Or perhaps her kid gloves had the effect of diminishing it.

"I'm very well, thank you," he replied. He felt almost desperate to tell her just how well her presence made him feel, but he didn't dare, not on such brief acquaintance, and certainly not in so public a place. Besides, he had no wish to make a fool of himself as he had with Charlotte Winter. "Will you do me the honour of joining me?" he asked, releasing her hand with reluctance.

Her hand flew to her mouth. "Oh, I—I'm not sure. I'm waiting for my..." She looked around at the doorway, just as a middle-aged gentleman entered the room. He was as tall for a man as Miss Radzinskaya was for a woman, with the same white, translucent skin stretched over the bones of his face, but his hair was as fair as hers was dark.

"I see you have met my—daughter," the man said with a smile that did not quite reach his pale golden eyes, which were, in their own way, quite as intense and as deep as Miss Radzinskaya's.

Rufus found himself thinking of the hawks he'd seen hunting at Ravenswood. And why that hint of hesitation when he announced Miss Radzinskaya as his daughter? With a feeling of disappointment, Rufus concluded she was probably his mistress. She certainly wouldn't be the first young lady to go about under such a guise. With the debacle of Charlotte Winter still vivid in his mind, he determined to do his utmost to tread cautiously, despite his strong attraction to Miss Radzinskaya.

She seemed to confirm his suspicion by saying, "Anton, Mr de Hunte has very kindly asked me to join him."

The man smiled, showing white teeth with the same indefinable peculiarity Rufus had noticed in Miss Radzinskaya's. Rufus found himself wondering if he dared hope this shared characteristic might mean they were related after all. "If he doesn't object to my company as well, perhaps we can both join him."

Rufus forced himself to smile politely. "But of course, I should be honoured, Mr...?"

"Ah, how remiss of me," the man said. "Do, please, excuse my lack of manners." He gave a slight, formal bow. "Anton Springer, at your service."

Rufus introduced himself, then, with somewhat mixed feelings, led the way to where he had been sitting. Once his guests were comfortably seated, he asked, "Would you care for some coffee or tea? I'm afraid they don't serve wine."

"Thank you, no," Springer replied, apparently for both of them. "Serafina and I desire nothing more than your company."

Rufus felt somehow less flattered than Springer's words suggested he should. He hid this, however, merely enquiring, "May I ask where you're bound?"

"Certainly," said Springer, with that smile that somehow wasn't. "We're travelling to the town of Auckland, in New Zealand."

"So am I!" exclaimed Rufus. "Have you business there, or are you seeking a new life?"

"Why, both, I believe," Springer replied, a gleam of something akin to amusement lighting his pale eyes.

"May I ask, Mr de Hunte," Miss Radzinskaya said softly, looking at him from under long, black lashes, "why *you* travel so far from your home?"

Rufus felt a sudden panic. Her eyes seemed to pierce through him until he could have sworn she had read his guilty secret. He found himself stammering, "I-I'm travelling to stay with—with my uncle."

"Indeed," she replied, with a teasing smile. "You must be very fond of your uncle to venture so far to see him."

"Oh—oh no." Rufus was uncomfortably aware, now, of Springer's sharp gaze on him. "I scarcely know him. That is— I—I..." He struggled to a halt.

"Perhaps Mr de Hunte is also in search of a new life," Springer said, not unkindly.

Rufus turned to him gratefully. "That's it, sir. That's it, exactly."

He drank a mouthful of coffee, which helped ease his embarrassment, and they continued to converse along less problematic lines until Rufus had finished his coffee.

"Well," said Springer, taking charge, "shall we go to the ball?"

Rufus nodded, rising to help Miss Radzinskaya from her chair. She laid her gloved hand on his arm as he led her to the ballroom. He caught a hint of her musky perfume and felt his heart quicken.

"Miss Radzinskaya," he said with a catch in his breath, "I do hope you'll do me the honour of dancing with me this evening."

She smiled at him. "I should have been severely disappointed had you failed to ask me," she replied before adding wistfully, "It seems so long since last I danced."

His heart leaping in anticipation, Rufus busied himself finding her a comfortable seat in the ballroom. Springer calmly surveyed the scene, apparently quite happy for Rufus to dance attendance on her. He began to feel hopeful that she was, after all, Springer's daughter, and not his mistress. The fact that they didn't share a surname was worrying, but they both had the same unusually pale skin, suggesting the likelihood of a blood relationship, and with that he must be content for now.

Once the dancing was underway, Rufus made sure he did his duty by the other young ladies, but he lived for the moments spent with Miss Radzinskaya in his arms. The touch of her soft skin was cool, yet electric, her perfume as intoxicating as the finest French brandy. Dancing with her was like being carried away on a tide of exquisite sensation. Never before had he felt so deliciously, intensely alive. He must, he concluded with excited trepidation, be falling in love. He had fancied himself in love a number of times before, most recently – and disastrously – with Charlotte Winter. But it had never felt like this. For the first time since boarding the *Orion*, Rufus was grateful for the length of the journey. It would give him time to court Miss Radzinskaya, and—please, God!—to win her heart.

All too soon, the ball drew to a close. As Doctor Wells announced the last dance, Rufus sought Serafina in the hot, crowded room. He planned to try to persuade her to accompany him onto the poop deck afterwards, to walk in the cool moonlight. But he could see neither her nor Springer anywhere. Disappointment gnawing at his heart, Rufus strode from the ballroom. Reaching his cabin, he flung himself onto his bed, wondering at the strength of feeling engendered in him by a minor disappointment over a woman he had only just met. At length, he fell into a sleep haunted by dark shapes that seemed both to tantalise and taunt him.

# CHAPTER FOUR

Some days after the ball, rumours began to circulate amongst the passengers of a mysterious illness that had afflicted several of their number. Some claimed it was an infectious disease, which must inevitably spread, making the *Orion* a plague ship. No port would allow them entry, and they would be forced, like Wagner's *Flying Dutchman*, to sail the seas until they were all dead. Others scoffed at these prophets of doom, insisting it was merely a few passengers who had succumbed to the rigours of the voyage. Still others insisted the whole thing was nothing more than baseless rumour.

While inclined to be sceptical of these wild theories, Rufus was nevertheless intrigued. The next time he saw Doctor Wells, with whom he had struck up a somewhat avuncular friendship – the surgeon being several decades his senior – he asked for clarification.

"The fact is," Doctor Wells told him, rubbing his whiskers with a meaty hand, "we don't quite know what it is. Several passengers have been found in a state of exhaustion for which I can find no obvious explanation. There's no sign of fever, which would indicate an infection, or of any injury. One lady, though, did have two welts on her neck. They looked a little like insect bites, but that's not possible out here in the middle of the ocean. And besides," the doctor gave a faint, ironic smile, "they'd have had to be damned big insects."

"But surely the victims themselves must have some idea what happened to them?"

"You'd think so, wouldn't you? But they've all been perfectly well one day, and the next in a state of near-coma. So far, thank God, they've all recovered with no apparent lasting ill effects. It's all very mystifying. Though if you ask me," the surgeon added, leaning towards Rufus with a conspiratorial air, "it's most likely nothing more than hysteria. Doctor Sigmund Freud is most interesting on the subject – you'll have heard of him, I dare say. In this case, I expect it's been brought on by living in such a confined quarters with strangers."

Rufus had, of course, heard of the Austrian psychiatrist, though mainly in terms of his being an unscrupulous charlatan who took advantage of the weaknesses of his largely female – and wealthy – clientele. He was also rumoured to be addicted to laudanum or some such, scarcely an endorsement of his already unlikely theories. However, he was far too polite to express such doubts to Doctor Wells, who was clearly a convert. Hysteria, though, certainly seemed as likely an explanation as the others circulating about the ship.

The shipboard rumours continued to make the rounds but, after a time, Rufus lost interest in an apparently unsolvable mystery. Besides, his energies were increasingly devoted to gaining the further company of the elusive Serafina Radzinskaya. Since the ball, he had not seen either her or Springer. Neither of them ever appeared for meals, so Rufus supposed they must dine privately, although why they should do so was beyond him. In an effort to discover the whereabouts of their cabins – for he felt certain they could not be domiciled with the hoi polloi below decks – he waylaid the ship's purser one evening.

"Excuse me, sir, but can you tell me in which cabin Miss Serafina Radzinskaya is staying? Miss Radzinskaya dropped a—a glove at the ball. I'd like to return it to her, but I haven't seen her since, and I thought perhaps I could take it to her cabin."

This purser gave him a look that suggested he considered himself more than equal to any tricks a love-struck young man might try on him. "Well, now, young sir, it'd be more than my job's worth to divulge such details to you, but if you'd like to bring the glove to my office, I'll see that the lady gets it."

Inwardly seething with frustration, Rufus thanked the purser and took himself off to pace the deck in the cool evening air. Why should he feel like this, he thought angrily, over a woman he scarcely knew? Why couldn't he just shake her off? He'd always been able to do that before. Even Charlotte Winter hadn't made him long for her company as Serafina Radzinskaya did. He felt as though he had found a part of himself he had not realised was missing, and was now desperate not to lose it again.

Engrossed in his feelings, he at first failed to notice a low voice calling his name. He looked up, annoyed at having his reverie interrupted, to see the object of his musings standing by the ship's railing. In an instant, his mood lifted to one of elation. He ceased his pacing and ran to join her.

"Miss Radzinskaya! How good it is to see you. I've missed you since the ball."

She gave her pensive smile. "How kind of you to say so, Mr de Hunte."

"Please," said Rufus, taking the hand she offered and bending over it. "Please call me Rufus, and—and may I call you Serafina?"

She gave a slight curtsey. "Indeed you may – Rufus."

Rufus relinquished her hand, deliriously aware that an important milestone in their relationship had just been passed.

"Would you care to take a turn about the deck with me?" he asked, offering her his arm. Serafina placed her pale hand on his coat sleeve and they began to stroll. "I do hope you've not been unwell," Rufus said. "There have been such dreadful rumours."

"Rumours?"

"Why, haven't you heard? There have been a number of mysterious illnesses recently. Passengers have been found quite insensible, yet with no clue as to the nature of their malady."

Serafina smiled at him; she was tall enough that she had no need to look up to meet his eyes. "What? No clues at all? That seems unlikely."

"Well, apparently one woman had marks on her neck – like insect bites, Doctor Wells said, only bigger."

"Goodness! A strange symptom, indeed."

"That's what I thought. Doctor Wells believes the afflicted passengers are just victims of hysteria."

"Ah. He's a follower of Doctor Freud, then?"

"I believe so. But must we talk of such distasteful things?"

Serafina smiled. "No, indeed we must not. Tell me, Rufus, do you still play the piano in the ballroom?"

"Yes, but it's not the same without my audience."

"Your—Oh, you mean me?" Serafina gave a soft chuckle. "But surely an audience of one is scarcely worthy of the name."

"It is if it's you!" declared Rufus, catching up both her hands in his. "Serafina, will you let me play for you again? Please say you will. I should love to hear you sing again."

She left her hands in his and stood looking at him, her dark eyes gleaming with a sudden fire that both excited and frightened him. He longed to take her in his arms and kiss her red mouth, but those eyes, inviting as they seemed, somehow held him at bay.

Then the moment had passed, and Serafina said calmly, "I should like that very much. When do you think would be suitable?"

"Why, now, if you'd like it."

Serafina sighed. "Oh, I'm so sorry, but Anton – that is, I'm to meet my father. It's already arranged, I'm sorry."

She looked so genuinely forlorn that Rufus took her hand again, saying, "I understand. Please don't upset yourself on my account. Perhaps you can join me tomorrow afternoon after luncheon, if your father can spare you. I've been practicing another of Rachmaninov's preludes."

"I should love to hear it, but would you mind very much if we make it later in the day? At five o'clock, perhaps?"

"Oh yes, five o'clock, thank you!" Rufus exclaimed, in such a state of delight that, without thinking, he raised Serafina's hand to his lips and pressed a fervent kiss upon it.

Her eyes blazed with a light that was alarming in its intensity. Again Rufus felt a thrill of fear and excitement. Though surely that glow must be a trick of the fading light?

Then it was gone, leaving him feeling oddly bereft.

"I'm sorry," he said, releasing her hand. "I shouldn't have done that."

"Why not, if you wanted to?"

Her words surprised him – shocked him, almost. He had never heard any other unmarried lady speak in such a manner. Even the most forward young ladies of his acquaintance would consider themselves sunken low, indeed, if they failed to make at least a pretence of modesty. Yet Serafina's words didn't seem at all immodest. Clearly of good breeding, she seemed simply to be operating from a different set of values from the ones he'd been bred to. But then, he thought, she was not English, so perhaps she'd been brought up to be this direct...

Serafina's words interrupted his speculations. "I must go now, Rufus. Until tomorrow, then, yes?"

"Oh, yes," breathed Rufus.

With a smile, Serafina turned from him and walked away across the deck. Rufus stood looking after her graceful figure until she disappeared down the stairway that led to the main deck.

\* \* \* \*

At half past four on the following afternoon, Rufus was already seated at the piano, but nervousness thwarted his attempts to practice his new piece. Because it now mattered to him more than ever, fresh doubts besieged him about the nature of Serafina's relationship with Anton Springer. Quite apart from the matter of their different surnames, he found it difficult to believe she'd refer to her true father by his

Christian name. It was unthinkable. Yet if she were his mistress, he dared not pay court to her for fear of how Springer would react. True, he'd evinced no sign of jealousy when Rufus had danced with Serafina, and no sign of wishing to do so himself. On the contrary, he had been pleasant and friendly throughout the evening. Still, something in his hawkish eyes told Rufus Springer would not be a man to cross.

As the hands of the large wall clock crept past five o'clock, Rufus began to fear Serafina would not keep their appointment. Springer must have forbidden her to meet him, he thought with a stab of jealousy. Or could it be that she'd been toying with him earlier? Could he have been wrong in his reading of what had seemed clear signs of her partiality? Were both she and Springer engaged in some cruel game with him, and if so, why? In a torment of frustration, anger and fear, he leapt up from the piano stool and began to pace about the room.

This calmed him somewhat, and he had just told himself for the third time that he would wait another five minutes and no longer, when Serafina appeared in the doorway. Her cheeks were slightly flushed, and Rufus thought she looked more enchanting than ever. As he looked at her, he wondered how he could ever have doubted her sincerity. He went to her and took her hand to raise it to his lips.

"I'm sorry to be so late," she said. "Thank you for waiting. I could hardly blame you if you'd quite given me up for a lost cause."

"No, no, not at all," Rufus protested, his anger quite dispelled by his pleasure in her presence. "Let me get you a chair."

41

Serafina smiled her thanks, and Rufus made sure she was comfortably seated before returning to the piano.

Although somewhat distracted by the tumult of emotions within him, before long the music began to work its usual magic. When he stole a glance at Serafina, she was sitting with her hands clasped in her lap, and seemed entranced. Was it just the music that enchanted her so, he wondered, or dare he hope he was included?

A sudden commotion outside the room startled them both. A man's authoritative voice called, "Fetch the surgeon, quickly!" followed by the sound of running feet. Rufus leapt to his feet. Serafina was already opening the door as he reached her side. Looking out, they saw one of the passengers – an elderly gentleman whom Rufus had seen at the dining table – lying slumped against a wall, his face the colour of putty. One of the ship's officers crouched at his side trying to loosen his starched collar. Rufus turned to Serafina, thinking to shield her from the grisly sight and to offer what comfort he could, but she was gone, apparently unable to bear it. He started forward to see if he could catch sight of her, but the officer barred his way.

"Stand back, please, sir. Give the gentleman some air. The surgeon will be here directly."

On cue, the rotund figure of Doctor Wells, carrying a brown leather case, came hurrying towards them from the end of the corridor. He stood with pursed lips, stroking his greying whiskers, as the ship's officer explained that the gentleman had collapsed suddenly, for no discernible reason.

"Humph." The surgeon squatted, with some difficulty, beside the recumbent form. He took the man's clammy wrist in his plump hand and felt his pulse. Frowning and shaking his head, he snapped open his case and drew out a stethoscope. Applying this to the man's chest, he shook his head again and levered himself to his feet. "Very little pulse," he informed the officer. "We'll have to get him to the sick bay so I can perform a more thorough examination, but it doesn't look good at all, I'm afraid."

Glancing briskly about him, the officer commandeered Rufus and one of the stewards to help him carry the inert figure to the sick bay, where they laid him as gently as possible on one of the narrow beds. While the officer stood by, ready to assist the surgeon, Rufus and his assistant withdrew.

As they left, he heard the officer's voice. "Same as the others, would you say, Doctor Wells?"

"Impossible to say for certain at this stage, but I fear you're right."

\* \* \* \*

The ship's rumour mills ground efficiently, as ever, and before long Rufus heard that the elderly gentleman – a Mr. Howard – had died. According to the general consensus of opinion, he was the first to die of the mysterious and frightening sickness sweeping the ship. The unfortunate victim had been travelling alone, and his sea burial was attended only by the captain, who read the service, the purser, Doctor Wells, and a few intrepid souls apparently determined to experience the full spectrum of shipboard life. For the most part, however, passengers seemed loath to venture forth, fearing to expose themselves to possible infection, despite the surgeon's assurances that there was no sign of the illness being infectious.

Rufus was disappointed, though not entirely surprised, to see nothing further of Serafina. In view of her hasty departure at the sight of the unconscious passenger, it was easy to believe she was afraid of contracting the disease herself. Indeed, with her cold, pale skin, she had often seemed to him to be not entirely well. He longed to be able to comfort and reassure her but, try as he might, he was unable to discover which was her cabin, so he had no choice but to wait for her to come to him. To this end, he took himself to the entertainments room most afternoons in the hope that his music would somehow attract her, but to no avail.

After a few days, passengers began once more to promenade on deck when the weather was fine. But Rufus saw no sign of either Serafina or Springer, and was forced to the miserable conclusion that either Springer did not want their friendship to continue, or, worse, that Serafina herself had no wish to see him again.

# CHAPTER FIVE

For some weeks, the *Orion* had been sailing into increasingly warm latitudes. As they passed the western coast of Africa, passengers crowded to the railings to marvel at the exotic perfumes wafted to them by the warm breezes, though the coast itself was but a distant blur on the horizon. Calm weather made progress slow, but Captain Standish had decreed that the auxiliary engines should not be used now they had passed through the doldrums. They would need them, he declared in ominous tones, once they reached the southern latitudes.

In the meantime, passengers and crew alike revelled in the balmy weather and calm seas. Clothes and bedding, damp from seawater seeping into cabins and musty from lack of airing, were brought on deck and draped to dry on any available beam or rope. By day, the decks were crowded. Men and women promenaded, chatted, read, or wrote up the journals they were encouraged to keep to ward off boredom, while children ran about, squabbled, and generally got underfoot. At night, many passengers came up on deck to view the magical sight of a sea glowing with the eerie luminosity of phosphorescence. One of the officers showed how a small object dropped overboard would create a veritable galaxy of starry lights as it splashed into the water, and this became a favourite evening pastime.

One evening, as Rufus was leaning on the poop deck railing to take in the cooler evening air, he caught sight of a group of young steerage passengers on the main deck, who were lowering a bucket into the water on a rope. As he watched, they pulled it up and began splashing its shimmering contents over one another, to shouts of good-natured laughter. His absorption in the happy scene was interrupted by a soft voice close behind him. His heart pounding, he spun round, expecting to see Serafina.

But it was Eleanor Fox, the young lady whose company he had enjoyed at the first dance held on board.

Rufus stifled his disappointment and took her outstretched hand with a smile. "How do you do, Miss Fox? I haven't seen you about for quite some time. I do hope you haven't been ill?"

"I'm afraid I have, rather, but I'm feeling much better now. Doctor Wells assures me it's nothing infectious, and it's such a lovely, warm evening, I just had to come out for some fresh air."

Rufus smiled. "I'm glad you're feeling better. A ship's cabin is no place in which to be sick."

"No, indeed." She gave him an impish grin. "Especially when one shares that cabin with a grumpy brother."

Rufus could not help responding to Miss Fox's wry good humour. "I can imagine! I certainly wouldn't want to be cooped up with my brother Humphrey on a long voyage – nor he with me, I dare say."

"Oh, do tell me about your family, Mr. de Hunte?"

"If you'll take a turn with me about the deck, I'll do my best, but I warn you they're a pretty dull bunch."

Miss Fox laughed. "Oh, I'm sure that's not true. I always

find the more one knows about people, the more fascinating they are. And I'd be delighted to walk with you." She placed her hand on Rufus's arm. "Does your family live in London?"

As they strolled arm in arm, Rufus did his best to make his family sound more interesting than he, himself, found them. Miss Fox responded with amusing anecdotes about her own numerous relations, and very soon they were conducting an animated conversation. After his disappointment over Serafina Radzinskaya, Rufus found the company of such a charming young lady as Miss Fox both gratifying and comforting. She was so open and unaffected, he could have no doubt that she was enjoying his company as he was hers. Although she and her family were clearly of much lower social standing that his own, she seemed not the least bit in awe of him, declaring, with a chime of laughter, that she had always wanted to live in a castle, and must make every attempt to ensnare him so her wish might be granted.

Rufus grinned. "I'm afraid you've chosen the wrong man on whom to work your wiles. I'm only a younger brother, so the estate won't be mine unless something unimaginable happens to Humphrey, and you seem altogether too sweet natured to carry out such a dastardly plan. Besides, it's not at all a romantic castle – especially in the depths of a Cumberland winter."

"Oh, dear, yet another dream punctured. But surely you have something of value to offer, Mr de Hunte? A magnificent town house designed by Mr Wren, perhaps, or a South African diamond mine you'll inherit from your eccentric Uncle Wilberforce?" Her brown eyes gleamed with mischief. "You disappoint me, Mr de Hunte, truly you do."

Rufus's lip twitched. "Yes, I'm generally regarded as

something of a disappointment."

"I find that very hard to believe," Miss Fox murmured, touching his hand lightly. Rufus gently removed his hand from hers. Much as he enjoyed her company, she was not the woman for him.

"Just you take your filthy hands off her!" A strident voice called out.

Startled, Rufus stepped away from Miss Fox and stared about him, half expecting to see Charlotte Winter's husband. Swaggering towards them, however, was the ferret-faced man Rufus had noticed earlier in the voyage. From the look of his dripping clothes, he'd been entertaining himself with the steerage passengers on the main deck. Reaching Miss Fox's side, the glowering young man took her arm in a proprietorial grip. Miss Fox tried to pull away.

"Ow! Let go of me, Toby. You're sopping wet. Just look what you've done to my gown."

"I leave you alone for two minutes and—blow me—if you're not up to mischief. Get back to the cabin, immediately." Miss Fox's assailant gave her an angry shove as if to emphasise his instructions.

"I take it you're Miss Fox's brother," said Rufus, refraining, by sheer force of will, from repeating the description of him the lady herself had used.

"Yes, I am, and I'll thank you to keep your hands off her in future," snapped Fox, rounding on Rufus with a glare that reinforced his sister's view of him. "I'm responsible for her, and I don't intend to deliver damaged goods to our destination."

"Damaged goods." Rufus could not keep a smile from his lips. "What a quaintly old-fashioned expression. But I assure you, Mr. Fox, I mean no harm to your sister."

"Hah! A likely tale. You toffs are all the same, think you're God's gift to women just because you've got a title or money. Well, don't think—"

Miss Fox, who seemed unfazed by her brother's outburst, spoke to him in a furious undertone. "Toby, stop making a scene. You're embarrassing me. Mr de Hunte and I were doing nothing that need worry you in the slightest."

Fox turned on his sister. "I'll be the judge of that, Nellie, thank you very much. Now, you heard me. Go back to the cabin. Go on. I won't tell you again."

Miss Fox sighed and rolled her eyes, but with a curtsey to Rufus, moved off to do her brother's bidding.

Fox gazed after her for a moment, a look of smug satisfaction on his face and then turned back to Rufus. "And that goes for you, too, Mr High-and-Mighty. Just you leave my sister alone if you know what's good for you."

"Certainly, since it means so much to you, though I'd have thought Miss Fox might have some say in who she chooses to talk to."

Fox said nothing to this, merely scowled at Rufus and repeated his warning. Rufus gave a formal bow and strode towards the stairs the main deck, leaving Fox glaring after him like an over-zealous guard dog.

Back in his own cabin, Rufus fell to wondering just why it was he always seemed to fall foul of disgruntled husbands and protectors. Of course, with Charlotte, he'd simply chosen the wrong woman. Had he had the slightest inkling that she was married, he'd never have become involved with her, regardless of how charming and beautiful she was. It occurred to him that his cousin, Edward, might have warned him, but then perhaps he didn't know, either. Rufus supposed a woman with a penchant for indulging in affairs would be unlikely to advertise her marital status to all and sundry. Then again, perhaps, like him, she'd been led astray by her feelings. Didn't everyone, at heart, want to be loved? Though apparently not Toby Fox, he amended with a grimace, if his behaviour tonight was anything to go by. It would be all too easy for a man to be swayed by sympathy for his browbeaten sister, but Rufus promised himself that that man would not be him. He had no wish to deceive her as he had been deceived, and besides, the last thing he needed was an enemy in the cramped confines of the ship.

Where Serafina was concerned, however, he suspected he'd be prepared to risk Springer's enmity for the right to hold her in his arms and to kiss her crimson lips. Just why she held such a powerful attraction for him, he was at a loss to say, and he supposed he'd never find out, now, since both she and Springer seemed to be avoiding him. Willing though he might be to risk Springer's wrath, if Serafina herself was determined to shun him, there seemed little he could do about it. Why did he seem fated to be attracted to women he was not permitted to have? Had he been born with some fatal flaw, or did the Fates just have it in for him?

With a sigh, he lay back on his bed, letting the gentle rocking of the ship, and the hint of a warm breeze filtering through the open porthole, lull him into a sleep mercifully free from dreams of threatening husbands or brothers.

# CHAPTER SIX

Although the *Orion* had crossed the Equator, and was steadily making her way south, the weather remained warm, rendering it stuffy and uncomfortable in the cabins, and even worse below decks. Like many of his fellow passengers, Rufus spent most evenings on deck taking advantage of the cooler night air.

Late one night, while strolling on the main deck, he heard voices nearby. He couldn't quite tell where they were coming from, but curiosity made him stop to listen. His heart gave a wild lurch as he recognised Serafina's voice. She spoke in a furious whisper.

"You can't expect me to obey you in this. Do my feelings count for nothing?"

"Of course they don't," came Springer's calm reply. "But surely you can see there's no other way. I cannot have you jeopardise our safety here."

"You cannot—!" Serafina's voice came to an abrupt halt, as though she were overcome by emotion. In a few moments she continued, her voice controlled, but still angry. "Just remember, Anton, this voyage was your idea. It's you who have put us in danger, not me. Besides, I'm my own person, not yours."

"Are you, Serafina? Are you sure of that?" His voice sank to a murmur, so that Rufus, feeling more than a little guilty, yet unable to stop himself, had to strain to hear it. "I know it can be hard, my dear, but did I ever pretend it would be otherwise? Unlike some of us, you came willingly, and with open eyes. This particular venture is vital to both of us. Whether we like it or not, Serafina, the world we inhabit is rapidly changing, becoming smaller, less safe for our kind. If we're to survive with some degree of security, we must accept this and adapt ourselves accordingly. Yes, it can be a lonely life, but really, all I require is for you to avoid putting us in danger. Surely that's not too much to ask?"

There was a pause, as Serafina apparently thought over what he had said. At length, she said with a sigh, "Sometimes it *is* too much, Anton. I hate all this constant travelling! Why can't we settle in one place? Others do."

"Believe me, Serafina, I wouldn't travel so much if it weren't necessary."

"But why is it necessary?"

"For God's sake, Serafina, can't you just accept what I say? I've already told you it's for our safety, yours as well as mine." Springer sighed and went on more calmly, "In the end, my dear, I dare say you'll do as you wish. But remember this – I made you. You are blood of my blood and nothing can change that – ever."

"Yes, you made me, but you can't control my feelings, Anton, any more than I can." Serafina's voice sounded as though she were on the verge of tears again.

"I assure you I could quite easily do that," came Springer's reply. "But, as you well know, that's not my way. Do not, however, give me cause to regret my leniency."

Rufus withdrew into the shadows as he heard Springer's footsteps, waiting until they had died away. He waited for a moment longer, then crept out again and looked about him. The deck appeared deserted. He stood there, both puzzled and disappointed. He could have sworn Serafina had not left with Springer. Then his ears caught the soft, but unmistakable sound of a sob. Turning towards it, he made out a dark shape hunched against one of the lifeboats.

"Serafina," he called out softly.

Her head lifted, and he saw her pale face, her great, dark eyes staring out at him like those of a frightened animal. For an instant, it seemed she might turn on him, but she merely lowered her eyes again. He hurried towards her.

"Serafina, what is it? Please let me help."

At his urgent whisper, she looked up again, tears sparkling on her long lashes. Rufus felt his heart contract at the sight of her.

"You can't help," she murmured. "No one can."

Instinctively, Rufus reached out to touch her cheek. It was as cold as snow. He quickly pulled off his jacket and draped it about her shoulders. "You're freezing! Let me take you to the dining salon. I have some brandy in my cabin."

Serafina looked up at him, a faint smile tugging at her mouth. "You're very kind, Rufus, and I truly appreciate it, but please don't trouble yourself on my account."

Rufus fixed his eyes on hers, still brimming with unshed tears.

"Nothing I could do to make you happy would be the least trouble in the world," he told her. "Oh, Serafina, it's what I want, more than anything. Since the moment I first saw you, I've thought of nothing else."

He caught up her hands in his and kissed her icy fingers, his eyes fixed on hers. Serafina returned his gaze, her eyes wide, and gleaming with a strange, wild light. A sensation like electricity surged through Rufus. His body pulsed with it; his blood sang to a music the like of which he had never experienced before, a music both dark and infinitely sweet. He had no power to resist it.

He pulled Serafina close, kissing her black hair, her eyelids, and her soft, smooth cheeks. She gave a little gasp as he kissed her mouth, then her lips, so strangely cool, parted beneath his. His kisses became more urgent, and Serafina responded with a passion as exciting as it was unexpected. They became lost to all but the sensations aroused by the explorations of hands, lips, tongues and teeth, their bodies clinging like two trees grown together.

"Oh, Serafina," he murmured at last, his voice rough with emotion. "I want you so much! Please say you'll be mine."

He moved to kiss her again, but she drew back, her eyes suddenly wary.

Rufus felt a stab of alarm. "What is it? What have I done to frighten you? You must know I'd never do anything to harm you."

Serafina shook her head, looking down at her hands. "No, no, I cannot—you cannot—you *must* not...!"

He took her hand and held it fast in his. With his other hand he raised her chin so that her eyes met his. She held his gaze, but it was as though she had withdrawn behind some dark, impenetrable wall.

"What is it?" he asked again, his voice gentle. "I know we've not known each other long, but I've wanted you since the first moment I saw you. I don't know yet if it's love, but I—I think it must be. It's as though I was incomplete until I met you. If you don't feel the same, just tell me and I won't trouble you any more, but if you do, won't you please give me the chance to prove myself to you?"

Serafina gave a sigh like the stirring of winter leaves. She lowered her eyes and bit her bottom lip as though grappling with some powerful dilemma. Then she raised her eyes again to his. "Oh, Rufus, if only things were that simple."

Rufus frowned, puzzled. "Is it Mr Springer? Is he your— your lover?"

Serafina laughed and shook her head. "No, Rufus, I can assure he is not my lover, but he..."

"I heard you arguing with him just now," Rufus said. "If he's worried about my intentions, let me speak with him. I'm sure I can—"

The look of despair she turned on him tore at his heart. When Rufus tried to put his arms about her, her body stiffened defensively.

"I'm sorry if I've upset you," he said stiffly. "I had thought my attentions weren't unwelcome, but it seems I was mistaken. Please accept my apologies; I'll trouble you no further."

He turned to leave her, all at once desperate for the privacy of his cabin where he could give vent to his feelings. But Serafina's hand on his arm held him back. Slowly, he turned to face her. At the sight of her, all his resolve fled. *Whatever the price,* he longed to tell her, *I'm prepared pay it – only say I may stay with you.*

But Serafina spoke first, her voice little more than a whisper, but her eyes firmly holding his. "Rufus, it isn't you who have upset me. Indeed, since first we met, you've been nothing but kind and considerate. I cannot, in truth, deny there's a bond between us. Yes, I've felt it, too. I didn't mean it to happen, but..." She paused and drew in a sharp breath, then continued rapidly. "Truly, I wish things were otherwise, but I cannot love you, Rufus. Indeed, I *must* not."

Rufus stared at her, his thoughts in turmoil.

"*Must* not?" he ground out at last, gripping her shoulders angrily. "This *is* Mr Springer's doing, isn't it?"

Flames kindled in her dark eyes, blazing forth until Rufus felt they would engulf him. He was at once repulsed, yet desperate to be consumed by their fierce heat, to become one with her, even though it destroyed him. Slowly, Serafina closed her eyes. When she opened them, the flames were gone. He must have imagined them, Rufus told himself, or perhaps it was just the way the moonlight had fallen on her eyes.

"It is Anton's doing, in a manner of speaking," she said, her voice deliberately calm. "But you mustn't blame him, Rufus. Truly, he's not to blame."

"How can you say that, when I heard him, myself, say you're bound to him? What did he mean, Serafina? Just what is the hold he has over you? Only tell me, and I'll help you break it. If necessary, we'll go where Mr Springer can't find us."

Serafina shook her head. "There is no such place, Rufus. Besides, Anton's right. I *am* bound to him – by ties that cannot be broken."

Rufus put a hand to his brow. His head throbbed from confusion and anger, and a terrible, desperate anxiety. He closed his eyes and breathed deeply in an effort to still the tempest within him. As if from a distance, he heard Serafina's voice.

"Rufus, I don't expect you to understand – just believe

what I say is true. We all make choices, don't we? And whether we make them from understanding or ignorance, those choices determine our future lives."

Rufus thought of what had led to his present voyage. There was no denying that, if he'd managed to resist Charlotte's charms, he'd still be in London, leading the uncomplicated life of a young man about town with his friends. He was seized by a sudden, aching longing for the life he had left behind. Then he opened his eyes and saw Serafina's strange, solemn face with its dramatic frame of night-black hair, and knew he'd gladly lose it all if only she were his.

"What you say is true," he said, "but we can make new choices. We don't have to be bound forever by one decision."

"Sometimes," she said simply, "we do."

"Let me talk to Mr Springer," he urged her. "I'm sure I can make him see how much we mean to one another. Surely he wants you to be happy?"

"Oh, Rufus, it's just not that simple." When Rufus made to urge her again, she placed one slender finger against his lips to silence him. "Please, you mustn't speak to Anton about this. He mustn't know of this conversation."

"Of course, if you wish it, but surely..."

She fixed her eyes on his, holding him in a gaze that seemed to fuse his will with hers, so that there was nothing left in all the world but Serafina.

"I do wish it, Rufus." Her voice remained little more than a whisper, but it now held a hint of the steel he'd heard in Springer's voice. "Promise me you won't tell him."

"I promise." His voice sounded strange in his ears, as though muffled by fog.

"Thank you. I'll never forget you, Rufus, but for your sake more than mine, you can't love me, and...and...and I can't love you. Please, you mustn't try to see me again."

To his surprise, she moved close to him and kissed him hard on the mouth.

Then she was gone, swallowed up by the darkness.

Rufus stumbled back to his cabin and flung himself, fully clothed, onto his bed. For a long time he lay there, staring unseeing at the panelled ceiling, still half under the spell Serafina seemed to have cast over him.

He must eventually have fallen asleep, as he awoke to bright sunshine and the first mate's voice overhead bellowing orders at the crew. Rousing himself to consciousness, he discovered his face and pillow were wet with tears.

Then he remembered why.

With memory came pain. At first a fire so intense it seemed his heart would shrivel like paper in the flame, it became by slow degrees a dull, cold ache in his breast, as though his heart were encased in ice. It stayed with him, a demon lurking at his shoulder, taunting: *She's gone, you've lost her, and there's nothing you can do.* Gradually, the pain transformed into a slow-burning anger. *She cares nothing for you,* his demon whispered then. *Why should you care for her? Show her how little you care. Show her!*

So began for Rufus a fury of self-enforced gaiety. If there were a concert, Rufus played. If there were a dance, he danced, flirting furiously with any young lady who gave the slightest encouragement – or none. He even sought out the company of the single men below decks, drinking or gaming with them with a recklessness they viewed at first with incredulity, and then with a sort of amused tolerance.

Of course it was impossible not to see Serafina and Springer from time to time, although neither of them spoke to him. In fact, whenever he did see either of them, it was at night, and they seemed so intent on some errand that they didn't notice him, even when he called out a greeting. One night, after a drinking session with his companions below decks, he was making his way back to his cabin when he caught sight of Serafina, also apparently returning to her cabin. Emboldened by cheap brandy, he decided to follow her. If he could only speak with her, perhaps he could persuade her to change her mind about him. She was some way ahead of him and, try as he might, he was unable to catch up with her. How could she move so quickly, with so little apparent effort? He increased his own pace until he was almost running, but was only just in time to see her disappear through the door of cabin twenty-three.

He was about to knock on the door when something stopped him. Some fierce, but nameless, impulse stayed his hand in the very act of striking the panelled wood. Confused, he turned towards his own cabin.

* * * *

Rufus's excursions below decks were unexpectedly curtailed by a serious outbreak of dysentery among the steerage passengers. Doctor Wells, disinclined to take chances with the rest of his charges, ordered all passengers to keep strictly to their own quarters.

This was less onerous for the cabin passengers, since they still had the use of the poop deck, which was, in any case, out of bounds to steerage passengers. But Rufus was in no state of mind to exchange pleasantries with these good folk, and kept to his cabin, the better to brood on his misery. This had the unintentional side effect of his being able, during more lucid intervals, to reflect on his situation. His budding love for Serafina was in no way diminished, he realised, and neither was the pain of losing her. It was gradually borne in upon him, however, that her rejection had not been of him, but of the very notion that they might love one another. Indeed, she had seemed not only to welcome his embrace, but to hunger for it as he did for hers. Would he ever forget her dark eyes, aflame with desire as her lips sought his? Could she have been dissembling? No, he couldn't believe it. Then why had she been so adamant that their love could not be? And what part had Springer played in her rejection?

Rufus's mind began to conjure up possible scenarios. What if she were already married, fleeing, perhaps, from a cruel husband, as Charlotte should have done from hers, had she only had the courage? This, however, begged the question of why Springer – whom Rufus was now almost certain was not Serafina's father – was helping her. Or perhaps she was a widow still in mourning. Although she was not wearing black, as any self-respecting English widow would do, it was possible, he supposed, that customs in her own society were different. It would explain her reluctance to enter into a relationship, though it hardly seemed to account for the passion she had shown him, and it still left the question of Springer. Try as he might, Rufus could find no explanation that took satisfactory account of so many apparent contradictions.

He came, at last, to the reluctant conclusion that he would

probably never discover the truth, and must now accept, however unwillingly, that Serafina was lost to him.

# CHAPTER SEVEN

It was not long before Rufus realised he could not continue to seclude himself in his cabin, if only because it would draw unwelcome attention to him. The last thing he wanted was to have some well-meaning person trying to find out what the matter was, or perhaps suggesting that Doctor Wells pay him a visit. For all that the rotund surgeon presented a bland face to the world, Rufus had the impression that a very sharp mind lay behind it. So he began to go about again, forcing himself to make polite conversation, and attending such entertainments as were organised, though his heart was not in them.

Alone in his cabin at night, he would find himself wondering just what could be wrong with him that his every attempt to find the love he so longed for seemed doomed to failure. Was it some fault within him that made him unattractive to women? With all due modesty, this seemed unlikely. After all, neither Elizabeth Fane nor Charlotte Winter had seemed to find him so, however flawed their motives might have been. Eleanor Fox had been happy to flirt with him, until her ghastly brother had ordered her off. As for Serafina Radzinskaya, the passion of her kisses left him in no doubt of *her* attraction to him. Yet something had made her draw back from him and run away, and it seemed to Rufus, that something could only be Springer, especially after the argument he'd overheard between them. What was it he'd told her? 'I made you. You are blood of my blood, and nothing can change that – ever.' It seemed a curious thing to say if all he meant was a blood relationship between them. It seemed to imply he had some power over her, and her fleeing from his embrace appeared to confirm it. Perhaps Springer was her father, after all. Rufus could think of little else to account for Serafina's refusal of a love she so patently wanted. But in that case, why hadn't she simply told him he must ask Springer for permission to court her? There must be some other hold he had over her – hadn't he told her he could control her if he chose to? But what form such control might take was beyond Rufus's powers of deduction.

So when Doctor Wells announced at breakfast that there would be an evening of card games in the dining salon that evening, he decided to join in. Of course there would be none of the betting allowed that he'd been used to at Hurst's and the other clubs he'd frequented back in London. But he'd long since realised he enjoyed card games far more for the skill than the money, so he knew he'd be perfectly happy to play for points.

Doctor Wells had taken care to cater for everyone, with a variety of games for the adults, and parlour games such as snap and fish that even the young people could enjoy. Rufus was invited to join several other men in playing euchre. It was not one of his favourite games, but the good humour of the others made it more enjoyable than he'd expected. However, when Eleanor Fox's brother made a move to join the group, the look he turned on Rufus carried such an obvious challenge that Rufus excused himself and went in search of a different game. He wasn't afraid of a challenge, but there was something of the bully about Fox, and this was neither the time nor the place for the sort of unpleasantness he seemed intent on provoking.

To his amazement, Rufus caught sight of the usually elusive Springer seated at the other end of the long dining table, engrossed in a game of bridge with three other men. This was his opportunity to speak with Serafina alone, and perhaps find an answer to the enigma that was destroying his peace of mind. Despite his trepidation, and his fear of what she might tell him, this might be the only chance he'd have, and he knew he must take it, come what might.

Waiting until he saw Springer bent over his cards, Rufus slipped out of the dining salon. A cold wind moaned through the rigging, making the ship's timbers creak so that the dark passageway took on an eerie quality that sent a shiver up Rufus's spine. As he approached Serafina's cabin, he heard the unmistakable sound of her voice. He felt a sudden rush of pleasure, and his gut tightened with a sensation somewhere between anticipation and apprehension. Then another sound reached his ears.

He heard the low murmur of a man's voice.

Serafina answered it with a soft ripple of laughter, and Rufus ground his teeth in anguish. He wanted to scream, but his breath seemed to have congealed in his throat. So that was the truth about Serafina. She was nothing more than another Charlotte Winter, using men for her own gratification, drawing them in with her hints and promises, but giving nothing. Yet again he'd been duped by a woman's charms, by her false air of vulnerability. Well, not any more!

There came a rustling sound from behind the cabin door, and then the door handle began to turn. Rufus flattened himself against the wall, hoping the darkness was deep enough to hide him, and that Serafina and her lover would not turn in his direction. His wish was granted as they moved off in the opposite direction towards the steps that led to the main deck. For a few seconds Rufus remained irresolute in the shadows, then, without conscious decision, he moved to follow them. He dreaded what he might see, but he had to know just who it was Serafina had chosen to replace him, and what qualities this new lover possessed that he, himself, lacked.

As the couple hurried along arm in arm, Rufus followed at what he hoped was a safe distance. When they took the steps down to the main deck, he hung back in the shadows, fearful of being seen or heard on the open expanse of the deck. To his relief, Serafina led the man into the dark seclusion of an area where coiled ropes were stacked against several lifeboats – not far from where he had overheard her quarrel with Springer – and Rufus was able to creep close enough to see the man's face. He recognised him, although he wasn't sure of his name – something like Hayes, he thought, or was it Mays? Serafina began to speak to the man in a seductive murmur, and, despite the sick misery that grasped him, Rufus found himself straining to make out her words.

"Don't be concerned." Her voice was soothing, hypnotic. "You will remember nothing of me, and nothing of what transpires between us this night. Nothing, do you understand?"

The man's voice drifted to Rufus, flat, somnolent, like one in a trance. "Nothing – I understand. Remember – nothing."

"Good." Her voice was a gentle caress.

Crouching in the cold darkness, Rufus saw Serafina's pale

fingers move to the man's neck. She seemed to be doing something with his clothing there, but the gathering wind was blowing clouds across the moon, and the shifting light made it impossible for him to see well. Suppressing a snarl of frustration, he moved, fraction by cautious fraction, until he could see more clearly. As he stared, mystified, Serafina raised her head to the sky, her skin gleaming like pearl in the moonlight, her hair a black cloud behind her, her lover a darker shadow before her. He heard the faint hiss of her indrawn breath, the silence as she held it for a long, long moment. Just for a second, she reminded him of Dante Gabriel Rossetti's *Beata Beatrix* – Blessed Beatrice – her rapt face raised in the exaltation of prayer. Then Serafina bent her head to the man's neck and seemed to inhale, as though his skin exuded some sweet incense, her body shuddering in apparent ecstasy. Oh, what wouldn't *he* give to feel that reverent breath on his own skin, to feel her body shiver like that against his! Sick with heartache, yet riveted to the scene before him, Rufus could only stare as her head lifted again, turning slightly so that he saw again that sudden flare of fire in her eyes that must, surely, be no more than an effect of the uncertain moonlight.

Then he saw...but no, it couldn't be! He thought he saw, in her open mouth, two fangs that gleamed like daggers in the moonlight. Her dark head swept down and she pounced – it was the only word he could think of – upon the man's exposed neck. He heard a soft crunch, like teeth biting into a crisp apple, followed by soft suckling noises. What on earth could she be doing? Then the clouds cleared from the moon and, by its stark light, he saw the stain of blood that had soaked into the man's shirt. More was seeping into it from a thin, crimson trickle running down from—from...

Rufus fled, barely managing to suppress the urge to vomit until he reached the poop deck, where he leaned out over the railing and retched until there was nothing left in him. Rushing to his cabin, he flung himself onto his bed, gasping for breath.

It was some time before he felt able to crawl from his bed to find one of the bottles of brandy he'd brought on board secreted amongst the linen in his cabin trunk. The White Star Line, owner of the *Orion*, strictly forbade the consumption of alcohol on board, but he'd thought a few bottles of decent Cognac might come in handy for emergencies and, if ever there were an emergency, this was surely it. Back on his bed, propped up against the pillow, he gulped down several mouthfuls, feeling its cleansing fire burn down his throat and gullet and into his stomach before replacing the cork and laying the bottle on the bed beside him.

He mustn't drink too much – he needed to think. But how could he think with the image still in his mind of Serafina biting into the neck of her – God! What should he call him? Lover? Victim? Prey? Why would she perform such an appalling act? Unless she was – he could scarcely bring himself to think the word – a vampire? But that was ridiculous. It was insane! Vampires didn't exist beyond the pages of a novel or the superstition of folklore. A thought almost too horrendous to contemplate entered his mind; perhaps Serafina *was* insane, a prey to some sick fantasy that made her believe she was a vampire and act accordingly. Had she committed such acts before, perhaps, and was Springer attempting to take her beyond the reach of those who would have her committed to an insane asylum?

He shook his head as though to clear it of such vile thoughts, uncorked the bottle and swallowed another mouthful of brandy. No, there were no vampires, and he refused to believe the Serafina with whom he had danced and conversed so happily, the Serafina who had kissed him with such passion, was insane. No, he had seen nothing more than some rather aggressive lovemaking. A rush of anger almost overwhelmed him at the thought of Serafina, whom he loved, and who knew he loved her, in the arms of another man so soon after such ardent kisses.

His mind returned to the argument he had overheard between Serafina and Springer. He had seemed to be forbidding her to do something – an injunction she had clearly felt was an infringement of her free will. Even from their brief acquaintance, he could readily believe Serafina valued her freedom, and would chafe under too firm a hand. What if she'd simply taken up with someone – anyone – to show Springer she would not be dictated to? If this were true, while it didn't make him feel any better about what he'd seen, he could see how it might have happened. Perhaps, even now, she was boasting to Springer of how she'd shaken off the shackles with which he'd sought to bind her.

But how could such behaviour, distasteful as Springer must surely find it, endanger them in any way? And that had seemed his major concern. Rufus pressed his hands to his brow in an effort to recall what Springer had said. What had it been? Something about the world becoming less safe for them? Yes, that was it: 'The world is becoming less safe for our kind.' What could he have meant by that, unless—unless both he and Serafina shared the same sickness, the same insanity? Try as he might, he could not bring himself to believe they were both insane when they seemed, the two of them, so rational.

Which left only the most insane explanation of all.

Those *were* fangs he'd seen, and that crunching sound had been those fangs biting into the man's neck. The suckling sounds were Serafina drawing blood from the wound she had made there. If she were a vampire, it made sense of her seductive voice commanding the man to forget the incident, as well as his trancelike reply. It made sense, too, of Springer's words to her, his unwillingness to countenance her becoming too close to anyone, even if it meant condemning her to loneliness. And the strange wasting sickness that stalked the ship, the welts Doctor Wells had found on a victim's neck, it made sense of them, too. It all made perfect sense – if the two of them were vampires. Ludicrous though it seemed, it fitted the facts as nothing else did.

And the worst of it was that he was still in love with Serafina. Even after seeing her in the very act that defined vampirism, he loved her, and, God forgive him, some part of him actually wished the neck her fangs had bitten had been his. Some terrible part of him longed with all his heart to feel her hunger for him as he hungered for her, to feel her body quiver against his with ecstasy as she drank his blood.

With a groan half-longing, half-revulsion, Rufus tore the cork from the brandy bottle and practically poured the liquid down his burning throat. What was wrong with him, for God's sake? How could he think such appalling thoughts? Yet how could he deny it? The plain truth was that he was in love with a woman he had every reason to believe was a vampire.

He knew he should do something – but what? If he told Serafina what he knew, she'd almost certainly tell Springer, and Rufus scarcely dared think what Springer might do, especially after his warning to Serafina. But what of the victims? How could he just stand by and let more passengers fall ill – or even die, as one had already? He felt sure he should tell someone – Doctor Wells, perhaps – but how could he expect anyone to believe something he found hard enough to accept himself, even after seeing proof? They might just as easily decide he was insane. Perhaps he was, though he had no desire to risk being locked up for the rest of the voyage. When he found himself contemplating leaving an anonymous message for Doctor Wells, Rufus knew he had reached the limits of what his mind could dredge up by way of a solution to his dilemma. His best plan now was to sleep – if he could. Perhaps in the morning his mind would be clearer.

He took a last mouthful of brandy, re-corked the bottle, and got up to replace it in his cabin trunk. As he opened the drawer, his eyes fell on the Bible his Aunt Fordyce had pressed on him before he had left for Glasgow. Like the other Bibles he'd seen at Glencrae House, it had a plain cover of soft black leather. Between its pages was a bookmark made of some stiff, blue fabric. Curious, he picked up the book and opened it. Someone – perhaps his aunt – had embroidered a cross on the bookmark with fine gold thread. It must be just his mood, he told himself, but he found it oddly touching to think of the austere old lady setting such delicate stitches. As he stood gazing at it, it occurred to him that such Christian symbols were reputed to be a protection against vampires.

Not that he believed in such mumbo-jumbo, but then, he hadn't believed in vampires, either, until...

Rufus gave an involuntary shudder and pushed shut the drawer of the chest, then carried the Bible to his bed and placed it under his pillow. He wasn't sure how much faith to place in its protective qualities, but he had seen for himself Serafina's ability to control a man. It seemed unlikely that Serafina would attack him. After all, hadn't she chosen to shun him rather than risk harming him? But who knew what Springer might do if he felt himself in danger of being exposed? Somehow, Rufus didn't think a mere locked door would be proof against Anton Springer. He was by no means certain a Bible would either – but it was all he had.

# CHAPTER EIGHT

Early the following morning, Rufus was roused from an uneasy sleep by the sudden clatter of hail on the poop deck above him, and the noise of sailors hurrying to furl the sails. The ship bucked, warning of an impending storm. As he sat up, yawning and rubbing his eyes, the memory of the previous night came flooding back, and with it the unsettling wash of anxiety. It was a wonder he'd slept at all. He certainly felt no better for it, or any closer to deciding what he should do.

By the time he had dragged himself through his ablutions and dressed, both hail and wind seemed to have subsided, so Rufus decided to take a walk on deck before breakfast in the hope that it would help clear the cotton wool from his head. The moment he left the relative cosiness of his tiny cabin, he became aware that the temperature had dropped considerably since the previous night. Shivering as he made his way along the narrow passageway, he heard voices issuing from the dining salon, and recognised one of them as belonging to Doctor Wells. Feeling rather guilty, but unable to resist eavesdropping after what he'd seen the previous night, he crept closer to the door, poised for a hasty retreat if necessary.

"I'm afraid so," the doctor was saying. "Mr Haynes collapsed last night on the main deck. Goodness knows what he was doing there at that time of night, but thank God one of the officers found him and brought him to the sick bay before he succumbed to the cold. He's young and strong, so I imagine he'll pull through all right, but in view of the number of passengers who've been taken ill already, I'm beginning to feel a quarantine might be in order."

"Hmm..." The answering voice belonged to Captain Standish. "I'd like to avoid that, if at all possible. Are you any closer to understanding what the malady is? Is it contagious?"

Doctor Wells gave a sigh of frustration. "I'm afraid I can't help you there. It doesn't appear to be like any disease I've come across before. There's no fever, no pattern discernible between the victims, no—"

"Just so," the captain interrupted. "Well, Doctor, you must do as you see fit, of course, but I must say I'll be much happier if we can avoid the inconvenience of quarantine."

"It's certainly not a decision I'd take lightly, Captain Standish, but I thought it best to bring the possibility to your attention sooner rather than later."

"Thank you, Doctor, much obliged," came the captain's brusque response. "But this hardly seems the place for such a discussion – breakfast is due to be served soon. Perhaps you'd like to breakfast with me in my quarters, and we can discuss the matter further?"

"Thank you, I'll be happy to do that."

"Good, good."

To Rufus's immense relief, the two men moved off in the opposite direction from where he was standing. Waiting only until they had left the dining room, he hurried to the sick bay, which, he recalled from when he had helped to carry the unfortunate Mr Howard there, lay between the men's and women's quarters below decks. Due, he assumed, to the inclement weather, the steerage passengers seemed to have confined themselves to their quarters, from which an unappetising melange of cooking odours reached his nostrils. Rufus wrinkled his nose in distaste as he negotiated the narrow passage that led to the sick bay, and tried not to imagine what the poor steerage passengers might be eating by this stage of the voyage. Outside the door of the sick bay, he listened intently for several moments, but heard no sounds of movement, so he opened the door a few cautious inches and peered into the room. As far as he could see, it was empty. He opened the door just wide enough to slip into the room, drawing it to behind him, and crept forward. In one of the narrow cots lining the two sides of the room, he made out the recumbent form of a man with dark hair. Hoping the patient really was asleep, Rufus tiptoed closer until he could make out his features. As he'd suspected, it was the man he'd seen with Serafina the previous night. His skin was as white as chalk, and on one side of his neck a gauze dressing showed two dark blotches of dried blood.

Rufus covered his eyes, breathing hard to allay his sudden panic, and turned away from the sight. On silent feet he crept from the sick bay, breathing a sigh of relief as he reached the deck without encountering Doctor Wells, or anyone else who might find his actions suspicious. The deck was slippery with the rain that fell in a steady drizzle, blown into misty drifts by a strong wind, and Rufus was forced to cling to the railings to avoid being swept into the sea that seemed to boil against the sides of the ship.

Back in his cabin, he stripped off his sodden clothes and

dried himself as best he could before dressing again in clothes that were dry, if somewhat grubby. While tying his bootlaces, he heard the gong summoning the cabin passengers to breakfast. The last thing he felt like was food; whether from the freezing temperature on deck or the quantity of brandy he'd drunk the previous night, his head ached abominably, and a sick horror lay coiled in the pit of his stomach like some venomous snake poised to strike. In the end, however, he decided his best plan was to behave as normally as possible in the hope that it might succeed in calming his overwrought senses.

Breakfast turned out to be unexpectedly diverting, due to the rolling of the ship on the choppy seas. Although the dining table was fitted with a ledge around its perimeter to prevent crockery and utensils from falling off in such conditions, they still had a marked tendency to slide across the table unless prevented by swift hands – much to the delight of the children and the chagrin of the adults. Nevertheless, breakfast was eventually accomplished with no more than one or two mishaps. Towards the end of the meal, Captain Standish arrived to announce that, due to the inclement weather, Sunday service would be held in the ballroom. Rufus groaned inwardly, wishing he'd stayed in his cabin after all. Sunday services were compulsory, so escape was impossible now he'd been seen.

The service, taken by Captain Standish, began with The Lord's Prayer, followed by a hymn, *Lead, Kindly Light*. Its unwitting irony, in view of what he had seen in the previous night's moonlight was not lost on Rufus as the voices swelled in ragged chorus. Then the captain, whose stentorian voice stood testimony to years of making himself heard over wind and weather – and the thunder of cannon-fire as well, for all Rufus knew – began a prayer for the safe recovery of Mr Haynes, who had been injured the previous night and was ill from loss of blood.

Rufus felt suddenly dizzy and unable to breathe. He forced air into his lungs and out again through teeth clenched against the nausea that threatened to overwhelm him. By the time he'd returned to some semblance of normality, the captain was reading a passage from the Bible. Rufus had missed the beginning of the reading, but with mounting horror he began to be aware of snatches of the Captain's words: "...he who eats my flesh and drinks my blood has eternal life...he who eats my flesh and drinks my blood abides in me, and I in him..."

Rufus clamped a hand to his mouth to choke back the bile scalding his throat. The woman next to him turned, a look of concern on her face. He forced a smile, then turned away from her, pretending interest in the captain's words. The rest of the service seemed to take forever, but at length it was over, and he turned to leave, wanting nothing more than his cabin and a swig or two of brandy to calm his nerves and settle his stomach.

As he made his way through the press of passengers, he glimpsed Toby Fox ahead of him, shepherding his hapless sister towards the door. Eleanor seemed to be hanging back, doing something with a book he assumed must be her Bible, or perhaps a hymn book. She raised her head and gave Rufus a quick smile before yielding to her brother's impatient hand on her arm. Rufus saw something small and white flutter to the floor behind her. Curious, he hurried forward to pick it up. It was a slip of paper, folded in four. He opened it to find a note scrawled in pencil and addressed to him:

*Dear Mr de Hunte,*

*Please meet me in the ballroom after luncheon.*

*E. Fox.*

Intrigued in spite of himself, as soon as luncheon ended Rufus slipped into the ballroom next door. Fortunately for his peace of mind, Toby Fox was nowhere to be seen. Probably standing guard over his poor sister, Rufus thought with a grimace of distaste, or hobnobbing with the steerage-class passengers whose company he seemed to favour. Although Miss Fox was charming and well mannered, and would not disgrace herself in any company, her brother seemed altogether more ill bred. Perhaps, for whatever reason, he had a penchant for low company, and had acquired the manners to match. Rufus had heard of the occasional scion of even the highest-born families who had gone the same way. He shrugged, dismissing the matter as of little importance, and sat down at the piano. He might as well entertain himself until Miss Fox arrived – if she arrived.

Before long, Rufus heard the door open and looked up to see Miss Fox standing just inside the room. With a swift glance at the corridor behind her, she closed the door and spoke in a low voice as if afraid of being overheard.

"I'm sorry I couldn't be here earlier. I had to wait until Toby had gone to meet his friends. Well, he calls them his friends, but they're more drinking and gaming companions, and I'm sure they'd fleece him as soon as look at him – not but what he doesn't deserve it."

Rufus rose, smiling, and took the hand she extended. "Never mind, you're here now. What was it you wanted, Miss Fox?"

With one of her quick smiles, she said, "Oh, I do wish you'd call me Eleanor. Miss Fox sounds so stuffy, don't you think?"

Rufus gave an answering smile, though he was wary of seeming too encouraging in case she assumed too much. "Thank you, and you can call me Rufus if you like. Now, what did you want to tell me?"

Eleanor looked down for a moment, biting her bottom lip, and then raised her eyes to meet his. "I expect you'll think me silly, but I wanted to apologise for Toby's behaviour the other day. He had no right to speak to you like that."

"Well, in all fairness, I suppose Mr Fox sees himself as in some sense your guardian."

"Yes, he does, and I really wish he didn't. I'm perfectly capable of looking after myself."

Rufus couldn't help smiling a little at her vehemence. He wouldn't have been surprised if she'd stamped her foot. "I'm sure you can, but that isn't quite the way society works, is it? You're both a long way from home, so I suppose it's only to be expected that a loving brother should want to protect you." Recalling what Fox had said to him, he gave an inward grimace at his own dishonesty. 'Damaged goods' sounded more like some Gothic villain than a loving brother.

Eleanor seemed to agree with him. "Oh, stuff and nonsense! He's not trying to protect me, and he's not even my brother, really." In response to Rufus's puzzled expression, she went on, a little less angrily, "Papa died when I was nine, and Toby was only a few years older when his mother died, and when his father married Mama, we became brother and sister by law, though not by blood. I never could like him. He used to pull my hair and put spiders in my bed when we were children, and twist my arm until it really hurt, just to show he was stronger than me."

"That's dreadful!" Rufus said with feeling. "It makes me glad my brother was already married when I was growing up – though at the time I thought a bossy elder sister was bad enough. Still, now you've both grown up, I dare say he does feel genuinely protective. If you were my little sister, I assure you I'd try my best to protect you."

Eleanor curtsied and gave an impish grin. "I dare say you would, though with a lighter hand, I imagine. But it's no use trying to show me Toby's good side, Rufus, he doesn't have one. He's a bully, and that's all there is to it. I don't believe he really wants to protect me at all, just to keep me for himself."

"You mean he wants to—?"

"Marry me? Yes, I think so, though he hasn't actually mentioned it. I have quite a respectable annuity coming to me from my father when I come of age, and Toby has a great love of gambling. Though I don't think he can be very good at it – he's always out of pocket. His father died a year or so ago, and ever since then Toby's been dead set on taking me to New Zealand, though he knows I don't want to go so far away from everything I'm used to." Eleanor pressed a hand to her mouth and blinked as though holding back tears.

Rufus moved to her side and caught her hands up in his in an effort to comfort her. "But what about your mother, surely she has some say in the matter?"

"I'm sure she would – if she were still alive."

"Oh, I'm sorry!"

Eleanor shook her head and conjured up a smile. "Oh, dear, I sound just like a penny dreadful, don't I? I don't mean to. Mama died some years ago of influenza. It was a great blow at the time, but, well, life has to go on – though I still miss her dreadfully. She made sure I had a good education, and I was going to try for a post as a schoolteacher until Toby got this bee in his bonnet about going to New Zealand. But he sort of is my guardian, since both of our parents are gone and I'm not yet of age, so it was difficult to say no to him without causing a scandal."

"Why on earth is he so keen to go there?"

"For the same reason as you, I imagine. It's supposed to be a land of opportunity. Isn't that why you're going?"

Rufus gave a rueful grin. "Well, no, not exactly. I'm—um— going to stay with my uncle who has an estate there. But surely, if you'd made it clear to your brother that you didn't want to go...?"

"You don't know Toby! Anyway, please don't worry about me." Eleanor leaned towards Rufus and lowered her voice to a conspiratorial murmur. "Toby doesn't know it yet, but I haven't the slightest intention of marrying him. I have plans of my own. I've been saving money from my allowance for some time now and, as soon as we reach Auckland, I plan to give him the slip and find myself a position as a teacher or a governess, or—or anything, really, short of becoming a lady of pleasure, just so long as I have my own income and can live independently."

Rufus grinned. "I'm glad to hear you don't intend to become a lady of the night, at any rate. You're very brave, you know, to undertake such a plan all by yourself, and in a strange country, too."

"I'm not brave," Eleanor said with a laugh, "just desperate! Rufus, I like you so much, and I really wish things could have been different between us. Perhaps they might have been, but for Toby. But, since I'm stuck with him, at least until we reach Auckland, I think it best all round if we try to ignore one another for the rest of the voyage. He can be very unpleasant if things don't go his way."

"I can imagine." If he was honest, Rufus was only too pleased to be able to avoid the Foxes without upsetting Eleanor, but he couldn't help feeling a twinge of guilt, since his real reason was Serafina. "Of course I'll do as you suggest though, under different circumstances, I'd have been proud to count such a plucky girl my friend. Thank you for explaining things to me, and I hope your plans succeed – though I've a feeling you won't need my good wishes."

Raising herself on tiptoe, Eleanor planted a soft kiss on Rufus's cheek. "I'm glad to have them, all the same. Thank you for being so understanding, Rufus, but I'd better go now, before Toby starts wondering where I am."

She ran to the door and opened it, peered both ways into the corridor, and then slipped out of the room. Rufus listened until the sound of her footsteps had faded away before leaving. There was no sense in arousing anyone's suspicions, in case word somehow got back to Fox. Then he made his way back to his cabin. Recent events had left him with a great deal to think about.

# CHAPTER NINE

Lying on his bed in his chilly cabin, his greatcoat draped over him for warmth, Rufus tried to make sense of all that had happened in the last few days. The rain had stopped, and the wind had died to a murmur that set the ship's rigging creaking and groaning so that he almost expected, if he looked out of his cabin, to see a white-draped ghost dragging its chains along the passageway.

"Thank you, Mr. Dickens," he murmured, smiling, "but I can do without further melodrama, if you don't mind."

He was no closer to deciding what he should do about Springer and Serafina – or, rather, about the passengers who'd fallen victim to their frightful appetites. He had no intention of giving the two of them away, if only to protect himself from their anger, though he knew his primary reason was to keep Serafina safe. He shuddered to think what would become of her if Doctor Wells, or worse, Captain Standish, discovered what she was. It seemed unlikely in the extreme that these worthy gentlemen would believe she and Springer actually were vampires. Most likely, they'd diagnose some mental aberration. Rufus had heard tales of men who believed they were wolves and ate human flesh from corpses they'd disinterred with their bare hands. In earlier times, they were believed to be werewolves, but these days they were thought to be suffering from a mental illness, and

Rufus had little doubt that would be the diagnosis given to Springer and Serafina. The thought of Serafina incarcerated in the sick bay for the rest of the journey, perhaps strapped into a strait jacket, was more than he could bear. God alone knew what they'd do to her once the *Orion* reached her destination. No, he could not bring himself to expose her – or Springer, for that matter – to such a fate.

But then, what of their victims, or of the quarantine Doctor Wells and the captain were considering? Rufus found himself wondering how this might affect the two vampires, and how they would fare without ready access to—to... Good God, what was wrong with him that he could even think of putting their welfare above that of the passengers and crew? Was he already that far gone with love for Serafina? Rufus could only come to the disturbing conclusion that he was. He always had been easily led by his emotions. The debacle of his involvement with Charlotte Winter stood testimony to that, but his feelings for Serafina seemed to be leading him into another dimension altogether, one he could neither accept nor relinquish.

With a snarl of frustration, he leapt from the bed and began to pace the cabin. How could he just do nothing and let other innocent passengers be injured? Yet how could he place Serafina in danger? He loved her and, despite her rejection, he was certain she loved him. How could he do that to her? What she and Springer did was undoubtedly evil, yet he'd seen with his own eyes, heard with his own ears how Serafina had sought to spare her—prey—he supposed he must call him, from physical and mental anguish. He continued to pace in his turmoil of indecision until he felt his head must explode, but there seemed no way to solve the conundrum. At length, feeling he must do something – anything – he pulled on his jacket and boots and left his cabin. Perhaps a walk in the cold air would clear his head and enable him to find a way out of his mental maze. Or, failing that, make him tired enough to sleep.

As he left the shelter of the rabbit warren of passageways that housed the cabins, the wind hit him like a wall of ice. The night was as black as pitch, with heavy clouds obscuring stars and moon. Buffeted by a freezing, southerly wind, Rufus made his way to the poop deck and clung to the railing while his eyes became accustomed to the dark. All around him was black on black, except for the watch house, illuminated from within by the soft glow of the watchman's lantern. Gradually, his eyes adjusted. He could just make out the middle and forward hatches, and the faint gleam of the main-deck railings washed by the heaving waves. It looked as though they were in for more bad weather. Hunching his shoulders against the cold, Rufus stared out to sea, listening to the wind screeching in the rigging and the waves slapping against the hull of the ship.

Then he heard another sound. It seemed to come from the main deck. He peered into the darkness, but could distinguish nothing. Pushing against the wind, he stumbled to the inner poop-deck railing and stared down. At first he could see nothing but the golden pool of light in the watch house. Then he caught a glimpse of movement towards the prow of the ship, not far from the forward hatch. As he watched, he thought he saw it again, just a flicker, moving towards him.

Perhaps it was Serafina or Springer about their dreadful business. On the spur of the moment, Rufus made up his mind to find out. If it turned out to be Springer he'd leave him to pursue his grisly objective, but if it were Serafina he'd try and speak with her. If she refused to hear him, at least he'd know he'd done his best to warn her. He made his way down the steps that led onto the main deck, and strode towards the forward hatch.

And walked straight into the arms of Toby Fox and two companions.

"Oh-ho," cried Fox, grabbing him by the arm. "If it isn't Mr High-and-Mighty de Hunte. I thought I told you to keep your hands off my sister."

"I've not laid a hand on Miss Fox," Rufus retorted, trying in vain to loosen Fox's vice-like grip. "Though I'd have thought she was old enough to choose her own company."

"Not laid a hand on her!" Fox exclaimed through gritted teeth. "Don't try that with me, sir, it won't wash. You were seen together in the ballroom."

"What of it?" asked Rufus, in what he hoped was a disarming tone. "We were conversing, that's all."

Fox leaned forward, thrusting his narrow face to within inches of Rufus's. "I told you to have nothing to do with her, didn't I?"

By now, Rufus was becoming afraid of Fox's aggressive manner, but he had no intention of letting him see it. If Fox had been alone, he'd have been more than happy to teach the bully a lesson, but he was outnumbered, and judged it best to try to defuse the situation, so he spoke as calmly as he could manage. "Look, I can understand your wish to protect your sister, but I can assure you I've no intentions towards her beyond mere sociability."

"You can call it what you like, Mr de Hunte, but I know

what you were doing. I warn you off her, and next thing I know she's seen kissing you." He turned to his two cronies. "Does that sound like mere sociability to you, lads?" The two men dutifully shook their heads. "I think it's time we taught Mr de Hunte a lesson, don't you?"

As though his words were a secret signal, Fox's companions lunged at Rufus and, before he quite realised what they were doing, they had his arms pinned behind his back. As he struggled against them, he saw Fox's features twist into a vicious snarl. Drawing back a little now that Rufus was helpless, Fox clenched his fist and drove it hard into his face. Rufus felt blood, hot and metallic, in his mouth, and kicked out at Fox, angry himself now, and determined not to succumb without a fight. His retaliation seemed to inflame Fox even more. With a roar of fury, he flung himself at Rufus, raining kicks and blows on his body and face as the others held him fast, until Rufus sagged in their grip, all but unconscious. They let him fall to the deck, where Fox swiftly rifled his pockets, taking his silver watch and chain, as well as what money he had on him. Then he yanked from Rufus's finger the gold signet ring that had been a gift from his father on his twenty-first birthday.

"These'll fetch a pretty penny once we reach shore," gloated Fox. "Come on, lads. Best scarper before the watch sees us."

As he left, Fox paused just long enough to administer a final vicious kick to Rufus's ribs. But Rufus was oblivious to further pain.

* * * *

Rufus could hear someone moaning, a low, anguished sound, and wondered vaguely who it could be. And why was he hurting so much? It seemed every inch of his body ached. Thinking it must be the lumpy mattress on which he lay, he tried to move, and agony licked through him like tongues of fire. He cried out, and realised the moaning had come from his own lips.

He felt a cool hand on his brow, and a soft voice spoke, "Hush, try not to move."

Wondering who on earth it could be, Rufus tried to open his eyes, but the lids seemed to be glued together, and the effort made his head hurt. He tried to speak, but his lips seemed too big for his face, and his throat felt as though someone had set fire to it.

"Shh, sleep now, you'll feel better presently," the voice said, soft, but somehow compelling.

He slept.

When he woke again, Rufus was able to open his eyes a little, and found himself in his own cabin, lying on his narrow bed clad in his nightshirt, but with no memory of how he'd come to be there. The last thing he remembered was going out for a walk on deck. He'd been trying to work something out, something important, but his mind refused to tell him what it was. He heard a faint splashing sound and turned towards it. What was that woman doing in his cabin? And who was she? He felt he ought to know. As he squinted through eyes that seemed unwilling to stay open, the woman turned towards him and smiled. It was Serafina. She was holding a glass in her hand.

"Do you think you could drink a little water, Rufus? No, don't try to speak, you're still very weak. Here, let me help you."

As she bent over him, he smelt her musky perfume. Very gently, she slid her arm beneath his head and lifted it, holding the cup to his lips. They were still swollen, and much of the water spilled and ran down his chin, but he managed to swallow a little.

Setting the cup down on the bedside table, Serafina took his hand in both of hers. Her skin felt cool against his. "Don't try to talk just yet," she told him with a smile. "You've been hurt quite badly, and have lain out on the deck for most of the night."

"But what...?" Rufus tried to ask, ignoring her instructions.

"I can't tell you exactly what happened, only that I found you lying on the deck early this morning. I think you've received a bad beating, but who might have done such a thing I don't know. I brought you here and cleaned your wounds, which aren't as bad as they no doubt feel, though I think you may have some ribs broken. There's a great deal of bruising on your left side."

Rufus squeezed her hand and whispered, "How long have I been...?"

"It was well after midnight when I found you, and they rang six bells a little while ago."

She turned anxious eyes towards the open porthole, where a faint lightening of the sky was visible. "I must leave you now, but I promise I'll return later and see what I can do to help you. I've filled your glass with water in case you feel thirsty. The best thing you can do now is to sleep." Serafina bent over Rufus and looked into his eyes so deeply he felt he must drown in the dark depths of her own. "Sleep now," she murmured, and hurried off.

* * * *

For most of that day, Rufus slept. It was late afternoon
before he was able to stay awake for more than a few minutes
at a time. Hauling himself painfully onto one elbow, he
looked about him, wondering what could have happened to
him, and why he was in so much pain. Then he remembered.
Fox! He and his accomplices had set upon him and beaten
him. But that had been outside on the main deck. Who had
brought him back to his cabin?

Now that he was fully awake, a strong thirst assailed him.
Noticing the glass of water on the table beside him, he picked
it up and took a few sips of the icy liquid, feeling it trickle
down his throat, cooling the fire that seemed to burn there.
After a few more grateful sips, he lay down again and pulled
the blankets – and his greatcoat, he noticed, with some
surprise – up to his chin. It was chilly in his cabin, and he
was beginning to shiver. As he lay there, rocked by the gentle
motion of the ship like a baby in a cradle, vague memories
began to filter through the fog in his mind. He could recall
nothing immediately after Fox and his cronies had beaten
him. Presumably he had been unconscious. He had no idea
how long he had lain thus, but it seemed to him that
someone had picked him up and carried him. He was sure he
could recall being carried, because of the pain it had caused
him. He could only suppose his rescuer had brought him
here, put him to bed, and cleaned his wounds. Now who had
told him that? Then it came to him. Serafina had told him
she'd found him and brought him here. But how could she

have carried him so far without help? She must have had help, surely, but who...? Then he remembered something else – something that wrenched him out of his torpor.

Weren't vampires supposed to have super-human strength? Rufus realised then that, even though he had concluded that Serafina must be a vampire, some part of him had resisted the notion; had clung to the comfort of believing he might be wrong. He had *wanted* to be wrong. But now, unless he could be sure Serafina had had help, he must finally accept that all such comfort was lost to him, that the woman he loved was, indeed, a vampire. His mind now working feverishly, Rufus began to wonder why Serafina had rescued him. Could he hope he'd been right to feel she wanted him as he wanted her? Or was her hunger of an altogether baser kind? Rufus was shaken by a deep shudder that had nothing to do with the cold. What if he'd been wrong all along? What if all she'd ever wanted from him had been...? In his mind he saw again her fangs glinting in the chill moonlight, heard her soothing, hypnotic words to Mr Haynes, her rapt expression as she bent her head to his neck.

Sick with horror, Rufus tried to pull himself to a sitting position. What was wrong with him that he could even contemplate loving someone—something—that could do that to a fellow creature? He must leave, now, before she returned, before she could suck out what was left of his will with those eyes of hers. He'd go to the sick bay. Surely he'd be safe under Doctor Wells's care. But his pain was such that he was unable to force his body to do his bidding. Trembling with fear, he sank back and waited for a few moments before trying again. On his third attempt, he managed to drag himself up onto his elbows. His left side was in agony.

Perhaps his ribs were broken after all. Panting and gasping from exertion, he waited for the pain to subside a little before making a further attempt. Then he heard a soft rapping on his door, and it began to open. He made another frantic effort, but collapsed back onto the bed, sobbing with pain and terror, and tried to cover himself with the bedclothes as though they might somehow protect him.

Soft footsteps approached his bed, and he heard Serafina's voice. "Rufus, what's wrong? Are you in pain?"

Trying in vain to quell his panic, Rufus pulled the blankets closer. He felt, rather than heard, Serafina bend over him, and covered his face with his shaking hands as she pulled back the bedclothes and stared at him.

"Rufus, please don't be afraid of me. Surely you must know I only want to help you."

Her voice was very gentle and, despite himself, Rufus found himself peering at her through his fingers. When he saw the look of concern on her face, he forced himself to lower his hands and take a deep breath, trying his best to ignore the pain that flared in his side and his throat. Serafina took his hand in hers and stroked it, gazing into his eyes, and he felt his panic subside and, with it, much of the pain.

"There," she murmured, like a mother soothing a frightened child, "that's much better, yes?"

Rufus nodded. He couldn't help but respond to Serafina's tender voice and touch. His mind felt strange, as though it were not his own, yet it harboured no doubt of her good intentions. With a sigh almost of contentment, he closed his eyes, ready to accept her ministrations.

\* \* \* \*

Something very strange was happening. It seemed to Rufus that some great cat had him in its grasp and was licking his face, though of course that was ridiculous. He must be dreaming, one of those dreams that are so vivid the dreamer is convinced of their reality, even while aware of their sheer absurdity. He tried to move his head to see what was happening, but found he could not. Nor could he open his eyes. He had no choice, it seemed, but to lie there and feel the soft, moist movement against his skin, the creature's tongue, or whatever it was, making its way from his face to his shoulders, then on down his body, lingering for what seemed a long time at his left side. Unable to prevent its slow, oddly sensual progress, Rufus gave himself up to it until at last he fell into a sleep too deep for dreaming.

How long he slept he couldn't tell, but it was dark night when he woke to find Serafina sitting on the edge of the bed holding his hand in hers. As his eyes opened, she leaned forward a little and brushed his forehead with a cool, gentle hand, her scent wafting over him like a fragrant breeze.

"How do you feel, now?" she murmured, smiling.

"Much better, thank you." And he did! As Serafina's words focused his mind on his body, he realised it hurt considerably less than before he had fallen asleep. Puzzled, he raised a hand to his face. He could feel where the skin had been broken, but the swelling seemed to have subsided along with the pain. He looked up into Serafina's pale, calm face, a sudden suspicion sharpening his gaze. "What did you do to me?"

She shook her head, smiling. "Don't be afraid, Rufus. It was nothing more than an old remedy I learned a long time ago. But I'm very pleased that you feel better. It will take a little time, I think, but I believe your wounds may heal quite well. Can you recall who did this to you?"

"Yes, it was a man called Toby Fox, and two others, friends of his I suppose. I think I've seen them before, but I don't know their names. They're most likely steerage passengers. That's the company Fox seems to prefer."

"But why should they wish to hurt you?"

Rufus looked away, unwilling to tell Serafina how he had incurred Fox's wrath. Now it seemed he had some proof of her feelings for him, if he told her about Eleanor how could he be sure he wouldn't incur her wrath as well? But he could sense Serafina waiting for his reply. He had to say something.

"I—I suppose I should tell someone about it," he blurted out, "Captain Standish, perhaps?" Serafina looked doubtful. "And I must tell Eleanor." The words were out before he could stop them.

Serafina gave him a sharp look. "And who is this Eleanor?"

"She's Fox's sister," Rufus said, feeling sheepish, yet at the same time pleased to have further evidence of Serafina's partiality. "Well, not really his sister. Her mother married his father after their other parents had died. At any rate, Fox is ridiculously jealous of her. Eleanor thinks he wants to marry her because she stands to come into a sizeable inheritance." He grimaced at the thought of Eleanor married to the brutish Fox. "He saw us talking together after church on Sunday, and I had the bad luck to run into him and his cronies that night when I went for a walk on deck." Rufus caught up Serafina's hand and carried it to his lips. "You've no need to be jealous, you know. I think Eleanor would have liked to become closer to me, but my heart is already engaged elsewhere, as well you know."

Serafina sighed, as though trying to expel something oppressive, but said nothing. Rufus squeezed her hand, which still lay in his.

"Please don't be sad. You know I love you."

"Yes," she whispered, "that's what makes me sad."

Rufus gave her hand another squeeze. "Let's not worry about that now. I'm sure Mr Springer will come round when he sees we're serious about one another."

Serafina shook her head. "I don't think so." For some moments, she sat in silence, apparently deep in thought. Then, as though to banish her despondency, she gave a little shake of her head and sat up straighter, smiling at Rufus. "But you're right, we shan't think of sad things." She picked up the copy of *David Copperfield* that lay on the bedside cabinet. "Would you like me to read to you?"

# CHAPTER TEN

Rufus must have fallen asleep while Serafina was reading to him. When he awoke again it was early morning and she had gone. On his bedside cabinet stood a plate containing bread and butter, and several slices of ham, and a glass of milk partially spilt from the rocking of the ship. Where she could have got them from during the night he had no idea, and wasn't sure he wanted to speculate. A rather damp note lay half under the glass. Rufus rescued it and read:

*Dear Rufus,*

*Here is food in case you are hungry. I will return later.*

*Serafina.*

Seeing food for the first time in almost two days made Rufus feel suddenly ravenous, and he made short work of the meal.

His next thought was to discover the state of his wounds. A thorough examination with the aid of his shaving mirror showed most of them were almost healed. Whatever treatment Serafina had used must be little short of miraculous. There was still a burning sensation in his throat and a tightness in his chest, which were worse if anything, but the only other pain he felt now was an occasional twinge in his left side.

\* \* \* \*

When Serafina returned soon after sunset bearing more food, she found Rufus burning with fever, alternately shivering and perspiring, and wracked by debilitating fits of coughing. She gave him water, and he managed to drink a few sips but, when she offered him the roast mutton and potatoes she had brought, he shook his head, telling her in a voice hoarse from coughing that his throat was too sore to eat. His nightshirt was soaked with perspiration, so she found one that was dry, if not perfectly clean, and helped him to put it on. Then she drew the blankets close about him, wishing she had some body warmth to give him. By midnight, he was delirious. If he had been a vampire, he would never have become so ill, but it seemed her vampiric skills had been insufficient to heal this sickness, or had even allowed it to develop, perhaps, by inadvertently interfering with his body's own healing processes. With all her heart, she hoped not, but whatever the cause, she knew she had no choice but to call the doctor to him.

Serafina found Doctor Wells in the sick bay, writing by the light of an oil lamp. With profound gratitude that no victims of the supposed wasting sickness were present, she explained Rufus's symptoms and then hurried back to his cabin with the doctor close behind her. If he thought it odd that a young lady should be caring for Rufus, he gave no sign of it.

Rufus lay as before, shivering and racked by bouts of coughing, a sheen of perspiration covering his corpse-pale skin. With an anxious Serafina hovering behind him, the doctor felt Rufus's pulse and forehead, then opened his brown-leather bag, pulled out a stethoscope and applied it to

Rufus's chest, nodding his head and pursing his lips as he listened to it. Next he took out a thermometer, shook it, and placed it beneath Rufus's tongue.

"Now, keep that there for a few moments if you can, Mr de Hunte."

Turning to Serafina, Doctor Wells said, "Can you tell me what has happened to Mr de Hunte, Miss...?"

Ignoring the doctor's tacit invitation to supply her name, Serafina thought quickly and said, "No, I'm afraid not. I found him lying on the main deck unconscious, and helped him back to his cabin." Looking straight into the doctor's eyes and willing him to believe her, she added, "I thought perhaps he had fallen and knocked his head."

The doctor nodded. "Yes, he has some bruising to the face, so I dare say that may be it."

He removed the thermometer from Rufus's mouth and held it up, peering at it through his gold-rimmed spectacles in the dim light. "Hmm, yes, I think he may have lain outside in the cold for quite some time before you found him. He has a fever, and his lungs are congested. I'll give him some laudanum now, to help him sleep, and I'll have another look at him in the morning. Don't worry if he's off his food, but he should have plenty to drink, and keep him warm." He gave Serafina a conspiratorial smile. "By rights, I should take him to the sick bay, but I don't think he's infectious. You appear to be giving him excellent care and I'm sure he'd rather look at your face than mine when he wakes up. Good night to you, Miss..."

* * * *

Doctor Wells arrived early the next morning to find Rufus considerably worse. Keeping his voice brisk and cheerful, however, he said, "Good morning, Mr de Hunte. How are you feeling today?"

Rufus could manage little more than a hoarse whisper in reply. "My head hurts...and my chest...and I can't...breathe...properly."

"Still coughing?" asked the doctor. Rufus responded with a paroxysm of coughing. "Are you coughing up phlegm?"

Rufus shook his head, wheezing as he tried to breathe.

After examining him and taking his temperature, Doctor Wells turned to Serafina, a grave expression on his rotund face. "I'm afraid Mr de Hunte has developed pneumonia, undoubtedly from taking a chill while lying out in the cold. There's not a great deal we can do other than to keep him as comfortable as possible. He should drink plenty of fluids, and I'll see that some broth is brought to him presently, as well as some breakfast for you. Keep him warm, but bathe his forehead with a cloth rinsed in cool water to help bring down the fever." He took a small, brown bottle from his bag and offered it to Serafina. "Give him a few drops of this every four hours. It'll help him to sleep, and sleep is the best thing for him right now. With any luck, the fever will break within the next day or two."

Serafina forced a smile. "Thank you, Doctor Wells, you're very kind."

"Not at all, Miss...I'll call back later."

He gave Serafina an encouraging smile and left.

She found it impossible to feel encouraged, however, with Rufus lying before her shivering and coughing, and, by the doctor's own admission, beyond human help. She wanted to scream from the frustration of being unable to heal him herself, and the guilt of knowing it might have been she who precipitated his condition, albeit unwittingly. But she knew she must present at least the appearance of calm for his sake, so she busied herself pouring water into the enamel washing bowl and finding a clean facecloth. Dipping it into the water, she wrung it out and gently applied it to Rufus's burning forehead. He moaned as it touched his skin, and Serafina murmured calming sentiments she did not feel.

As the morning wore on, she began to long for the sanctuary of her own cabin where she could sleep until daylight began to ebb, but she dared not leave Rufus unattended, and she did not feel able to beg the services of anyone else. She and Anton had striven to keep themselves, if not completely unnoticed, at least largely unremarked by the other passengers, to avoid the possibility of being recognised by those from whom they must feed. Their vampiric mind control was their main weapon against recognition, but Anton preferred to leave nothing to chance, and Serafina was happy enough to bow to his greater experience. So far, their stratagems had worked. No one had even remembered what had happened to them, let alone who had been responsible, but to approach any of the other passengers now could put both of them in danger of discovery. She could not ask Anton for help. For one thing, he would be deep in vampiric sleep by now, almost literally dead to the world, and for another, he'd be furious if he knew she was helping Rufus. Although he'd been happy enough to indulge her desire to dance with Rufus at the ball, as soon as he had become aware of her feelings for him, he'd been adamant that she must give him up.

Yet how could she, when her desire for him tortured her almost as though the hunger were upon her? It was all very well for Anton to make such decrees. He seemed not to need love at all, yet the pain of losing Francois almost a century ago had lain like ice in her heart down all the long years since – until Rufus had begun to melt it away. The fact that Anton was right about the dangers of loving humans was of no consolation whatsoever. She knew there were small colonies of vampires, usually in relatively out-of-the way places where local superstition was strong, allowing the vampires to play on it to control the human inhabitants. She had even heard of vampires who kept groups of subservient humans to fulfil their needs, much as humans kept cattle, or pets. But what chance had they of meeting such kindred spirits when Anton insisted on living the life of a nomad? Serafina sighed. She was sick to the heart of travelling. Anton was solitary by nature, and had spent most of his adult life, prior to becoming a vampire, as a soldier, so he was used to being posted all over the place. But she was not. She longed to settle down somewhere, to have a place called home. Now she found herself longing to have Rufus there with her, to feel his kisses, his strong arms about her, as she had that night after her quarrel with Anton. She wanted him so badly she thought she could even bear the inevitable loss if only she could have his love for the span of his human life. Now it seemed even this was to be denied her, not by Anton, but by that villain Fox and his friends and, worse still, perhaps by her own attempt to heal him.

Blinking back tears of despair, Serafina bent and kissed Rufus's burning forehead, his eyelids, his mouth. He moaned faintly in his sleep, and she laid her cheek against his. "Oh, my darling," she murmured, "how can I lose you so soon?"

As she lay there, feeling his skin burning against the chill of her own, an idea came to her. An idea so audacious it all but stopped her breath. If only she dared carry it out, in one fell swoop she could restore Rufus to health, remove Anton's objections to her loving him, and have his love forever. But did she dare? Serafina leapt to her feet and began to pace the length of the tiny cabin, fear and excitement bubbling up in her like molten rock in a volcano. Could she do it? At one moment her heart said yes; at another her head said no. What if Rufus didn't want it? What if he came to curse her for what she had done, as Anton cursed his maker? But then, she reminded herself, Anton was not brought across by one who loved him, but by one whose only desire was to escape discovery, not caring what pain and despair he inflicted in the process. But if Rufus wanted her as much as she wanted him...

She sat by his side again, reaching her mind out to his to discover what was in his thoughts. But his mind was filled with pain and confusion, overlaid by the soporific effects of laudanum, and she could glean nothing. Yet perhaps he did feel her mind touch his, for he opened his eyes and whispered her name. Serafina brushed away the damp hair from his forehead and touched her lips to it.

"Yes, my darling, I'm here. Would you like some water?" He nodded, and Serafina lifted his head and put the glass to his lips. He took a few sips, and then lay back, exhausted.

"Serafina," he whispered again, "am I...going to...die?"

Serafina blinked back the cold tears that sprang in her eyes. What should she tell him? Should she lie? Or should she turn the lie into truth?

"Rufus," she murmured at last, "I love you so much! Do you love me?" Rufus nodded, reaching for her hand and attempting to lift it to his lips. "Doctor Wells says you're very ill, but if I could find a way to make you better, would you take it?"

"Like the way you healed my wounds?" he whispered. "Can you...do that?"

"Yes. And we could be together, too, for as long as you wish it."

"Forever!" Rufus declared hoarsely, and then was overcome by a paroxysm of coughing.

Serafina lifted him up, cradling him with one arm as she gave him more water. "Yes, if that's what you want. But you must really want it – I can't do it otherwise."

As he gazed up at Serafina, Rufus's eyes seemed to burn with some deep hunger. Or was it only fever? She held his gaze with hers, and saw that his hunger was for her – for her love, her heart, her soul – as hers was for him. *Yes*, she thought, *I'll do it! I must!* But caution told her *not yet, not just yet*. She couldn't let Rufus endure his first hunger during daylight, when it would be impossible for them to hunt in safety. Besides, she was so weary she felt halfway dead herself.

"We must rest first," she said. "Just for a while."

She bent to kiss Rufus's lips, and then looked deep into his eyes, willing him to sleep.

When she was sure he was asleep, Serafina first secured the cabin door, then, not wanting to disturb his slumber, lay down on the floor beside his bed and sank into the heavy sleep she would soon be able to share with him.

\* \* \* \*

Soon after sunset, while Serafina was enjoying the vivid, almost surreal dreaming that often marked the period just prior to a vampire's awakening, a brisk rapping at the cabin door brought her rushing into full consciousness. She scrambled to her feet, quickly smoothing back her hair and straightening her clothes, and opened the door to find Doctor Wells standing there. She had forgotten he was due to call. Giving silent thanks that he had arrived before she was able to carry out her plan, and not while it was in progress, she smiled and ushered him inside.

"How's our patient this evening?" he asked, with his usual friendly smile.

Serafina judged this to be a rhetorical question, so she said nothing, but stood back to allow him to pass.

Rufus, who had also been woken by the doctor's arrival, did his best to seem cheerful, but it was as clear to Doctor Wells as it was to Serafina that he was no better. If anything, his breathing was more laboured than it had been that morning, his face pale and haggard, and his eyes sunken and red-rimmed, the surrounding skin seeming almost bruised. As Doctor Wells took Rufus's temperature and made his examination, Serafina reached her mind out to his. What she found was not comforting. It was clear Rufus was dying, and there was only one way she could be certain of saving him – if the doctor would only finish his business and leave.

When, at long last, her wish was granted, Serafina heaved a great sigh of relief and hurried to lock the door. Then she went to sit beside Rufus on the bed. The sight of him so ravaged by his illness almost broke her heart.

"My poor, brave darling," she murmured, her lips against his burning forehead. "Now I shall make you well, if you'll trust me. Do you trust me, my love?"

"Always!" Rufus's voice was like the rustling of the leaves in the trees before the winter winds take them.

Very gently, Serafina took him up into her arms, turning his head so that he faced her, and drew him into her steady, hypnotic gaze, speaking to him in a voice like warm honey, willing him to be calm and to feel no pain. When his eyelids began to droop, her voice became the murmur of soft music carried from far away, slow and rhythmic, drawing him more and more deeply under her power. She felt the familiar tingling in her gums as her fangs began to emerge, and drew in a deep breath, letting it out in a soft sigh of anticipation as she bent her head towards him.

Despite the spell she had woven around him, Rufus cried out when her fangs pierced his neck, his body writhing in an effort to be free of her embrace, but she clasped him tighter against her. As his blood began to trickle into her mouth, sweet, warm, and metallic, her lips worked against his skin, turning the trickle into a flow. She could taste the faint tang of laudanum, and of his fever too, but Serafina did not care. She was drinking her beloved Rufus into herself! She could feel him flowing over her tongue and down her throat and into her body until she tingled and glowed with his life, so warm and precious. Soon she would give him new life, and they would be free to share their love.

Serafina knew it would be all too easy to lose herself in the ecstasy of feeding, and to drain Rufus completely of life. But she must leave him a little blood or she would lose him. At a little less than two centuries, she was still young as vampires went but, under Anton's tutelage, she had quickly learned not to take too much from those from whom she fed, leaving them weak and light-headed perhaps, but with no lasting ill effects. Indeed, vampiric mind control was able to impart a sense of well being, a feeling of having just experienced something delightful they could not quite recall. With Rufus it was different. She must take enough of his blood for her own to become dominant when he drank it, yet not enough to kill him outright. It was a fine line to judge, especially since she had never before brought anyone across. Because he had been made against his will, Anton had not wanted to bring her across – or anyone else, for that matter – and had only overcome his horror of it when it became evident that he could not guarantee her safety by any other means. From the start of her life as a vampire, he had insisted she cause as little harm as possible to the humans from whom she must feed, and that on no account was she to introduce any human to the existence he regarded as a curse. Even with Francois, the young French nobleman with whom she had been so enamoured she had helped him to escape France and the guillotine, she had obeyed Anton and resisted the temptation to bring him across. But what had that brought her? She had lost him. Anton had seen to that, dragging her away from England and leaving Francois behind. Years later, she had heard of his marriage to the daughter of an English duke.

But she would not let it happen again. Anton would not stop her this time. She would not lose Rufus!

She raised her head and stared at his bloodless face, then down the length of his emaciated body. He was so still! So pale! But a little blood still trickled from the wound in his neck, and her fingers found the faintest of pulses in his wrist. There was no time to waste.

She sat up and practically tore undone the buttons of her left sleeve. She pushed it back from her wrist and bit into a vein there. She lifted Rufus's limp body, unceremonious in her haste, so that he lay across her lap, supporting him with her right arm as though he had been her baby. She held her wrist close to Rufus's mouth, but it was closed, and the blood merely trickled over his lips and down his chin. Desperate now, and afraid she might have taken too much of his blood, Serafina grasped his hair and pulled back his head, forcing his mouth open. She practically shoved her wrist into it, reaching around his head with her other hand to squeeze more blood from the vein. She had no clear idea of what she was doing. Anton had described the process to her once, but she'd never seen it done, and Anton had said nothing about how awkward it was.

Then, after what seemed an eternity of willing him to drink, Serafina saw his throat convulse, and knew he was swallowing the life-giving fluid. She expelled a breath she had not realised she was holding, and the release of tension relaxed her enough for her blood to flow more freely, and for her vampiric instincts to take over. When she sensed Rufus had ingested enough, she laid him back down on the bed and prepared to keep vigil until he reawakened. She could only hope it would not be too long.

# CHAPTER ELEVEN

Rufus opened his eyes to find himself alone in the darkness. How long had he been asleep? he wondered. His last waking memory was of Doctor Wells visiting him. Serafina had been there, too. After that, his recollections were so bizarre they could only have been fever dreams.

He seemed to recall looking down a tunnel, smooth-walled, almost like living tissue and infused with a faint glow, stretching away before him as far as he could see. Then he had been moving inside it, wafted along by some unseen force towards a light just visible at the end of the tunnel, as though a sun were rising there and he was watching its first golden rays. It called to him – not with a voice, but with something that seemed to hum soundlessly inside him. He could not feel his body. Although he had some vague recollection of pain, it seemed to have receded, and he was floating, floating towards the light...

Then someone had snuffed out the sun.

A voice had murmured to him, low and soothing, telling him not to be afraid, and he had felt something in his throat, something warm and thick that trickled across his tongue and down his gullet until he thought it would choke him, but the muscles in his throat had tightened, convulsed, swallowed the salty, metallic liquid until a pool of it lay heavy and viscous – and strangely satisfying – in his stomach. He had become aware of his body only when he had felt it being moved. Then he was lying down, the strange stuff in his stomach spreading out like a pool of treacle. Then, while he was still wondering what on earth was going on, something else had happened.

He had begun to change.

Not on the outside – at least he didn't think so – but on the inside. His stomach was altering, and his heart, and other parts he couldn't even identify, all stretching and contracting, transforming like an insect larva inside a chrysalis. A sudden panic had flooded through him and his body had begun to writhe, his arms and feet to flail about unbidden, as though seeking to shake it off. But the weird and terrifying transformation remained beyond his control. Again he had heard that soft, comforting voice, and eventually his body had become still, apparently accepting the changes of which his mind could make no sense.

Rufus could only conclude that these bizarre sensations had, indeed, been a product of his fever. Which was gone now, he realised with a start. In fact, he felt remarkably well – and hungry! How long he had gone without food, he had no idea, but right now he was ravenous enough to make short work of a three-course meal. He sat up and looked about him, half expecting to find himself back in England, so different did he feel, but his eyes made out the now familiar wood panelling of his tiny cabin, his cabin trunk – all the usual trappings of daily life aboard the *Orion*, although someone had fastened the brass cover over the porthole. That must be why it was so dark. Jumping out of bed, he opened the porthole cover to see a choppy sea beneath a lightening sky. It must be early morning. No wonder he was so famished!

It appeared someone had thought of this eventuality, however; on his bedside table was a tray containing two slices of buttered bread, now curling at the edges, a wedge of hard-looking cheese, and a rather wrinkled apple. He seized one of the pieces of bread, but the very smell of it made his gorge rise. What on earth was going on? Granted, the food was not particularly appetising, but still...

He picked up the piece of cheese and bit off a chunk, but was forced to spit it out again as his stomach rebelled at the taste and the feel of it on his tongue. Puzzled, and more than a little annoyed, Rufus threw the cheese back onto the plate. Perhaps he wasn't yet as well as he'd thought. He'd heard of people who had gone for some time without food losing their appetite for it, at least temporarily. He'd have to ask Doctor Wells on his next visit. In the meantime, he supposed he might as well get dressed.

It was while he was attempting to ferret out some clean underwear that it occurred to him there might be another explanation for his sudden aversion to food. What if Serafina had...? But she wouldn't – not without his agreement. Would she? With a moan of horror, Rufus staggered to his bed on legs suddenly weak, and fell onto it, fear and hunger contracting his gut until the pain was all but unbearable. He curled himself into a tight ball, hands clasped about his knees as he lay gasping in agony. Then he heard footsteps approaching the cabin. Assailed by a fresh wave of panic, he turned to stare at the door, flinching as it began to open.

To his amazement, it was not Serafina who stood there, but one of the young ladies with whom he had danced at the ball, although he couldn't recall her name. What on earth was she doing here, especially without a chaperone, and what was wrong with her? She appeared to be sleepwalking – but that was ridiculous. Then he saw Serafina. She was standing close behind the girl, propelling her into the room. All at once things became completely – horrendously – clear to Rufus. Serafina had been part of what he had mistaken for fever dreams. It was her voice murmuring comforting words to him while he...while she...

Feeling sick to his core, he demanded, "What have you done to me, Serafina?"

Her eyes slid away from his. "I've made you well, Rufus. You were so ill, I thought you would die. Doctor Wells thought so, too. He said you had pneumonia, and there was nothing he could do. How could I leave you to die when I could make you well again?"

Rufus glared at her. "And what else have you made me?"

"But you know, don't you?"

"Say it! Tell me what you did!"

"Oh, please don't be angry, Rufus." Tears welled up in Serafina's eyes and began to slide down her cheeks. "I love you so much, and I couldn't bear to lose you. I sat there and watched you in pain, dying, and I couldn't bear it! Then I thought if you were as I am, you wouldn't be ill, not ever again, and all Anton's arguments against my loving you wouldn't matter any more. Can't you see, my love, now we can be together always, and Anton can't have any objection to it, can he?"

"Oh, I imagine he might have one or two." Rufus's voice was hard with anger and misery. "Do you think he'd approve of your just going around making people vampires, willy-nilly? Do you? Good God, Serafina, how could you be so—so *selfish*?"

Serafina's eyes widened. "Selfish? How—?"

"Did you stop to consider what I might want?"

"But I asked you. You said you wanted to be with me forever. You said you trusted me to bring you across safely, and I have!"

A note of defiance had crept into her voice that merely served to increase Rufus's anger. "For God's sake, Serafina, I was delirious with fever! I could have said anything!"

"But you didn't," she pointed out. "You told me you wanted to live."

"Well, of course I did! It doesn't mean I wanted to spend the next God knows how long having to drink human blood, having to creep about in the shadows for fear of being found out! Serafina, I don't give a damn what *you* are, I love you anyway. But—this?" Speechless, he spread his hands as though presenting to her the full horror of what she had done to him.

Serafina looked at him, her dark eyes brimming with love as well as tears. "I know you feel strange just now. You're still becoming vampire. Your body has changed – you'll already have felt that – but the mind takes a little longer. Soon you'll leave your human fears behind, but until then, please know I'm with you. I'll teach you what you need to know, I promise."

During this exchange, the young woman had continued to stand stock still, deaf to their voices, staring ahead of her with unseeing eyes. Rufus, however, had felt the gnawing inside him grow until it seemed to radiate out in waves from the very hub of his being, engulfing him in a hunger so fierce it seemed beyond endurance. It was as though he were being consumed from the inside by something so ravenous it must surely eat him alive if it was not fed. He gazed at the girl and realised she smelled utterly delicious, her blood warm and sweet in her veins, inviting him to partake of it. He could hear her heart beating with the soft rhythm of a drum. He felt a sudden, fiery surge of excitement. He looked at Serafina, unsure what to do next. She smiled and led the unresisting girl towards the bed, pushing her down onto it. Another great wave of hunger engulfed Rufus so that he almost cried out with the pain of it. Serafina smiled encouragement and gave him a little push forward. Simultaneously terrified and excited, Rufus sat down beside the girl and pushed her heavy brown hair back from her neck. He stared at the bluish veins throbbing there just beneath the soft smoothness of her skin, at once fascinated and repulsed. Then both revulsion and hesitation gave way to a fierce, desperate longing as his new senses filled with the scent of sweet, warm blood. At the same time, he felt a sharp tingling in his gums, and his canine teeth elongated into the needle-sharp fangs he had seen in Serafina's mouth. Instinctively, he bent to the girl's neck and sank them into a vein and felt the hot blood flow into his mouth.

How delectable it tasted, how sweet, the pure life force pouring into him, spurting against his throat, flowing over his tongue with the texture of warm honey and tinged with the taste of metal, awakening such a sharp, thrilling pleasure in him that he wanted it never to stop.

He became aware of something shaking him, tearing him away from the source of his delight. With a snarl, he raised his head to see Serafina smiling down at him, her dark eyes gleaming with something akin to pride.

"No more," she whispered, "or you'll kill her."

Disappointed, Rufus sat back, light-headed from the blood rushing through his veins. Serafina pulled the girl to her feet and straightened her gown where Rufus's grasp had creased it.

"I'll return soon," she whispered, and led the girl from the room.

Moments later, she was back. Closing the door softly, she smiled and held out her arms to him. Rufus went to her and she held him close and kissed him, her tongue delicately gathering up the traces of blood that still clung to his lips, every touch sending sweet sparks of fire shooting along his nerves.

"So," she said at last, with a mischievous smile, "I have a new brother."

"Not a brother. I want you too much for that."

"You're vampire now," she said, tracing his lips with her finger, and licking it with the tip of her tongue. "We share the same blood, you and I. You're my brother, my child, *and* my lover. We'll always be together."

"Yes!" breathed Rufus, for the first time gaining some inkling of what this meant.

He felt a tingle of fear ripple through him, not just fear of what being a vampire might mean for him, but of Serafina herself. The gaze she turned on him was filled with such intensity it seemed he might drown in her eyes. Yet along with fear came excitement. A sensation akin to electricity pulsed between them, prickling along the surface of his skin until all he could think of was Serafina's lips against his. As though she had read his thoughts, she drew him close and kissed him again, not the tentative kiss of an inexperienced girl, but hard and passionate, her tongue and lips caressing his mouth as her hands caressed his body.

Somehow he managed to manoeuvre both of them to the bed, tugging at the buttons of her gown with clumsy fingers as he did so. Serafina smiled, and gently disengaged herself, her deft fingers accomplishing what his could not. He helped her to remove her gown, his hands caressing her, savouring the smooth lines of her body and the delicious longing it aroused in him. Kneeling before her, he quickly unlaced her black-patent boots and pulled them off, running his hands up the curves of her legs beneath her petticoats, seeking the garters that held up her stockings. As he rolled the first stocking down, he pushed back her petticoats and kissed the inside of her knee. Serafina gasped, and he felt her hands grasp him tightly by the shoulders. Seconds later, both stockings lay on the floor. Rufus's jacket soon followed. Serafina pulled open his shirt, pushing her hands inside it, caressing him as she removed it. Her touch was like cool water flowing over his skin, yet it seemed to fill him with liquid fire until he was consumed by such a longing he felt he must die unless he could melt into Serafina and become part of her.

As though reading his thoughts, she turned so he could unlace her corset. She pulled it off and flung it to the floor. As his hands slid inside her soft linen shift, she held up her arms so he could remove it. It joined the rest of their clothes. Her hair had fallen loose, and Rufus lifted it back so he could gaze at her. Slowly, his eyes drank her in, delighting in the long, straight lines of her slim body. He reached out and ran a finger along her cheek and down her neck, tracing the line of her collarbone and the slight swell of breasts so tiny they were almost like those of a girl. Her skin was as white and smooth as a statue, but it no longer felt cold to his touch. His hand continued to trail down her body until he reached the dark triangle of her pubic hair. Just above it was a tiny constellation of moles, and he bent to kiss it. Serafina drew in a sharp breath, releasing it in a sigh of longing.

"So much clothing," she murmured, touching her hand to the only part of his body still clad, and squeezing gently so he could be in no doubt of her meaning. Then she undid the buttons and helped him to pull off his trousers.

With his eyes closed, Rufus savoured her hands stroking him until he was forced to stop her, gasping, "No, please, I won't be able to..."

She laid a finger across his lips. "Hush. Look at me." Rufus opened his eyes and she gently pulled his face down to hers, and he was lost once more in the depths of her dark eyes.

"Now," she whispered, "now, please!" She took his hand and pulled it to her, pushing it against her so he could feel she was ready for him, giving little gasps and moans as his fingers slid inside her, gently stroking the delicious softness of her. "Oh, please!" Almost roughly she thrust herself against him, her fingers guiding him to where he longed to be.

As he plunged himself deep inside her, he felt as though he was penetrating the very core of her being, her soft, moist flesh surrounding him, telling him he was home at last. Very slowly, he withdrew again, prolonging the delightful sensations of her softness moving against his hardness, Serafina's low moans assuring him that she shared his pleasure. When he was almost completely withdrawn, she thrust herself against him, pushing him inside her again. And so they helped one another to greater and greater heights until all at once it seemed to Rufus that Serafina melted around him, wave after wave of her pulsing against him, each wave drawing a cry from her parted lips, until he knew he could bear it no longer. He thrust himself hard inside her, feeling himself explode in a burst of pleasure so fierce it was scarcely distinguishable from pain.

Gasping, he collapsed against Serafina, her breast rising and falling against his. Raising himself up on one elbow, he kissed her on the mouth. Her lips moved against his, but in a way that was almost chaste compared with their former endeavours.

For some time they lay in each other's arms, content to enjoy their closeness in silence. Then Serafina murmured, "The sun is up now. We must sleep."

"So it's true that vampires can't abide daylight?" Rufus asked, not at all sure he wanted to hear the answer. Despite the fact that he now seemed able to see as clearly by night as he had by day, and despite the heightened senses that had so intensified their lovemaking, he didn't think he wanted to forgo daylight altogether, though he feared he might have no choice in the matter.

Serafina smiled, and traced the outline of his cheek with her finger. "Not precisely. Daylight doesn't harm us physically, as some have claimed but, like any hunting creature, our powers are greatest at night. Also, of course, it's much safer for us to hunt under cover of darkness, so it's natural for us to sleep during the day. For most of us, this becomes our normal pattern. It's unusual for us to feed in the early morning as you did, but that was because of the time it took you to change. The first hunger is so intense you couldn't have waited until tonight."

Rufus nodded. A deep weariness had, indeed, settled over him, although he thought this was most likely because of all he'd been through recently. In the space of just a few days, he'd been severely beaten, brought to the brink of death and back again, had his insides rearranged into those of a vampire, drunk human blood, and made love with Serafina for the first time. He felt as though he'd been caught up in a vortex of new ideas and sensations and whirled about until he scarcely knew what he felt or thought any more.

As a new fear swept over him, he asked, "What about Mr Springer? What will *he* think of what you've done?"

Serafina made a not entirely successful attempt at bravado. "I shall tell him he has a new family member. He may not like it, but he'll accept it."

Rufus looked dubious. "What do you mean, 'family'?"

"I'm blood of his blood, and you're blood of my blood." Serafina shrugged. "The same blood flows in the three of us – in vampire terms, that makes us family."

"That certainly gives a whole new meaning to 'blood relations'," Rufus said, his voice teetering on the brink of hysteria. "But doesn't that mean I've been making love to my sister?" He pulled away from Serafina, his face registering horror.

Serafina made a sound that could only be described as a gurgle of laughter. "Hardly any vampires are related in that way, Rufus. Our blood ties are of a different kind. We can't breed, so why should we be affected by such – human considerations?"

As the tide of his blood ecstasy began to ebb, the full

import of all that had happened struck Rufus with the force of a heavy blow. He was a vampire. One of the un-dead. Forever!

Although he had to admit he had not wanted to die, had longed for some way to be with Serafina, had even harboured fantasies of becoming her willing victim, this was so far beyond anything he could have imagined that his head spun from attempting to comprehend it. Worst of all, as horrifying as the prospect of being a vampire was, there was some part of him that was excited by the new path that stretched before him.

A sudden realisation broke through Rufus's reverie.

"Doctor Wells! He's coming back to check on me this morning. We can't sleep until he's been."

Serafina heaved a sigh and sat up. "You're right. I must dress, and you should put your nightshirt on." She reached over the side of the bed and picked it up, an expression of distaste spreading over her face as she surveyed the crumpled and sweat-stained article. "I'll get you a clean one."

Throwing the offending garment into a corner with the rest of Rufus's clothes, she jumped out of bed, found one in his cabin trunk that, if not precisely clean, had at least been somewhat aired, and tossed it to him before gathering up her own clothes.

Doctor Wells arrived to find Rufus sitting up in his nightshirt and Serafina perched on the edge of his bed looking demure. As they had arranged between them, they told the doctor Rufus's fever had broken during the night and he was beginning to feel better. Rufus had been terrified Doctor Wells would want to examine him, and would find abnormalities, but Serafina had reassured him that could easily be dealt with.

"You must watch what I do when he arrives," she had told him in a tone that had reminded him of his nanny when he was a little boy. "What I do, you can do also when you need to."

As soon as Doctor Wells entered the cabin, she rose to meet him, gazing deeply into his eyes as she held out her hand in greeting. It was only for a moment, but, as she had told Rufus, the doctor made no attempt to examine him.

"You certainly do look as though you're on the mend, now, and if you take things quietly, I should think it won't be too long before you're up and about again. But I must say you've had a pretty narrow escape. If you'll take my advice, you'll steer clear of the decks at night from now on, at least until we're out of Antarctic waters. The wet planks can be very icy. Now, I expect you'd like something to eat and drink. I'll ask one of the stewards to bring you something."

"No, there's no need," said Serafina quickly. "I'll fetch food for both of us."

"Very well. I'll pop back this evening before dinner and see how you are."

"Thank you," Rufus said, feeling an unexpected stab of guilt at deceiving the man who'd been so kind to him throughout the voyage.

After the doctor had left, Rufus lay down to sleep. When Serafina made to join him, however, he sat up again.

"I'd like to sleep alone," he told her.

She pushed herself up on one elbow, a look of surprise on her face. "But, why? Don't you love me any more?"

"Yes, of course I do." He longed to be able to find the words to explain to her how he felt, but they eluded him.

"Is it so terrible," Serafina asked in a small voice, "to see beauty in the darkness, to taste life more fully than you ever have before, to read minds and shape thoughts, to—to make love as we did? Don't you find these things beautiful?"

"Yes, but they're terrible as well, and the hunger was awful. It was like being eaten up from the inside."

"But it won't be like that again. I promise it won't. The first time is always the worst."

"But feeling it at all, and knowing the only way it can be satisfied is by drinking people's blood? How can I ever get used to that? Serafina, for most my life I've felt a hunger for something, for love, I think. My Mama died when I was eight, and my feeling of being loved died with her. But good God! To hunger for human blood! I knew someone who was addicted to laudanum, and it—it just used him up until he might as well have been dead. How is this any different? Except, I suppose, I *am* dead," he ended, his voice bleak.

The ghost of a smile haunted Serafina's lips. "Is it really so different from the hunger for food? Blood isn't a drug, Rufus. It's our food, that's all."

Rufus looked sceptical. "I don't believe I've ever felt intoxicated after eating," he said harshly, "but that's what drinking blood did to me."

"Do you mean to tell me you've never been intoxicated by wine or spirits?"

"But that's different."

"Is it?"

"Of course it is! It's not made from blood, for a start."

Serafina gave him a quizzical look. "But meat is, and you eat that."

"That's completely different, and you know it. Even

carnivorous animals don't drink the blood of their own kind, and neither do people – at least not normal ones. You can say what you like, Serafina, but it isn't right, and the feelings it induces aren't, either, however wonderful they might be at the time."

Serafina placed a gentle hand on his arm. "You're still very new, Rufus, and there's a great deal to get used to. I'll sleep in my own cabin if that's what you want, but I'll come back this evening. You still have a great deal to learn, and it's my duty as your maker to teach you. And my pleasure, too." The look on her face almost vanquished Rufus's resolve. "If I've done wrong, I'm sorry, and if you hate me for it, that's something I must learn to live with. But you do need my help, Rufus, for your own safety, so you must deal with me whether you like it not."

"I don't hate you, Serafina," Rufus said with a sigh. "I don't think I could, and believe me, it's not for want of trying, but I need to deal with what's happened in my own way, and that means alone."

Serafina nodded, looking more resigned than happy with the situation. "You'll need to hunt tonight, so I'll come back then, but I won't stay unless you wish it."

After she had gone, Rufus lay down again, pulling the bedclothes over himself from habit, although he no longer seemed to feel the cold. A great wave of weariness engulfed him, and within seconds he was deep in slumber.

# CHAPTER TWELVE

Rufus woke soon after dusk, physically refreshed, but no clearer in his mind. As he sat combing his hair into some semblance of neatness, a knock at the door signalled Serafina's arrival. She was wearing her favourite crimson silk gown, and it occurred to him for the first time that it was the ideal colour for concealing bloodstains. He looked at her, his eyes taking in the rosy flush that infused her cheeks, her lips as dark and lustrous as cherries. She must recently have fed, he thought, startled by a sudden stab of jealousy towards whomever it was who had had the privilege of giving her the gift of life.

She came to sit beside him. "Don't be jealous, Rufus. Those others are mere sustenance. It's you I love." She smiled at his look of surprise. "I can read your mind, remember? And very soon you'll be able to read mine just as well." She reached out to caress his cheek with her hand. "You must be hungry by now." Rufus nodded, trying his best to suppress a response that hovered uncomfortably between passion and outrage. If Serafina read his thought, she gave no sign of it.

"Come," she said, and took his hand.

Together, they made their way along the dark corridors between the cabins, both silent as they sniffed at the musty air. From every cabin came the alluring scent and the steady pulsing of blood coursing through human veins. Rufus felt the hunger rise in him, and the tingling in his gums as his fangs began to emerge in anticipation of satisfying it. But Serafina led him on until, outside one cabin, her mind reached out to his, telling him this was the one, as it held only one passenger, who was fast asleep. Slowly she turned the handle and silently opened the door. Rufus found himself looking into a cabin somewhat larger than his own, and containing two bunks, one above the other. On the lower bunk he made out the outline of a body. A wave of excitement flooded through him, and he crept closer, his senses delirious with the smell of fresh blood and the rhythmic beating of the heart that pumped it through a myriad of tantalising veins. As he crept up beside the bed, he saw the occupant was a woman, her fair hair flowing like sand over her pillow. He bent over her, willing her not to wake, and gently pushed back the golden tresses from her neck. He felt his stomach contract as the hunger took him over. His fangs, now as sharp as daggers, longed to sink into the vein he could see in the woman's neck. He bared his fangs and lowered his head.

Only when he raised his head at the insistence of Serafina's touch did he realise he was looking at Mariah Hamilton, with whom he had danced it now seemed so long ago and in another life. He drew back with a gasp, sickened by what he had just done to her. But her blood raced in his body, filling him with such excitement that as soon as he turned away from her, he forgot his momentary misgivings.

Back in his cabin, he went immediately to his trunk and took out his mirror. His reflection told him what he'd suspected: the pallid skin of his face was infused with the same flush he'd seen in Serafina's. He turned to her and gazed into her dark eyes, and the part of him that loved her reached out to her. She answered with both mind and body, and together they fell onto the bed, their mouths locked together in a deep and sensuous kiss. Rufus could taste the blood in Serafina's mouth as his tongue explored the sweet softness there. Then his hand was sliding up her long legs towards that other sweet softness. He heard Serafina's gasp as he found what he sought, felt her hands tugging at his trousers as she pressed herself against him. Their need for each other was too urgent for the removal of any but the most necessary garments. With impatient hands, Rufus pushed back Serafina's petticoats, and then he was inside her, clasping her hard against him, each movement wresting gasps and moans of delight from her open mouth.

In moments it was over, another hunger sated. In Rufus's mind, the two had somehow merged, flesh and blood together crying out to feed and be fed.

As they lay in one another's arms, Serafina murmured, her lips against Rufus's cheek, "Do you see how wonderful it can be?"

Rufus nodded, and kissed her hair. "It still doesn't seem quite real, somehow."

"That's because you're not yet used to feeling as a vampire feels. All our senses are heightened, not just those required for hunting."

"Did you know that before you were brought across?"

Serafina shook her head, her soft hair brushing against Rufus's face. "No, I just wanted to be free of the need to fear men and their animal lusts."

"Are we really so dreadful?"

"Not all, of course. But I'd had more than my fill of the worst of them."

Rufus hugged her to him as though to offer the protection she had lacked back then. "Is that why Mr Springer brought you across?"

"That was part of it, but his consent wasn't easily won." Serafina moved against Rufus, snuggling into him like a child seeking comfort. "He believed he was laying a curse on me, but to me it was a blessing. Rufus, you can't imagine how wonderful it felt to know I need never again let any man hurt me – and that was before I discovered the pleasures of the hunt, the sweet taste of blood, the heightening of the senses. You've felt that now, you must know what I mean."

"I do." Rufus stroked Serafina's hair, teasing out the tangles with absent-minded fingers. "But, however enjoyable it is at the time, once I've had time to reflect on its cause, I can't seem to feel anything but disgust."

"Even for me?" When Rufus said nothing, Serafina pulled back from him, frowning. "Rufus? Do I disgust you? Do I?"

Rufus drew back to look deep into Serafina's eyes. "No, not you. No matter what you are or what you do, I can't feel anything for you but love. It's me I'm disgusted with. I've done some things in the past I'm not proud of, but this...how can I feel anything but revulsion? You should never have brought me across, Serafina, especially without my knowledge."

"Even though you were going to die?"

"Yes, even so. No one has the right of life and death over anyone else, Serafina. Can't you see that?"

Serafina jumped off the bed, her eyes sparking with indignation. "I did it because I love you and wanted to save

125

you! You were going to die, remember?"

Rufus sat up, staring angrily at her. "You did it for yourself, Serafina, admit it. *You* didn't want to lose me, never mind what *I* wanted."

Serafina rounded on him, her eyes filled with angry tears. "Is that so terrible?"

"It's understandable, of course, but don't try to present it as an act of nobility, because it wasn't. You did it for yourself, not for me."

"Why are you saying such things to me?" Serafina demanded. "Surely you can't deny that being a vampire has brought you wonderful things already. I've watched you feed, and I know how much you enjoy it, how reluctant you are to stop. And what about our lovemaking? Don't try to tell me it wasn't better than you've ever experienced before."

"No, of course it was wonderful. When I'm with you, when I drink blood, I feel as if those are the only things I want – the only things I've ever wanted, the most glorious, marvellous things in the entire world. But afterwards, when I'm no longer delirious with blood and with you, I feel sickened by what I've done. That girl I fed from earlier, Mariah Hamilton? I've danced with her, Serafina. I've played cards with her, talked with her, yet I didn't even notice who she was until afterwards. How can you expect me to accept living with that – and living forever, doing it over and over and over again?" Rufus leapt to his feet, his hands clenched. "I'm a monster, Serafina. That's what you've made of me. I wanted your love, and I wanted to give you mine, but..."

"Oh, Rufus, I'm sorry I was angry with you!" Serafina ran to Rufus and threw her arms about him.

Overcome with self-loathing and desperation, Rufus

thrust her away, snarling like a cornered animal, not realising his new strength until she fell to the floor. He backed away in horror as Serafina scrambled to her feet, her eyes wide with surprise, and a hint of fear.

"Don't hate me, Rufus, please! I couldn't bear it!"

"I don't hate you, Serafina, I've already told you that. I just don't feel over the moon, as you clearly do, with the prospect of hunting innocent people and drinking their blood for the rest of time. How anyone could feel good about that is beyond me."

"Then let me help you to understand. Let me tell you about my life, and how I was brought across."

Rufus shook his head. "Not now, Serafina. For God's sake, just go. I need to think, and I can't do that with you here."

Serafina turned away from him, choking back her tears. Then she drew herself up to her full height, put her head in the air and strode from the cabin.

# CHAPTER THIRTEEN

After Serafina's departure, Rufus lay down on his bed again and tried to induce something approaching order into the seething mass of half-digested thoughts and feelings that crowded his mind. But he could still smell Serafina, and the scent of her inflamed his senses so that thinking was impossible. He got to his feet and began to pace back and forth, but that only made him feel even more like a caged tiger. Perhaps some fresh air would help. In the act of opening the cabin door, he drew back. What if he was overcome by blood hunger? What if, without Serafina to restrain him, he failed to stop in time, and...? Rufus shook his head violently as though trying to dislodge such a horrific thought, yet he knew all too well it was a distinct possibility. With a hiss of impotent fury, he slammed the door shut again and strode across the cabin to stand by the porthole, scowling and clenching and unclenching his fists. He was trapped! Trapped forever in a nightmare of blood and death and self-loathing, unless he could find some way to kill himself, and, most despicable of all, he didn't think he possessed the courage for that.

A knock at the door startled him out of his dismal musings. Thinking it must be Serafina, he strode to the door and wrenched it open, ready to vent his anger on her. But it was not Serafina who stood there.

It was Springer.

As Rufus stared at him, Springer inclined his head in greeting. "May speak with you?"

Seeing the surprise and fear in Rufus's face, he added, "No need to be afraid of me, Rufus, I'm not angry with you. Indeed, I believe we have a great deal in common."

"We have?" Rufus blurted out in surprise, and then swiftly collected his wits. "I—I beg your pardon, sir, do, please, come in."

Springer closed the door behind him and leaned against it, arms folded, a faint smile on his lips. "As you've no doubt already surmised, I'm aware of what Serafina has done and, believe me, I'm quite as disapproving as you must be. Useless as they are in the circumstances, please allow me to offer my deepest apologies. I wouldn't have wished such a dire fate on you – or anyone else, for that matter. I think I have a fair idea of what you must be going through, and I'd like to do what I can to make the – *transition* easier for you than it was for me. So if there's anything you'd like to ask me, I'm at your disposal. Though I must warn you I shan't gild the lily as Serafina may have done."

Rufus, who had been standing by the bed, his mouth agape with surprise, collapsed onto it. "I—I hardly know where to begin, sir. But – why would Serafina do such a thing to me when she says she loves me?"

"Ah," said Springer, a sudden gleam lighting his eyes. "Serafina and I have very different opinions on the experience of being a vampire."

Rufus nodded. "Yes, sir, I'd gathered that, but – why? Surely it's the same experience for both of you?"

"The difference," Springer told him, "lies in the

interpretation – much as it does with human experience, yes?"

"I—I suppose so, but I still don't understand why she'd do something so—so..."

"Drastic?"

"Yes—and permanent, and without even asking me if it was what I wanted."

Springer's eyes glinted with irony. "Believe it or not, I think she did it precisely *because* she loves you. She knew I disapproved of her liaison with you, and so she did the one thing she believed would overcome my objections." Rufus thought back to the argument he'd overheard between them, recalling Springer's plea to Serafina not to put them in danger, and her impassioned refusal to co-operate. It now seemed they'd been referring to Serafina's feelings for him. "It wasn't you I objected to, *per se*," Springer went on. "Let me make that clear. Liaisons between vampires and humans can be dangerous for both, but it's not just that. Such relationships, if they involve genuine love, invariably lead to heartbreak for both parties. Indeed, Serafina herself has experienced this in the past. Vampires don't age, you see, and, of course, humans do. Then there's the matter of our radically different lifestyles and—er—habits. And even if the human lover could overcome his natural horror of what we must do to stay alive, others almost certainly would not. In the past, we were hunted down like dangerous beasts. These days, I imagine incarceration in a lunatic asylum would be more likely. Imagine that, Rufus, to be locked up forever in such appalling conditions, deprived of the one thing we must have, reduced to a skeleton covered with skin, yet unable to die."

"But I thought vampires had superhuman strength. Couldn't you just escape?"

Springer gave an abrupt laugh. "Even vampires have their limits, and asylums are used to dealing with inmates whose very madness lends them great strength, at least temporarily. At any rate, I doubt if such considerations led to Serafina's decision to bring you across – that's what we call the process, by the way. I imagine she did it to circumvent what she saw as my unfair objections to her happiness with you." He gave a rueful shrug. "But then, Serafina always was distressingly self-willed."

"So," said Rufus with a quizzical lift of his brow, "in forbidding a relationship with me, you were trying to save Serafina from herself."

Springer's lip twitched. "Something like that, though I must admit to a fair degree of self-interest. Quite apart from the potential dangers, I haven't the slightest desire to share such cramped quarters for weeks on end with a woman in the throes of heartbreak, and Serafina can be a trifle— intense, as I daresay you've noticed."

Rufus had. Her passion was one of the things he particularly loved in her, but he said nothing of this to Springer. "I do love her, sir, in spite of—of what she is. I tried not to, but I can't seem to help it. I can see your point about vampires and humans, and I'd never have wanted to hurt Serafina or put her in danger, but—but being a vampire myself...Serafina tells me it's wonderful, yet she says you see it as a curse. I don't know what to think!"

Springer nodded. "I do understand – probably more than you can imagine. Serafina and I were brought across in very different ways, and for very different reasons, and I dare say that's coloured our views. If you think it might help, perhaps I can tell you something of how I was brought across."

Rufus rubbed his brow as though to smooth away the frown lines gathered there. "Perhaps. I suppose so."

"You really must learn to curb your enthusiasm," Springer observed, the ironic gleam returning to his eyes.

Rufus gave a rueful grin. "Sorry, sir, I didn't mean to sound churlish, but I really have no idea what might help me at the moment. God! I suppose I'll have to go hunting again, and I don't know if I can face Serafina just yet."

"Don't worry," Springer said. "The hunger won't affect you so badly after the first time. After a while, you'll even find you can defer feeding for several days if you need to, though I don't advise making a habit of it. If you sup little and often, there's less danger of accidentally killing someone."

"What about Mr Howard? Is that why he died?"

"Mr...? Oh, you mean the elderly gentleman. That was my doing, I'm afraid. I regret his death more than I can tell you, and it certainly wasn't intentional. I've always made it a point of honour to do as little harm as possible to those on whom I must feed. I can only assume he was already ill." He looked at Rufus, noting his expression of distaste. "I share your abhorrence, Rufus. Unfortunately, regret is all that's left to me now. Perhaps hearing my story will give you a little more understanding."

"Yes, I think perhaps it might."

"Very well, I'll fetch a chair from the dining room. Even a vampire likes his creature comforts."

Springer set his chair down against the cabin trunk, lowered his lean frame onto it, leaned back and stretched out his legs, which were long enough to span the space between his chair and the bed.

"I was brought over in fifteen-twenty-one," he said, "but my story really begins two years before that. I was stationed with my regiment in Berlin, having been for many years a cavalry officer in the army of the Hapsburgs. When Charles the fifth inherited their lands and became Emperor, I felt I was too old, too set in my ways, to switch allegiance to a new master, so I took an honourable discharge. However, I soon had cause to regret my decision. I'd been a soldier since the age of sixteen, you see, and had never married. Not that I'd ever wanted for female company – or male, for that matter, which I soon realised was my preference – but marriage and family were not something I'd ever wanted. I preferred a life of adventure.

"So there I was, alone in Berlin, no longer young, with no source of income other than my small army pension, and no skills but those of a soldier. For a time, I was able to live on my savings while I sought suitable employment, but it seemed my skills were not much in demand outside the military, and before long I was reduced to gambling in taverns to keep body and soul together.

"At some point, I fell in with a young Austrian called Stefan, whose dress and manner suggested high birth, although he followed the life of an adventurer. Since he appeared to have an endless supply of ready cash, I cultivated his friendship – rather more assiduously than does me credit, I must confess – and we soon became lovers.

"Through Stefan, I gained an *entree* into a better class of gambling establishment and, since I allowed myself to be more or less kept by my young lover, I managed to amass, if not a fortune, at least rather a tidy nest egg. Invested wisely, it soon afforded me quite a comfortable existence. But by now I'd become used to a more luxurious lifestyle. When Stefan's father died and he inherited the family estates near Innsbruck, I followed him there, where, to the horror of the rest of his family, we maintained an extravagant – not to mention bohemian – court, attended by musicians, artists, alchemists, courtesans, and a variety of other hangers-on. It was a strange existence we led, sleeping by day, carousing by night, and a far cry from the austerity of the army. Indeed, I gradually became ill from excesses I was no doubt simply too old to sustain. To his credit, Stefan spared no expense in his efforts to return me to good health, but to no avail. To this day, I don't know what ailed me, but I became chronically ill, at times virtually bedridden.

"There came into our lives a man who called himself Doktor Walther von Dunkel. Dunkel, I should tell you, is the German word for 'dark'. He must have devised the name himself; it's not a name form that would normally exist in Germany. But it certainly suited him. Hair, eyes, clothes, everything about him was black, except for his face, which had the form and complexion of the recently dead. Indeed, he looked in need of a doctor himself. It was on account of his skill as an astrologer that he was invited to join our court, and he soon became a favourite, particularly with the ladies, whom he was careful to flatter with the charts he drew for them. Not long after he joined us, a mysterious wasting sickness began to afflict the court."

Springer broke off with a sardonic grin at Rufus's gasp. "I see you recognise the symptoms. As I said, Stefan was determined to find a cure for me, so when von Dunkel claimed that I, too, had the wasting sickness, and that he knew how to cure it, Stefan begged me to allow him to try his skills on me. By now, I felt I had little to lose save perhaps my life, and I wanted to please Stefan, so I agreed, though I found the doctor quite repulsive, without really knowing why.

"He came to me that evening and drew off some blood, claiming it was to relieve me of my fever. This left me very weak, but it did seem to reduce the fever somewhat. If I had misgivings, I stifled them for Stefan's sake. So began a regimen of regular bloodletting. Stefan, because he wanted to, believed von Dunkel's claims that I was recovering, and I didn't have the heart to disillusion him. But I knew I was becoming weaker with every session of bleeding, and I fancied von Dunkel was taking more than he should, but by this time I was too weak to protest.

"Meanwhile, the wasting epidemic continued unabated. Most of its victims seemed to recover eventually, but there were a number of relapses, and one or two deaths. Still, untimely death was by no means uncommon in those days, so no one found it remarkable. Somehow, however, I couldn't rid myself of the suspicion that it was in some way connected with the arrival of the doctor. As you can imagine, I had ample time for reflection on the subject, bedridden as I was." Springer's smile was devoid of humour. "One night, when von Dunkel had left with yet another bowl of my blood, I dragged myself out of bed and crept after him on legs unsteady from the blood loss. Fortunately, his room wasn't far from mine. He closed the door after him and locked it, but he didn't leave the key in the lock, so I was able to watch through the keyhole as he raised the bowl – the bowl containing blood still warm from my veins – to his lips, and drained it. In horror, I watched as he lowered the bowl, his lips still rimmed with its dark contents, on his face the look of a predatory animal sated – for now.

"I was, as I'm sure you'll appreciate, appalled. Had I had more religion left in me, or even a touch of superstition, I might have realised then what von Dunkel was. As it was, after a life of fighting and killing, and generally living on my wits, I no longer had much in the way of beliefs of any kind. But I knew von Dunkel was evil, and I knew what I must do, both for my own sake and those of his other victims. My soldier's weapons had long since been sold to buy food, but I did have a steel knife whose blade I kept well honed. Making my way back to my room, I placed it under my pillow and waited.

"A few nights later, von Dunkel appeared once more, bearing, as usual, a surgeon's knife and a small bowl. As he bent over me, I summoned what little strength I could and grasped his wrist. Sheer determination must have lent me some force; his knife fell to the floor, clattering against the flagstones. At the same time, I pulled my knife out and held it to his throat.

"'I know what you're doing,' I hissed through teeth clenched against fear and revulsion, 'and I intend to stop you.'

"To my amazement, he merely knocked the knife out of his way, giving a mocking smile as he ran a thin finger along its sharp blade, apparently careless of injury. Then he bent to pick up his knife as though nothing had happened. After a moment of confusion, I took advantage of this, drew back my knife, and struck as hard as I could in my weakened state.

"But, quick as I was, von Dunkel was quicker. Almost before I had made my move, he had my wrist in a grip so tight the knife fell from my fingers. With a strength that would have overcome the most hardened soldier, let alone one weakened by soft living and illness, he pinned me to the bed, his arm like an iron band across my throat. In the other hand he brandished the glinting surgical knife and sliced open a vein in my wrist. This time, he drank my blood in front of me, sipping it slowly as though it had been a particularly fine wine, mocking me all the while with his devilish smile. Only when the last drop had been drained, the last vestige licked from his lips, did he leave.

"It was clear to me now there was no way I could overcome von Dunkel physically, so I decided to denounce him, hoping Stefan and the others of his retinue might manage to overpower him. Stefan had left on a hunting trip five days previously. He'd been reluctant to leave me while I was ill, but I knew how he loved hunting, so I overcame his qualms. He was due to return at the end of the week – I would tell him then.

"In my fear and detestation of my tormentor, however, I made a fatal mistake.

"Perhaps I hoped to prevent his dreadful attentions. Perhaps I thought I could persuade him to flee, and leave us all in peace. Whatever my confused motives might have been, the next time von Dunkel came to me, as he bent over me I told him I had a plan for his downfall. Foolish, I know. Perhaps I just wanted to feel he didn't have complete power over me. I could not have been more wrong.

"His eyes began to glow like smouldering embers. His thin lips drew back in a snarl, showing teeth suddenly sharp and wolf-like. But his voice, when he spoke, was as soft as a lady's silken kerchief.

"'In that case,' he told me, 'I have but one remedy.' He placed his bowl on my bedside table, carefully laying the knife beside it.

"He bent over me, clamping his hand tightly over my mouth. 'I cannot risk your alerting others,' he murmured, 'especially when the pain starts,' though by then I was so terrified I doubt if I could have made a sound. I felt a sharp, pricking sensation just above my collarbone, and I shuddered to my core as I realised he had bitten into me with those dreadful fangs to open a vein. I felt hot blood trickle down my neck. Then he laid his lips to the vein and began to suck out my blood. I was sick with horror, but I couldn't move. Indeed, I could scarcely think as his mouth moved against my neck, making soft, suckling noises like a babe at its mother's breast. Before long, I began to find it strangely sensual. I think this terrified me most of all.

"I had thought his plan must be to kill me by draining me entirely of blood, but at last it seemed he was done, and I was still alive, if only just. He sat up, the red glow in his eyes slowly subsiding. Blood – my blood! – reddened his mouth, trickling in slow rivulets down his chin. I stared up at him, too weak now to move, yet unable to drag my eyes away.

"'A little more,' he murmured, 'and then it is your turn.'

"I still hadn't grasped what he was about, but I was in no state to think about it. Once more he bent to the open vein in my throat and began to suck. Before long, I had all but lost consciousness.

"Through a haze of pain and nausea, I saw him pull back his sleeve to expose his right wrist. He bent over it for a moment. When he drew back, I saw dark blood welling up, but still I was mystified. Von Dunkel thrust his arm out close to my mouth and pinioned me with his black eyes.

"'Drink!' he commanded.

"My eyes widened in horror as I finally began to realise what he was. 'No,' I managed to whisper, 'I will not!'

"'Oh, but you will!' His voice was little more than a whisper, but as cold and relentless as vengeance. 'You must. It is the only way. If I make you as I am, then you cannot expose me without exposing yourself. And you know as well as I do that exposure means death at the stake, for you and your patron – preceded by torture, of course, for 'tis common belief that we vampires are creatures of Satan. Now drink! Unless you want both yourself and your beloved Stefan burnt to death.'

"At his mention of Stefan, all my resolve fled. I'd come to love him with all my heart. How could I expose him to such a fate? For his sake, I must endure von Dunkel's ghastly ritual. Holding me motionless in his cold, hypnotic gaze, the doctor bit his wrist once more to make the blood flow, and held it against my lips. I made a feeble attempt at sucking his blood, but I was very weak, and the mere thought of what I was doing froze me with dread. With a snarl of rage, von Dunkel stretched his arm out over the bowl on the bedside table. Together, we watched his blood drip into it, he with evident satisfaction, I through a haze of nausea.

"At length he must have judged he'd drawn enough, as he put his tongue to his wrist and licked at the vein. I stared in disbelief as the wound began to close over. In a matter of moments it had completely healed, leaving nothing more than a thin, red scar glaring against the pallor of his arm.

Flicking his sleeve back into place with exaggerated fastidiousness, von Dunkel picked up the bowl of his blood, sniffing it as though savouring a nourishing broth.

"'Now,' he said, his voice as soft as water, but his eyes as cold and hard as ice. 'You will die. But fear not, for you shall rise again from the dead, miraculously cured by the great Herr Doktor von Dunkel. And when you do, you will be as I am. You will be bound to me forever, blood of my blood, so you will no longer dare to harm me.'

"With his left hand, he took hold of my hair and wrenched my head back so that my mouth was forced open. He shoved the bowl against my lips and tipped its contents down my throat. I spluttered at the salty, metallic tang of it, coughing as I breathed the ghastly liquid into my lungs. Drops of it splattered von Dunkel's face and hands. I watched in disgust as he lapped the stuff up, licking his lips with apparent relish. However, enough must have made its way down my gullet, as von Dunkel put the bowl down and let go of me. I must have fallen unconscious then, because the last thing I remembered was a wish for death to take me.

"When I awoke, von Dunkel was gone. I had no idea how much time had passed, though I think it was still the same night. The first thing I noticed was that I no longer felt weak and ill. Instead, I was infused with a sense of well being I'd not felt since leaving the army. I realised I'd merely been drifting since then. Now, for the first time in years, I felt completely, totally alive, though I had no idea why. Everything I looked at seemed sharper, richer, more colourful than before. I could hear sounds previously inaudible: the faint sighing of the wind outside, the movement of a bird's wings as it flew by, a mouse scurrying somewhere overhead, the beating of the hearts of folk asleep in other rooms of the castle. I could hear my own blood – or rather, von Dunkel's blood – coursing through my veins. The candle that had been burning by my bedside had gone out, but I had no need of it. Like a cat, I could see as clearly as if it were day.

"For a time I just lay there, taking it all in, trying out my new senses. Then I became aware of another sensation welling up from deep within me. At first I didn't recognise it. I'd never experienced such a hunger before, not even on campaign, when we sometimes went for days at a time without food. This was a hunger not just of the stomach, but of the very soul and being. It was like a longing – a feeling that some part of me had been torn out and I must replace it at all costs. I'd never felt the like – not even when Stefan was away for great lengths of time, as he sometimes was. At that moment, I began to comprehend what von Dunkel had done to me. I felt sick with horror.

"But that awful hunger would not be denied, so I got up from my bed and, like a wild animal, I went hunting.

"I padded silently along the dark corridors, instinctively sniffing the air like an animal, listening to the beating of hearts until I felt myself drawn to one in particular. I listened at the door of the room, hearing only the steady breathing of the one within. Slowly, I turned the door handle, pushed the door open, and crept in. The area of floor I must cross to the curtained bed seemed immense. I was terrified its occupant would wake and raise the alarm, and still more terrified at the hideous act I was about to perform. Yet the hunger drove me on. I drew back the curtain, and was relieved to find the bed occupied by a man I didn't recognise. Mercifully, he had his head turned away from me so I was not obliged to look at the face of my victim. His cry of pain as I bit into the vein at the base of his neck was bad enough. Despite my deep revulsion – not to mention inexperience – I set about satisfying my hunger as best I might. To my amazement, it quickly became an act of extreme sensuality, as though I were drinking in life itself in all its rich beauty. By the time I left the gentleman, dawn was almost breaking, and an immense weariness overcame me. I barely managed to drag myself back to my bed to sleep through the day."

Springer moved his long legs to a more comfortable position and smiled at Rufus. "You'll already have some inkling of what I felt."

Rufus, sitting on the edge of the bed, nodded. "Yes, sir, I think I have. I don't want to seem intrusive, but I can't help wondering what happened next. Are you still bound to von Dunkel?"

Springer sighed, though Rufus heard no sense of relief in it. "I never saw Stefan again. By the time he returned, I was long gone. It broke my heart to leave him, but how could I see him embroiled in the horror that was now my life?

"As for von Dunkel, he soon realised that, far from becoming his willing acolyte, I loathed him with all my being, so he was glad to see me go, and hoped to turn the situation to his advantage. But although I dared not tell Stefan the truth, I couldn't bear to see von Dunkel's plan succeed, so I left Stefan a note telling him von Dunkel was responsible for my leaving. I later heard that he'd banished von Dunkel from the castle.

"As soon as I heard of this, I determined to find him, to take vengeance for what he'd done to me. I had little in the way of money – just the horse Stefan had given me, a few clothes, and my knife. Using my newly enhanced faculties, and the tracking skills I'd learned in the army, I eventually ran von Dunkel to earth in the back streets of Vienna, where he preyed upon prostitutes and other refuse of society. By now, of course, I was little better than him, but I had no awareness of that at the time. It does me no credit, but my only thought was revenge."

"But, sir, surely that's understandable after what he did to you," said Rufus, and then fell silent as the parallel between him and Springer struck him.

Springer's lip twisted. "Perhaps I did the right thing by the world, but I can't pretend I did it for the right reason. At any rate, I eventually found von Dunkel in a rundown part of the old city. He was sleeping rough in the back room of a disused apothecary's shop, one of a row long-since abandoned. It was shortly before sunset, and he lay asleep on the floor, curled up like a dog in a nest of old sacks. He appeared to be unarmed. As I crept towards him, my knife in my hand, he awoke, instantly alert. But he stretched his limbs in a leisurely way, his black eyes mocking me.

"'I thought it would not be long before you came to me,' he sneered.

"Before he could rise to his feet, I threw myself on him, plunging the blade of my knife into his breast with all my vampiric strength. Such a wound would have killed any ordinary man, but von Dunkel merely pushed me aside and sprang to his feet. As he stood there laughing at me, I saw the gaping wound begin to heal over. Within minutes, the only signs of injury were a livid scar and his torn and bloodstained shirt. I had missed the heart I'd been aiming at.

"'That really is no way to use a family member,' he said, reaching for his doublet and drawing it on in a leisurely way.

"'You're no kin of mine,' I spat at him.

"'Oh, but I am,' he replied. 'Are we not – *blood* brothers?'

"Snarling, I made to spring at him.

"He laughed. 'Please, spare yourself the trouble of wounding me again. I shall only heal, you know, for that is the vampire's nature. And now, time for some supper, I think. I would ask you to join me,' he gestured at his bloodied shirt, 'but it would seem you don't enjoy my company.'

"He deliberately turned his back on me and strolled towards the door. I wanted desperately to attack him again, but I realised it would be futile. I should have to find some other means of destroying him.

"As if reading my thoughts, he half-turned at the door, taunting me with his black eyes, 'Ah, yes, I forgot to mention that we vampires are immortal.'

"With that, he was gone, leaving me to ponder the ghastly import of his words. I finally left von Dunkel's den more determined than ever to destroy him if I could. At first, I thought the task would prove impossible, but for all that, I found myself fascinated by the creature who'd destroyed the life I'd loved so much. I couldn't resist following him like a wolf stalking its prey, though I loathed, with all my heart, what I saw.

"As my understanding of my new nature grew, I came to loathe myself as well. But the need for blood was a craving that would not be denied. I was as much a slave to it as the opium addict is to his drug. For that, and the loss of Stefan, I hated von Dunkel. Besides finding ways to feed in safety, destroying him became my obsession. Several months later, however, I seemed no nearer to my goal. One night, as I stood in the shadows near the door of some low tavern, watching as von Dunkel sought to lure a young prostitute away to become his unwitting sustenance, a fight broke out nearby. Before the landlord could summon help to quell it, someone knocked a lantern flying, setting fire to one of the curtains. As the flames leapt up and the tavern patrons scrambled to escape, I saw stark terror in von Dunkel's eyes. I knew I'd found his weak spot at last.

"In the confusion, I slipped away unseen, waiting nearby until I saw von Dunkel rush out of the burning tavern, his intended 'supper' forgotten in his desperation to escape the flames. I followed him back to the apothecary shop and waited to see if he would re-emerge. His dealings with the prostitute suggested he was in need of blood, and I hoped he might be weakened – or at least distracted – by that need. I waited, crouched by the window of the shop next door, where I could see if he left his lair. The fire must have frightened him badly, as by the first rays of sunrise I had caught no sight of him. If my own experience as a vampire were anything to go by, he'd sleep the day away. A plan began to form in my mind.

"It was a very rudimentary plan, and depended on my being able to stay awake long enough to carry it out. I waited until the sun was well up, and then crept into his den, carrying my knife in my right hand, and in my left a lighted taper formed from a twist of some yellowed paper I'd found lying around.

"But von Dunkel was nowhere to be seen.

"I stared about me in alarm. How could he have escaped

while I was keeping watch on him? Or was invisibility another of his foul tricks? Once my panic had abated, however, I noticed what looked like a trapdoor in the floor of the room. I crept across to it and saw there was no dust or detritus on or immediately around it, though both lay thick on the rest of the floor. I took hold of the iron ring bolted onto it and pulled it up, inch by careful inch, taking great care not to make a sound. For the first time, I found myself grateful for my new strength and senses. The open trapdoor revealed a narrow staircase leading down to a small cellar. Even from the top of the stairs, I could smell von Dunkel down there. Creeping down the stairs on silent feet, I quickly made out his inert form in the cellar's farthest corner. To my huge relief, he lay in a deep sleep, curled up on one side on an old mattress with his back to me. As I stood over him, he seemed to me to be dead. I could sense no pulse, no stir of blood in his veins, and his skin was like ashes. For a second, I paused to wonder if I looked like that during my daytime sleep. Then I bent over him and drove my knife hard through his ear and deep into his foul brain.

"I scarcely dared hope this would kill him, but with luck it would disable him long enough for the rest of my plan to work. As I left, I used the taper to set light to the mattress on which he lay, and to whatever detritus I thought might catch fire quickly. I raced up the stairs and jammed the trapdoor shut with a length of wood I tore from the decaying shop counter. I hadn't counted on von Dunkel having retreated into the cellar, and could only hope his mattress would produce enough fire to consume him. But I set fire to the shop as well, so even if he managed to escape from the cellar, he'd still have to run a gauntlet of flame.

"Within minutes, all the dry, rotting wood in the building was ablaze. Despite the brightening sunlight, and my desperate need for sleep, I forced myself to watch until the fire had burnt itself out. I could never be certain, but I think, through the roar of the flames, I heard a thin, high scream, not just of agony, but of sheer, unadulterated fury. So perhaps, before he died, von Dunkel knew I'd had my revenge."

Springer stood up, pushed his chair back against the cabin trunk, and went to stand by the porthole, staring out through its thick glass at the night sky. After several minutes, he turned to Rufus. "Perhaps now you can see why I feel my vampirism to be something of a curse."

Rufus had been sitting with his knees drawn up to his chin. Now he unfolded them and swung them over the edge of the bed. "I can, sir, yes," he said in sombre tones. "To deprive you of mastery over your life for the sake of his own safety, that was a terrible thing to do."

"It would have been bad enough if it were only that," Springer's voice was filled with bitterness, "but I believe it was as much for his amusement as his safety. Can you wonder at my reluctance to bring Serafina across? Being what von Dunkel had been, how could I be certain of my own motives? Oh, I know it was what she wanted, but I'm not sure I'd have agreed, had it not been for that dreadful business in Paris with the Compte de Mar. Has Serafina told you about it?"

Rufus shook his head. "I think she wanted to, but I thought she was just trying to excuse the inexcusable."

Springer smiled. "Well, you clearly have her favour. It's not something she likes to talk about, even with me. It's not my tale to tell, but perhaps you should listen to Serafina when you feel up to it. It never hurts to have more than one perspective. At any rate, after that, I realised Serafina was far too naïve for her own good. There are creatures like de Mar everywhere in society preying on innocent young women, and others with even worse proclivities, so I felt she'd be safer as a vampire. At least then she'd have the means to deal with them. I admit my decision was also to my own benefit. I reasoned that if Serafina became a vampire, she'd become more independent, leaving me freer to pursue my own objectives. It wasn't long, however, before I saw she'd been so damaged by the appalling uncle into whose care she was given after her father died, that she ran the risk of becoming nothing more than a predator hell-bent on vengeance."

"Like von Dunkel?" asked Rufus, inwardly shuddering at the idea.

"Not exactly," Springer said. "He was opportunistic and cruel, but I don't think revenge was his motive. I think he enjoyed it for its own sake. The one I had in mind was...well, never mind that now. The important thing was that I should teach her to retain as much of her humanity as possible, for her sake as much as to appease my own conscience. In those days, they still hunted vampires, attempting to burn us with crosses or fumigate us with garlic." Springer wrinkled his nose at the memory. "Neither of these worked, of course. Vampirism itself has nothing to do with either religion or evil. However, a stake through the heart would certainly do the trick, just as it would with anyone. In some of the more backward areas they were still burning us to death when they could capture us, and I had no wish to expose Serafina to that. She is, after all, my family."

*Blood of my blood*, thought Rufus. Those were the words Serafina had used.

Springer nodded, as though he'd heard Rufus's thought. "It's certainly made things easier for us since, though when I think of what I've denied her – marriage, children, the joy of growing old with someone she loves – I'm not sure I'll ever forgive myself. I can only hope you don't come to resent her for depriving you."

Rufus said nothing. He'd been hoping the same thing himself.

# CHAPTER FOURTEEN

As Serafina had promised, the hunger was never again as ferocious as that first time. Scenting and approaching suitable victims—he still found it difficult to think of them as anything else—continued to cause him considerable apprehension, but this was invariably banished by the sheer, animal pleasure of drinking in their warm, pulsing life force. At first, he found it necessary to have someone on hand when he fed, to prevent him from inadvertently killing his prey. However, despite his undiminished love for Serafina, he couldn't bring himself to forgive her and, for her part, Serafina kept her distance. So it was Springer who helped him learn how to scent and hunt prey, how to subdue them by mind control, and to use it to ensure afterwards they'd remember nothing of what had happened. Also, perhaps most important of all, he learned how to know when he'd taken enough blood, by recognising such signs as shallower breathing and the subtle cooling of skin.

While he was flush with new blood, Rufus positively gloried in the heightening of his senses. Standing by the poop-deck railing, he could smell not only the piquant tang of the sea, but the fish beneath its waves. He could sense the approach of seabirds long before they came within human view, could feel the air parting to flow round their bodies, and hear their tiny hearts beating as they flew past. On the sea winds, he could scent the aromas of unfamiliar plants growing on unseen islands. All around him he heard the beating of human hearts, the movement of joints and muscles, the soft, alluring surge of blood in veins and arteries. He longed for Serafina's touch, and the musky scent of her skin, with a hunger that all but eclipsed even his need for blood. At such times, it was as much as he could do to keep from abandoning his resolve and begging her to forgive him for sending her away.

Yet once the intoxicating tide of fresh blood had ebbed, he would find himself once more prey to doubt and self-recrimination. Part of him detested Serafina for what she had made him, while part desired nothing more than to hold her in his arms. Between the two, he found himself thoroughly confused. He had never thought of himself as religious, but what he had become seemed to make nonsense of even such basic concepts as good and evil. Was he suddenly evil because he was no longer human, or was he now subject to other laws altogether? Or were the very concepts pointless? These and other questions besieged him whenever he was not preoccupied with satisfying the one hunger he could not deny.

Somewhat to his surprise, Rufus found himself missing food less than he had expected, although this might well have owed something to the fact that by this stage of the voyage the meals had become less than appetising. Conversely, he missed the ordinariness of human company more than he'd imagined he might. Of course, he could still have attended evening entertainments such as the concerts and games evenings Doctor Wells continued to organise from time to time, but he felt unexpectedly self-conscious, as though people would see through his human exterior to the vampire within. Or worse, that those from whom he had fed would recognise him. Even the piano was effectively denied him for fear of attracting an unwanted audience.

The thought of Serafina hunting drove Rufus half-mad with jealousy. He would find himself picturing her seducing men into her arms in ways he was still human enough to resent. He knew perfectly well that by no means all her victims were men, and that most of them were steerage passengers, since there was less chance of being recognised by them, yet this knowledge did little to ameliorate his torment. But then the hunger would take hold of him and he would prowl the dark ship until he scented what he needed. Sometimes it would be a lone passenger asleep in his or her cabin. These were the easy ones, although now he took the precaution of ensuring they were not personal acquaintances like Mariah Hamilton before he began his dreadful task. At other times he found it necessary to approach crew or passengers on deck, luring them, as he'd seen Springer and Serafina do, with a combination of mind control and honeyed words and phrases. While he was hunting or feeding, his mind would become so focused, so intent upon his task, that he would sometimes find himself back in his cabin again with only the vaguest memory of how he had got there.

Much of the time, he found himself terrified by desires so overwhelming he seemed always on the brink of being swallowed up until there was nothing left but the shell of his body, inhabited by something alien and elemental – and monstrous. What if it demanded so high a price that it must claim everything he had been? And, when there was nothing at all left of his old self, what then? Would he become like von Dunkel? As much as he might remind himself that neither Springer nor Serafina had so succumbed, he seemed unable to shake the suspicion that he might not be so strong.

One night, Rufus's prowling led him to a young steerage passenger, a girl hurrying back from an assignation with one of the officers, her thin coat clutched about her, her mind and body still so filled with the pleasure of her encounter that she easily fell prey to his powers. Standing in the drizzle in the shadow of one of the lifeboats, he held her in his arms, drinking in her sexual enjoyment along with her blood, sweet with the rum her lover had given her, and the smell of lavender water and pipe tobacco on her skin and hair. Afterwards, he watched as she scurried across the deck to the hatch leading down to the women's quarters before returning to his cabin.

Still half-ecstatic from the fresh blood in his veins, he flopped down on his bed. His mind swirled with a kind of delirium combining both pleasure and a cold, prickling anxiety. Like an opium addict after his pipe, he must have dozed off, as he woke feeling stale and sluggish, yet restless and irritable at the same time. Too ill at ease to concentrate on reading, he decided to go for a walk.

On the main deck, Rufus raised his head instinctively to scent the cold night air, heedless of the drizzle that was fast turning to sleet-laden rain. He could see the watch house by the flickering light of the watchman's lantern, but even his enhanced sight could see little more through the drifting curtains of rain. He began to pace about the deck, icy water sluicing over his body unnoticed. How could he bear this half-life to which he'd been condemned? A great wave of despair engulfed him, pressing in on him until he felt scarcely able to breathe. For the first time since his stark introduction to boarding school as a small boy, he felt utterly alone. All but unaware of his actions, he wandered over to the railing and stared down into the heaving, oily mass of water pitted by half-frozen shards of rain. His enhanced sight picked up faint glints like dark rainbows on the waves, but he saw no beauty in them. He seemed to see through them into the stygian depths of the sea. Below the uneasy surface, it seemed so calm, so peaceful. He felt himself drawn to the cool serenity it appeared to offer. It seemed to Rufus then that everything he'd hoped for in life had come to nought. Even the love he had hoped for with Serafina had been ruined, not just by what she'd done, but by his own inability to accept it. And now he was condemned to live forever as some kind of demon. Why shouldn't he just be done with it, once and for all?

"I shouldn't, if I were you," a soft voice murmured just behind him. "Not unless you really fancy drifting about the ocean until you fetch up on some bleak, deserted island with no sustenance but the blood of seabirds. Unless, of course, you're eaten alive by sharks before you get there."

Rufus turned to see Springer, wrapped up against the rain in a voluminous greatcoat and with water dripping from the wide brim of his hat. "Come," he said, taking Rufus by the arm. "This isn't the answer."

Still feeling half dazed, Rufus allowed himself to be led back to his cabin, where Springer instructed him to take off his sodden clothes, pulling off his own coat and hat as though by way of example. While Rufus meekly obeyed, Springer hunted through his cabin trunk for some dry garments and a towel.

"That's better," Springer pronounced, once Rufus stood before him in dry shirt and trousers. "Here." He tossed Rufus his dressing gown. "And a little brandy, I think. I'm sure I saw a bottle in there somewhere." He turned back to the cabin trunk.

Rufus stared at him. "Brandy? But I thought you—I mean we—couldn't...?"

"We certainly can't process food," Springer said over his shoulder. "Ah, here it is." He turned to face Rufus, the bottle in his hand. "But small amounts of liquid from time to time seem to do us no harm, and in this case I think will be positively beneficial." He poured a little into the glass that still stood on the bedside table from when Rufus had been ill, and proffered it to him. Rufus took it and gave the contents a cautious sniff. "Drink it," urged Springer. "I assure you it won't harm you."

Rufus sipped the brandy, feeling its heat spread through him, warming him from the inside.

"Good." Springer sat down on the chair that had somehow never found its way back to the dining salon. "Now, Rufus, I think you and I need to have a little chat. Don't worry about Serafina," he added, reading Rufus's unspoken question. "Right now, she's back in our cabin reading one of the lurid Gothic romances she seems to favour."

"But why hasn't she...?"

"Visited you? My dear Rufus, is there any reason why she should live in your pocket?" Rufus shook his head, looking petulant. "It may surprise you to know that Serafina hasn't been finding things much easier than you have. In some ways, she's still quite naïve, and she really hadn't counted on

155

your reacting as you have to joining our family." He held up his hand to forestall Rufus's reply. "Believe me, I don't blame you, and if she'd taken my advice...well, she chose not to, and since it's now a *fait accompli*, you have no choice but to try to come to terms with it."

"That's easier said than done," Rufus muttered in sullen tones.

"Undoubtedly, but that's hardly the point, now, is it?"

Rufus hunched his shoulders. "I suppose not."

Springer sat up straighter on his chair and looked Rufus in the eye. "Quite. Now stop acting like a sulky child and pay attention. I'm going to tell you a few home truths, and if you don't want to spend the rest of a very long life making yourself and everyone around you miserable, I advise you to take note of them."

"Yes, sir," said Rufus, feeling very much as though his headmaster were about to give him a lecture.

Springer nodded, pursing his lips. "First, you're going to have to come to terms with what you are. I've already counselled you to retain as much as you can of your humanity, and I still advise this, no matter how difficult it might be, if only to avoid becoming the rabid monster of your fears. However, you're not human any longer, and the sooner you accept this, the better for your state of mind. When Serafina brought you across, you underwent a number of physical changes as well as the mental ones that are still settling into place. As we've already discussed, your body can no longer process food – fortunately, this change is compensated for by a corresponding lack of appetite for it."

Rufus nodded. "I've already noticed that. What I really miss is ordinary human company."

"That will pass in time, or at least abate considerably. Personally, I find it easier not to consort with those I must look on as potential sustenance, unless I need to transact business with them. But then I've never been the convivial type. Serafina, on the other hand, still craves some of the human pleasures, especially dancing and music. But mixing with humans can be dangerous – and not just for them. The simple fact is it's a very rare human who can face the existence of vampires with anything approaching equanimity – fear of the 'other' runs far too deep in them for that. And what people fear, they usually seek to destroy. The life of a hunter, Rufus, is a lonely one and filled with dangers, yet it does have its compensations."

"Such as?" asked Rufus, fixing Springer with a sceptical gaze.

"I've come to believe," Springer told him, "that nature has compensated us for our loss of humanity by giving us not only superior mental and physical powers, but also an enhanced enjoyment of the very thing that makes us vampires."

"Drinking blood you mean?"

"Precisely. You'll have noticed how...delicious that can be."

Rufus looked down at his hands, which he had been clenching without realising it, and slowly uncurled them. "But awful, too, sir. However wonderful it may feel at the time, and even afterwards, it's an appalling thing to do. Surely you must acknowledge that."

"Indeed," said Springer. "From a human perspective it is. Have you ever been on a pheasant shoot?"

Rufus stared at him, startled. "Of course I have, on my

father's estate. What's that got to do with anything?"

"And you enjoyed it?"

"Yes, it's good sport."

Springer shrugged. "How do you think the pheasant feels as your bullet tears into its flesh?"

"But that's completely different!"

"Is it? You shoot pheasants because their flesh is your food. We bite humans because their blood is ours, and unlike humans, who can become vegetarians if they find killing fellow creatures unacceptable, we have no choice in the matter. We do what we do because it's the only sustenance we're capable of taking. The most we can do is to ensure we do as little harm as possible, and that we leave our prey with no unpleasant memories. If nature has seen fit to make the experience a pleasurable one for us, why not enjoy it? What I'm trying to tell you, Rufus, is that you have no real choice but to accept what you are and make the most of it. As I've already pointed out to you, there's no point in trying to kill yourself. You almost certainly won't die, unless you manage to throw yourself onto a bonfire, or drive a stake into your own heart." He paused, staring up at the ceiling as though deep in thought, then shot Rufus a sudden hawk-like look. "Of course, cutting off your head would also kill you, but I fancy that could be a little tricky without help..."

Rufus burst out laughing. "Enough, sir, enough! You've got your point across. I don't think it'll be easy, but I will try to come to terms with being a vampire."

"Good. And while you're about it, I advise you try your best to overcome your anger towards Serafina. I, of all creatures, understand it, but I also understand that, however imperfect her reasoning might have been, Serafina did what she did because she loves you. So if you've any sense at all, you'll forgive her and then get on with being happy with her. Oh, and it's pointless torturing yourself with jealousy whenever she feeds from other men. It should be obvious to you by now that those are the easiest prey for her, just as women are for you, and if you're going to resent that as well, we're all going to have a very miserable time of it. I could, of course, use mind control to change your feelings, but frankly I think it's better if you come to terms with them yourself. You're no longer the pampered son of a wealthy aristocrat, so the sooner you get used to standing on your own feet, the better. I'm sorry if you find that harsh, but I urge you to give it some very serious thought."

"I will, sir," said Rufus, when he finally found his voice. "Though in all fairness I feel I must point out that I was hardly pampered, at least not after my mother died. I don't suppose you're familiar with English public schools, but I can assure you they don't go in for pampering."

Springer gave a wolfish grin. "*Touché*. However, I stand by the rest of what I said." He unfolded his length from the chair and walked to the door, gathering up his coat and hat on the way. "I'll bid you goodnight, now, or rather good morning, since dawn is approaching."

Rufus stood and went to shake Springer's hand. "Goodbye, sir, and thank you. I do appreciate what you've told me, and I promise I'll try to do better in future."

Springer flashed another, rather more kindly grin and left.

# CHAPTER FIFTEEN

Several nights later, not long after Rufus had returned from hunting, there was a knock at his cabin door. It was Serafina, biting her lip and twisting nervous hands together.

"Are you still angry with me?" Her voice sounded stiff and wary, as if she was uncertain what to expect. "If you are, I'll go away. I don't wish to quarrel with you any more."

Rufus stood back to let her enter the cabin, closed the door and offered her the chair to sit on before returning to his perch on the bed. "Serafina, I'm trying to come to terms with what I am, but it goes against everything I've been taught was right. I don't want to quarrel with you either, but I'm not going to pretend everything is fine just to keep the peace."

Serafina's gaze softened, and a tentative smile touched her lips. "I do see now it was wrong of me to bring you across as I did. I was so afraid you'd die, and there didn't seem any other way to save you. But you were right to call me selfish. I brought you across because I didn't want to lose you."

"If I'm honest with myself, I didn't want to lose you either and, from what Mr Springer has told me, it would have been next to impossible for us with me human and you vampire. I'm not finding it easy. I've never experienced anything so completely overwhelming, but I promised him I'd try my best to adapt, and...what?" He broke off as Serafina collapsed into giggles.

"Mr Springer!" she spluttered. "Why do you keep calling him that? It sounds so—so *English!*"

"I *am* English," Rufus protested. "I was only being polite. What am I supposed to call him?"

"Anton, of course! Mr Springer!" She dissolved into another fit of laughter.

By now, Rufus had caught her amusement, and the two of them tumbled together on the bed clutching at each other and giggling like children. Before long, Rufus's arms were about Serafina's waist and the blood ecstasy was singing through him. He kissed her, and tasted fresh blood on her lips. At that moment, he didn't care whose it was or where she had been. With impatient fingers they undressed. Rufus ran the fingers of one hand down Serafina's spine, and felt her body arch against his in response. Before he became quite overwhelmed with desire, he recalled their first time, and how Serafina had used her mind control to stay his urgency. Could he do the same? He felt Serafina's wordless response telling him how to accomplish it. So they made love, every smallest nuance of passion enhanced and extended beyond anything Rufus would have believed possible, like the slow movement of a symphony that reached sublime heights again and again before rising to a final crescendo that left Rufus breathless and complete.

This time, when the blood music subsided, instead of fear or depression, Rufus was left with a languorous sense of wellbeing and the tentative beginnings of an acceptance of himself as a vampire.

\* \* \* \*

As the *Orion* continued to sail northeast, the temperature became noticeably warmer, despite the fact that she was sailing into the Southern Hemisphere winter. In keeping with the season, the weather was often damp and cloudy, confining passengers indoors for days at a time, and so few passengers went abroad at night that Rufus often had to hunt among the steerage passengers.

One night, as he was setting out to hunt, he caught sight of Eleanor Fox sitting alone in the darkened dining room. She seemed to be crying. As Rufus entered she looked up, her face red and streaked with tears.

"Rufus! You shouldn't be here with me. Toby..."

Rufus shook his head and went to sit opposite her. "Where is he? What's he been doing to you? If he's hurt you, I'm going straight to Captain Standish, as I should have done before."

Eleanor shook her head, dabbing at her eyes with an already sodden handkerchief. "No, he hasn't hurt me – at least not physically. He's just...he goes drinking with those two friends of his – though I can't imagine where they get their alcohol from – and then there's just no reasoning with him at all. I'm frightened of him, Rufus, and I don't know what to do!"

Rufus reached out and placed his hand over hers, but she withdrew it as though afraid her stepbrother might walk in on them. "Are you afraid he'll hurt you?"

"Yes—no—oh, I don't know! I just hate it when he's like that. He—he rants at me, and orders me about, and nothing I can do or say seems to stop him!"

"I wish there was something I could do," Rufus said, feeling helpless to act for fear of making matters worse. "Is there one of the other women passengers you can talk to, or perhaps Doctor Wells? He's very kind, and he might be able to help you. I'm sure he'd like to know about the drinking – it's against ship's protocol, you know." A twinge of guilt pricked at him as he thought of his own concealed store of brandy.

"I know." Eleanor stared down at her hands, twisting her damp handkerchief. "But if they try to stop him, he'll know it was me who gave him away, and then he'll be worse than ever."

Rufus said nothing for some minutes, trying to think of some feasible way of helping her. With his strength, he had no doubt of his ability to deal with Fox, but administering a beating would be certain to make things worse for Eleanor in the long run. "You know," he said at last, "if you were to make some discreet inquiries, it wouldn't surprise me if you could arrange a position you could take up as soon as we reach Auckland, or at least a family with whom you could lodge. A number of the families on board have young children, and one of them might well value your help. I know it's probably not ideal, and it doesn't help you during the rest of the voyage, but at least you'd have an escape route planned for when we disembark."

Eleanor looked at him with a watery smile. "Rufus, that's a wonderful idea. Or it would be if only Toby would let me out of his sight for long enough. He doesn't leave me alone for a minute during the day."

"Perhaps you could ask Doctor Wells if he can make inquiries on your behalf. I dare say he knows as much about the passengers as anyone else on board. Surely your brother won't object to your seeing the doctor if you have, let's say, a sick headache?"

"No, but he's bound to insist on coming with me."

"Hmm, then you'd better make it 'women's problems'. That should keep him away. It certainly worked with my father. The slightest hint of women's ailments and he'd suddenly find an urgent need to be elsewhere."

Eleanor gave a throaty chuckle. "Yes, I should think that'll do the trick. Thank you so much, Rufus."

Rufus took her hand and gave it a sympathetic squeeze. "Not at all, I only wish I could have been more helpful."

"Oh, but you have! I think I can just about put up with Toby now I have a plan for getting rid of him once we reach Auckland. But I'd better go now. He's out with his horrid friends again, and if I'm not there when he gets back, there'll be the devil to pay and no pitch ready."

With these colourful words, Eleanor thanked Rufus again, wiped her tears away with the sleeve of her gown, and hurried off.

When Rufus returned to his cabin, he found Serafina curled up on his bed reading his book of Shelley's poems. She looked up as he entered and replaced the book on the bedside table.

"You took a long time. Did you have trouble finding someone?"

Rufus shook his head. "I wasn't just hunting." He gave her a brief account of his conversation with Eleanor, explaining that she was Toby Fox's sister. Serafina gave a hiss of anger. "What a cruel, horrible man! He deserves to be taught a lesson!"

Rufus nodded, grim-faced. "He certainly does, and I'd happily do it myself if it could be done without making things worse for Eleanor."

Serafina said nothing. The frown creasing her brow suggested she was deep in thought, though Rufus could gain no inkling of what those thoughts might be. At last, she looked up at him. "I need to hunt now. Will you come with me?"

Rufus and Serafina made their silent way through the shadowy passageways between the cabins, hoping to find some lone person asleep in one of them. But it seemed no one was asleep yet except children and babies. From almost every cabin came the murmur of conversation. Serafina signalled to him that they should try on deck – the night was so fine and clear that surely someone would be out walking. To their surprise, however, the deck was completely deserted, apart from the dimly lit watch house, and the sounds emanating from there suggested it was occupied by more than one person. Creeping closer, they saw two sailors playing cards, and smelled the sweet, heavy odour of rum. After a few moments, they decided it was too risky to approach the two unless they were left with no other alternative.

Slipping away through the shadows, Rufus and Serafina turned their steps towards the steerage quarters, always something of a last resort due to the stench created there by the combination of unwashed bodies and clothing, primitive cooking facilities and latrines, and a lack of fresh air. At first they heard nothing but the usual snoring, coughing and stirring of bodies indicating the inmates were sleeping; so much the better for their purposes. Then there came a sound like a rusty gate, and the hatch covering the women's quarters began to rise slowly, emitting a gust of warm, foul-smelling air. Serafina glanced at Rufus and the two of them shrank bank into the shadows cast by the watch-house walls, drawing in their energy fields to make themselves invisible to the figure now emerging from below decks. Somewhat to their surprise, it revealed itself to be a man.

Not one of the officers, surely, Rufus thought, wrinkling his nose at the odour still wafting up from below. Perhaps it was one of the male steerage passengers. Although the men and women were supposed to be strictly segregated, he imagined at least some of them were enterprising enough to find a way to skirt the rules, just as some of the women did with the crew. At that moment, the moon glided from behind the clouds, throwing a pale beam onto the lone figure weaving its drunken way across the deck. Rufus stifled a gasp as he realised who it was. Serafina shot him a swift look.

*It's Toby Fox*, he told her without speaking, *Eleanor's stepbrother!*

# CHAPTER SIXTEEN

Serafina looked at Rufus, a terrible smile on her bloodless face as she slid out from the shadows, signalling for Rufus to stay hidden until she had Fox in her power.

Rufus watched as she approached Fox, who halted, swaying on his feet and staring at her in surprise. Serafina returned his gaze, murmuring a greeting that was also a seductive invitation. Fox, looking as though he couldn't believe his luck, reached out for her, but she held him at bay with her eyes until his face took on the entranced look now familiar to Rufus. Serafina turned, beckoning to Fox, who began to follow her towards the railings against which the lifeboats were lashed. At the same time, she reached her mind out to Rufus, indicating that he should follow them. He hesitated, reaching out to Serafina's mind: *I've already fed. I'll keep watch for you.*

*We said someone should teach him a lesson,* Serafina replied, *and what better teacher than you, my love?*

As Serafina held Fox in trance, Rufus looked with loathing into his pinched, ferret face, and nodded. He'd already fed, but as soon as he smelled the man's blood, he felt his fangs emerge. As the blood hunger began to envelop him, he felt the familiar uneasy mix of pleasure and disgust, this time with the added ingredient of his abhorrence of Fox. Making no attempt to be gentle, he tugged Fox's filthy shirt away from his equally grubby neck, shoved his head to one side and plunged his fangs into the exposed flesh. He felt Fox stiffen. Although no sound came from his lips, it was clear he was in pain. Rufus raised his eyes to Serafina's. The look on her face told him she had no intention of sparing Fox the horrors of their depredations. He would feel every second of agony. A sensation equal parts fury and satisfaction flooded through Rufus. Then the hunger engulfed him completely and he began to drink, only vaguely aware of Fox's body writhing and shuddering with pain.

Sated at last, Rufus raised his head from Fox's neck. His skin was now the colour of dirty chalk, his thin lips drawn back from his teeth in a rictus of pain and terror. Rufus licked Fox's blood from his lips, savouring the satisfaction of vengeance against the man who had sought to kill him. Serafina took his place at Fox's neck, her raven hair falling like a curtain over his shoulder and down his arm as she fed. As Rufus watched, Fox's body began to sag like an empty sack. He plucked at Serafina's arm anxiously, but she did not respond.

"Serafina," he hissed, "you'll kill him."

Still no response – either she was too deeply in thrall to the hunger, or she was ignoring him. Alarmed now, he took hold of her arm and shook her. She growled deep in her throat, but continued to feed while Rufus, unable to do more for fear of rousing the watchmen, stared at her with growing dismay. When at length she raised her head, throwing her hair back from her face and running her tongue around her bloody lips, Rufus saw that Fox was little more than a skeleton covered with sagging, greyish skin. In one swift movement, Serafina jerked his head back sharply. Rufus heard the crack of breaking bones. Serafina let go of Fox's body as though discarding refuse, and it fell to the deck with a muffled thud.

"What did you do that for? You've killed him!" Rufus said in a horrified whisper.

Serafina placed a warning finger to her lips and cast a swift glance towards the watch house. Reaching her mind out to his, she said: *Of course I've killed him. Isn't that what one does with vermin?*

*But that's murder! I thought we were going to hurt him, to teach him a lesson, not to kill  him!*

Serafina shrugged. *Why should a creature like this—* she pushed at the limp body with a disdainful toe *— be left to continue hurting people? And Eleanor will be free, now, don't you see?*

*That's a damned sight more than we will, once his body is found!*

Serafina smiled, showing fangs that were just beginning to recede. *But it won't be.*

She stooped and picked up Fox's limp body, lifted it above her head and tossed it far out to sea. The splash as it entered the water was scarcely discernible from the washing of the waves against the ship's side.

"My God!" Rufus gasped aloud.

"No one will find him, now," Serafina said with evident satisfaction.

"But Eleanor's bound to wonder where he's gone, and I dare say she'll report his disappearance to—to whoever one reports these things to on a ship. Questions will be asked. What are we going to say?"

"There's no need for us to say anything," Serafina pointed

out. "Without a body, there's nothing to incriminate anyone. Although," she added with a sly smile, "if you wanted to, you could say you saw him on the main deck, very drunk. Then everyone will assume he fell overboard."

"My God," Rufus exclaimed, "have you no conscience at all?"

Serafina's eyes flashed sparks of anger. "Not where creatures like Toby Fox are concerned. Why should I feel guilty at ridding the world of such a brute? Did he care whether *you* lived or died? Do you think he would have cared about his stepsister, either, once he had her inheritance?"

"I suppose not," Rufus was forced to admit. "But killing him just makes us as bad as him. Is that what you want, to sink to his level?"

Serafina looked at him, her face harsh, and somehow less human than usual. "Please don't preach human ideals to me, Rufus. The vampire code is at least as old as humans, and a great deal more rational."

"An eye for an eye?" said Rufus with a curl of his lip.

Serafina's eyes flashed fire. "No, nothing so petty as that. Vampires see further and deeper than humans. Believe me, the world is a better place without the likes of Toby Fox."

Rufus shook his head, but said nothing. He could think of nothing to say that would change Serafina's mind.

"I told Anton we'd visit him tonight," she said as they approached the cabin area. At Rufus's look of horror, she smiled and patted his arm. "Don't worry, we can hide our thoughts if we need to."

"From Mr—from Anton?"

Serafina shrugged. "It'll be all right, you'll see."

Rufus very much doubted that, but he felt well out of his

depth in the alien world he'd been thrown into, and judged it best to hold his peace.

By now they were outside the cabin. Serafina opened the door and walked in, tugging a reluctant Rufus after her. Springer lounged on his bed smoking a Turkish cigarette, dressed in an elegant silk-brocade dressing gown of deepest blue that made his hair look even paler than usual. As Serafina and Rufus entered, he got to his feet with a lithe suppleness that made Rufus think of a great cat.

"Ah, I trust all is well with you both?"

"Of course it is," said Serafina, standing on tiptoe to give him a peck on the cheek. "Why shouldn't it be?"

Rufus, who had caught the sudden gleam in Springer's eyes, said nothing, trying to hide his anxiety, not least from himself.

After a long and rather awkward silence, Springer spoke, his voice languid but his pale eyes like ice. "You might as well tell me, you know. There's no point in trying to hide it from me. Besides, confession is good for the soul, isn't that what they say?" He sat down on the bed, stubbed out his cigarette in a silver ashtray on the bedside table, and, with a meaningful glance at Serafina, patted the spot beside him. Serafina, with an air of studied innocence, sat down. There being nowhere else to sit, Rufus leaned against the cabin trunk opposite them.

"Of course," Springer added, taking great care over flicking an invisible speck of ash from the collar of his dressing gown, "I use the word 'soul' figuratively, since the common consensus seems to be that we vampires don't have them." He shot Rufus a sudden, sharp look. "What do you think, Rufus?"

"I don't know, sir," Rufus stammered, unwilling to meet Springer's gaze.

"Then again," Springer continued as though Rufus had not spoken, "perhaps the entire concept of the soul is false. There are those who claim so, and I must confess it would make life a great deal simpler – and death, of course. Take young Toby Fox, for example." He ignored Rufus's sudden start of surprise as well Serafina's carefully wooden expression. "A vicious and unscrupulous young man, as we all have cause to know, and I dare say one not greatly missed by the world at large. Now, if the soul doesn't exist, his death might simply be seen as a good thing all round. If, on the other hand—"

"Oh, for God's sake stop it, Anton!" cried Serafina, thumping Springer's arm with her fist. "You know I killed him. Why don't you just say so?"

Springer shrugged his shoulders, holding Serafina gently but firmly at bay. "Why didn't *you* just tell me? Did you really imagine I'd give a damn about the death of a creature like Fox?" He released her, and smiled his chilly smile. "I take it you got rid of the evidence?" Serafina nodded. Springer looked up at Rufus, who had been staring, mouth agape, at the bizarre vignette unfolding before him. "Why so shocked, Rufus? Or are you one of those who believe in hellfire and damnation?"

"N-no, sir, I mean—"

"And let's dispense with the 'sir', shall we? I'm not your headmaster. Look, Rufus, for all that I try not to harm the humans who provide me with sustenance, I can't pretend sorrow at the death of vicious brute like Toby Fox, any more than I grieved over von Dunkel. The world is a better place without them, and I dare say their deaths have prevented a great deal more evil than that of the act of killing them. I'm sorry if that shocks you, but it doesn't make it any less true."

"But it's not our decision to make!" cried Rufus.

Springer gave Rufus a quizzical look. "You mean, 'the Lord giveth, and the Lord taketh away?'"

"No, of course not, but we can't just take the law into our own hands like that! We're supposed to be civilised, aren't we?"

"So they say," countered Springer, "though I'm not sure how – or even if – the concept applies to vampires. Like you, Rufus, I didn't choose to be a vampire. Nevertheless, that's what we are. Like it or not, that *is* what we are. By our very nature, we have a different perspective on the world—on life—than humans do. Immortality does rather enable one to take the long view."

"So all your fine words about retaining our humanity were just—just—?"

"Lies? Sham? No, of course they weren't but, for all that, we're *not* human, not completely, not any more. Besides, what desirable human qualities did Fox exhibit, hmm? He beat you up and left you for dead, merely for being friendly with his stepsister, and bullied her and planned to marry her so he could waste her inheritance on gambling and drinking. And who knows what other evil deeds he's done, or would have done?"

Rufus gave a snarl of frustration. "But if we go around killing people because they've ill-treated us, or because they're bad people, surely that makes us just as bad as them."

"In general, yes, I suppose, but perhaps, sometimes, a bad deed might become a good one if done for a good reason?"

"Such as?" prompted Rufus, unconvinced.

"Such as, for example, letting a man feel the full—unpleasantness—of a vampire taking his blood? You seemed to have few qualms about that." Rufus stared at him. Was there nothing Springer didn't know? "Very little," Springer smiled, "when it comes to my family."

"Family!" Rufus made a derisive gesture. "How can you call what we are family?"

"But we are, Rufus, in our own way," said Serafina. "And family is very important to our kind, even more so than to humans, since we can't create families in the way they can. Vampires are bound to each other by shared blood. Whole lines of us share exactly the same blood, and that creates a bond that lasts for as long as we live. Ultimately, it overrides all other considerations. That's why *I* sought revenge for what Toby Fox had done to *you*. You're part of me, Rufus, blood of my blood. Besides, killing him was the only way I could think of to save Eleanor from him." Rufus frowned at her, puzzled. "I wanted to save her," Serafina told him, tears filling her eyes, "because I know what it's like to be bullied and frightened by cruel men."

"What do you mean?" asked Rufus, still confused. "Is that what you were going to tell me the other night?"

Serafina pressed her lips together and said nothing.

"Things will become clearer in time," Springer assured him. "In the meantime, you'll find it considerably easier if you simply accept what you are, and learn about what it means for you, rather than trying to keep hold of what you used to be. After all, what can't be cured must be endured."

"You sound just like my nanny, when I was a little boy," Rufus said, a fledgling grin alighting on his lips.

The hint of an answering smile warmed Springer's eyes for a second. "Just don't tell me I look like her, that's all. Now you two run along. I have a book I want to finish. And for God's sake try not to quarrel."

Neither Rufus nor Serafina spoke as they walked back to their cabin.

Once there, Rufus sank onto the bed and put his head in his hands. "Why can't I just do what Anton says? Why is it so difficult?"

Serafina went to sit beside him. She put her arm about him, drew him towards her so his head rested on her shoulder, and began to stroke his hair. "You have vampire blood now, but your mind still clings to what you used to be."

"Was it like that for you?" Rufus asked, his voice muffled against Serafina's gown.

"Yes, but perhaps not as much. Most of my memories I was more than happy to leave behind. Besides, I'd been travelling with Anton for some time, knowing what he was, before he brought me across. For you, the transition has been much more abrupt, and—and unexpected. I'm sorry if it's not what you wanted. For your sake, I'd undo it if I could, even though it would mean losing you, but—but..."

Rufus lifted his head to look into her eyes. "If you'd asked me straight out whether I wanted to be a vampire, ill as I was, I'm certain I'd have said no, but it's not that simple any more, is it? It just seems so... *huge*, living forever, and all the feelings I have that I don't understand. When I was drinking Fox's blood, I didn't care a jot that I was hurting him. I *wanted* to hurt him, to pay him back for what he'd done to me. But when I saw you were killing him, I felt that, whatever evil Fox had done, killing him was wrong.

175

Everything about it was abhorrent to me, and I hated you for it. So, was I a vampire when I was drinking Fox's blood? Was I human when I hated you for killing him? I don't know what I am any more, and I'm frightened! How can I accept what I am—what you and Anton are—if I can't even understand it?"

Serafina sat back and thought for several minutes. Then she took Rufus's hand and looked into his eyes. "You're a vampire all the time, Rufus, but it's not as simple as being either human or vampire. All vampires began as humans, and they don't suddenly lose their humanity when they're brought across. It's more like having new qualities added. I don't know what you were taught, but you must try not to see the two aspects as being opposed. And it's not a matter of vampires being evil and humans good. Despite what superstition and the church would have you believe, vampires come in as many variations as humans do. Is Anton evil? Am I?"

Rufus shook his head. "No, but I can't help feeling that some of the things you do are."

"It's a matter of perspective, that's all. As a vampire, it's in your interest to unlearn some of the fairytales you've been taught."

"What do you mean, 'fairytales'?"

"For a start, that humans are superior to all other creatures. It should be clear to you by now that, at least in some respects, vampires are superior."

Her words forced a smile from Rufus. "But does that mean they're morally better?"

"Does it mean they're morally worse? Who decides? What are morals, after all, but rules devised by humans for their own benefit?"

"That's true, I suppose," Rufus said, looking thoughtful. "There's no denying humans have done some pretty appalling things to other human beings in the name of religion."

Serafina nodded. "You see? They don't even follow their own rules, yet they want to force them on us. When I was first brought across, Rufus, in some regions people still hunted vampires. They burned us to death or beheaded us, or drove stakes through our hearts, and said it was to save our souls, just as they did to people accused of witchcraft. There were all sorts of claims made about us: that we ate babies, and were hell bent on turning everyone into vampires. They had lists of ways to recognise vampires and to fend them off."

"Like garlic and crosses?"

Serafina smiled, but her eyes were sad. "Yes, and even sillier things, such as that we cast no reflection in a mirror, and can transform ourselves into bats and wolves, or even dissolve into fog. People are very prone to demonising what they can't understand, Rufus, but we aren't all monsters, any more than all humans are saints."

"Yes," said Rufus, "I can understand that. When were you brought across? You never told me."

"I was going to," Serafina said, "but you didn't want to listen."

"I was too angry before, but I'll listen now if you'd like to tell me. I do want to understand."

"Very well, but I must warn you my story contains some very wicked humans."

Rufus smiled. "I suspected as much."

# CHAPTER SEVENTEEN

Serafina settled herself more comfortably on the bed, facing Rufus, her legs tucked under her voluminous skirts. "I'll begin by telling you a little of my early life, as it has some bearing on later events. I was born in Moscow in sixteen-ninety-five, and was named after my mother, who died giving birth to me. My father was a talented musician and composer, from which he made a reasonable enough living by touring Russia with one of the minor orchestras. After my mother died, he hired a nurse, Katya, who travelled with us and took care of me. I came to love Katya as though she were in fact my mother, and by the time I was ten I'd travelled widely, met all sorts of interesting people, and was in a fair way to becoming an accomplished singer. Then, shortly after my eleventh birthday, my father contracted influenza. He quickly developed pneumonia, and within a fortnight it took him from us.

"When several of the other musicians also fell ill, Katya was afraid we might succumb, so she took me back to Moscow to my Aunt Anya – my father's elder sister – and her husband, my Uncle Sergei. My uncle was very wealthy, and he and my aunt had an elegant town house as well as an estate in the country, so when Uncle Sergei agreed to take me in, Katya felt she'd done very well by both of us. However, my uncle quickly dismissed her, saying I no longer needed a nurse. So, for the first time in my life I found myself alone.

"But Aunt Anya treated me kindly, and I soon came to love her. Uncle Sergei was away from home a great deal, but when he was there, he, too, seemed kind, sitting me on his knee to offer me sweetmeats or trinkets he'd brought back from his business trips, and calling me his little blackbird, because of my hair. He also loved to hear me play the piano and sing. Gradually, the pain of my loss began to fade and I settled into my new life.

"Soon after my thirteenth birthday, however, my new world was also shattered.

"Uncle Sergei had been away on business for several weeks, and during this time I became aware that Aunt Anya was becoming increasingly unhappy. I'd walk into a room to see her hurriedly tucking her handkerchief away, her eyes red from crying, and she'd snap at me over the slightest thing. "Late one night, long after I'd gone to bed, the sound of Uncle Sergei's carriage clattering into the courtyard in front of the house woke me. Shortly afterwards, I heard Aunt Anya's voice. This surprised me, since he was often out late, and she never waited up for him. For some time I could hear their voices, apparently raised in anger, but my room was too far away for me to make out what they were saying. Much later, I learned that Aunt Anya had discovered a letter in a coat of my uncle's that she was taking to be mended – a letter from his mistress.

"She was so shocked by his betrayal that although they continued to live in the same house she refused to have anything more to do with him. She refused even to speak to him, let alone share his bed. His mistress, a highborn lady, also rejected him, fearing the scandal their continued liaison might now bring.

"At the time, of course, I knew nothing of all this, only that an unaccountable pall of anger and sadness hung over the house. As time went on, this took its toll on me, and I fell into a great melancholy. One evening, Uncle Sergei came home to find me sitting on the staircase, crying.

"'Why, what's this?' he cried. 'Why is my little blackbird so sad? Dry your eyes, my sweet. Come and see what I've brought you.' From his pocket he drew a tiny painted lead figure and held it up for me to see. "Come and give your Uncle Sergei a kiss, and you shall have this pretty little princess."

"I knew Russia had its own princesses, but I'd read all about princesses in fairytales, and they were my idea of a real princess, so I wiped away my tears with the sleeve of my gown, and went to my uncle to see which of these he'd brought me. To my surprise, he caught me up into a strong embrace and kissed me full on the lips. However, I got my little princess – as near to a true fairy princess as any I'd imagined – and went to bed happy, thinking no more about it.

"Not long after that, he began coming to my room after I'd gone to bed to hear my prayers and kiss me goodnight. I was surprised, but not alarmed. Aunt Anya had retreated almost entirely to her room, so I assumed Uncle Sergei was trying to make up for her lack of attention.

"During the summer, my aunt and uncle used to go to Uncle Sergei's *dacha*, his house in the country, where the heat was less oppressive, and where he could hunt and fish. This summer, Aunt Anya refused to go, so Uncle Sergei declared we should go without her. I wasn't very happy with this, since I sometimes found my uncle a little intimidating, but there was nothing I could do about it. To my surprise, however, I had a lovely time there. I milked cows under the tutelage of Ivan, my uncle's aged retainer, picked vegetables and fruit from the garden for dinner and helped his equally aged wife, Alena, who looked after the house, to make bread. Best of all, I was allowed to play the harpsichord that stood in a corner of the parlour.

"Uncle Sergei spent most days out hunting or fishing, returning in the late afternoon carrying a couple of rabbits, or perhaps some fish, for our supper. After supper we'd play cards, or I'd play and sing for him. To my great delight, he allowed me to stay up late. However, the nightmares that had begun after my father died still haunted me sometimes. On one such night, I woke to find Uncle Sergei sitting beside me on the bed, stroking my hair. 'I heard you cry out,' he said. 'You had a bad dream.' He kissed me and made to leave, but I was afraid to be alone. So Uncle Sergei picked me up and carried me to his bed.

"After that, when bedtime came he'd ask me whether I felt up to sleeping alone. Somehow, although I was uncomfortable about sharing his bed, I felt that to refuse would seem ungrateful. I was very innocent, despite my unusual life with my father, so I went along with what he was careful to represent as his wish to protect me from my fears. Before long, however, his true motive became clear. He began a sexual relationship with me. It began very gradually – I think he wanted me to believe it perfectly natural for him to comfort me in this way. But I didn't. In all the time I'd travelled with my father, he'd never done anything of the kind.

"With Uncle Sergei, I felt terrified. How could he hurt me so, and say it was because he loved me and wanted to take away my fear? After a time, though, I stopped crying when he hurt me. I hated what he did, and I hated him for doing it, but I somehow learned to go into a secret place where I felt nothing at all. It didn't stop him, of course, but it made it a little more bearable. Naturally, I wasn't to tell Aunt Anya, as she wouldn't understand how truly innocent our 'little secret' was. Indeed, I couldn't tell anyone. How could I risk Aunt Anya becoming as angry with me as she was with Uncle Sergei? Besides, by now I was too frightened of him to go against his will.

"As time went on, my uncle's demands became more frequent – and more unpleasant. I loathed him with all my being, but I felt powerless to escape, and I loathed myself for being such a weakling. How I longed to see my father again, or Katya."

Tears welled up in Serafina's eyes, and Rufus put his arms round her, stroking her hair soothingly while she sobbed out her grief. At length she turned her face up to his. "Thank you," she said, with a smile that all but melted Rufus's heart.

"Please, don't go on if it causes you pain."

Serafina shook her head. "Thank you, but they're old tears, and should have been shed long ago."

She went on, "When I was about eighteen, my uncle fell ill, and at last I had respite. At first, I simply luxuriated in the freedom from his visits, but when he began to be on the mend, my terror returned even worse than before. I was desperate to escape, but had no idea where I could go that my uncle wouldn't find me. I knew no one now except friends of my uncle and aunt, and I had no money of my own.

"One evening, a foreign gentleman called at the house demanding to see my uncle. Uncle Sergei's manservant, Petrov, told him the master was too ill to see him, at which the gentleman declared he would wait until he was well again, as he was owed a great deal of money. Petrov begged me to deal with the visitor, since he dared not pay out the master's money and the man refused to leave without it. I knew it was useless to send Petrov to Aunt Anya, so I agreed to talk to the visitor. Over tea in the parlour, he told me he'd been involved in some financial speculation with my uncle, who was refusing to pay him his share of the proceeds, despite several entreaties by correspondence, forcing him to come in person to retrieve the debt. I knew Uncle Sergei was a miser, both with the household expenses and the servants' wages, so I had no difficulty in believing the visitor. Besides, I'd begun to formulate a plan. It was risky, but if it worked I'd be free of my uncle and have money as well.

"'Very well,' I told the gentleman, 'you shall have your money if I can obtain it, but on one condition.'

"'And what might that be?" he enquired, a faint smile of amusement playing about his lips, though his eyes weren't smiling at all.

"'You must promise to take me with you. And you must promise not to touch me.'

"'That's two conditions,' he pointed out, smiling, though not unkindly.

"'Well,' I insisted, my voice sharp with the fear that he might refuse me, 'those are my conditions. If you want the money, you must agree to them.'

"'You must be desperate, indeed,' he said, 'to place such trust in a complete stranger.'

"'I don't trust you,' I said, 'or any other man, but you're right, I am desperate. And whatever you may do to me, it can't be worse than what I've already endured from my uncle.'

"'You need have no fears on that score.' He smiled. 'My taste, such as it is these days, is for men, not women. Give me my money and I'll take you with me. Though you mustn't blame me if you find you've jumped from the frying pan only to find yourself in the midst of the fire.'

"I made Petrov get me the key to Uncle Sergei's safe. Inside were many, many roubles –more than I'd known existed – in bundles of notes, and a large amount in francs. I counted out the amount my new ally said he was owed, and took what I thought I might need for myself. I went upstairs and quickly packed some clothes in my valise, placing the money underneath them. Then I put on my warmest cloak and my fox-fur hat and ran downstairs again.

"Five minutes later, I climbed into the gentleman's carriage and was on my way to freedom. I expect you've already guessed that the gentleman was Anton."

"When did you realise he was a vampire?" Rufus asked. "And how did *you* come to be one?"

"Oh, that didn't happen for some time. As I told you, I was very naïve, and I just accepted Anton's unusual lifestyle. We travelled about Europe a great deal, but after my early years with my father it didn't strike me as odd that Anton lived such an unsettled life. He seemed to have the knack of fitting into any company, and I felt quite safe with him, which was an enormous relief after the previous five years. However, I was growing into a young woman, and I suppose it was inevitable that men should take an interest in me.

"One night in Paris, we were attending a *soiree* given by some grand lady Anton knew. He liked to cultivate such people, partly for financial reasons, but also, I think, because, like any true bourgeois, he enjoyed being seen in elevated company. Her salon was filled with the cream of Paris society, and I'd been asked to play the harpsichord and sing for them. I was a great success, and at the dancing afterwards I was besieged by gentlemen begging me to dance with them. Naturally, this flattered me but, although I loved the dancing, I couldn't bring myself to respond to their flirtation.

"One in particular, who seemed quite old to me, although I suppose he was in his forties, and who reminded me unpleasantly of my Uncle Sergei, was particularly assiduous in his attentions, sending flowers, gifts and invitations to our hotel each day. I returned the gifts and declined the invitations, but it made no difference. I begged Anton to take me away from Paris, and from this Compte de Mar, who was beginning to frighten me with the intensity of his pursuit, but he said he had business to complete there so I'd have to be patient for another week or so. However, he readily agreed to my staying out of society, claiming I was indisposed.

"One afternoon, I was alone in our salon practising some new songs while Anton attended one of his business meetings, when the Compte de Mar somehow managed to gain entry. I imagine he'd bribed one of the servants – it certainly seemed his style. He must have been standing at the door listening to my singing, and came forward as I finished.

"'Ah, my dear Mademoiselle Serafina,' he gushed, bowing over me and kissing my hand in a way that quite unnerved me. 'How delighted I am to see you well again. I was quite devastated when Monsieur Springer said you were ill. I came at once to extend my condolences. And when I heard such divine singing, why, I was convinced the angels had come to bear you away with them. Imagine, then, my joy at seeing you here as lovely as ever.'

"From his manner, I felt certain the Compte knew I hadn't really been ill, as well as the reason for my subterfuge. However, I decided to go along with Anton's story, hoping I might be able to put him off without arousing his anger.

"'Why, thank you,' I said. 'Indeed, I am feeling a little better, although I believe I may still be infectious.'

"'Really?' he asked, lifting one perfectly painted eyebrow. 'May I enquire as to the—ah—nature of your illness?'

"Of course, I had no idea what to tell him. It had never occurred to me that he might contrive to visit me. I stammered out something, but I could tell he wasn't deceived.

"'My dear Mademoiselle,' he said, his voice as smooth as polished steel. 'I do believe you've been trying to avoid me.'

"'Oh, no, indeed, Monsieur,' I lied, striving to conceal my alarm.

'How happy I am to hear you say so,' he said. 'I should be quite desolated to think you didn't wish to see me. Life without my delightful little seraph would be utterly unbearable. And yet,' he continued as though to himself, 'I'm not entirely convinced.'

"'Monsieur,' I said, anger lending me some degree of

courage. 'I'm sorry if you don't believe me, but since you don't, then I cannot imagine how I'm to convince you.'

"Of course, that was completely the wrong thing to say, as I realised the minute the words had left my lips. A greedy look came into his eyes that made my blood run cold.

"'Can you not?' he enquired silkily. 'I can imagine quite a number of ways, each of them equally delectable. But a kiss will serve – to begin with.'

"'But Monsieur,' I said desperately, as he came towards me. "Didn't I tell you I may be infectious? I shouldn't wish to infect you, Monsieur. Indeed, I shouldn't.'

"'Oh, but my dearest Serafina, you already have. You've infected me with love. Why, my pulse races at the very sight of you.'

"'Oh no, please!' I cried, backing away from him.

"But he lengthened his stride and caught hold of my wrists. I tried to pull them away, but he had a surprisingly strong grasp, and he held me fast.

"'Come, come, my dear,' he said, his voice becoming as hard as granite. 'Such coyness does not become you. You must know how much I want you. I adore you, Serafina, and I must have you!'

"'But,' I gasped, by now almost speechless with terror, 'I don't love you!'

"He laughed. 'Oh, but you will, my sweet little innocent. I'll teach you to love me, and this shall be your first lesson.'

"He pulled me to him so tightly I could scarcely breathe, and kissed me. Oh, Rufus, it was horrible! In my mind, I was suddenly a child again, and the Compte was my Uncle Sergei. I was so frozen with fear I could do nothing to stop him as his lips and his hands invaded me. I hated him for violating me, but I hated myself even more for being unable to stop him."

Serafina broke off, gasping convulsively as the memory overcame her. Rufus took her hands in his, stroking them and murmuring soothing words until she regained some calm.

"Please," he begged, "don't upset yourself for the sake of my foolish curiosity."

"I didn't mean to tell you so much," she said. "But now that I have, I should like to finish. Perhaps it will help me to lay these old ghosts to rest, as well as helping you to understand me better."

"Well, only if you're quite sure..."

Serafina nodded and took a deep breath. "I don't know what I should finally have done, but at that moment Anton arrived home. The Compte's momentary distraction allowed me to break away from him and call for help. In an instant, Anton was in the room. Taking in the situation at a glance, he seized the Compte with one hand in a grip that made him wince, and with his other hand gently pushed me out of the way. I ran to the far side of the harpsichord, as though its solid bulk might somehow protect me.

"The Compte began a blustering attempt to explain away his behaviour, but Anton quelled him with nothing more than a look. It was quite wonderful to see! Keeping the Compte in a bone-crushing grip, Anton turned to me.

"'Don't be afraid, my dear,' he said. 'I shan't let this—creature—harm you. Now, what would you like me to do with him?'

"'Make him go away,' I whispered. 'Please, just make him go away!'

"He smiled. I'd never seen such a terrible smile before, yet I wasn't afraid. I knew, in that moment, that Anton, who'd agreed to help me purely for the sake of money, would protect me as de Mar would never do for all his protestations of love and adoration.

"Anton picked up the Compte as though he were a child's toy and threw him clear across the room. His body struck the wall with a sort of liquid thud, and I heard the crack of bones before it slid to the floor. His mauve-powdered wig had fallen off, revealing a shiny, bald head with skin all mottled and speckled like an old trout. I wanted to laugh, but I was afraid I'd be unable to stop.

"Anton turned to me and bowed. 'I don't think he'll bother you again, my dear,' he said, as though he had merely sent the Compte away with a flea in his ear instead of killing him.

"I know I should have been shocked, but I wasn't. I felt only an immense gratitude, swiftly followed, I must confess, by a quite unseemly curiosity.

"'How did you do that?' I demanded.

"'All will be revealed,' Anton replied mysteriously, 'but first, I must get rid of this.' His gaze rested contemptuously on the Compte's lifeless form. 'Then I think it will be in our best interests to leave France as soon as possible. The ubiquitous Compte de Mar has many powerful friends, and his absence from society is bound to be remarked before long. Pack your things, my dear; we leave within the hour.'

"I have no idea how he contrived to get rid of de Mar's body, but when I came downstairs again there was no sign he'd ever been there.

"During our long, furious drive out of Paris and north to Calais, Anton explained to me something of the source of his immense strength. Again, I found myself unshaken. Recalling that I'd never seen him eat, and seldom even drink, I merely marvelled at my own poor powers of observation. But Anton explained that this was, at least in part, due to his vampiric ability to make people see only what he wished them to.

"How I longed to be a vampire, too! To have such powers, such strength! Never again to need fear any man! Over the following months I begged and begged Anton to take me across. Of course, he refused. He didn't tell me his full story – I think he still found it too painful – but he tried his utmost to convince me it was a curse I should avoid at all costs. I remained unconvinced. To me, men like my uncle and the Compte de Mar were a curse, whereas the life of a vampire seemed to offer only freedom and power.

"Eventually, and with many misgivings, Anton agreed to do as I wished, though he made me promise I'd never reproach him for it, no matter what it might bring me. Of course, I was only too happy to agree. Oh, Rufus, I can't describe my feelings when I awoke again. It was as though a film had been lifted from my eyes and I finally saw the world as it really was, in all its dark splendour – and I was its mistress!

"Before long, of course, the hunger came upon me. Anton took me on my first hunt, and together we drank our fill from some poor vagrant we found lying in an alley. It's strange: to this day, Anton seems to feel a need to apologise for what we do, yet to me it's always seemed as natural as eating and drinking once were, and in its own way quite as deliciously sensual as fine food and wine. I'm sorry if this shocks you, Rufus, but at least now you know how I feel about it."

"And why," said Rufus, drawing Serafina closer to him. "You're right, people like your uncle and the Compte de Mar are truly wicked. I can appreciate now why you wanted so much to heal me, after what happened to your father."

"You're not angry with me any more?"

Rufus hugged her to him and placed a gentle kiss on her lips. "How can I be, knowing what you've already endured? I don't know if I'll ever feel the same as you do about being a vampire, but for your sake – and with your help – I promise I'll do what I can to make the best of it."

With a great sigh of relief, Serafina laid her head on Rufus's shoulder, and they held one another until it was time to sleep.

# CHAPTER EIGHTEEN

Serafina's story touched Rufus in more ways than he had expected. Little by little, with help from her and Springer, he found the turmoil within him abating as he developed a genuine appreciation of his new senses and skills. His old life as a human came to seem more and more remote and, rather to his surprise, he discovered how little he missed it. Where at first he'd craved the ordinary interactions and rituals of human life, he began to find them pointless and without meaning. Like the customs of an alien culture, they were interesting in their way, but irrelevant to his real life. Hence he slept by day – more often than not with Serafina beside him – and hunted by night. Afterwards, euphoric from fresh blood, he and Serafina would make love, although 'love' seemed to Rufus a pitifully inadequate word to describe such an ecstatic melding of bodies and minds.

As Serafina had assured him, Toby Fox's death was ascribed to his falling overboard while drunk, and his loss caused even fewer ripples among the passengers than his body had in the sea. Rufus began to find a new perspective on Serafina's part in Fox's death, and to see how limited his views of right and wrong had been. As both she and Anton had tried to tell him, nothing was as black-and-white as he'd once believed.

For the most part, Springer left Rufus and Serafina to

their own devices, but Rufus sensed he was aware of them, and ready to step in if necessary. Sometimes he would visit them – or they him – and they'd play cards or talk through the night. Although Springer was no more academically inclined than was to be expected of someone who'd left home at sixteen to become a career soldier, he was extremely well travelled and had a great wealth of practical experience, both from soldiering and from four centuries as a vampire, so their conversations were wide ranging and frequently enlightening. Rufus came to respect and admire Springer as much as he loved and admired Serafina.

* * * *

Late one afternoon, a great shouting up on deck roused Rufus from sleep. He sat up, rubbing eyes that seemed reluctant to open. Beside him, Serafina lay curled against his side like a cat. Gently, he pushed back the strands of hair that had fallen across her face. She stirred and opened her eyes, blinking at the light.

"What's all that noise?" she muttered, still half asleep.

Rufus shook his head. "I don't know. Shall we go and see?"

Serafina groaned, but she sat up and shook back her hair. Rufus brought water, and they quickly washed and dressed and climbed up to the poop deck. All along the railings passengers were crowded, pointing and chattering in great excitement. Looking down, they saw it was the same on the main deck.

"Come on," said Rufus, taking Serafina's arm and ushering her to the railing. "What is it?" he asked the gentleman standing beside him.

"We're in sight of New Zealand!" the man exclaimed, pointing to a faint blur on the horizon. "The First Mate tells us we'll reach Auckland in a matter of days!"

At these words, another cheer went up from the assembly.

No wonder, thought Rufus. After a voyage that had at times seemed interminable – though in reality it had been a little less than four months – and fraught with storm, cold, sickness, and sheer, mind-numbing boredom, they'd all be glad to reach their destination at last. But when he thought of his own journey, and what might be in store for him and Serafina in a strange town in a strange land, with little more to sustain them than their love and their vampiric senses, he couldn't help feeling apprehensive. He felt Serafina's voice in his mind: *Don't worry, my love, Anton will take care of us. And we'll take care of each other, you'll see.* But he found it difficult to be so confident.

As they turned to leave, Rufus caught sight of Eleanor Fox's dark curls amongst the crowd on the main deck. Like everyone else, she was craning for a glimpse of their destination. Even from some distance away, he could sense she was happier, her bearing lighter, and he felt glad for her sake that Fox was dead.

That night, after they had both fed, Rufus and Serafina went to Springer's cabin. He wasn't there when they arrived, but appeared not long afterwards, the faint flush of his skin indicating a successful hunt.

"Ah, and to what do I owe this visit?" he asked, his smile still showing the last vestiges of his fangs.

"We'll be reaching Auckland soon," said Serafina, "and we

need to discuss what we'll do when we get there."

Springer nodded, pursing his lips. "Indeed, our situation has changed somewhat. I take it you won't be going to your uncle, Rufus?"

It took Rufus a moment to realise he was being teased. He grinned. "I hardly think I'd be welcome, under the circumstances."

"Quite. I hadn't made any very definite plans, but I do have business to transact, both in Auckland and Australia."

"Anton has business interests all over the place!" Serafina interposed, her voice betraying a degree of resentment as well as admiration.

"Yes, well, as Serafina may have told you, I like to keep on the move, and having irons in many fires, so to speak, provides me not only with readily available funds, but also a discreet *pied a terre* wherever I go. I intend to acquire one in Auckland, but I'll probably rent something, or perhaps stay at a hotel, until I can assess the possibilities. Naturally, you'll stay with us, Rufus. You still have a great deal to learn, and you'll be much safer with your own kind."

*My own kind*, thought Rufus, and realised it no longer seemed so strange to think of himself as something other than human.

"And with those who love you," added Serafina, caressing Rufus's cheek.

"You really ought to stop reading those penny dreadfuls," Springer admonished her with a faint curl of his lip. "They appear to be addling your brain."

"Oh, rubbish!" Serafina retorted.

"Isn't that what I just said?"

Serafina pulled a face at him, but followed it by blowing

him a kiss. He pretended to ignore it, but Rufus saw the warmth that softened his pale eyes.

\* \* \* \*

Two days later, the *Orion* began its long approach to the port of Auckland. Slowly it passed green islands and headlands basking in sunshine beneath a cobalt sky flecked with picture-book lamb's-wool clouds, until it sailed into the massive harbour. Even Springer braved the sunlight to stand with Rufus, Serafina and the other passengers crowding the railings, gazing at a sight like nothing they had seen before. On either side, sparkling waters of intense blue spread away into the distance, an azure cloak fringed with the soft lavender of misty hills.

It was late afternoon when they reached the inner harbour and the town of Auckland lay sprawled before them. The soft light lent an air of mystery to the buildings lining its wharves, although the warehouses, hotels, and other trappings of a bustling seaport were not unlike those of any European equivalent, except for their comparative modernity and an extensive use of timber in their construction. Darkness was falling before the passengers began to drift back to their quarters, chattering together in great excitement.

That night, as they were returning to their cabin after hunting, Rufus and Serafina felt Springer's mind-call for them to join him in his cabin. They found him looking very well fed, smoking one of his fragrant Turkish cigarettes and sipping a glass of port wine. Two empty glasses – purloined from goodness knew where – and the wine bottle stood on the bedside table.

"Ah, there you are," he said as they entered. "Since we disembark tomorrow, I thought a small celebratory drink might not be out of order. Will you join me?" Rufus and Serafina expressed their approval of his offer, and Springer poured a measure of the garnet-hued wine into each of the empty glasses. "A toast—" he announced, lifting his glass, "— to family."

"To family," they repeated, raising their glasses, and for the first time it began to seem real to Rufus.

"Now," Springer turned to Rufus. "I believe the disembarkation begins early tomorrow morning, so if you haven't yet packed your belongings, I suggest you do it tonight while you have the energy."

"I will," said Rufus. "But will we need to leave the ship that early?"

"I shouldn't think so, the process will take quite some time, but it always pays to be prepared, don't you think?"

Rufus thought back to when he'd first come aboard, when the boarding of the steerage passengers alone had taken an entire day. How far he'd come since then, in so many ways.

"I'll help you pack," said Serafina. "Anton, will you come for us tomorrow when it's time to leave?"

Springer blew a lazy smoke ring and watched it unravel as it rose to the ceiling. "I will, but I expect you to be ready."

Back in Rufus's cabin, he and Serafina made short work of his packing. Most of his possessions he crammed into his cabin trunk, packing a few clothes and necessities for immediate use into his large carpet bag. Then Serafina, sitting cross-legged on the bed, asked, "What do you want to do first, once we reach Auckland?"

"Have a nice, long bath," Rufus said without hesitation, "and then put on clean clothes – if I still have any. What do you want to do?"

"A bath and clean clothes will be wonderful, yes," Serafina said, "and I want to make love with my darling Rufus in a lovely, big, soft bed!"

Rufus went to sit beside her and kissed her. "Do you think you could make do one last time with a narrow, hard one?" he murmured.

Serafina's reply was all he could have wished for.

\* \* \* \*

Auckland proved both unexpectedly familiar and deeply, sometimes disturbingly, exotic. Since meeting Serafina, Rufus had given little consideration to what he might find there, but he discovered he was quite unprepared for rough, dusty streets bustling with gentlemen and ladies dressed in fashions already *passé* years before in London, and loud with the rumble and clatter of carriages and the 'clip-clop' of horses' hooves. He was even less prepared for the sight of brown-skinned Maori dressed like their British counterparts, but some – even the women – with alarming facial tattoos. Least of all was he prepared for the foul odours that hung in the air, the combined stench of sewage and unwashed humanity, redolent of the less salubrious districts of London. The streets near the harbour, their very names – Quay Street, Commerce Street, Custom House Street – describing their nature, formed a thriving commercial precinct. Beyond this lay a haphazard conglomeration of shops and houses, and the farriers, chandlers, millers, and other tradesmen necessary to a thriving seaport. Rufus had never before seen so many wooden buildings in one place. Even the ramshackle hotels and grog shops – of which there seemed an inordinate number – and other commercial buildings lining Queen Street, the town's main thoroughfare, were built of wood.

All this Rufus and Serafina saw, gazing with equal measures of fascination and horror from the windows of the carriage Springer had hired to take them to their hotel. He had decided they would stay at the Concord Hotel in Wyndham Street, off Queen Street.

"I'm assured it's very well appointed," he told them, "with lounges and sitting rooms, and even a cafe and a restaurant and a billiards room – though I hardly think we'll have need of them. I've taken a suite of rooms that includes our own sitting room, and I believe they have excellent views of the harbour. More to the point, though, the hotel is both central and private."

"How do you know what it's like?" Rufus asked. "I thought you hadn't been to New Zealand before."

Springer was not forthcoming on the subject, merely tapping the side of his nose with his forefinger.

"Well," said Rufus, surveying his grubby and rumpled clothes with distaste, "as long as it has a decent bathroom."

The bathroom, it turned out, boasted a large porcelain bath with cold running water and a gas geyser to provide hot water, so Rufus and Serafina were able to luxuriate in a real bath for the first time since leaving Britain, although, Rufus was surprised to discover, his body no longer tolerated much in the way of heat. When Springer finally knocked on the door, reminding them they weren't the only ones anxious to bathe, they wrapped themselves in the large, white, rather scratchy hotel towels and hurried to the bedroom Springer had designated as theirs.

"Oh, thank God, a double bed!" said Rufus, surveying the room's somewhat oppressive grandeur.

Serafina ran to the bed and threw herself onto the puce satin quilt. "And it's lovely and soft!" she said, holding her arms out to Rufus, heedless of the towel that slipped from her body.

In a moment, Rufus had joined her. They kissed, and he felt desire stir within him – not the wild urging of the blood ecstasy, but a gentler longing, filled with tenderness. Together they rediscovered one another's bodies – now smelling deliciously of soap – with kisses and caresses until they seemed almost to melt into one. Almost. Rufus slid his hand down the smooth white skin of Serafina's belly and between her legs. She opened herself to him, arching her body to meet his, drawing in her breath as he slid inside her, then letting it out in a long sigh as he began to move within her. Without the rush of fresh blood, they needed no mind powers to prolong the pleasure they took in each other, and the culmination, when it came, seemed to Rufus to possess a deeper, richer note, like a cello concerto compared to the wild exultation of a gypsy violin. Did he prefer one to the other? They were both born of his love for Serafina, and he adored them equally.

# CHAPTER NINETEEN

When Rufus and Serafina made their way to the parlour, they found Springer already there, stretched out on the red-plush settee, wearing his blue dressing gown over shirt and trousers, and reading a newspaper.

He looked up as they entered. "Ah, I take it you managed to occupy yourselves while I was out?" His carefully bland expression told them he knew exactly how they'd occupied themselves. "I presume you haven't dined yet?" Serafina and Rufus shook their heads. "Then I suggest we go now. Afterwards, we can take a walk about the town and familiarise ourselves with it."

Springer accompanied them as far as the harbour, where he turned west and Rufus and Serafina made their way east along the seafront on Custom House Street, turning inland as they caught the scent of a large number of people close by. Before long, they came upon the Albert Barracks, shining like a beacon amidst the ill-lit streets. Fog drifting in from the sea combined with sulphurous chimney smoke to form a clammy pall that clung to their skin and clothes. Inside the high, stone wall of the barracks, they could sense only a few men moving about, most likely, they thought, on watch duties.

"Shall I bring one of them to us?" Serafina murmured as they stood in the wall's deep shadows. "Or shall we try elsewhere?"

"You're not going to go in there?" asked Rufus in alarm.

"Of course not, I can call one of them. I'll do it and you can link your mind with mine and see how it's done."

Rufus nodded and joined his mind with Serafina's. She reached out with her mind until it connected with that of one of the soldiers, and began to draw him towards her, insinuating into his thoughts the idea that he had an important assignation to keep with a lady waiting just beyond the barracks gates. When one of his fellow soldiers called out to ask him where he was going, Serafina gave him the words to say to put the man's mind at ease. Very soon, the gates opened and a stocky young man in uniform slipped through them. Serafina drew him to her like an angler reeling in a fish, his eyes becoming glazed and dull, his face devoid of expression as he stared into dark eyes that held him captive. Rufus felt his gums begin to tingle, but he signalled to Serafina that the man was hers. As he watched, she pressed the soldier against the wall into the shadows, pulling his jacket and shirt loose at the neck as her fangs grew long and sharp. Rufus barely suppressed a gasp of shared pleasure as Serafina's fangs sank into the man's neck and she began to drink. Part of his mind he kept attuned to the barracks yard in case one of the other soldiers decided to find out what his companion was doing, but none came.

As Serafina finished, she licked at the wounds she had made to clean them and help them to heal quickly, then she sent the soldier on his way, the dazed smile on his face showing she had left him with happy, though vague, memories of his encounter. She and Rufus stood silently in the shadows as he slipped back through the gate and shut it behind him, waiting until his footsteps had died away before continuing their hunt.

"Where there are soldiers, there should be prostitutes nearby." Serafina smiled, linking her arm with Rufus's. Taking a few moments to scent the air, they retraced their steps along Military Road and onto Princess Street. A short walk along Princess Street brought them to Chancery Street, where they found what they sought. A number of women of varying ages, their tawdry attempts at allure proclaiming their profession, wandered about or leaned against shop fronts waiting for customers. All looked frozen to the bone in the chill, dank fog. Serafina slipped into the shadows cast by a tall building.

*I'll stay here out of sight while you draw one of those women to you. Bring her into the shadows here and I'll keep watch for you.*

Rufus nodded and strolled a few steps down Chancery Street, where he stopped and reached out with his mind to the nearest woman, a rather stout blonde of uncertain provenance, and she began to move towards him. As she came closer, he saw she had attempted to disguise the marks of smallpox by applying large quantities of makeup that gave her the appearance of a grotesque china doll. But he didn't care. He could smell her blood, feel it pulsing through her veins, and once again he felt the tingle of his fangs emerging and the tugging at his gut of the deeply sensual thrill that always accompanied feeding.

The woman came to stand close to him, murmuring, "Interested in a bit of business are you, sir?" in what Rufus assumed was intended to be a seductive tone.

He smiled, carefully concealing his fangs, and gazed into

her eyes until he saw her face go blank, then led her into the shadows. Holding the woman in his arms, he let the blood tide rise within him until his entire body seemed to vibrate with it, then he bent over her neck and bit into her plump flesh. She gasped when his fangs pierced her, as though responding to a lover, and then gave a shuddering sigh as Rufus began to drink. He felt her pleasure, bequeathed by his control of her mind, and drank it in with her blood, but his mind was filled with thoughts of Serafina. When the shallowness of the woman's breathing told him he'd taken enough, he raised his head, licking away the last trickles of blood from her skin, lowering her almost unconscious body to the pavement and leaning her against the wall. She gave a contented sigh and her head lolled onto her chest. Anyone seeing her would think she was sleeping off an over-indulgence in strong drink.

Rufus turned to Serafina and joined her in the shadows, pulling her into his arms and kissing her. Their kisses became more passionate as the blood ecstasy took hold of them, and Rufus felt his hunger for her grow strong. He pressed her against the wall, his body hard against hers, his breathing fast and rough with excitement. *Not here!* Serafina spoke into his mind. *We might be seen.* But Rufus crushed his mouth against hers, kissing her with such force that he could feel her half-retracted fangs through her lips. She pulled away. "No, not here!" she repeated, this time in a fierce whisper. The woman slumped beside them began to stir. Serafina grabbed Rufus's hand and tugged him after her, and they ran back to their hotel.

On discovering Springer had not yet returned from his own hunting, Serafina turned to Rufus, fires of passion burning in her eyes. "Interested in a bit of business are you, sir?" she murmured in near-perfect mimicry of the prostitute they had left in Queen Street.

"I'll need to know your terms," Rufus responded, grasping her by the shoulders, practically pushing her into their bedroom and shoving the door closed with his foot.

His passion rising as it had in Queen Street, Rufus pressed Serafina against the door and began to kiss her, one hand entwined in her hair, the other pulling up her long skirts. He gasped as he felt her hands against him, her fingers busy unfastening his trousers as she returned his kisses.

"Oh, God, Serafina! I want you so much I can't bear it!" With something close to desperation, Rufus grasped Serafina and lifted her up so he could slip inside her, revelling in her sharp cry of pleasure, and they made love with a fierce intensity that left them both shuddering and gasping for breath.

Somehow they made their way to the bed, shedding clothes as they went, savouring the touch and scent of each other's bodies as they employed every sense at their command to explore each other with a slow and sensual thoroughness that took them almost to the limit of endurance before they gave themselves up to ecstasy.

Afterwards, they lay with their bodies twined together, needing no words to tell each other of their feelings.

At length, Rufus raised himself on one elbow and gazed at Serafina's face, as pale as a spring blossom framed by her raven hair. "Darling Serafina, how did I ever live without you?"

"As I lived without you, my love – incompletely. But we've

found each other now, and we need never be parted again."

"Please God!" Rufus's voice was muffled against Serafina's lips as he bent to kiss her.

*Please God!* Serafina's response echoed in his mind.

When they emerged from their room, they found Springer in the sitting room, once more immersed in the pages of the *Evening Star* newspaper.

"I thought it best not to disturb you," he said with a knowing smirk, and Rufus found himself wondering how he dealt with the blood ecstasy. "An iron will, honed over centuries," Springer murmured from the depths of his paper.

It was some minutes before he closed and folded the paper, placing it neatly on the arm of the settee. "Now," he said, rising to his feet with the grace that still surprised Rufus, "shall we take a tour of the town?"

The three of them spent some hours wandering about the Auckland streets, aimlessly to anyone seeing them, but taking in each detail. A brisk breeze arose, blowing away much of the sea fog and driving wisps of cloud across the dark sky so that the moonlight seemed to flicker like a fitful candle flame. As they walked, Rufus and Serafina pointed out to Springer the Chancery Street area where prostitutes plied their trade, and the Albert Barracks with their supply of soldiers. Springer guided them around the harbour area whose murky taverns, brothels, and grog shops were the haunts of sailors and prostitutes and the usual rogues found in such areas, as well as a number of hostelries further afield whose patrons might provide sustenance for a vampire in need. By the time they returned to the Concord in the small hours of the morning, each had a mental map of the town, with the most likely areas for successful hunting marked.

Rufus had also noticed a number of respectable-looking gaming establishments where he thought he might earn a useful income by supplementing the skills developed in the London clubs with his new abilities. Part of him was inclined to be squeamish at the thought of using these for such a purpose, but he knew the money he'd brought with him would not last long, and without the income from his father – which would doubtless be stopped in any case once his father learned he'd failed to arrive at his uncle's estate – he suspected it might be his best option. Thoughts of his family and his friends in London made Rufus aware of how far he'd come – in every sense – since leaving England, and he was overcome by an unexpected wave of nostalgia for the life he'd left behind.

*You have us, now*, came Serafina's thought into his mind, and she slipped her arm about his waist and kissed him.

*Yes*, he thought, *this is what I have now. I couldn't go back if I wanted to.* And, with his cheek against Serafina's raven hair, he knew he had no wish to do so.

\* \* \* \*

Somewhat to Rufus's surprise, Springer approved of his plan to make money from gambling, even offering to go with him on his initial forays so that they could compare notes and Springer could give the benefit of his expertise, both as a gambler and a vampire. Serafina, however, was considerably less than happy when she realised she was not to be included in these outings.

"They're not gentlemen's clubs, so why shouldn't I go with

you?" she demanded, a scowl on her face and her eyes flashing sparks of anger. "I used to when we lived in Europe. I even wagered money and won, more often than not."

"This is not Europe," Springer reminded her. "In New Zealand, it's not the custom for women to go gambling – at least not women with any pretension to decency. You'd be far too noticeable in such an establishment."

Serafina jumped up from her seat by the parlour window and began to pace about the room. "I told you we shouldn't have come here, damned uncivilised place!" she flung at Springer.

"And I told you why we should," said Springer. "Besides, I'm not going to be with you all the time, and Rufus needs an income for when I'm away. This offers the dual advantages of suiting his skills and fitting in with our lifestyle. You know I don't respond well to fits of the sulks, my dear, so you might as well accept the situation with good grace."

Rufus, who had been sitting on the settee listening to this exchange with amusement, held out his arms to Serafina. "Sweetheart, don't be angry. You know I'd take you if I could, but I can take you to a play or a concert. You'd like that, wouldn't you?"

"If they have concerts in this godforsaken place," Serafina muttered ungraciously, but she stopped pacing and went to sit beside Rufus.

He put his arms about her and kissed her. "Of course they do. Just the other night I saw the billing for a concert at the Choral Hall in Symonds Street. I dare say it's not quite what you've been used to, but there was an operatic singer from England on the bill, and a Beethoven concerto."

Serafina did her best to remain mutinous, but the gleam

in her eyes at the mention of music told Rufus a different story.

"Do you promise to take me?"

"I promise."

"All right, but just remember how bored I'll be while you two are out gallivanting."

Springer got to his feet and gave Serafina a pained look. "Let me assure you I have never gallivanted in my life or, indeed, my unlife."

Serafina's frown began to melt into a smile. "I can believe that! Off you go, then, but don't be surprised if you come back to find I've died of boredom."

Martin's, the gaming house Rufus and Springer had chosen for their first visit, was a sizable two-storey establishment just off Queen Street, run, according to the gilt lettering above the door, by Mrs Honoria Devine. Mrs Devine proved to be a rather dashing woman in her forties with chestnut hair that owed little to nature and shrewd, sapphire-blue eyes. Business was flourishing, if the quantities of gilt, velvet, and heavy carved furniture were any indication. Various rooms on both floors were given over to a number of different games: backgammon, *vingt-et-un*, poker, piquet, euchre, even a roulette table. There was a supper room on the ground floor, where a string quartet played soft music and refreshments were served throughout the evening.

They were greeted at the door by an older gentleman with the look and manner of a butler fallen on hard times. Mrs Devine herself directed them to an upstairs room where poker was being played and, before long the two of them were engrossed in a spirited, fourhanded game.

Throughout the game, Springer remained unengaged as far as mind powers were concerned, allowing Rufus to discover his own capabilities. In fact, Rufus found it surprisingly easy to probe the minds of the other two players to learn what cards they held and the strategies they were planning. He suspected his efforts at mind reading were not yet particularly subtle, but his subjects gave no sign of awareness. Nevertheless, he decided he would be wise not to win too much or too often, since this would arouse suspicion as no amount of mind-probing seemed likely to do. It was scarcely a high-stakes game but, two hours later, when the others decided to try their luck at roulette, Rufus was almost twenty pounds the richer.

"Well, that wasn't too difficult," he said as they strolled down the thickly carpeted staircase.

"No," admitted Springer with a smile. "Some of your abilities could use a little refinement, but there's no doubt at all of your skill at cards."

"Thank you. Perhaps next time you can do the honours and I'll observe. I do want to learn all I can."

Springer made a slight bow. "Excellent. What shall it be this time?"

They had reached the ground floor, where a small crowd was gathered around the roulette table. "I wonder," murmured Rufus almost to himself, "if our powers extend to manipulating inanimate objects?"

Springer spoke into his mind: *Alas, no. Apart from control of our own bodies, they're powers over the mind alone. And please, if you know what's good for you, don't ever say such things aloud, hmm?*

*Sorry,* returned Rufus, *I'll be more careful in future.*

Aloud, he said, "Shall we try our luck at euchre, then?"

"Certainly." As they made their way to the tables, Springer caught the attention of one of the servants. "Could you bring us a bottle of claret and two glasses? We'll be at the euchre tables."

\* \* \* \*

"Tell me all about it!" Serafina demanded, steering Rufus toward the settee. "What was it like? Who was there? Were any of them ladies? Tell me! Tell me!"

"Serafina!" Springer's voice carried a warning.

"But I've been so bored, cooling my heels here all alone while you two were out on the town. The least you can do is tell me about it."

Springer pursed his lips and murmured, "I note, however, that you didn't expire of your boredom."

"All right, all right," Rufus laughed, pulling Serafina onto his knee and kissing her.

"Martin's is a very well run house, presided over by Mrs Honoria Devine, who's forty if she's a day, and must be quite wealthy judging by the way the place is decorated. It's all velvet and oak and mahogany, and gilt everywhere. It has upstairs and downstairs rooms with a roulette table, and tables for all sorts of card games as well as dice and backgammon and..."

"What did you play?"

"Poker, and euchre and piquet."

"And were there ladies there?"

"Only a few, apart from Mrs Devine herself, and none of them ladies in whose company you'd want to be seen."

"You mean in whose company *you'd* want me to be seen," retorted Serafina.

"Aren't you going to ask about the entire point of the evening?" drawled Springer, opening his cigarette box and extracting a cigarette and matches.

Serafina frowned at him. "I was getting to that! So, my love, how much did you win?"

"Not as much as I could have won," grinned Rufus. "But I didn't want them to think I was cheating – or, rather, I didn't want them to *know* I was cheating." He dug his hands into his pockets, pulled out fists full of notes and flung them onto the couch. "I think there's around forty-five pounds there – more than enough for the theatre, I should think."

Serafina picked up handfuls of the notes, staring at them in delight. "Rufus! So much money! Oh, you *are* clever!"

"Well, I did have something of an advantage."

"No false modesty, Rufus." Springer sent a thin stream of tobacco smoke towards the ceiling and watched as it curled upwards in a widening spiral. "You're a very talented card player. I only wish I'd had you with me in Berlin. It could have saved me a great deal of—ah—trouble."

Rufus, guessing he was referring to his friendship with Stefan, and what it had led to, said nothing.

Springer, his face devoid of expression, continued to smoke his cigarette for some minutes, then, crushing the remains of it into his silver ashtray, he rose to his feet. "I'm for my bed, now," he announced. "Dawn is not far off. Tomorrow, I intend to start looking for a house for us."

# CHAPTER TWENTY

Late the following afternoon, Springer woke Rufus and Serafina with the news that he'd made an appointment for them to view several houses in Epsom, a district on the outskirts of the city, where many fine houses had been built. An hour later, they were standing in Wellesley Street outside the premises of A. R. Manning and P. G. E. Harper, Esquires, Estate Agents. Telling the others to wait for him, Springer went inside, emerging moments later accompanied by a trim little man with a waxed moustache, whom he introduced as Mr Anthony Manning. Before Springer had finished introducing them, a smart, if rather dusty, carriage drew up beside them, pulled by a pair of solid-looking chestnut horses and driven by a skinny youth in a black suit. Rufus handed Serafina into the carriage and he and Springer and Mr Manning followed. Soon they were bowling along the unpaved streets in a choking cloud of dust.

Rufus's initial excitement soon turned to disappointment and boredom, as one after another property failed to meet Springer's exacting standards. All, it seemed, were too small, too large, or – most important of all – not private enough. Dusk was darkening the sky when at length Mr Manning's carriage drew up outside the last of his offerings. From the street, nothing of it was visible, being hidden by a high wall of grey stone that reminded Rufus of the one encircling the

Albert Barracks. Springer shot a glance at Serafina and Rufus that made clear his approval so far.

Mr Manning opened the wrought-iron gate to reveal a square, two-storey house with a veranda across the front, its roof forming the floor of a balcony with a balustrade of white-painted wrought iron. "As you can see," he said, "it's built of stone, so it's good and solid. Ideal for a gentleman like yourself, Mr Springer, who's away on business much of the time. Really, it'll pretty much take care of itself, and it's very private, just as you wanted."

Springer gave a noncommittal nod and, with the others, followed the estate agent up the long, curved path to the wooden verandah. Mr Manning opened the front door and led them into a high, square, wood-panelled hallway with three doors off it and an elegant wooden staircase rising at one side. Mr Manning led the way, the others trailing after him through the parlour, sitting room, dining room, kitchen and pantry downstairs, and three bedrooms upstairs, along with a bathroom. A spirit of ease and comfort seemed to infuse every room. The large grounds – almost half an acre, Mr Manning told them with enthusiasm – were well enough fenced to ensure complete privacy, and plantings of well-grown trees added to the sense of seclusion.

"The furniture can be bought with the home, if required," the estate agent told them as one delivering the winning argument in a debate.

Rufus, who had noticed a piano in the parlour, decided there and then that this was where he wanted to live – if only Springer would take the furniture along with the house.

While Mr Manning busied himself locking up the house after their tour, Springer conferred mentally with Rufus and

Serafina. *I think this will suit us, don't you? It's as private as we could wish for, and will be comfortable enough to live in – though I dare say it doesn't quite match what you've been used to, Rufus.*

Rufus grinned. *You never saw my rooms in London.* He showed Springer and Serafina a mental image, and it was Springer's turn to grin, and Serafina's to grimace.

*We're agreed, then?*

Rufus and Serafina nodded.

Mr Manning, having ensured everything was secure, came down the steps to join them, his moustache all but quivering with the expectation of a successful sale.

"Yes," Springer told him, "this will suit us quite well." To Rufus's delight, he added, "And we'll take the furniture as well, provided the price is not too steep."

The estate agent fingered his moustache for a moment as though afraid he might have left it behind in the house. "Oh, I think you'll find the vendors very reasonable. They're anxious for a sale as they want to make extensions to their own house – expanding family, you know. I'll visit them this evening after I've taken you back to town and, if you'd care to call on me tomorrow, we can conclude our negotiations then."

The estate agent's carriage set them down outside the premises of Manning and Harper. As they walked to the corner of Wellesley and Queen Streets, Springer said, "What an exhausting business that was. I'm so famished it was all I could do to keep my hands off the estimable Mr Manning."

"Rubbish!" snorted Serafina. "I've known you to go for days without feeding."

"At any rate," returned Springer, refusing to rise to her bait, "I don't intend to do so tonight. I'll see you back at the hotel. We've a lot to discuss." He set off along Queen Street towards the harbour, the dim and flickering gaslights burnishing his pale hair to a golden sheen.

It would not do for the three of them to hunt in close proximity, so Rufus and Serafina walked in the opposite direction to Springer, scenting the smoky air as they went. They turned left into Wakefield Street, making for the domain, hoping they might find some lone soul wandering there. But it seemed the citizens were all snug indoors; all they saw were a few policemen trudging their beat. At Symonds Street, however, they picked up a promising scent, their senses becoming alert and focused as they followed it. Before long, they reached the Grafton Gully cemetery. Rufus felt the stab of excitement that told him they were closing in on their target, and he felt Serafina's excitement, which served to increase his own. Glancing across at her, he saw her lick her lips like a jungle cat anticipating a kill, and his mouth watered in response. They seemed almost to have become one in the intensity and focus of their quest.

Ahead of them, among the crowded tombstones, Rufus caught sight of a man staggering through the rank, wet grass, steadying himself against the monuments as he went. Rufus and Serafina quickened their pace until they came level with him, and Rufus saw he was quite young, no more than twenty or so, and very, very drunk. Serafina took him by the arm and turned him to face her. The man stood swaying on his feet, mumbling unintelligible words that Rufus, looking into his rather confused mind, interpreted as expressing a mixture of surprise and conviviality. Serafina stared into his bleary eyes, running her tongue over her lips in a gesture that was almost lascivious, and Rufus felt desire and hunger lick along his nerves like flames.

Grasping the man by the arms to hold him steady, Serafina continued to gaze into his eyes. Within moments, she had control of his mind and he willingly followed her to the shelter of a small stand of trees. Once there in the shadows, she pushed him against a tree trunk and pinned him there with her eyes. As Rufus watched, Serafina's eyes began to glow red and her fangs emerged. He felt the tingle of his own fangs forming, and then Serafina was in his mind, inviting him to join her. Just for a second, he wondered at the wisdom of the two of them taking blood from the same man, but the thought was lost as the blood hunger overwhelmed him. As Serafina stood poised above the man's neck, Rufus grasped his wrist and pushed back his grubby sleeve, and at the same moment their fangs pierced his skin and they became engrossed in the flow of blood, hot and salty, and as intoxicating as the alcohol they could taste in it. When they finished, the man slid to the ground unconscious. Alarmed, Rufus bent to feel his pulse. It was weak, but his heartbeat was regular, if a little slow. He straightened up again and turned to Serafina, holding out his arms to her. Their fangs still sharp in their mouths, they kissed, licking blood from each other's lips.

A coach rumbled by on the street, its lamps sending flickers of light dancing over the tombstones as it passed. Rufus pulled Serafina further into the shadows, murmuring, "Have you ever made love in a graveyard?"

Serafina grimaced in disgust, her teeth gleaming white in the darkness. "No, I haven't, and I don't intend to start now."

Rufus pulled her against him, his hands moving down her back, feeling her lithe body through her gown. "Don't make me wait, Serafina. I want you so much I can't bear it. Serafina, don't you feel it, too?"

"Yes," she whispered, drawing back from him with a smile. "Humans hunger for many things, but in most vampires all hungers are subsumed into two – blood and physical love. You and I are lucky, Rufus, we can satisfy that other hunger with someone we truly love. Not all of us can do that."

"What do they do, then? Suppress it, as Anton does?"

"Some do, but many will satisfy it with whoever is to hand, be they vampire or human, often with those from whom they feed. That's why people through the ages have believed us to be succubi or incubi – demons that prey on them in the night. I suppose we do, when there is desire without love. That's why some vampires have formed communities, so they can be true to their nature, yet protect themselves from the risk of being discovered by humans. This has its own risks, though, mostly because of the intensity of our feelings, which is why some vampires prefer to keep humans – rather as humans keep pets – so they can satisfy both desires."

"And the humans don't mind?"

Serafina shrugged. "They're kept controlled, I imagine. They provide the blood the vampires need, and I suppose the satisfaction of desire is mutual."

"Sounds just like an Arabian's harem to me," said Rufus with a grimace of distaste.

Serafina smiled. "Yes, I suppose it is similar, though I hadn't thought of it that way before."

"Have you come across any of these groups?"

"No, Anton refuses to have anything to do with them, though he's never told me why. Sometimes, when I've been lonely, I've thought how pleasant it would be to be with others like me, but I couldn't bear to use anyone in that way, not after my—my..."

"It's all right," Rufus murmured, stroking her hair. "You can let all that go, now."

Serafina smiled at him. "Yes, I can, now I have you. Oh, Rufus, I love you so much!" She wrapped her arms about his neck and kissed him. "Let's go home, darling. I want you as much as you want me, but not here among dead people and derelicts."

Rufus nodded, and they climbed up the grassy bank and hurried back along Symonds Street.

The wind blew chill from the sea, carrying the tang of salt and fish and odours of rope and tar and oil, and a variety of cargoes from the ships that lay berthed at the wharves. Low clouds raced before the wind, their bellies turned sickly yellow by the light from the streetlamps, the same glow washing over everything like an old coat of varnish, except for the shadows skulking beyond the reach of the gaslights.

All at once Serafina stopped, her head raised like a pointer scenting a bird, a puzzled frown furrowing her brow.

"What is it?" Rufus asked as she took his arm again.

"There's another vampire nearby."

"Are you sure?"

"Yes, I think so."

Rufus stopped, probing about him with his mind. "I don't sense anything."

"No," said Serafina, "it'll take a while for your senses to

develop fully, and besides, it was only for a moment. I suppose whoever it was wants to remain hidden."

For some moments Rufus looked thoughtful, then he asked, "Why would another vampire want to hide from us? I'd have thought they'd be pleased to find a kindred spirit."

"I don't know," Serafina said with a shrug. "Perhaps he just prefers to keep to himself. It's very easy for creatures who must live off others and hunt by night to come to prefer their own company – and to be wary of strangers, even other vampires."

"You say 'he'. This is a male vampire, then?"

Serafina shook her head. "I can't be certain. The contact was too brief. I'll tell Anton about it later, but the chances are we'll never know."

# CHAPTER TWENTY-ONE

Springer's response when Serafina told him what she had sensed was non-committal. "I'm a little surprised to find another of us in such an out-of-the-way place, but I dare say it's of no importance, especially if he, or she, as the case might be, doesn't wish to be known to us."

"But aren't you curious?" asked Rufus.

Springer shrugged. "In a general way, yes, but if a vampire chooses to remain hidden, there's little I can do to satisfy my curiosity, is there? Of course I'll be on the alert, as should the two of you, and I think it would pay to keep ourselves hidden, just to be on the safe side, but, as Serafina says, we may never find out who it is. Besides, we have more immediate concerns. I've bought the house, and we can move in as soon as the transfer of title is completed."

Serafina ran to hug Springer, and then Rufus. Rufus shook Springer's hand. The touch of his skin conveyed nothing more about the vampire Serafina had sensed, yet Rufus couldn't help feeling Springer was keeping something from them. Still, he reflected, if there were any cause for concern, surely he'd have told them.

\* \* \* \*

They had been in the new house for just over a week when

Rufus and Serafina went downstairs soon after sunset to find Springer in the sitting room standing by the fireplace, a thoughtful expression on his face.

Serafina immediately went to him. "What's the matter, Anton? It's not that other vampire is it?"

Springer shook his head, smiling. "No, nothing like that, it's just that I need to go to Australia sooner than I expected. I'm sorry we have to leave so soon after moving in here, but—"

"Leave?" Serafina interrupted. "I don't want to leave! Please don't make me go, Anton. I'm so sick and tired of travelling. Why can't I stay here with Rufus?"

Springer sighed and rolled his eyes, then turned to Rufus. "And what does Rufus want?"

Rufus, taken aback both by Springer's announcement and Serafina's reaction to it, stammered, "I—I don't know. I'm a stranger to both countries, but I won't leave Serafina. If she wants to stay here, of course I'll stay with her."

Springer's expression made it clear this was not the answer he had wanted. "Don't you think you'd both be safer with me?"

"Perhaps," said Rufus. "I've no know way of knowing but, either way, I won't leave Serafina."

"Your loyalty is commendable, at any rate," said Springer, "but I'd very much prefer to have the two of you where I can keep an eye on you."

"Then you stay!" said Serafina. "Why do you have to keep travelling all the time?"

"I have business interests to take care of, you know that," Springer told her, but there was something about his carefully controlled voice and expression that made Rufus think this was not the whole truth.

Serafina glowered at him, her eyes sparking with anger. "Business! That's what you always say. You care more for your damned business than you do for your own family!"

"Yet you're happy enough to use the proceeds for fine clothes and other trinkets," Springer pointed out, his voice gentle, but his eyes as cold as a winter frost.

"Well, I won't then, not if it means I have to follow you round the world like a—like a pet dog!"

Springer strode across the room and took her by the shoulders, but she refused to look at him, keeping her face averted, even when he tried to lift her chin to make her eyes meet his.

"No," she said fiercely, "I won't let you control me!"

With a hiss of anger, Springer let go of her, almost pushing her away from him. "How dare you, Serafina? You know I've never done that, not to you." He strode back to the fireplace, grasping the mantelpiece with both hands, and breathing hard as he tried to master his feelings. When he turned back to Serafina, his face was like granite. "I refuse to talk with you while you're in such a mood. Rufus, I'm sorry you've had to witness this."

He turned his back on Serafina and left the room, shutting the door with such care it was clear to Rufus he was making a deliberate effort not to slam it. A moment later, Rufus heard the front door open and close.

As soon as Springer was gone, Serafina flung herself onto the nearest settee and began to pummel it with clenched fists, howling like a wild animal. For several minutes, Rufus stood aghast, uncertain how to deal with a side of Serafina he had not seen before. Then, unable to bear her distress any longer, he went to sit beside her, putting his arm about her shoulders. Serafina turned on him, her eyes flashing, her lips drawn back in a snarl, and her fangs beginning to grow as though she meant to attack him. Leaping up in alarm, Rufus backed away from her, his hands raised ready to fend her off, staring at her in astonishment, not only at what she seemed to have become, but also at what might lie dormant within him. Then tears filled her eyes and her stark face crumpled. She jumped up and ran to him, throwing herself against him wracked by convulsive sobs, her tears falling like rain after a thunderstorm. Rufus gathered her into his arms and held her, trying to exert what will he could muster to calm her. As he reached into her mind, he saw not the enraged creature that had snarled at him and shown its fangs, but a young woman torn by conflicting loyalties. She really did long to settle down with him, her lover, yet she was afraid that if she didn't keep travelling with Springer, her maker, who had been more truly her father than any human had ever been, she would lose him. That fear had been the source of her anger. Through the turmoil in her mind, Rufus spoke to her without words, telling her she was part of Springer as he was of her, that the blood that linked the three of them formed a bond that could never be broken, and for the first time he began to feel for himself the reality of that bond.

Gradually, Serafina's tears abated. She raised her head, wiping her face with her sleeve. "Oh, Rufus, forgive me! I never meant to attack you like that. It's just..."

Rufus kissed her gently. "It's all right, darling, I understand. But you won't lose Anton, you know. In his own way, he loves you as much as I do, and he wants to protect you from harm."

"But I can't come to any harm here with you, can I?"

"I'd like to think not, but I suppose he wants to be sure."

Serafina sighed. "But I'm so tired of travelling. I don't think we've stayed anywhere for more than a few months at a time since I first left Moscow, and Anton won't even tell me why we need to keep moving. He just says it's better for us."

Rufus shrugged. "Perhaps it is. After all, Anton's been a vampire for longer than either of us, so he probably has a better understanding of the potential dangers."

"Then the least he could do is tell me why."

"If you like," said Rufus, "I'll have a talk with him later."

"Oh, would you? I'm sure he'll listen to you."

Rufus was considerably less certain, but he smiled at Serafina and kissed her gently. "Of course I will, sweetheart," he said, adding, in an attempt to lighten the mood, "but right now, I think we should go and hunt. I don't know about you, but all this excitement has made me ravenous."

It was well after midnight when Rufus and Serafina heard Springer return. They had already fed and bathed, and had decided to spend the hours until dawn in the sanctuary of their room, curled up together in their bed, talking. As soon as he heard Springer downstairs, Rufus sat up.

"I'll go and talk to Anton now," he told Serafina, trying to sound more sanguine than he felt. He got out of bed and pulled on his dressing gown, then bent to kiss her.

"I should go with you," she said, though it was clear from her face that she didn't want to.

Rufus shook his head. "No, you stay here. I shan't be long."

With considerable trepidation, Rufus made his way

downstairs. Outside the sitting room he stopped, listening intently, trying to gauge Springer's mood, although he made no attempt to reach out to his mind, fearful of exacerbating an already delicate situation. As he stood there trying to think how to approach him, Springer called out, "Do come in, Rufus. I shan't bite, you know."

Smiling in spite of himself, Rufus pushed open the door to find Springer standing by the window smoking one of his Turkish cigarettes. He turned to face Rufus, who was heartened to see his face looked less stony than before, his eyes less arctic.

"How is Serafina?" he asked, exhaling fragrant smoke.

"She's feeling better," Rufus said. "I promised her I'd speak to you."

Springer raised one eyebrow. "About...?"

"Well, about her staying here with me."

"And...?"

"Anton, she really doesn't want to keep travelling, but she's afraid that if she doesn't go with you, she might never see you again."

"But that's ridiculous!" exclaimed Springer, angry sparks flashing in his eyes. He took a deep breath, then went on more calmly, "I don't intend to go away forever, just until it's—until my business is concluded. I do believe that she—that both of you—will be safer if you're with me, but I suppose I can't blame Serafina for wanting to be more independent, especially now she has you. It's just that..." Springer seemed to withdraw into himself, his forgotten cigarette dripping ash onto the rug. After several minutes, he murmured, as though to himself, "After all, it's me she wants, not..." Then he seemed to collect himself. "Please tell

Serafina I'm not angry with her, just concerned for her welfare. I won't pretend it's what I think is best, but since she wants to stay here so much, then she has my blessing. Just make sure you take good care of her, Rufus, or you'll have me to answer to. Is that understood?"

"Yes, sir, thank you. Do you know yet when you'll be leaving?"

"As soon as possible. I fear I may already have stayed too long." Rufus wanted to ask Springer what he meant by such an odd statement, but Springer turned away to stub out the cigarette he'd barely smoked. When he looked at Rufus again, it was as though he'd drawn shutters over his eyes. "I'll say good morning, now, if you don't mind. Tell Serafina I'll talk to her this evening."

Rufus nodded, bade Springer good day, and walked back up the stairs. He felt sure Springer was hiding something from him and Serafina, but he couldn't imagine what it might be.

# CHAPTER TWENTY-TWO

Three days later, on a grey and humid afternoon, Rufus and Serafina accompanied Springer to the wharf, where he boarded the Union Steamship Company vessel *Waitemata*, bound for Australia. At first, Serafina had refused to go, declaring she couldn't bear to see him sail away. But at the last moment, as Springer and Rufus were about to step into the carriage Springer had hired, she came racing down the stairs with no coat on, imploring them not to leave without her. So the three of them stood at the quayside surveying the ship – a singularly unattractive vessel it seemed to Rufus, with three masts and a tall, thick, ugly steam funnel sticking up from the deck – while the baggage was loaded.

When the time came to board, Springer shook Rufus's hand. "Goodbye, Rufus, I hope to see you again before very long. Remember, I'm trusting you to look after Serafina while I'm away."

"I will, I give you my word on it. *Bon voyage*, sir, I hope your business goes well."

"Thank you Rufus. I hope so, too. Careful, or you'll have me in the water!" This last was to Serafina who had flung herself into his arms in a flood of tears and kisses.

"Oh, Anton, I wish you didn't have to go. I shan't know how to go on without you."

Springer fended her off as best he could, but gently, for he was clearly almost as affected as she was beneath his veneer of calm. "My dear," he said, stroking her cheek. "Of course you will, you have Rufus now."

"But I'll miss you so much."

"And I'll miss you, too, my dear. For someone who never wanted children, I've become remarkably fond of you, despite your capriciousness."

"Me? Capricious?" Serafina exclaimed. "You're a fine one to talk!" Springer smiled, and Rufus felt sure his words had been calculated to jolt Serafina out of her tearfulness. If so, the ruse worked. Serafina slapped Springer lightly on the cheek. "You're a wicked, wicked man," she declared, laughing and kissing the cheek she had struck. "I'm going to close my eyes now, so go quickly before I start crying again."

Springer turned and went aboard. Seconds later, he was lost to sight among the other passengers.

Rufus put his arm about Serafina and hugged her to him. "You can open your eyes now, love. Let's go home, shall we?"

As they walked away from the quayside, they heard behind them the hoarse breathing of the ship's engine and the thin, lonely cry of its horn as it drew away from the quay.

\* \* \* \*

At first, both Rufus and Serafina found themselves missing Springer's enigmatic presence in the house. Serafina would sit for hours at a time in his favourite chair, breathing in his scent and reaching out her mind in the hope of finding his. But, by the second day, the *Waitemata* had carried him beyond mind reach. Rufus did his best to make her happy, taking her to plays and concerts, and for moonlight walks around the harbour or to the top of Mount Eden, from where they could see the entire town sprawled out beneath the blanket of coal smoke that made its lights seem like embers in a dying fire. Rufus's chosen source of income remained a bone of contention between them, but he was adamant that he would not take her to gaming houses, where she would attract unwanted, and possibly dangerous, attention.

One night, about a month after Springer's departure, Rufus found himself embroiled in yet another round of the same conflict.

"For goodness's sake, Serafina," he told her, his voice sharp with exasperation, "it's not as though I go every night. Surely you can find something to amuse you while I'm there."

"I don't want to amuse myself. I want to go with you."

"Well, you can't, and you know very well why, so the sooner you accept it, the happier we'll both be." Aware that he was beginning to sound like Serafina's parent rather than her lover, he made an attempt to mollify her. "Look, I won't be there for more than an hour or so. Why don't you meet me outside at, say, nine o'clock? Then you can come with me while I hunt, and afterwards we can walk home together. I promise you, you won't have to amuse yourself then."

But Serafina was not inclined to be appeased. "You'd better not be late," she told him, "or I might find myself some other entertainment."

"I won't be, I promise. Come on, we can walk together as far as Queen Street."

At nine o'clock, fifty-five pounds richer, Rufus left Martin's, which had become his favourite establishment, to find

Serafina already waiting for him. She looked even more enchanting than usual in the new gown Springer had purchased for her before he left, a simple, but elegant creation in the deep crimson that suited her so well.

"Where did you go tonight?" he asked, kissing her cheek and slipping his arm about her waist.

She slid out of his grasp, determined to show he was still out of favour. "I went to the Albert Barracks, and found a very handsome young soldier there. I was quite tempted to keep him."

"If you're trying to provoke me, Serafina, I assure you it won't work," Rufus told her, though in truth he had felt the prick of jealousy she'd intended him to feel.

"I could still go back and get him." Serafina gave him a sidelong glance to see what effect her words were having. "After all, it was you who said I should find something to amuse me, and I'm sure a pretty soldier boy could be most amusing."

"Serafina!" Rufus stopped and stared at her. "Why are you talking like that? It's hardly my fault if places like Martin's don't accept women. You know I'd take you with me if I could. Or would you rather we became destitute?"

"We won't. Anton will take care of us. But if you absolutely must make your own money, why can't it be from something that doesn't exclude me?"

Rufus turned and grasped Serafina's shoulders, repressing a strong desire to shake her. "What would you suggest? Prostitution? Highway robbery?"

"Now you're just being silly." Serafina glared back at him, sparks of anger glinting in her eyes. "And let go of me, you're hurting."

With a sigh, Rufus removed his hands. "Why are you being so unreasonable? It's my duty to provide for us now, not Anton's, and I'm only trying to do it as best I can."

Serafina continued to scowl at him, her face hard and angry. He wanted to take her in his arms and kiss away her anger, but the blood hunger was beginning to tear at him, and he couldn't guarantee the patience needed to make a good job of it. "I must feed now," he said, keeping his voice low, although there were few people about besides the usual vagrants and drunkards. "Come with me, and afterwards perhaps we can come up with a solution that suits us both."

"I don't think so," Serafina flung at him, "since you're determined to shut me out of your 'men's business'. Anton has never treated me like that, and I won't accept it from you. Go on, then, go and feed. Do whatever you like. See if I care!"

She tossed her head and stalked off down the street.

Rufus started after her. "Serafina, come back. Please!"

Serafina ignored him and began walking faster. He began to run after her but, at that moment, a young woman standing near the corner of a narrow alleyway between a bakery and a run-down hotel walked towards him. He felt the familiar tightening in his gut as the hunger surged through him, stopping him in his tracks. For a long moment he stood there, torn between making peace with Serafina and feeding his hunger.

"Good evening, sir." The young woman's voice was low and sultry, inflaming not the lust she intended, but the blood hunger that clamoured within him.

She came to stand close to him, her eyes, fringed by dark lashes, half closed as though with passion. Her lips were full, and painted scarlet. Her perfume smelled of musk and roses. The moment Rufus turned to look at her he was lost, consumed by his need for blood. He took her arm and led her into the darkness of the alley, backing her up against the brick wall and staring into her eyes. They were the colour of seawater, so that looking into them was like looking at the ocean on a clear day. As her eyes lost their depth and became expressionless beneath his gaze, he felt his fangs emerge and his entire being focused on the girl's soft, pink neck and the veins pulsing just below the surface of her skin. Holding her in a tight embrace, he raised his head, almost in a gesture of reverence, and lowered it to a succulent, throbbing vein. Then there was nothing besides blood, sweet and thick, spurting into his hungry mouth and filling him with life.

Afterwards, Rufus hurried home anxious to make amends with Serafina. He hadn't realised until tonight just how strongly she felt about being unable to accompany him to the gaming houses. But now he did, he was prepared to concede the point and, since he really couldn't take her to places like Martin's, to look for some other way to make money, though he hadn't the slightest idea what that might be. But nothing, he felt, was worth upsetting Serafina for. Besides, she might well feel more complaisant about it when she had had more time to come to terms with Anton's absence. It must be a considerable wrench to her after they'd been together for so long.

He arrived home to find the house in darkness, but this didn't surprise him, since of course Serafina could see perfectly well in the dark. She was probably waiting for him in the parlour, or in bed. His body stirred in anticipation. Unlocking the door, he stepped into the dark well of the hallway. The house felt strangely empty. Puzzled, Rufus reached out his mind to Serafina – and found nothing. Unwilling to believe what his senses were telling him, he raced from room to room, turning on lights as though their glare might reveal what he already knew was not there. Desperate now, he dashed out to the back garden. He even searched the tumbledown shed. Inside and out, the house was completely empty. Where could Serafina have gone? No matter how angry she might be with him, surely she wouldn't have left him. Would she? He strode back inside and flung himself onto a couch in the parlour, racking his brains for some clue as to where Serafina might have gone. Then he recalled her remark about amusing herself with a handsome young soldier. He hadn't thought she was serious at the time, and he still thought it unlikely, but then he'd never seen her so angry and resentful before. Well, he had to start looking for her somewhere, and the Albert Barracks seemed as good a place as any.

During his hurried walk to the barracks, Rufus kept his senses open to any hint of Serafina's presence, but he caught no sign of her. Nor did he find the slightest hint of her at the barracks, nor at any of the other places she favoured for hunting. As a last resort, he made a tour of the gaming establishments he frequented, but to no avail. At last, he turned his steps towards home, hoping Serafina would be there when he arrived.

But the house stood as empty and still as it had before.

Frantic with dread, Rufus climbed the stairs and threw himself onto the bed, but leapt up again immediately because he could smell Serafina there, and it was more than he could bear. He dashed downstairs again and spent the rest of the night either pacing about the parlour or sitting with his head – which seemed simultaneously filled with pain and as empty as the house itself – in his hands. He could think of no possible reason why Serafina would have left him so suddenly – and so completely. Yes, they had quarrelled, but they'd quarrelled before and she hadn't left him. Besides, where could she go without money? No, something must have happened to take her away – but what? Into his mind came the picture of Serafina standing, brow furrowed, sensing the fleeting sign of another vampire.

He sat up, his heart pounding. That must be it, surely. Who else would have the power to take Serafina from him? He could not even remotely imagine why some unknown vampire would take her, but every instinct told him it must be the answer.

Rufus dragged himself to his feet. "I will find you, Serafina," he vowed through gritted teeth. "I don't know where you are, or why you've been taken but, by God, I swear I'll find you and bring you home!"

# CHAPTER TWENTY-THREE

Serafina woke to find herself lying on a velvet-covered chaise longue with a plump, velvet cushion beneath her head. She was still fully clothed, though someone had thought to cover her with a rug. But where on earth was she? And why was she here? She cast her mind back, but found no memory of coming to this place – wherever it was. Her last memories were of walking away from Rufus along Queen Street, of someone calling her name – and of a pair of black eyes as deep as forever...

In sudden panic, she sat up and stared about her. She was in a spacious and opulent room decorated in scarlet and gold. Throwing back the rug, she stood up and began to pace about the room in agitation. It was certainly a lovely room, with its sumptuous red oriental rugs, its elegant furniture and beautiful paintings and ornaments. Above the massive tiled fireplace, two highly polished military sabres hung on the wall in a cross formation, and a variety of swords and knives lay on shelves in a wide, glass-fronted cabinet to one side of the fireplace. A bookcase covered the wall on its other side, and two large armchairs faced each other in front of it.

But why was she here, and where was Rufus?

She went to the windows, hoping for some clue in the street outside. As she began to part the gold velvet curtains, she heard a soft, sensuous voice behind her and recognised it as the one that had called her name.

"Ah, Serafina, welcome to my humble abode."

Serafina whirled to see, standing just inside the doorway, a tall, voluptuous woman in an elegant gown of wine-coloured silk, cut low across her white bosom. The profusion of black hair curling over her shoulders and down to her waist, her dark, sloe eyes and exotic features, reminded Serafina of pictures she'd seen of ancient Minoans, except that her skin was pale and translucent, with a smooth, almost waxy quality. She looked to be about thirty years of age, but instinct told Serafina the vampire was far older – older, even, than Anton.

Serafina drew herself up to her full height and glared at her. "Who are you, and why have you brought me here?"

The woman's full, blood-red lips curved in a smile, though her eyes remained cold and rapacious. "You don't recognise me?" Her voice was rich and seductive. "But no, I suppose not. However, I certainly recognised you. Or rather, I recognised the lovely necklace and earrings you wear. They were given to you by Anton Springer, weren't they?"

Serafina gasped. Her hands flew to her neck where her silver and jet necklace lay. This must be the vampire she'd sensed, this creature with smiling lips, but eyes like a bird of prey.

"Of course I don't recognise you," she snapped, using anger to mask her fear. "How could I, since we've never met? Who are you? How do you know my name?"

"Oh, Serafina, such a naive question. You really should know better. How do you think I discovered your name? Mine, by the way, is Viviana Alexandreu, but you may call me Viviana."

"Why have you brought me here?" Serafina demanded, her tone making it clear she had no desire to be on intimate terms with her captor. "And what have you done with Rufus?"

"Rufus? You mean the young man you brought across? Why, nothing. I've no interest whatsoever in *him*. But come, let us be comfortable." Viviana walked with a slow, sinuous gait to sit in a wing-backed chair by the fire, looking at Serafina and indicating the chair opposite.

"I prefer to stand, thank you," Serafina informed her stiffly.

"As you wish, my dear."

"Don't call me that! I am not your 'dear' anything."

Viviana shrugged. "A pity, you're really rather delectable. Ah well, I hope we may still be friends."

"I hardly think so. Friends don't go about abducting one another. What do you want with me?"

"What a little spitfire," murmured Viviana, taking a heavy silver box from a side table and turning it this way and that to study its ornate embellishment. "Still, I'm sure it's nothing I can't deal with." She slowly closed one slender hand around the box and crushed it between her fingers.

As she tossed the mangled ornament carelessly into the fireplace, Serafina felt her throat constrict with fear. She swallowed hard, determined not to show it. But she was not surprised to hear Viviana say, "No need to be afraid, Serafina, I've no wish to harm you. I merely need your help, that's all."

"What—what help?" Serafina had to force her voice to do her bidding by sheer willpower.

"I have a great desire," Viviana replied in a voice like

satin, "to see my old...friend, Anton Springer, once more. When I saw you, and recognised the jewellery he gave you, I thought, why, Serafina will surely be able to help me find him. Did he tell you how he acquired that lovely jewellery, by the way? No, I suppose not, since it hardly redounds to his credit."

Serafina ignored this barb. "Since you were able to find me and bring me here without my knowing it," she retorted, her voice scathing, "I should think you'd be able to find him yourself."

"Sadly, things are not always as simple as one could wish." Viviana stood and turned to face Serafina, fixing her eyes on hers. "Where is he, Serafina?" she asked, dropping her voice almost to a whisper. "You must tell me!"

"But I don't know," Serafina stammered.

"Come, come, my dear. Where Serafina is, can Anton Springer be far away?" Her seductive voice had acquired a dangerous undertone.

"I truly don't know. He left for Australia well over a month ago. I believe he had some business to conduct there."

"Don't lie to me!" Viviana's voice was low, but her eyes flared red with fury. "Springer knows how to conceal himself – I'm only too well aware of that – and clearly he's taught you a few of his tricks. But you're no match for me, Serafina, be assured of that. I want Anton Springer, and you're going to help me find him."

"How can I tell you what I don't know?" Serafina's voice was sharp with fear as well as anger. She stood facing Viviana, inwardly quaking, but with her head held high. "You boast of your great power. Read me. See that I'm telling you the truth."

Viviana fixed her eyes on Serafina's, and Serafina felt the probing of her mind. She gritted her teeth to suppress a shudder of disgust as Viviana crawled, cold and relentless as a snake, through her thoughts and feelings. When she was done, Serafina gave a great sigh, realising she had been holding her breath.

"There, you see? I don't know where Anton is."

"No," smiled Viviana. "But still you may lead me to him."

"But how—?"

Viviana held up a hand to silence her. "For almost four centuries, I've been seeking Anton Springer, ever since I discovered it was he who murdered my beloved Walther."

"Anton is not a murderer!" Serafina protested angrily.

"Ah, but he is, and ungrateful, too. How else would you describe someone who kills the one who gave him eternal life?"

Serafina's eyes grew wide with astonishment. She opened her mouth to speak, but Viviana forestalled her.

"Just so," she said. "The vampire who brought Anton Springer across was himself brought across by me. Springer knew him as Doktor von Dunkel, but when I met him, he was Walther Hummel, a Doctor of Philosophy at the University of Frankfurt. He was also an alchemist, and it was this that led him to me. He sought the key to immortality, you see – true immortality, not the pathetic sophistry peddled by religions. Naturally, I didn't reveal myself to him at once, though I knew as soon as I saw him that we were kindred spirits, and so we became, in blood. Of all the dear children of my blood, I loved Walther the best. We were in perfect harmony, he and I." Viviana licked her lips slowly as though recalling something sensual and intimate. "Indeed, so strong was our bond that the moment he died, I knew it, and I vowed, in my grief, to have my revenge on his killer. And so I shall, Serafina, if it takes four centuries more. After all, what is time to such as we?"

Stunned by these revelations, Serafina remained silent for a time. At last, she stammered, "But how can I find Anton for you? I've already told you, I don't know where he is. Besides, he's not a murderer. Von Dunkel was very cruel to him. He brought him across against his will in the most heartless way, and took him from the one he loved. That's why Anton killed him. You, of all people, should understand that."

"Oh, I do," Viviana assured her, a note of boredom in her voice, as though the precise reason for her vendetta were no longer of any great import. "But I've sworn to have revenge, and, one way or another, I will have it. As for how you can help me, I'm not sure of that just yet. I had hoped you'd be able to tell me Springer's whereabouts, and I could have sent you back to the loving arms of your Rufus, and no harm done. As it is, however..."

Viviana broke off to go and tug at a brocade bell-pull that hung by the wall. Somewhere in the depths of the house, a bell clanged faintly.

"You can't keep me here!" Serafina cried in panic. "I can't help you, and even if I could, I won't!"

"You'll do precisely as I tell you," Viviana's voice put Serafina in mind of a crouching panther, "and believe me, Serafina, that's no idle boast. Thirteen hundred years as a vampire have given me powers you couldn't even imagine."

"Then do your own dirty work," hissed Serafina.

"If only I could," Viviana sighed, as though indulging a difficult child. "Unfortunately, there's just one small problem. Springer won't come to me, you see. For some unaccountable reason, he doesn't trust me. You, however, his beloved little sister...you see, Serafina, I really do need your help."

"Of course Anton trusts me," Serafina replied. "But even if I found him for you, he'd know straight away that he was in danger. I wouldn't even have to tell him."

"Oh, I'm sure I can overcome that little difficulty," purred Viviana, and Serafina shivered as she felt her mind invaded once more.

Viviana withdrew, however, as the door opened and a young woman came into the room. With a shock, Serafina recognised the girl she and Rufus had seen in the alley off Queen Street – was it earlier that night or the night before? Viviana must have sent her out deliberately to act as a decoy. Serafina felt sick with apprehension.

Viviana spoke to the blank-eyed girl, "Elizabeth, take Serafina to her room, then return here to me."

"Yes, ma'am." Elizabeth nodded her compliance.

Viviana came to stand in front of Serafina and stared into her eyes. At once, Serafina felt herself bombarded by wave after dark wave of pulsing energy.

"Go with her," Viviana ordered. "I'll send for you later."

Serafina tried to fight her, but the black waves engulfed her and pulled her under. Like a sleepwalker, she turned and followed Elizabeth.

Elizabeth led her up a wide, curving staircase to a kind of gallery with an ornate wooden balustrade on one side overlooking the vast hallway, and on the other a stained glass window depicting trailing vines and blood-hued roses. Turning right, she continued down a long hallway with heavy doors on either side. She halted before one of these and opened it. Serafina saw a large room furnished with a double bed with a carved oak headboard, a massive oak dressing table and wardrobe, and two chairs upholstered in bottle-green brocade. Heavy green plush curtains were drawn across the room's high windows, and the bedclothes on the bed were turned down as though for an expected guest. As though in a dream – or a nightmare – Serafina followed Elizabeth into the room.

"Sleep now," the girl said. "You must be tired."

With a shudder, Serafina realised that the voice was Elizabeth's, but the words were those of Viviana Alexandreu.

The girl left, closing the heavy door behind her, and Serafina heard a key grate in the lock, and the scraping of heavy bolts. Viviana clearly had no intention of allowing her to leave. Yet somehow she must get away from this place and find Rufus again. Perhaps then they could fight Viviana together, or at least have some chance of warning Anton.

It occurred to Serafina that the large window at the far end of the room might offer a means of escape. Although she was on the upper floor of the house, with her vampiric agility she felt sure she could find a way down to the ground if only she could manage to open it. She ran to the window and pulled back the curtains.

The window was barred.

It was covered on the outside by a heavy metal grille. The window itself was locked shut, but Serafina was able to wrench off the lock and push up the sash. Grasping the bars, she began to shake them with all her strength. They did not give at all. She slammed the window shut. How long had Viviana been planning her capture? Or was she not the only one to be kept prisoner here? The thought made her shudder.

Staring out through the metal grille, she made out a sweeping driveway and an expanse of grass dotted with trees and clumps of shrubs. Beyond this, the trees grew closer together, almost like a small wood or copse. Through the treetops she could just make out a high wall topped with spikes. Even if she managed to escape the house, it seemed breaking free of this vast property would be impossible. Viviana had thought of everything; there was no way out at all.

Feeling sick and defeated, Serafina crept back to the bed.

Viviana's mind intrusions had left her barely able to think, and now it was almost dawn. She sank onto the bed, pulled off her boots, gown and corset, and slipped between the cool, white sheets. Her last thoughts, as she drifted into sleep, were of Rufus – she refused to let herself think of Anton in case her captor should pick up some clue that would lead her to his whereabouts.

\* \* \* \*

Somewhere quite near, a bell was ringing. Its deep, sonorous tone dragged Serafina up through dark clouds of sleep. Still only half awake, she heard soft footsteps hurrying outside her room, but by the time she had fully roused herself, they had all but faded away. She sat up, sleepily rubbing her eyes. In a rush, the events of the previous night came back to her and tears pricked at her eyes. She dashed them away in anger. She must hide her fear and despair, even from herself, or Viviana might discover her weakness and use it against her. Or even against Rufus, if she realised just how dear he was to her. With this stern self-admonishment, Serafina climbed out of bed and pulled on her clothes.

It was well into the night, she thought, so she must have been exhausted. She still felt a trifle lethargic, though this was probably due to the lingering effects of the mind control Viviana had used on her. Equally, it could be the hunger that was beginning to gnaw at her gut. She began to pad about the room in her stockinged feet, discovering that a door she had not previously noticed led to a bathroom. Thick towels hung on wooden towel rails, and a shelf above the bath contained fragrant soap and a small stack of neatly folded facecloths. From a hook on the door hung a crimson satin dressing gown. Abruptly aware of how grubby she felt, Serafina turned on the bath tap. Lying in water up to her chin, she tried to imagine she was cleansing her mind of Viviana's unwanted intrusion as she cleansed her body of grime.

* * * *

All that night and the next day, as the hunger grew ever more insistent, Serafina saw no one, and heard nothing but the occasional dull clang of the bell, and footsteps hurrying to answer its summons. Of Viviana there was no sign.

Sitting on the bed, Serafina tried to sense Rufus, and to contact his mind with hers, but the house seemed to be surrounded by a great, invisible shield that nothing could penetrate. No doubt this was how Viviana avoided notice, despite living in such a grand and opulent house. Serafina had not felt so alone, or so helpless, since she was a child living in Moscow.

Hugging her knees to her chin she weathered another pang of hunger and clenched her teeth against the pain. If only there were something she could do. As the wave of pain receded a little, she slid off the bed, padded across to the door, and began to tug on the brass doorknob until it almost came away in her hand. The door remained locked fast. With one last, furious thump of her hand on its polished surface, she began to pace about the room in a fury that only barely concealed the stark terror lurking beneath. For, despite her elegant human veneer, Serafina knew Viviana had made no attempt to retain her humanity. She was all vampire. Her primitive hunting instinct honed over a thousand years and more, she would stop at nothing to get what she wanted. And she wanted Anton.

Eventually, pain drove Serafina back to her bed, where she lay tightly curled beneath the covers until she finally found some refuge in a sleep haunted by dreams of death and blood and a great beast gnawing at her gut.

\* \* \* \*

The scraping of the bolts on the door of her prison roused Serafina from her uneasy slumber. She heard the key turn in the lock, and then the door swung open. As she sat up, rubbing her burning eyes, she saw a young Maori woman standing just inside the door.

"Viviana wants to see you," she said, her pretty face and brown eyes devoid of expression.

All at once, the sound and scent of the girl's blood overwhelmed Serafina as she sensed the pulsing rhythm of the blood in her veins, rich and warm and inviting. Her eyes were drawn to the girl's slim neck where the jugular vein traced a faint blue line beneath her brown skin. Instinctively, she moved forward, her lips curled in a feral smile. No longer did she see a young woman staring back at her; she saw only deliverance from pain, from weakness, from hunger...

Sharp agony seared through her so that she cried out, doubling over with the shock of it. But it was not the hunger. Nor did it come from the girl, who stood just as before, one hand on the door handle, her brown eyes as blank as those of a corpse. It was Viviana. But why did she torture her so, when she must know she could not give her what she wanted? Or did she derive some perverse pleasure from it? Well, Serafina would not give in to her. She would not put Anton, her dear protector, in danger, no matter what this monster did to her.

The girl spoke again, "Come."

In a desperate bid to conceal her fear, Serafina tried to make her mind as blank as the girl's as she followed her along the corridor and down the stairs.

Viviana stood by the fireplace in the room where Serafina had first woken – was it only two days ago? As Serafina followed the Maori girl into the room, Viviana turned and came toward them as though approaching a lover. Ignoring the girl, she took Serafina by the elbow and steered her towards the sofa. Serafina longed to shake her off, but her captor's grip was strong, and she was distracted by hunger. And she must not betray her feelings.

"Good," Viviana said, once she was seated. "I dare say you're feeling hungry."

"You know I am!" Serafina replied through gritted teeth.

"Yes," said Viviana with a sharp little smile. "I must apologise for having left you for so long – I'm afraid I've been rather busy. *Nil desperandum*, however – relief is at hand."

Without taking her eyes from Serafina, Viviana beckoned to the Maori girl, still standing by the door. "Come here, Rebecca."

Without a word, the girl obeyed.

"There you are," Viviana said with a careless wave of one elegant hand. "She's all yours."

"But..." Hungry as Serafina was, she was suspicious of Viviana's motives. If she had intended to feed her all along, why not simply let her feed in her room? Or was this another ploy to demonstrate her power?

"Oh, don't worry," Viviana's tone was offhanded, "she's used to it." As Serafina still hesitated, the vampire's forehead creased in an impatient frown. "I have no intention of leaving you alone here," she said sharply, "so you'd better get on with it before I regret my hospitality and send you to bed without any supper."

Serafina had no difficulty believing her captor would make good her threat. She moved towards Rebecca, who stood motionless and quiescent before her. As Serafina approached, the girl put her head to one side, exposing her neck. Clearly, as Viviana had claimed, she was used to providing sustenance. Perhaps Viviana kept her and Elizabeth for that very purpose.

She clasped Rebecca's arms and drew her closer. The tang of her blood was overwhelming, its pulse as hypnotic as the beat of a drum. Behind her, as she tasted the first drops of the girl's blood, she heard Viviana move away towards the window. Then there was nothing but warm, sweet life flowing into her, making her whole again, making her strong.

The next thing she knew, Viviana's voice behind her was saying, "That's enough!" and hands were on her shoulders, pulling her away from Rebecca. Serafina's lips drew back in an instinctive snarl, and her eyes blazed red as she turned on Viviana.

Viviana gave a soft, appreciative laugh. "I know," she said, "but she's no use to me dead, you know." She led Rebecca to the sofa, leaving her there to recover while she escorted Serafina back to her room. "You see," she said, "I'm not so bad, after all." Ignoring Serafina's expression of disgust, she stretched out her arms to encompass the luxurious room.

"You could live like this all the time, you know, both you and Rufus. No more creeping round alleyways and cemeteries feeding off whores and drunkards and worse. No, you could live surrounded by beauty, safe from the prying world, your every need catered for. All I ask in return is a little cooperation, a little help."

Serafina said nothing, but held herself erect and fixed Viviana with a haughty stare.

Viviana shrugged elegant shoulders. "As you wish. But remember, Serafina, what I give I can just as easily take away. And I *will* find Anton Springer, with or without your help."

"I wouldn't help you," spat Serafina, "even if I could."

"Such ingratitude!" Viviana gave an exaggerated sigh, shaking her head as though despairing over a recalcitrant child. In her eyes, however, red sparks of anger glinted like hot coals. "Ah, well, perhaps you'll be in a more compliant frame of mind tomorrow."

Before Serafina could reply, Viviana turned on her heel and walked out of the room, closing the door firmly behind her. Serafina heard her turn the key in the lock and push the bolts home, and then there was nothing but the sound of her soft footsteps retreating into the distance.

For some time Serafina stood there, hearing nothing but the silence that hung like a pall over the house.

How many young women, she wondered – or men, come to that – did Viviana keep like milch cows in a beautifully appointed dairy to satisfy her need for blood? And for what else? Who could tell what perverse desires she might have developed over the course of her long life? She seemed to have suppressed all but the faintest veneer of her human side – or was that how it became for all vampires in time? But no, she refused to believe that. After all, Anton, who had been a vampire for four centuries, had been successful in retaining his humanity. Indeed, he had more of it in his vampire's heart than Uncle Sergei had ever had in his human one. And yet even Anton had dragged her all over the world with him, and had left her in danger – for how could he not have known about Viviana? – just to pursue his wretched business deals. Why, he cared more for money than ever he had for her! In the midst of these bitter recriminations, it was borne in on Serafina that they were not her thoughts at all. Viviana, whom she had foolishly allowed access to her mind, was now using her past to poison it against Anton, to make her more willing to betray him. She shook her head as though to rid herself of Viviana's influence. She must not think of Anton, or Viviana might somehow glean from her mind some fragment of knowledge that would help her in her vile quest.

Instead, she must somehow devise a way to escape.

Perhaps, now her strength was renewed by fresh blood, she would be able to dislodge the bars on the window. She strode across the room. Pulling back the heavy curtains, she pushed up the sash window. She examined the iron grille, but could find no point of weakness, and the bars were too close together to allow her to lean out and see how they were attached to the outside wall of the house. Using all her strength, she tugged, and pushed, and rattled, and finally kicked with all her might, but the grille remained firmly in place. But she would not despair, Serafina told herself. Somehow there must be a way to escape. Next time one of Viviana's minions came to fetch her, she would overcome her, and at least break free of her immediate prison. There was bound to be a back way out of the house. Of course, that still left the problem of how to scale the high wall. Sadly, real vampires lacked Count Dracula's ability to climb sheer walls. Still, a number of the trees growing close to it were tall enough to allow her climb up and drop down on the other side. And if she tore herself on the spikes, so what? Her flesh would soon heal. She had no idea where she was, but somehow, however far Viviana had brought her, she would make her way back to Rufus.

She peered out between the bars into the darkness. A blanket of cloud hid the moon and stars, but Serafina's eyes could clearly make out the silhouetted roofs of houses standing in rows like broken teeth, and the grey sinews of road lit by the soft glow of street lamps. To the left loomed a dark hump that must be a hill. Somewhere in her memory, something stirred. Then she noticed a darker shape in front of it, a wall of some sort, perhaps? She frowned. It was all strangely familiar, but why? As she stood there, puzzled, the moon edged out through a gap in the clouds, its wan light revealing the dark mound in greater detail.

Then she remembered. It was Mount Eden, and the wall must be the one surrounding the Mount Eden Stockade where prisoners were incarcerated. She was so close to home, yet so completely cut off from it – and from Rufus. Tears trickled from Serafina's eyes, but she dashed them away. She must be strong – for Rufus if not for herself – and watch for a chance to escape from this velvet prison. After that, it would take her no time at all to make her way back home.

# CHAPTER TWENTY-FOUR

Two days dragged by before Serafina saw Viviana again, long enough for the pangs of hunger to bite cruelly once more. This time she came in person, accompanied, to Serafina's surprise, by a young Maori man. A very beautiful young man he was, with shining black curls and sultry eyes, and a full, sensual mouth. Although Serafina had seen both Maori men and women about Auckland, she had never seen any so well built and handsome. Closing the door behind her, Viviana stood close to the young man, running a sensuous hand up his muscular arm and over his shoulder and chest, gazing at Serafina through half-closed eyes. The young man stood silently beside her. His eyes were on Serafina, but he gave no sign that he was seeing her.

"Well, Serafina," Viviana purred, "and how are you this evening?"

Serafina's lip curled, but she said nothing.

Ignoring this slight, Viviana went on, "Are you hungry?"

Serafina remained silent, but her eyes strayed instinctively to the young man, whose veins enticed her through his warm, sepia skin.

"Ah," said Viviana with a smile. "I thought you might be. Bored, too, I imagine. That's why I've brought Tamati to meet you. He's very pretty, don't you agree?"

"How very generous of you." Serafina's voice was heavy

with sarcasm.

"Oh, Serafina," Viviana said in mock disappointment. "Why are you so distrustful? It's very hurtful, you know, when I've offered you so much." Her eyes lingered on Tamati for a moment before returning to Serafina.

"Oh, yes," said Serafina. "At a price."

Viviana spread her hands in a gesture of resignation. "Why, that's just the way of the world, Serafina, you must know that. You give me what I want, and I'll give you Tamati. I think that's very fair, don't you, especially considering how fond I am of him? I'm sure you'll find him as entertaining as I do – and much more, besides."

"How dare you!" Serafina's eyes flashed sparks of fury. "First you ask me to betray Anton, and now you want me to betray Rufus as well! What kind of creature do you think I am?"

Viviana gave a throaty laugh. "One who is hungry, Serafina, and who will become hungrier. Come, Tamati."

Without so much as a glance at Serafina, Viviana ushered the young man from the room and secured the door behind them.

Serafina began to pace about the room. She felt like screaming, but she would never give Viviana the satisfaction of hearing her vent her fury and despair. Gradually, her anger subsided, leaving in its wake a heavy lassitude. Dragging herself over to the bed, she sat down and tried to clear her head.

Somehow – *somehow* – she must find a way to escape. What Viviana wanted of her she simply did not possess, yet it was certain she would show no mercy in her attempt to gain it.

\* \* \* \*

Serafina's fears proved well founded. No one came near her for days.

How many days, she could not tell. As her hunger grew, so the boundaries of her awareness constricted until she became incapable of focusing on anything beyond her need for blood. Day by day, her reflection in the mirror showed her paler and more haggard, until her cheekbones cast shadows on the wrinkled parchment of her cheeks, her lips shrank back from teeth that seemed too large for her mouth, her fangs ever present with her need for blood, and her hands, once elegant, resembling the curved talons of a bird of prey. Unable to bear the thing she had become, with a hiss of impotent rage she pulled the mirror from the wall and dashed it to the floor so she could no longer see what Viviana had done to her. Sometimes, staring longingly out of the barred window, she would lift her head and sniff the night air and howl like a wolf baying at the moon, scarcely even aware that the high, keening sound issued from her own lips. But no answering call reached her. The house was cocooned in a silence so profound it seemed to have swallowed her whole.

When she became too weak even to howl out her hunger, and lay day and night curled in her bed like a dying animal, Viviana came to her. This time she was alone.

Serafina scarcely heard the scratch of the key in the lock. When Viviana softly called her name, it took all her feeble strength to lift her head from the pillow and stare at her from dull eyes in shrunken lids.

"Come, Serafina," she said, her voice gentle as she lifted Serafina up to sit leaning against her arm. "I've come to set you free. But first, you'd like to feed, yes?" Serafina tried to speak, but all that emerged was a faint, rasping breath. "Of course you would," Viviana said soothingly, stroking her tangled hair back from her brow.

Viviana placed pillows behind Serafina, since she was incapable of sitting unsupported, then sat back and unbuttoned her gown, pulling her chemise open to expose her breast. Her lips curved in a voluptuous smile as she lifted one hand and raked a sharp fingernail across her pale flesh, gasping as though responding to a lover's touch as she slashed her skin. Blood welled up, thick and dark, and Serafina instinctively strained forward, her lips working hungrily. Calmly, Viviana held her at arm's length.

"Ah, but there is a price to pay," she murmured. "Always, there is a price."

A faint, whimpering sound came from Serafina's lips. She moved her head as though searching for the source of the sound, then her eyes returned to the blood slowly trickling down Viviana's alabaster skin.

"Hush now," said Viviana, as though reassuring a child. "I promise you you'll be fed. But first, I need something from you. Come, look at me."

Serafina felt her captor's hand beneath her chin, the fingers soft but insistent. Scarcely able to comprehend her words through the fog of her weakness and hunger, she dragged her eyes painfully away from the tantalising crimson gash, and lifted them to Viviana's face. Her black eyes bored into Serafina's. Before Serafina could think to stop her, Viviana was inside her mind, ruthlessly pushing aside her thoughts and imposing others of her own devising. It was like being raped. She whimpered like the frightened child she had once been but, as she had been then, she was powerless to stop the onslaught. At last, even her fear and revulsion were pushed aside and replaced with the blind, unquestioning devotion of a child for its mother, its source of love and nourishment.

With a triumphant smile, Viviana drew Serafina close, stroking her hair as she lapped greedily at her breast as though she were, indeed, her mother.

"Ah," she breathed, "now you are truly mine! You will find Anton Springer for me. If you fail, I will avenge myself by destroying his kin as he destroyed mine. I will destroy your will, your very love for those you most care for. Perhaps that will be the sweetest revenge of all."

After a few minutes, she pushed Serafina away, laughing softly as she sat there hungrily licking her bloodstained lips.

"I'll send someone to you soon," she said. "But first, tell me who I am."

Serafina stared at her, a look almost of wonder in her eyes. "You are Viviana," she said, her voice a dull monotone, still harsh from long fasting.

"And what am I?"

"You are my mistress."

"Good. And what will you do for me?"

"I will find Anton Springer. I will bring him to you."

"And what about Rufus?"

Serafina's brow creased in a puzzled frown. She shook her head. "I don't know any Rufus."

"Excellent!" Viviana stood up, buttoning her gown over the livid wound that was already beginning to heal, and left the room.

Within moments, there was a soft rap at Serafina's door and Tamati entered with a fair-haired young woman Serafina had not seen before.

As she stared from one to the other, Tamati said, "This is Catherine. Viviana said you were hungry, so she sent us both."

"Yes," Serafina whispered, reaching out her skeletal, white arms. "Hungry."

Catherine came forward, meekly presenting her soft, pink neck as she sat down on the bed. With a low cry, Serafina fell on her and began to feed. Warmth began to suffuse her body. She could feel herself growing younger, stronger, as the life-giving blood rushed through her starved veins.

She felt a tug at her shoulder and lifted her head, blood dripping onto her chin from her crimson-rimmed lips, her eyes flashing red sparks of anger. Tamati stood there, clearly excited by the sight of her. As Catherine slipped from Serafina's grasp, he quickly took her place. Still fast in the grip of her bloodlust, Serafina scarcely heard his moan of pleasure as she bit into his neck, or felt his hands on her body as she drank his blood.

Sated at last, she lay back on the pillows, eyes closed, savouring the delicious sensations afforded by the fresh blood flowing once more through her body. She ran her hand along her arm, revelling in the soft, cool smoothness of her skin. She touched a finger to her lips. They were soft and full once more. Ah, it was good to feel young and strong again!

When she felt Tamati's lips on hers and his warm hand on her thigh, her response was purely physical. No thought, no emotion adulterated the animal lust with which she returned his kisses, pulling him to her, feeling his hardness thrusting against her. Frantically she tore at his clothing, desperate to feel his skin on hers, to feel him inside her, to slake that other most primitive of hungers.

Through the heat of desire that possessed her, Serafina became aware of something else in her mind, its tread so delicate she had not noticed it at first. With a cry of disgust, she thrust Tamati away from her. Viviana must have known the effect the blood ecstasy would have on her after starving her for so long. Now she was using the mind connection created when Serafina had drunk her blood to share her enjoyment of him. Nausea overcame her, and with it a cold fury.

She leapt off the bed, screaming at Tamati, "Get out! Just get out!"

His face registered shock, but he pulled up his trousers between fearful glances at her, lifted Catherine – who had been leaning against the bed half unconscious – to her feet and dragged her with him to the door. With one last, wide-eyed stare at Serafina, he and Catherine left.

Serafina stood gazing after them, trembling with horror, listening to Viviana laughing softly in her mind as she enjoyed the deception she had used. How could she do something so—so depraved? Serafina tried to close her mind, to deny Viviana entry, but found it impossible. Again she heard Viviana's crooning voice. *Now you are truly mine!*

With a sob of anguish, Serafina turned away from the door. Her eyes fell on the mirror lying face down on the rug. Wondering vaguely what it was doing there, she stooped to retrieve it and propped it up on the dressing table, staring at her reflection. The young woman who looked back at her was tall and slim, her body lithe and her skin moonstone-pale and translucent. But her raven hair was wild and tangled, her wide, full lips rimmed with blood. Dried blood streaked her face and her breasts. And the eyes that stared back, huge and dark, into hers were almost devoid of intelligence, the eyes of a creature more animal than human. Tears welled up and spilled down her cheeks, tracing lines through the caked blood – tears of sorrow for a loss she could scarcely comprehend.

She snatched up the mirror and turned it to face the wall. Whatever it was that was looking out at her, she did not want to see it.

She dragged herself to the bathroom and turned on the bath tap, half mesmerised by the water flowing into the tub. For a long time she squatted in the freezing water, scrubbing at her hair and body, desperate to cleanse herself of defilement.

* * * *

Certain now of her submission and obedience, Viviana no longer kept Serafina under lock and key. When she grew hungry, she was fed. If she needed clothes, they were provided. And if, sometimes, gazing out over the grounds of Viviana's mansion, feelings came to Serafina of a vague and undefined longing, they remained unexplored, for she no longer had any idea what to do with them.

One evening, shortly before sunset, Serafina was woken from slumber by an irresistible sensation that Viviana wanted her. Dressing quickly, she made her way down the wide staircase to the scarlet-and-gold sitting room where

Viviana waited in her customary chair by the fire. As she entered the room, Viviana beckoned to her. With no thought but to obey her, Serafina went to stand before her.

"My dear Serafina," Viviana's voice was as smooth as finest wine. "I do apologise for waking you early. I trust you're well enough rested?" Without waiting for Serafina's reply, she motioned to her to sit in the chair opposite her, and went on, "I've been wondering, my dear, how you might begin to repay me for all I've done for you. I think it's time, don't you?"

Again she went on without waiting for Serafina's response. "My initial reason for bringing you here was to draw Anton to rescue you, for how could such a fond sire as he is not come to rescue his beloved Serafina? I'm still persuaded he cannot be far away, but I'm sure you'll agree the results to date have been disappointing, to say the least. I've been at something of a loss over this. Could the so moral Anton Springer really care so little about you as to abandon you to his worst enemy? Surely not!

"But inspiration has come to me, Serafina! Of course Anton wouldn't come to me, not even for your sake. He knows it would be far too dangerous to try to rescue you from me directly. Whatever else Anton Springer may be, he's no fool. He'll not risk confronting me in my stronghold. However, if you were somehow to – break free, why then he might come to you. If he believes you've escaped me, surely he'll try to save his precious little sister.

"Of course," Viviana added thoughtfully, "he may well realise, as indeed he should, how very unlikely it is that anyone *would* escape me. But it's a new and rather intriguing variation of the game, don't you agree?"

Serafina said nothing, knowing no reply was either needed or wanted, but waited for Viviana to reveal her new plan and the part she would play in it. She did not have long to wait. Viviana rose from her chair and took Serafina's hand to pull her to her feet. She placed her hands on Serafina's shoulders and stared into her eyes. Serafina returned her gaze, allowing Viviana to speak to her mind to mind.

*Serafina, from now on you will go out when I tell you to. You will walk where I direct you until sunrise, and then you will return here. You will not attempt to communicate with Anton Springer, or, indeed, with anyone. Whatever is necessary, I shall do through you. Do you understand?*

Serafina nodded. "Yes, Viviana."

She saw Viviana smile, but her mind, controlled by Viviana's, did not register the look in her eyes of a cat preparing to toy with its prey.

And so Serafina went out to do her mistress's bidding, returning at sunrise to sleep the day away in her freshly made bed. If she came back empty-handed, Viviana showed no anger. After all, she could afford to wait.

# CHAPTER TWENTY-FIVE

Despite his vow to find Serafina, and his efforts to fulfil it, the weeks went by with Rufus no closer to discovering her whereabouts. She seemed to have vanished off the face of the earth. Night after night he searched the town, both physically and mentally, but not the faintest glimmer of her reached his distraught senses. Day after day, fearful dreams ravaged his sleep. Only blind animal craving forced him to drag himself out to feed yet, more often than not, he ended up roaming the streets for hours afterwards, not caring where his footsteps led him, so long as he could put off returning to a house empty of Serafina.

One night, after satisfying his blood hunger with one of the Chancery Street *habitués*, Rufus wandered to the end of Queen Street and across Custom House Street to the wharf. He stood staring out over the sea, listening, without really hearing, to the cries of gulls and the creaking of the ships berthed at the wharf. From somewhere out in the sea mist came the hoarse moan of a foghorn. For what seemed the thousandth time, he tried to imagine what could have happened to Serafina. Despite their quarrel, he remained certain she would not have left of her own volition, so someone must have taken her, and whoever it was must have powers beyond the merely human, or Serafina would never have succumbed. Once again, he saw Serafina's face frowning as she caught the fleeting sense of another vampire. It had to have been him – or her. Serafina hadn't been sure. But what could some unknown vampire possibly want with her?

Perhaps his certainty was misplaced. Perhaps, after all, Serafina had simply become tired of their quarrelling. Why had he been so determined not to let her go to Martin's with him? Had it really been for her sake, or because he didn't care to stand out from the crowd, as if the opinions of a bunch of colonial gamblers mattered a damn compared to Serafina? It wasn't as though any of them were friends, or even social acquaintances. They were nothing more than a means to make money. And he'd put that before his duty to Serafina. He'd failed Serafina, and he'd failed Anton, whom he'd promised to take care of her. A strangled cry escaped his lips.

Startled by the sound of his own anguish, Rufus leapt to his feet and began to stride along the waterfront. The mist had turned to a soft rain that draped the gaslights with gossamer drifts of mist and turned the ground to sticky mud that seemed to clutch at his boots as though seeking to drag him down into itself like some monster of the deep. With a snarl of impatience, he crossed back over Custom House Street and onto Hobson Street and began to walk away from the harbour, although there was little difference underfoot. Somehow, he told himself, he had to find Serafina, but where could he search, with no clue to her disappearance beyond a few seconds' awareness of an unknown vampire who might or might not have abducted her? It did seem likely that this vampire was Serafina's abductor, if only because no one in Auckland knew them, though what his or her reason might be Rufus couldn't begin to imagine. Besides, any vampire who knew Serafina presumably also knew Anton, and he could have had no sense of danger, or why would he have left them? Despite the anxiety for the two of them to go with him to Australia that had caused such friction between him and Serafina, surely he wouldn't have left if he'd thought she might come to harm. The entire situation was insane, not least because he couldn't sense Serafina anywhere, although the entire town of Auckland was small enough to be within range. Unless, of course, she was no longer in Auckland. And if that were the case, then his quest must surely be hopeless.

Or maybe his senses just weren't yet well enough developed to sense her. After all, he'd failed to sense the unknown vampire when Serafina had. Perhaps, he thought as he turned into Wellesley Street, he needed to work on developing his senses further, although the thought of putting off his search for any reason made him sick with apprehension. On the other hand, none of his searching so far had borne fruit. He was no further ahead than when he'd started. The rain began to fall harder, and he quickened his pace. It was a long walk back to Gillies Avenue. He had no great desire to go home. It felt empty there without Serafina, though he'd have to be somewhere safe by the time dawn arrived. By the time he came to Symonds Street, he had half decided to find a hotel room for the day. He began to trudge down Symonds Street, uncomfortably aware of the rain dripping from his hair and trickling down his neck, and the squelching of his sodden boots in the slippery mud. As he walked, it occurred to him that no decent hotel would be likely to take him in – he must look like a tramp, and a half-drowned one at that. But he had to get out of the rain, at least for a little while.

A short way ahead of him he saw, through the driven rain, what looked like a public house, or perhaps one of the rough grog shops that abounded in the town. As he drew closer, he saw it was, indeed, a public house, The Fitzgerald, according to the sign creaking in the wind above its door, and the light spilling out onto the street told him it was open for business. Rufus decided to go inside. At the very least he could sit somewhere dry for a while and have a glass of wine to fortify him for the rest of his journey. There might even be a fire where he could dry himself off a little, although the idea of so much heat was unappealing to his vampiric sensibilities. Judging by the hubbub drifting from within, the place was well patronised. All the better, since he could find himself an out-of-the-way corner and remain anonymous. From somewhere inside there came the strains of a piano tinkling out a tune he didn't recognise. Rufus pushed open the glass-paned door and found himself in a long, high-ceilinged room with a bar running most of its length along one wall. The atmosphere, dimly lit by oil lamps hung from the ceiling, was thick with their acrid fumes as well as tobacco smoke and the smell of warm human bodies in varying degrees of unwash. Even more overpowering to Rufus was the beating of human hearts and the pulsing of blood through human veins. They seemed to blend with the tinkling music and the hubbub of voices to form a bizarre sort of music that he found oddly comforting.

He pushed his way to the bar, taking care to make himself as unobtrusive as possible, and ordered brandy, since only beer and spirits seemed to be on offer. There was no fireplace such as he might have expected to find in an

English public house, so he took his drink to a corner table near the door, but out of the draught created by the comings and goings of patrons. The customers were overwhelmingly working-class males: raucous young men intent on becoming as drunk as possible in the shortest possible time, groups of middle-aged men with the air of having escaped domesticity for a few hours to indulge in a game or two of cards or dice along with their beer, and a number of down-and-outs making their grog last as long as possible. Rufus thought the few women present, laughing and chattering – and occasionally quarrelling – in small groups, were most likely prostitutes snatching some brief respite from the rain-swept streets. It had never occurred to him before just how weather-dependent their incomes must be, and he felt a strange kind of fellowship with them. After all, weren't they all hunters of a sort, depending on the streets for their prey?

Distracted by these thoughts, Rufus didn't notice that someone had come to his table until he heard a soft voice speak his name. He looked up, his eyes widening in surprise.

"Good God, Eleanor! What are you doing here?" His gaze flicked to a group of women laughing over pots of ale. "You're not...?"

Eleanor shook her head, chuckling. "No, I haven't sunk to that, after all. I work here as a barmaid."

"Didn't you find a position teaching, then?"

"I did for a while, as a governess, but I didn't like it. Not that I want to make myself out to be better than I am, but I was expected to be nursemaid and teacher combined to four horridly over-indulged brats, and all for a pittance and with not much higher regard than the scullery maids." Eleanor wrinkled her nose in disgust. "It's hard work here, but at least I'm paid what I'm worth and valued for what I do."

Rufus grinned. "Well, it's good to know you haven't been reduced to being a lady of pleasure, at any rate."

"Pleasure! One would have to be desperate, indeed, to take on such employment –especially on a night like this! I take it you didn't go to your uncle, after all?"

A warning note sounded in Rufus's mind; he must take care how he answered Eleanor's question. "No," he said. "In the end, I found Auckland a more attractive proposition than a farm in the middle of nowhere."

"Yes, I can see that. I'm afraid Auckland's quite primitive enough for me. And the smell! I thought I'd left that behind in London."

Rufus smiled in sympathy. "Not to mention the dust in the streets, and the smoke from the house fires. And I thought London was dirty! But tell me, do you think you'll stay here, or will you return to England?"

"I can't afford to go back, not yet, at any rate, though I'm saving as much as I can. I have a room upstairs here, which means I don't have to pay so much rent. Besides, in spite of the dust and the smell, and the other drawbacks, there's a kind of freedom here that I never felt in London. Oh, I know there's poverty here as well. One only has to walk about the town to see the beggars and vagrants, and the poor, hungry little children sitting in the dust. But here a person can rise above the station into which they were born in a way that rarely happens in England. There, I'd have been nothing if I hadn't married. Here, I can be my own woman. Oh, I know I'm only a barmaid at the moment, but I don't intend to stay one forever."

"Good for you! And what do you intend to become?"

"I don't know just yet. Perhaps I'll own my own public house one day, who knows?"

"Well, whatever it is, I wish you well."

Eleanor smiled and patted Rufus's hand. "Thank you, Rufus, it's been lovely to see you again, but if I'm to climb the ladder of success I'd better go and do some work now."

"Of course." Rufus took her hand and drew it briefly to his lips. "And I must go, too. I hadn't intended to stay for this long, but I've so enjoyed talking to you it's seemed no time at all."

Eleanor stood up. "Good night, Rufus. Do pop in again sometime, won't you?"

Rufus got to his feet. "Thank you, I will. Good night, Eleanor."

The rain had eased, although the ground was still slippery with mud, but Rufus felt sufficiently restored – as much by seeing a friendly face as by the brandy – not to mind the long walk home.

\* \* \* \*

Rufus continued to trudge the streets of Auckland hoping to find a clue as to Serafina's whereabouts, but with no more success than he'd already had. Somehow, without really intending to, he quite often found himself in Symonds Street, outside The Fitzgerald and, despite a niggling feeling that he was somehow betraying Serafina, he would go inside, promising himself he'd stay for just one drink, but would end up nursing the drink until closing time. There Eleanor would find him, and they'd talk until she was too tired to keep from her bed any longer. Then Rufus would walk home, his spirits lifted by her companionship.

Little by little, although he did not stint in his search for Serafina, he found himself looking forward to his talks with Eleanor; they were like a tiny oasis of pleasure in the never-ending desert his life seemed to have become. Even hunting and feeding gave him little of what they had once provided. What had given him such *joie de vivre,* such delight in all his senses, without Serafina merely made him nervous and irritable. He would walk for hours in an effort to shake off his despair, but in the end the only thing that made sense was the time he spent with Eleanor Fox. If it weren't for the blood hunger and the immense weariness that overtook him each dawn, in her company he could almost have persuaded himself he was still human. But, with the gradual passing of winter, the sun rose a little earlier and set a little later each day, its relentless cycle reminding him of his true nature.

One night, after slaking his thirst with a drunken sailor by the New Wharf, he made his way to The Fitzgerald, ordered himself a brandy and settled down at his usual corner table to wait for Eleanor. As he waited, he amused himself by reaching into the minds of whichever patrons took his fancy. As Serafina had told him, this was not as easy as with other vampires, but he looked on it as practice to hone his vampiric skills until he could sense Serafina or her captor.

All at once, he sensed something familiar.

Oh, God, could it be Serafina? He was sure he could smell the musky scent she always wore.

His heart pumping like a piston, Rufus stared about him. He knew, because Serafina had told him, that her scent had been created especially for her by a Paris *parfumier* who owed Anton a favour; it even bore her name. It was impossible that anyone else could be wearing it. Yet, for all he could smell her perfume, he had no sense at all of Serafina's physical presence. He closed his eyes and concentrated on tracing the scent to its source. When he opened them again, he found himself staring at a young woman he'd never seen before. She was eating a slice of meat pie that she washed down with hearty draughts of ale, though she seemed more interested in finishing her meal than in enjoying it. Very gently, Rufus reached into her mind. It was blank, just like...his eyes widened as the realisation struck him. Her mind was blank – exactly like the woman from whom he'd been feeding on the night of Serafina's disappearance!

Rufus could barely contain himself until the woman stood up to leave, pulling a grey knitted shawl about her thin shoulders. As soon as the door had swung shut behind her, he slipped out after her. He was careful to withdraw into himself so that whoever was controlling her – and it had to be another vampire, nothing else made sense – wouldn't sense him as he slipped through the shadows to avoid the woman herself seeing him. She set off along Symonds Street travelling south, not hurrying, but not looking about her either. It was clear she wasn't just strolling home after a night out. She had some purpose in mind. Or, rather, whoever controlled her did.

At the lower end of Symonds Street, the woman turned into Mount Eden Road. Where on earth was she going? Rufus wondered. She continued past the high, stone wall of the Mount Eden Stockade until she came to a tall laurel hedge above which the silhouette of a roof loomed black against the sky. Withdrawing into the shadows, Rufus

271

watched as she opened the wrought-iron gate and disappeared through it. He heard her footsteps crunch on a gravel path, climb three steps and cross what was presumably a veranda or porch. Then he heard the rap of a doorknocker. Moving silently to the gate, he peered around the hedge. A worn-looking woman in a dressing gown of faded pink brocade was standing in the open doorway, and the two of them were conversing in low voices. Still completely withdrawn into himself, Rufus allowed his hearing to pick up what they were saying.

"Have you got it?" the woman he was following asked.

The woman in the doorway nodded. "I'll just go and fetch it." She disappeared, returning moments later with what looked like a large pouch or a small satchel made of some stiff fabric. "It's all there," she said, handing the pouch over.

The other woman said nothing, but opened it and peered inside. Focusing on her intently, Rufus almost caught her thought before it was snatched away by whoever was controlling her. He supposed her controller must have been reading her thoughts for information about the pouch's contents. As she nodded and turned to leave, Rufus ducked back out of sight, standing still and silent in the shadows until she had passed him. Then he continued his pursuit. Just what was in the pouch the woman now carried tucked inside her shawl? he wondered. From the brief conversation he had overheard, he imagined it was probably money, and that she was taking it to her controller – who was most likely Serafina's captor. That had to be the reason he'd sensed Serafina through this unknown woman. She had presumably been in contact with Serafina and had picked up a hint of her scent, and the link between them must surely be Serafina's captor, the unknown vampire. His stomach tightened with excitement at the thought, and with the hope that his suspicion might prove correct.

Continuing down Mount Eden Road, the woman turned left into Epsom Avenue. With a shock of recognition, Rufus realised they were not far from Gillies Avenue. Could Serafina really be this close to home without his being able to sense her at all? Forcing down his excitement in case it gave him away, he followed at a safe distance, flitting through the shadows thrown by buildings and hedges until the woman stopped outside a high stone wall. Forbidding-looking iron spikes marched along the top of it and an ornate wrought-iron gate was set into it. That he could sense nothing whatsoever of what lay behind the wall served only to increase his excitement. Either the property was completely uninhabited, and had been for some time – or someone was deliberately keeping all sign of life hidden from the outside world. It must be the latter, he reasoned, or why would someone be delivering a satchel there in the middle of the night?

The young woman opened the gate and slipped through it, closing and latching it behind her. From his vantage point nearby, Rufus listened to her footsteps receding. Judging by the time it took until he heard a door opening and shutting, the house must be set well back from the road. With the closing of the door, the house and grounds retreated into silence – a strange, oppressive, unnatural silence, as though no creature dared stir there.

Consumed with curiosity, Rufus crept to the gate and peered between the curlicues of wrought iron. He saw a veritable mansion. Built of cream-painted timber, it rambled over a considerable area and rose two stories high, topped by a domed tower and a grey slate roof whose ridges were crowned with spikes like the ones adorning the top of its surrounding wall. The house was set in large grounds dotted with trees and shrubs, and more trees grew round the perimeter – oaks, beeches, elms, and a number of others he didn't recognise. If it weren't for the gate, the entire property would be cut off from the outside world – ideal for a vampire, especially one involved in skulduggery of some kind, and he was becoming increasingly certain this was the case. There might be all sorts of unsavoury reasons for one vampire to kidnap another, but strange packages changing hands at dead of night smacked of an entirely more mundane variety of wrongdoing.

He could discover nothing more here at present, but he'd return tomorrow night and watch to see who went in and out. Just what he hoped to find, he was by no means certain yet. But he now had a focus for his search.

# CHAPTER TWENTY-SIX

Soon after sunset the following evening, Rufus woke with the excitement kindled by the previous night's discoveries still burning bright. He hurried through washing and dressing, deciding to hunt closer to home rather than lose time by walking into town and back again. Quite close by stood a small park, and Rufus made that his first port of call. However, it seemed the very proper residents of Epsom were all inside at their dinners, and the vagrants he might have expected to find in the town were not in evidence in such a genteel neighbourhood. In almost every house he passed, lamps or candles spread their golden glow through curtained windows, and he could hear the murmur of conversation. But not one soul among them could be glimpsed outside. With a hiss of annoyance, Rufus turned and made his way back up Gillies Avenue. It seemed he must go into town after all. Still, at least the rain had stopped. There were even a few stars shining between the ragged clouds.

Near the corner of Gillies Avenue and Epsom Avenue, he picked up a scent, following it to a tract of the scrubland that still covered much of outer Auckland. Making his way through the rough grass and tangled bushes, he saw at last two shabbily dressed men in a gully partially sheltered by a stand of small trees and bushes. One was recumbent in the long grass – passed out from over-indulgence in drink, judging by the fumes that reached Rufus's nostrils. The other sat leaning against a tree trunk warbling tuneless snatches of some unidentifiable tune in between swigs from a green bottle clutched in his claw-like hands. Skirting the area on silent feet, Rufus crept closer to them, hidden by the clump of trees beneath which they rested. He sent out his mind to the conscious one of the two, who clambered to his feet and stumbled towards him, clutching at tree trunks and branches of shrubs to keep himself more or less upright. It took no more than a moment for Rufus to mesmerise the man, as alcohol had done most of the job for him. He drank until he heard the man's breathing become shallow, then emptied his semi-somnolent mind of all but vague, pleasant memories that he would most likely attribute to the quantity of cheap liquor he'd consumed. Then Rufus hurried on towards his destination.

On reaching the mansion in Epsom Avenue, he cast around for somewhere to hide. He settled on a piece of rough ground on the opposite side of the road and perhaps twenty yards along from the house, crouching behind a clump of thorny bushes from where he had a reasonable view of anyone coming or going. Looking across the street, he was startled to recognise the house he and Serafina and Springer had looked at before deciding on the one in Gillies Avenue. Lucky for them they hadn't ended up living almost next door to what he was now convinced must be a highly unpleasant vampire. About an hour before dawn, he finally gave up his vigil. Not one person had gone near the place all night, much less issued forth from it. Frustrated, Rufus made his way home.

Over the following nights, he made it a point of honour to

spend almost all of the hours of darkness keeping watch on the silent mansion from his vantage point behind the bushes. Hunting became something to be accomplished as quickly as possible, rather than something to be savoured. He resented every moment not spent in keeping his lone vigil. Yet, at the end of a week, he'd observed no one entering or leaving the premises, and he began to wonder whether, despite all his efforts at concealment, he'd somehow given himself away. Not to the young woman or others like her – and he felt certain there were others – but to whoever was controlling them. His conviction became stronger than ever that this must be Serafina's captor, the vampire she'd sensed so fleetingly all those weeks ago.

One night, after yet another fruitless watch, he was about to leave when he suddenly sensed Serafina. And she was not far away. His heart pounding, he waited, certain she would appear at any moment. When she failed to do so, Rufus crept from his hiding place and up to the gates of the mansion. Peering through the wrought-iron gates, he saw only the empty expanse of the grounds and the dark silhouette of the house, but his sense of Serafina had become so strong he was certain she must be somewhere in the house. Almost without conscious thought, he opened the gate and slipped inside. For several minutes he stood in the silent darkness willing himself to be calm. Then he began to walk across the grass towards the house. At first it seemed the entire building was in darkness but, as he drew closer, he noticed chinks of light escaping from around the edges of blinds or curtains in a few windows, and two long rectangles of light shone faintly through the panes of stained glass on either side of the front door. Making his way across the flowerbeds to avoid stepping on the gravel where the sound of his footfalls might give him away, Rufus climbed onto the porch and peered through one of the glass panes. He saw nothing but a spacious foyer with doors leading off it and a staircase rising at one side. He crept from window to window across the front of the house, noticing that all of them were barred. Whoever was inside the house was not intended to escape.

As he made his way around the side of the house, his sense of Serafina suddenly became stronger still. It seemed odd to Rufus that he sensed her so strongly, yet he could discern no trace of her physical scent. Perhaps it had something to do with the cloak of – he could only think of it as absence, as though the place had no existence in the real world – that seemed to swathe the entire property. But Serafina was near, of that he was certain. He had almost reached the back of the house when a beam of light sliced through the darkness just ahead of him. Someone had lit a lamp in one of the rooms. Rufus hurried towards it, crouching low under the windowsill, every sense alert and focused. He heard the low murmur of a woman's voice, and his heart gave a violent lurch. It was Serafina! Biting back the urge to call out to her, Rufus raised himself on his haunches until he could just see into the room.

The light came from an oil lamp on a table beside a low divan upholstered in scarlet plush. On the divan lay Serafina, looking even more beautiful, to Rufus's starved eyes, than he remembered her. Her wrap of rich red satin fell in smooth folds over the contours of her body. His heart was beating so hard it seemed she must surely hear it, but she did not look his way. She was gazing into the darkness beyond the lantern's light, and she seemed to be talking to someone in a low voice. She reached out her hand, and Rufus saw another hand grasp it. Then the owner of the hand came into view, and it was as much as Rufus could do to smother a cry of horror. It was a man, a young Maori man with features that seemed carved from some rich wood polished to a smooth sheen, and black hair curling onto his broad shoulders. Rufus knew he should look away, but something held him staring in anguished disbelief as the handsome young man sat down beside Serafina and began to run his strong, brown hand over the white skin of her thigh where her wrap had fallen open. Then he lowered his mouth to Serafina's and pulled her into his arms as her body arched to meet his. Her eyes were closed, and her face bore a look of – oh, God, how could he bear it? – a look of rapture.

With a supreme effort, Rufus tore himself away from the scene and fled back across the grass and out through the gate, not stopping until he reached home.

Racing up the stairs, he flung himself onto his bed and lay there gasping, trying in vain to banish from his mind the picture of Serafina in the arms of—of her lover? Could she have forgotten him so soon, so completely? Had all her protestations of love been empty? Or was it her way of punishing him for his intransigence over taking her to gaming houses? He found it hard to imagine her taking such a cruel revenge for such a petty offence, but then perhaps it wasn't so petty to her. Then again, perhaps it was somehow the doing of her captor – but for what possible reason? How long Rufus lay there trying to make sense of it all he had no idea, but eventually the pangs of hunger grew so intense they forced him out to hunt.

He found sustenance among the vagrants sleeping rough

in the Grafton Gully cemetery, but he took no pleasure in feeding, and left as soon as his hunger had abated. As he strode along Symonds Street, he found himself wishing Fox and his cronies had killed him outright that night on the *Orion*. It would have been a suitable end for such a hopeless life as his had turned out to be. Everything he touched seemed to turn to dross. Even Serafina, who loved him as no other woman had done, had been driven into the arms of another man by his stupid stubbornness. Maybe he should just kill himself and be done with it all – except that he'd be bound to botch that, too. All of a sudden, Rufus found himself engulfed in hysterical laughter. The whole situation was too insane for words! What he needed was a good dose of normality. Realising he was not too far from The Fitzgerald, he decided to treat himself to a drink in its warm and smoky atmosphere amongst the down-to-earth humanity of its patrons.

He ordered whisky instead of his customary brandy, and turned to find his usual seat in the corner, but two rather raddled middle-aged women – and a younger one who seemed well on her way to reaching the same state – were in possession, so he found himself a place towards the back of the room. Eleanor looked up for a moment from serving customers and smiled at him. He raised a hand in salutation and settled down to enjoy his whisky. After an hour or so, she joined him.

"Hello, Rufus, I'm sorry I can only stay for a moment. We're very busy, as you can see, but my shift will be over in half an hour, and I was wondering if you'd like to come upstairs for a chat and a drink – or tea if you'd prefer it? There's a sitting room there where we can be nice and cosy and quiet."

Startled, Rufus asked, "Are you sure? I mean, are you allowed...?"

"Probably not, strictly speaking, but I don't think anyone will notice, much less mind, and frankly, I've just about had my fill of noise and tobacco smoke and the sweat of honest toil for tonight. Do say you'll come."

Rufus hesitated, but only for a moment. The company of someone as sweet and uncomplicated as Eleanor seemed exactly what he needed, and if a hint of revenge for what he'd seen earlier lurked in his mind, he ignored it. He smiled. "Thank you, I'd like that."

Eleanor patted his shoulder. "Lovely. I'd better go now. I can see Mrs Morris looking daggers at me."

She slipped away through the throng, and Rufus saw her speak briefly with a stout, middle-aged woman in a stiff brown dress and a frilled apron – presumably Mrs Morris – before returning to serving the patrons clustered along the bar.

The sitting room, which was up a narrow, dark staircase, was, indeed, cosy, with its lived-in furnishings, oil lamps, and a fire flickering in the grate.

"What would you like to drink?" Eleanor asked. "We have sherry or port or beer – unless you'd like me to make you some tea?"

Rufus shook his head. "No, nothing for me, thanks. I think I've had my quota for the night."

He looked at Eleanor, acutely aware of the warm, human scent of her, and the warm, human blood pulsing within her. Her dark hair was pulled back into a bun at the nape of her neck, but strands had come loose, framing her face in waiflike curls. He'd forgotten just how enchanting she was. They no longer had her vicious stepbrother to worry about, and it was obvious Serafina didn't want him any longer, so why shouldn't he have a little pleasure in his life for a change?

"Do come and sit down, Rufus." Eleanor indicated the spot beside her on the sofa.

Rufus hesitated. The fresh blood racing in his veins, enhanced, perhaps, by the whisky he'd drunk, made him wary of being too close to her. But he felt equally unable to refuse her invitation, so he smiled and sat beside her.

"So, Rufus," Eleanor said, "how are you enjoying life in the colonies?"

"Oh, well enough, though it's very different from what I was used to."

Eleanor gave a throaty chuckle. "I can imagine! I'm sure you were quite the man about town back in London."

"I suppose I was." A hint of wistfulness tugged at Rufus. "Still, it's quite an adventure, don't you think?"

"That's one way of putting it."

"What would you have been doing if you'd stayed in England?"

"Lord, that doesn't bear thinking about, not if Toby were still in the picture!" She gave a little gasp, and her cheeks reddened. "Oh, dear, I do beg your pardon. One isn't supposed to speak ill of the dead, is one? Still," she added with a grimace, "I can't help being glad he's not around any longer. I can't tell you how much more pleasant life is without him!"

A sudden image of Serafina tossing Fox's lifeless body into the sea came into Rufus's mind, but he pushed it aside, saying, "I'm glad you're happy, Eleanor. You certainly didn't seem so during the voyage."

"Thank you, Rufus. You've contributed greatly to my happiness, you know."

"I have?"

"Of course you have. You were so kind to me, even though it put you at risk from my—from Toby. I'm glad I've met you again, Rufus. I've wanted so often to tell you how grateful I am."

She leaned towards Rufus and surprised him by kissing him softly on the mouth. A sudden thrill ran through him, fanning to a flame the blood ecstasy he'd been keeping at bay.

Eleanor looked at him, her eyes shining in the lamplight. "I'm afraid that was rather forward of me," she murmured, "but I've wanted to do it for so long. I hope you don't mind."

As Rufus gazed at her, all his fear and despair and loneliness were suddenly subsumed into the blood ecstasy. He was overwhelmed by a desire for warmth and comfort – in short, for Eleanor. He drew her into his arms and kissed her, gently at first, and then with growing passion as the blood tide flooded through him. As she responded, Rufus drew her ardour into himself, feeding his own until he was lost in sensations of pure delight. With some part of him, he knew it was not what he felt for Serafina, yet it satisfied some longing within him that had gone unfulfilled since her disappearance, a gnawing hunger that even blood failed to nourish. A shudder ran through him as Eleanor's body pressed against his, the scent of her warm skin was as sweet and intoxicating as champagne. Rufus pulled her closer, crushing her against him as his lips and tongue explored the contours of her face and her soft, warm neck. Instinctively, he licked at the skin beneath which her veins – her beautiful, tempting veins – beat out their rhythm against his tongue. He felt the familiar tingling in his gums.

"Oh, God, no!" he gasped, pushing Eleanor away as he realised what was happening. "No, it's not you," he insisted, seeing the look of hurt on her face. "It's just...oh, I can't explain! I'm sorry, I'm so sorry, please forgive me, Eleanor, I must go!"

Eleanor stared at him, uncomprehending. "Rufus, what's wrong? If I've offended you in some way..."

"No, it's nothing you've done, I swear it, but I can't—I can't...oh, forgive me, Eleanor!"

Rufus leapt to his feet and rushed from the room, stumbling down the dark stairs, half blinded with tears of shock at what he'd almost done. At the foot of the stairs, he stopped only long enough to get his bearings, then he shoved open the back door and found himself in a small yard crowded with barrels and wooden crates of empty bottles. Ahead of him was a narrow wooden gate. He yanked it open and propelled himself out into the street, where he stood gulping in the smoky air and trying to will his mind to stop spinning and his heart to stop thudding. He had half expected Eleanor to follow him, but she didn't. On reflection, he was hardly surprised. The poor girl probably never wanted to see him again, and who could blame her? Of course he could never explain himself to her, so he mustn't see *her* again, either. He could only hope she'd find someone who would love her as she deserved.

Tears started in his eyes again as he thought of Serafina. Was he condemned—albeit by his own stupidity—to be alone for the rest of his life? However long that might be?

With a shake of his head, part anger and part despair, he turned to make his way home, then halted as he sensed something familiar nearby. It wasn't Serafina – that was too much to hope for – and yet it seemed to have a hint of her about it. He noticed two women huddled together near the entrance to The Fitzgerald, deep in conversation, and the sense of the familiar grew stronger. Rufus drew back into the gateway he'd just left, where he could watch without being seen. Facing him was one of the raddled women he'd seen in the bar, but it wasn't her who was familiar or he'd have sensed it earlier. It must be the other one, but she had her back to him so he couldn't be sure. He reached his mind out to hers, but it was blank. Just like...good God, it was just like the woman he'd followed the other night! How many of them were there, controlled by—well, perhaps this time he'd find out who it was.

His mind a ferment of hope and anxiety, Rufus focused all his attention on the two women, every sense alert to their murmured conversation.

"You must have it all by Friday." the woman facing away from him was saying in an urgent whisper. "Otherwise she's going to be angry. And you don't want that, do you?"

The older woman, clearly tense and worried, replied, "I'll have it. I've already said so haven't I?"

The younger woman gave a curt nod. "Well, you'd better hand over what you've got, then. I can't go back with nothing."

She held out her hand, and the other fished into the neck of her gown and pulled out a brown paper package. As she offered it to her companion, she said, "I swear I'll have the rest for you by Friday, come hell or high water."

"You'd better, or you may find that those are the easy options."

As the woman spoke, Rufus realised with a start that the words were not her own. Someone was speaking through her—or at least telling her what to say—just like the woman the other night. This was beyond coincidence. They must both be under the sway of whoever had kidnapped Serafina. He withdrew further into the shadows as the woman turned and began to walk in his direction. She was tucking the package into the bosom of her gown, and as the light above the tavern door shone on her face, Rufus suppressed a gasp. No wonder she had seemed so familiar. She was the woman from whom he'd been feeding when Serafina had vanished!

With that realisation, pieces of what had seemed an insoluble puzzle began to fall into place. What if she'd been a decoy, sent to distract him while someone else went after Serafina? Who else but a vampire would know so well how best to distract him, and when? So it must have been a vampire who had taken Serafina, and who else could it be but the vampire she had sensed for those few, mystifying seconds? How could he have been so stupid as to believe for a second that Serafina would willingly have betrayed their love? Far from being a willing party to what he'd seen earlier, she must have been acting under the control of her captor. Rufus was overcome by self-loathing to think he'd been so close to her, yet had left her in danger because his precious feelings had been hurt.

But this was no time for self-recrimination, however well deserved. He was no closer to understanding why Serafina had been taken, but here was a possible information source, and he must not let her escape him. Withdrawing further into himself, lest the woman's controller should sense him, Rufus began to follow her down Symonds Street.

# CHAPTER TWENTY-SEVEN

The young woman seemed to be following the same route as the previous girl, and Rufus decided to do nothing beyond keeping her in sight and himself unnoticed until they reached the outskirts of town, where the unlit areas of rough land offered better cover should he need it. Meanwhile, he set himself to considering how he might break the mind control she was under, since he knew he'd get nothing from her while she was in thrall to some other vampire. The trick would be to free her without allowing her controller access to his own mind, assuming that was possible.

Along Symonds Street they went, past the Grafton Gully cemetery where he and Serafina had fed together, and past the mean houses of Newton to Mount Eden Road. Unlike the other woman, however, instead of skirting the Mount Eden Stockade, she continued striding down Mount Eden Road. It seemed likely to Rufus that she was going straight to the Epsom Avenue mansion. He would have to act quickly. They were approaching an area between the road and the stockade that had been cleared of native bush but allowed to grow wild again since. It was very poorly lit, so Rufus decided to act on the only idea that had come to him; he could only hope it would work. Veering off into the murk beyond the streetlamps, he swiftly cast about him for something he could use as a weapon. There were a number of fallen branches lying about, but they were from the thorny bushes that seemed to grow everywhere, and were too spindly to be useful. If he didn't act now, however, he'd miss his chance; he'd just have to improvise. He began to stamp on the dry branches, hoping the girl – or the one controlling her – would think the noise worth investigating.

He was in luck. Almost immediately, she left the road and came towards him across the open ground, stumbling a little over the uneven surface, heedless of the thorny branches tearing at her gown. Rufus ducked behind some bushes, breaking another branch with a sharp crack to draw her to him. Then, when she was almost upon him, he leapt out and knocked her to the ground, using all the force he could muster. It was not that he wanted to harm her, but he'd decided his best chance of releasing her from mind control was to render her unconscious. She gave a cry, half pain, half surprise, as she fell, then lay still among the fallen branches and weeds. Rufus bent over her, then, seeing her eyes begin to flicker open, struck her hard on the side of the head with his fist. She gave a grunt and her head lolled to one side. He shuddered, hoping he hadn't done too much damage. Hitting a woman was not something he had ever thought to do, even in the hope of releasing her from a form of hypnosis. He got to his feet, and then bent to pick her up. A sudden panic assailed him as he wondered where on earth he could take her. He couldn't very well interrogate her where they were, much less on the street, but he was reluctant to take her home in case she later recalled where she'd been and gave him away. Still, if he could change the memories of those from whom he fed, he supposed he could do the same with this girl. At least he hoped so.

Making sure to avoid going anywhere near the mansion, Rufus sped home, carrying the girl in his arms. Instead of taking her to any of the rooms he and Serafina habitually used, he carried her to the small sitting room next to the dining room and sat her down in an easy chair. He didn't light a lamp. He could see perfectly well in the dark, and the less she saw the better. Pulling up another chair, he sat opposite the girl and reached his mind out to hers. It seemed he had been successful; instead of her mind appearing blank, he could now read it with relative ease. By sifting through her thoughts and memories, he was able to build a picture of her life in the household of the vampire who had controlled her. It was a chilling picture: an ancient vampire, far older than Anton, with almost no humanity left beyond her physical form, who seemed to keep a number of humans as slaves and playthings, toying with them as a cat would a bird, using them to do her will, and revelling in the control she had over them. There was no disputing, though, that her physical form was beautiful. She looked to have been brought across in her mid-thirties, with long, night-black curls cascading down to her waist, a pale, sensuous face and dark sloe eyes, and a voluptuous figure. She reminded him of pictures he'd seen on Grecian pottery at the British Museum, where his tutor had taken him on a number of occasions in an effort to improve his mind. But inside that lovely exterior lay a being filled with the vilest desires, the power to fulfil them as she pleased – and no conscience whatsoever.

Her name was Viviana. Rufus laughed inwardly at the irony of that name, she was so far from any meaningful concept of life. He could only hope he never reached such a state.

Before he could glean more from the girl, her eyelids fluttered and she gave a moan and opened her eyes. To Rufus's surprise, the seawater eyes he remembered from their previous encounter showed not fear, but cool appraisal.

"Ah," her voice was a seductive murmur. "I see now the reason for Serafina's devotion."

"What!" Rufus exclaimed, startled. Then, as she continued to stare at him, her eyes like deep pools in her expressionless face, he suddenly realised she was not speaking at all. Someone was speaking through her. And that someone could only be—"

He felt rather than heard a languorous sigh. "Oh, well done, Rufus! Clever as well as pretty!"

"What do you want from me?" Rufus demanded with a snarl.

"And spirited, too – an admirable quality, though a trifle awkward at times, as your beloved Serafina has discovered."

"What have you done to her?"

"Oh, nothing more than a little—persuasion, and she's been well rewarded for her compliance, as you saw for yourself..."

Rufus grasped the sides of his chair with all his might as he tried to resist the urge to attack Viviana's mouthpiece. "Why have you kidnapped Serafina?" he shouted. "What do you want with her? Or is she just another of your damned playthings?"

His words were answered by low, sensuous laughter that seemed obscene coming from the lips of the young woman before him. "Oh dear, you really do love her, don't you? Well, Rufus, since I'm in a generous mood tonight, I'll give her back to you. But you must give me something in return."

"What? What is it you want?" Rufus whispered, barely able to speak for the warring emotions of hope and dread that seemed to choke him.

"Just a little help, Rufus, that's all. You see, I thought Serafina would be able to help me, but she's proved to be of no use at all, and nowhere near as amusing as I'd hoped. Quite frankly, I'm growing bored with her."

"What do you want me to do?"

"Why, to find Anton Springer, of course. Once I have him, I assure you neither you nor your precious Serafina will be of the slightest interest to me. So, do we have a bargain?"

"I don't know where Anton is any more that Serafina does. We know he went to Australia, but he didn't tell us any more than that."

"Oh, but I dare say he won't stay away for ever."

"No, I suppose not, but—"

"But nothing, Rufus," Viviana's voice took on an edge of steel. "Either you agree to help me, or you'll never see Serafina again."

Rufus longed to scream at Viviana that he'd never betray Anton, but how could he, in the face of such a stark ultimatum? He had little doubt of Viviana's ability and will to carry out her threat. What choice did he have but to agree to her terms? He'd just have to hope that Anton, when he returned to Auckland, would be able to find some way to deal with her. He was quite certain he couldn't do it himself. Yet he daren't risk losing both Serafina and Springer.

"How do I know I can trust you?" he demanded with a sang-froid he was very far from feeling.

"If you want Serafina, you'll just have to take the risk, won't you?"

"And what about her mind, will you return that to her?"

Viviana laughed. "It's of no use to me. I thought we'd already established that. Agree to help me, and Serafina will be with you before dawn. Though of course she must never know of our bargain. I don't trust either of you any more than you trust me. If one word of it reaches her...well, let's just say there'll be consequences, and I don't think you'll find them pleasant."

"All right, I agree!" His words sounded strangled, as though his throat wanted to prevent them from forming. "When Anton returns to Auckland, I'll let you know."

"Oh, don't worry," gloated Viviana, "I'll know. From the moment you and Serafina are reunited, I'll be there in your minds, waiting. You won't feel me, but never doubt that I will be there, as often as I wish, until I have what I want."

Rufus nodded, gulping in air and finally relaxing his grip on the chair. "What about...? He glanced at the girl, who still sat blank-faced before him.

"Elizabeth? By all means send her back to me. Unlike your Serafina, she's still of some use, and a great deal less trouble."

As abruptly as she'd arrived, Viviana was gone.

Elizabeth stared around the room as though wondering how she came to be there, her hand pressed against the side of her head where Rufus had struck her. For a few moments, her face relaxed and she looked human again. Rufus reached his mind out to hers, but was met by a force that hit him like a blow from a club, knocking him to the floor. He seemed to hear faint, mocking laughter, and then Elizabeth stood up and made for the door. Rufus clambered to his feet just in time to hear the front door open and close.

* * * *

"How long have I been away?"

Serafina and Rufus were sitting together by the fire in the parlour, Serafina staring into the flames. Neither of them needed the warmth, but Rufus had insisted on lighting a fire as soon as Serafina had arrived, thinking to make the room look cosy for her. She'd arrived in the early hours of the morning, knocking at the door like a visitor as Rufus sat waiting, tense with the fear that she might not come at all, and terrified that if she did she'd immediately realise the appalling bargain with which he'd bought her freedom. But she hadn't. Instead, she'd run into his arms and covered his face with kisses and tears. Yet, he thought, watching the flames reflected in her eyes, she was changed, in ways he had yet to understand.

"Almost four months," he told her.

Serafina nodded, her eyes not leaving the fire. "It was so easy to lose track of time." She turned to Rufus. "I still can't quite believe she let me leave. I was afraid she never would."

"Why do you think she did?" asked Rufus, hating himself for pretending he didn't know, but desperate to avoid giving himself away.

Serafina gave a short, bitter laugh. "I was no use to her any more, since I'd done nothing to deliver Anton to her. That's what she told me. The worst of it is I think I would have helped her if I could. Not at first, but afterwards, after she..."

Rufus leaned across to touch her cheek. "Try not to think about it, darling, not just yet. I'll go and draw you a bath."

When Rufus returned to fetch Serafina, he found her wandering about the room, touching various objects as though reacquainting herself with old friends. She turned when she heard him, and ran to him, wrapping her arms about him and kissing him.

"I can scarcely believe I'm home at last!" she exclaimed. "I feel I've been living in a nightmare."

"So do I, darling," Rufus said. "But we're both awake now. Come on, your bath is ready."

In the bathroom, Serafina ran a critical eye over Rufus's clothes, muddied from his encounter with Elizabeth, and his dirt-streaked face and hands. "I can't imagine what you've been doing, but you're more in need of a bath than I am," she told him with a hint of her old, mischievous smile. "You'd better bathe with me."

Rufus needed no second bidding. Together the two of them shed their clothes and climbed into the water. For a time, they simply lay there, savouring each other with their eyes. Then Rufus took up the soap and facecloth and gently and carefully washed Serafina's body as though to cleanse it of any last traces of Viviana's influence. As Serafina washed him in turn, Rufus realised just how much he had missed her, how empty his life had been without such gestures of caring. He drew her against him and kissed her, pouring all his love and longing into her, and feeling her love flooding into him, feeding him as even blood could never do.

Scarcely bothering to dry themselves, they hurried to their bed and made love, minds and bodies melding as they shared the sweetness of being together once more.

Afterwards, Serafina gave a great sigh, and smiled at Rufus. "Oh, I've missed you so much! And I didn't even realise it until I saw you again. How could I not have realised?"

"Don't be upset, darling. It wasn't your fault. It was Viviana. I've missed you too, dreadfully. I was terrified I might have lost you forever." Serafina's response was to burst into tears. Rufus held her, stroking her damp hair with gentle hands. "I'm so sorry," he murmured. "We should have gone with Anton, at least he would have kept you safe."

To Rufus's astonishment, Serafina began to laugh. "Oh, Rufus, if only you knew the times Anton has led me into danger, the times we've barely escaped with our lives. Not that I blame him," she added. "If there's one thing I've learnt from Anton, it's that a vampire is always in danger. Wherever we may travel, there will always be those who wish us harm." Her face grew sombre. "In the end," she said, almost to herself, "we may not even be able to trust our own kind." Rufus felt a stab of fear. Had Serafina already found him out? "Oh, Rufus, it was terrible! I tried to withstand her, truly I did, but she's more powerful than I ever dreamed possible." Her voice sank to a whisper. "I did try, Rufus, I truly did, but she was too strong for me."

"Hush, darling," Rufus murmured, his voice gentle and reassuring. "You're free of her now, and that's all that matters."

But Serafina was unable to stop. "She wants Anton, Rufus, and she thought I could lead her to him. I tried to tell her I don't know where he is. I even let her into my mind so she could see I wasn't lying, but she's determined to find him, no matter how long it takes. She's been after him for four centuries, now."

"And that's why Anton keeps travelling all the time?"

Serafina nodded. "I suppose it must be, though he never said so, or even allowed me to read it from his mind."

"But why does she want him?" Rufus asked. This was something to which Viviana hadn't thought to make him privy.

"You remember Anton told you about von Dunkel?" Rufus nodded. "Well, Viviana was his creator. He was the love of her life, according to her, and she wants revenge on Anton for killing him."

"After all this time?"

"Yes. I truly believe she's mad, Rufus, perhaps from losing her lover, perhaps from having lived for so long, or perhaps she was always mad. I don't think she even cares about the reason any more. She's sworn to have revenge, and she won't stop until she succeeds."

A wave of horror engulfed Rufus as he thought of his part in Viviana's plan. He pushed the thought down into the deepest reaches of his mind and smiled at Serafina. "It's almost dawn now. We should sleep. Time enough tonight to think about Viviana."

# CHAPTER TWENTY-EIGHT

When Rufus woke just after sunset, Serafina was still asleep. He propped himself up on one elbow and gazed at her mask-like face. Her skin had the smooth, waxen quality of a mannequin or an embalmed body. Once, this would have horrified him. Now it was just another phase of the vampire's daily cycle. He knew he looked the same when he slept.

When Serafina woke, they dressed and went out to hunt. Serafina was eager to resume old, familiar habits.

"I missed the hunting," she told Rufus, her voice wistful. "Feeding is about so much more than just drinking blood."

Perhaps not to the likes of Viviana, Rufus thought, but he said nothing to Serafina.

On reaching town, they made their way to the harbour. A ship had lately berthed at the New Wharf, and Serafina drew one of its crewmen to her, handing him over to Rufus as soon as he was suitably compliant. Rufus, half afraid that Serafina might be stolen away from him again, despite Viviana's promise, kept her close to him as he drank fresh blood tinged with rum from the young sailor. Afterwards, he kissed Serafina with bloodstained lips, almost swooning with delight at the sensation of her tongue lapping up the blood there.

They walked further along the harbour side and Rufus found another sailor for Serafina, watching as she fed, his mind linked with hers so he could enjoy her pleasure as she had enjoyed his. Afterwards, she came to him and kissed him with her blood-reddened lips.

"Come," she murmured against his mouth. "Let's go home."

In the hallway, Rufus turned to Serafina in the darkness that was filled with the rich light and colour of their vampiric sight, pulled her into his arms and kissed her again. The blood ecstasy was flooding his body and mind with the most delectable sensations, and it seemed every part of his being was filled with Serafina – her scent, her taste, the touch of her body, and her mind joined with his. Together they hurried up the stairs and into their room, their fingers tugging at buttons and ties with a mixture of impatience and laughter. Their lovemaking was passionate and fierce, as if they must re-establish their claim on one another.

Afterwards, Serafina said, "I felt your fear, Rufus, when I was feeding."

"I'm afraid every moment that Viviana might snatch you away again. I know she said she had no more use for you, but what if she changes her mind?"

Serafina was silent for some moments, then she said, "There might be a way to protect ourselves from her." She told him how Viviana had starved her and then fed her with her own blood to bind her to her. "Perhaps we might do something similar with each other."

"Do you really think it'll work?"

"I think so, especially now I'm free of Viviana's control. As her blood bound me to her, so our blood in each other will bind us together and strengthen our protection against her. Come, give me your wrist."

Rufus felt the blood ecstasy rise in him again. "No," he whispered, and offered his neck.

Serafina smiled and pulled him towards her. "I love you so much," she whispered, and touched her lips to the vein he presented.

A wave of excitement rushed through Rufus as he saw Serafina's fangs grow long and sharp, and heard her sigh of longing, of reverence for his gift of blood. He closed his eyes and gave himself up to the intertwining sensations of pain and ecstasy as her fangs pierced his flesh and she drew his blood into her mouth, her lips cool and soft as they moved with a soft rhythm against his skin. After a few moments, she withdrew, licking at the wound she had made. She lifted her dark hair with one hand and pulled it back to expose her neck. Her eyes were like black opals with rainbow fires glowing in their depths. Rufus felt the familiar tingling sensation as his fangs emerged. Just for a moment, he held back, gazing at her white neck with its delicate tracery of veins. It seemed almost a pity to sully it. But he felt Serafina in his mind, felt her excitement as she urged him on, and he bent and plunged his fangs into a vein, all but overcome with elation as her blood spurted into his mouth. It was cooler than human blood, but more complex, somehow, and more delicate on his palate.

All at once, Serafina pulled away from him with a hiss of anger. "Rufus, how could you do such a thing? To betray your own kin?"

Gasping from the shock of her sudden withdrawal, Rufus stared at her in horror. "Oh, God, no! Serafina, I—I didn't—"

"You did!" Serafina's voice was little more than a whisper, but it seared Rufus like hot iron. "I felt it! I heard it! You've betrayed Anton—betrayed us—to that creature! What did she promise you, Rufus? What prize did you take for giving Anton to her?"

Unable to meet her furious gaze, Rufus stared down at his tightly clenched hands. "I—I didn't want to. I couldn't help...Serafina, you of all people know how powerful she is."

"Don't make excuses! You didn't have to live with her! She didn't make you drink her blood!" Serafina leapt from the bed and practically flung herself across the room as though unable to bear being close to Rufus. "How could I have trusted you? How could I have been so stupid as to love you, to believe you loved me? I defied Anton for your sake, and this is how you repay me!"

She had had her back turned to Rufus. Now she wheeled about and ran at him, raining blows on his head and shoulders, snarling like a wild cat, her fangs growing sharp, not with hunger but with rage. His hands raised in an attempt to ward off her blows, Rufus tried to roll away from her. She crawled after him on all fours, reaching out to grasp him with clawed hands, her lips drawn back from her fangs, her eyes burning like hot coals. Panic held him immobilised as she clawed her way up his body, her fingernails leaving long, bloody streaks on his skin. Then his own anger began to bubble up from somewhere deep inside him. He felt it grow hotter and hotter until it boiled over like hot lava from a volcano. With all his strength, he thrust Serafina off.

"You want to know Viviana's price?" he flung at her. "It was you, Serafina! It was the only way I could get you away from her." His voice rasped in his throat, and hot tears rose in his eyes.

As Serafina stared at him, at first in angry disbelief, and

then in horror, Rufus explained how he had crept up to Viviana's house and seen Serafina and the young Maori, how Viviana had spoken to him through Elizabeth, and what had led him to make his devil's bargain with her.

"I did it because I love you, Serafina, and I was afraid of what else she might do to you. She said I'd never see you again if I didn't do what she wanted. And I couldn't bear that, Serafina. I simply couldn't bear it! Even if you want other men, I'll try to accept it as long as I can have at least a little of your love." His voice sank to a whisper. "I didn't want to betray Anton, but I can't live without you."

For a long time, Serafina was silent, staring at her hands as they twisted at the bedclothes. When she looked up at Rufus, there were tears in her eyes. "Oh, Rufus, forgive me! I should have known. After all, I brought you across for love, because I couldn't bear to be without *you*. And I don't want anyone else but you, I promise. I confess that I did, once..." Serafina lowered her eyes again, and took a deep breath. "But it was only because my mind wasn't my own. It was after Viviana had starved me and fed me with her blood to make me her creature. She sent others to me because I needed more blood than she was willing to give me, and one of them was her favourite, a Maori called Tamati, and—oh, please don't hate me, Rufus! I was so carried away by the blood ecstasy that I...and she was in my mind, experiencing him through me! As soon as I realised what was happening I made him stop, I swear it! But what you saw at her house the other night didn't happen. Please believe me, it was just something Viviana put into your mind to torment you."

"Oh, Serafina, my poor darling! How could I blame you for that monster's depravity?"

He held out his arms and Serafina crept into them, and they clung to each other in silence for a long time.

At length, Serafina said, "We've both fallen into her power, Rufus, but we mustn't give in to it again. Somehow, we're going to have to find another way of dealing with her."

"Dealing with whom, might I ask?" a familiar voice said from the open doorway.

Rufus and Serafina turned to see Springer standing there in his topcoat, his hat in one hand, his silver-topped cane in the other.

"Anton!" Serafina, heedless of her nakedness, rushed across the room and flung herself into Springer's arms.

"I've missed you, too, my dear, but is this any way to greet me, almost knocking me off my feet? And please, I beg of you, cover yourself up." Springer turned away from her as though in embarrassment, but the warmth in his eyes belied his admonishment. "I'll wait for you in the parlour."

Serafina threw on her dressing gown and raced downstairs. Rufus followed suit, but more slowly, wondering how he was going to tell Springer about his promise to Viviana. He didn't for a moment imagine he could keep it from him. He found Springer standing by the fireplace, his arm around Serafina's shoulders.

Springer inclined his head in greeting. "Good evening, Rufus, I trust you're well?"

"Yes, thank you. Welcome home. I hope your business went well."

"Oh, well enough, thank you. And how goes the gambling? I dare say you're a wealthy man by now."

Rufus, doing his best to erase all thoughts of Viviana, said, "Oh no, I haven't dared to win too much, for fear of gaining notoriety."

Springer smiled his icy smile, his pale eyes seeming to penetrate to Rufus's heart, but all he said was, "We'll have a glass of wine and a chat presently. Right now, I need to change out of these clothes and wash away the grime of travel. These modern steamships may be fast, but they're downright filthy to sail in!" With a slight, formal bow, he turned and made for the staircase.

Rufus and Serafina seated themselves on the settee. For some time, neither of them spoke. Then Rufus said in a whisper, as though afraid Springer might hear him, "He knows already, doesn't he?"

Serafina nodded. "Oh, yes, it wouldn't have been possible to keep it from him."

Rufus quailed inwardly. "No, I suppose not."

Serafina squeezed his hand. "I dare say he'll understand," she murmured, though Rufus found little comfort in either words or gesture.

"Understand what?" came Springer's voice from the doorway. Serafina and Rufus both gave a guilty start. Springer, wearing his dressing gown over shirt and trousers, strolled across to the sideboard. "A little wine, I think." His voice was bland, but his eyes were as cold and as sharp as icicles. He took Rufus and Serafina their glasses, and they accepted them in silence. "Now," he said, seating himself in his favourite armchair. "A toast. To understanding, yes?" He sipped his wine, gazing at them both over the rim of his glass before focusing on Rufus. "I take it you intended telling me at some point," he said at last, "or did you really think you could keep it a secret from me? Even you should know better than that by now."

Serafina glared at him, placing a protective arm around Rufus's shoulders. "If you'd been here, you might have stopped her, but no, your wretched business deals were more important."

Springer pursed his lips. "Without my 'wretched business deals', we'd all be a great deal poorer. And if it was, perhaps, unwise of me to leave you as I did, you could have come with me, you know, both of you. You were the ones who insisted on staying here."

"Only because you didn't see fit to tell us we were in danger!" Serafina snarled at him, her eyes flashing. "How could you do that, Anton, when you must have known full well what she's like? Well, so much for family!"

She spat out the last word through bared teeth. For a moment, Rufus thought she was going to hurl her wine glass at Springer. Instead, she flung it across the room, where it shattered against the fireplace. Then she burst into tears. Rufus put his arms around her and held her against his shoulder as she sobbed. He fixed Springer with an angry stare.

Springer hurried to kneel beside Serafina, stroking her hair with a gentle hand. "Please forgive me, my dear. I thought it was only me she wished to harm. I had no idea she'd try and get to me through you, much less through Rufus."

"Do you mean to tell me," said Rufus, his voice frigid with anger, "that in all the years you've carted Serafina about the world willy-nilly, you never thought to tell her why?"

"*Mea culpa*, I'm afraid." For the first time since Rufus had met him, Springer seemed discomfited, his voice very low, his eyes staring across the room. "At first, before I brought

Serafina across, I felt it would frighten her unnecessarily to tell her why I must be always on the move. How could I tell her Viviana was hunting me to exact revenge for killing one of her kin, especially when she still went in fear of her uncle? Afterwards, to my shame, I just didn't know how to tell her. It's not as though I felt proud of what I'd done to von Dunkel, and I genuinely believed that if I could outrun Viviana for long enough, she'd give up trying to find me. I thought I'd been successful until she turned up in Dublin, where we were staying at the time. As soon as I realised she was there, we slipped across to England and took the first ship I could find to the South Pacific, where I already had one or two business interests that needed my attention. I finally realised, when she followed me here to Auckland, just how wrong I'd been. That's why I was so insistent that you both come to Australia with me. I knew it would be no more than a short-term remedy, but at least if you were with me I might have some chance of protecting you. But when Serafina was so adamant that she wanted to stay here, I'm afraid I persuaded myself that as long as I was out of the picture, the two of you would be safe. I know now just what a forlorn hope that was."

"But why didn't you kill Viviana long ago?" Rufus demanded. "It's not as though the concept was new to you, not after von Dunkel, not to mention your years in the army."

Springer gave a thin smile. "True, though as I said before, von Dunkel's death, at least, was scarcely a matter of pride to me. Besides, Viviana is not so easily killed. She's managed to survive for over a thousand years – no mean feat, even for a vampire – and she has powers you could scarcely imagine,

Rufus, and little compunction about using them."

"Yes, I've had my own insight into that," Rufus's voice was grim as he recalled his recent encounter, "as I dare say you already know. But you should have told Serafina. She deserved that much, surely?"

"Yes," Springer admitted, "she did, and I truly wish I'd handled things differently. All I can offer by way of excuse is that my long years in the army had taught me to be secretive. In war, it can be fatal to be too open, to admit too much."

"You still should have told me," Serafina said, raising her head from Rufus's shoulder. "You could have taught me how to protect myself from her."

"I'm not sure there is a way to protect oneself from the likes of Viviana. Wherever she goes, she gathers around her slaves made willing by her mind control to defend her to the death. Once upon a time, they were other vampires, for she was as indiscriminate in creating family as she was in satisfying her other appetites. But there are fewer of us, now. Despite our potential immortality, our lives are precarious enough that most of us don't reach five centuries, let alone a millennium. Besides, under her control, humans can achieve much of what vampires can, and are far more expendable, from her point of view. Why do you suppose she keeps those strong young men?"

"Well, from what Serafina told me—" began Rufus.

"Oh, that as well," said Springer with a harsh laugh. "Viviana was brought across in less, shall we say, civilised times than we enjoy today and, as I said, she's never seen the need to control any of her appetites. By now, the demands of her blood ecstasy are as strong and as constant as her hunger for blood."

Serafina gave an involuntary shudder, recalling Viviana's lascivious enjoyment of her mindless coupling with Tamati. Rufus squeezed her shoulder in a gesture of sympathy.

"But she also keeps them to defend her, controlling their minds rather than engaging, herself, in the grubbier aspects of conflict."

"But if she's as powerful as you say," Rufus said, "why does she need anyone to fight for her? Why did she force me to...?" His voice trailed away as he realised what he was about to say, and he stared fearfully at Springer.

"To betray me to her?" Springer's voice showed sadness rather than anger. "She enjoys controlling people, Rufus. If she could, she'd bring the entire world under her sway, and even that would probably seem insufficient before long."

Serafina nodded. "She told me if I couldn't help her to destroy Anton she'd destroy me, his kin, instead, not physically, but by binding me to her with blood and then destroying my mind, and I think she might have succeeded if Rufus hadn't—hadn't..."

As her voice faded to nothing, Springer looked at Rufus, and Rufus realised he was waiting for his confession. He swallowed hard.

"I captured one of her humans," he said. "I thought—hoped—I'd be able to release her from Viviana's hold and find out how to rescue Serafina. I knocked her out and brought her back here. But when she came round she was still under Viviana's control. Viviana was using her to speak to me, and she told me if I didn't promise to deliver you to her, I'd never see Serafina again."

"I see," said Springer. "Well, for what it's worth, Rufus, under those circumstances I don't blame you for what you did."

"Thank you. She promised to free Serafina from her control and I hoped once we were all together again we might find some way to deal with her."

"You see," Serafina said, "she doesn't care how she hurts you, Anton, or who she uses to do it. And she's never going to stop. She told me herself she has all the time in the world, and no reason to hurry."

"I know." Springer's voice was grave. "That's why we must leave here immediately!"

# CHAPTER TWENTY-NINE

"Leave?" Rufus and Serafina spoke as one. Their faces bore identical expressions of horror.

Springer spoke calmly, but his face was taut, his eyes as impermeable as granite. "Yes, of course. What else can we do? I dare say Viviana already knows I've returned."

He made no mention of Rufus's bargain, but Rufus squirmed inwardly, recalling Viviana's telling him how she would know of Springer's presence.

"But surely we must stay and fight her!" he declared.

"As we should have done long ago!" Serafina added accusingly.

Springer got to his feet and began to pace about the room. It was the first time Rufus had seen him so agitated. Springer went to the fireplace, seized the poker and began to poke viciously at the skeleton of the fire Rufus had lit for Serafina. At length, he turned towards Rufus and Serafina, letting the poker fall with a dull clang onto the hearth tiles.

"You're quite right," he said to Serafina. "I should have dealt with Viviana. But I didn't, and now it's too late. She's too powerful now. You've both seen what she's like, and I dare say that was only a fraction of what she's capable of doing. The best thing—the *only* thing—we can do is flee."

Rufus stood and faced Springer, nervous yet determined. "I know I'm guilty of giving in to her, but if we just leave her to carry on as she is, none of us will ever be safe from her, not to mention the humans she enslaves. She used Elizabeth as a decoy to keep me occupied with feeding while she kidnapped Serafina. Humans like her are not just food to Viviana. She uses them for amusement as well as to collect money for business transactions of some kind. We're all just toys to her, and from what she told me through Elizabeth, I don't think she'll even stop at murder if it suits her purposes."

"And how, precisely," Springer enquired, "do you propose to deal with a thirteen-hundred-year-old vampire with powers beyond what *I'm* prepared to face?"

"We must kill her!" Serafina declared, rising to stand at Rufus's side. "She has to be stopped for good, and that's the only way to do it."

Springer turned his icy gaze on her. "I repeat, just how do you propose to accomplish this?"

"I don't know yet. All I know is that it must be done. Somehow, it must be done, and we're the only ones who can do it."

"My dear," Springer said, his eyes softening as he looked at her. "I'm full of admiration for your spirit, but I assure you it can't be done. If it could, I'd be more than happy to do it myself, but she'd sense any of us long before we got close enough to behead her or burn her to death, and those are the only ways to be certain of killing her. Before we even reached her house, she'd have her minions at the ready, quite possibly armed, and she'd be using mind control to give them extra strength and speed."

"But there'd be three of us, all vampires," said Rufus, adding, with more hope than certainty. "Couldn't the three of us overcome a bunch of humans, however well controlled?"

Springer, who had been leaning against the mantelpiece, pushed himself away from it and fixed Rufus with a frosty stare, though it seemed to Rufus that something lurked behind it – could it be fear?

"There won't be three of us, Rufus, because I have no intention of taking part in whatever fanciful scheme the two of you might concoct. I shall be leaving Auckland as soon as I can book my passage, and unless you want to end up completely dead, or worse, I strongly advise you to do the same."

"But Anton!" Serafina cried, running to him and taking his arm.

Springer brushed her aside and strode from the room.

Serafina made to run after him, but Rufus pulled her back. "Let him be. Perhaps he'll feel differently after he's slept."

"I don't think so. He's obviously been afraid of Viviana for a very long time – frightened enough to keep her existence from me. He means to leave, and he wants us to go with him."

Rufus stood staring at the floor for a moment, then looked at Serafina. "But we can't, can we? Anton's been running from her for four centuries, and if we don't stop her now, we'll be doing the same, forever, unless she succeeds in bringing us under her control. So we'll be fugitives or slaves for the rest of time." He took a deep breath and let it out slowly. "Our only real option is to kill her."

"I know," Serafina said softly. "It terrifies me even to think of it, but we cannot let that— *creature*—continue her evil work without a fight."

Rufus took her hand in his. "We'll face her together, Serafina, with or without Anton. I owe you that much, at least. If I hadn't been so damned stubborn about taking you to Martin's, she'd never have got hold of you in the first place."

"No, my love. I was the stubborn one. But that's all over now. We'll face Viviana together."

Serafina reached out to stroke his cheek. Rufus saw fear in her eyes, but also a fierce determination, and hoped his own showed the same.

"Let's sleep now," he said. "Tonight we can start making plans."

When they awoke that evening, Springer was already up and gone. Rufus and Serafina chose the harbour area in which to hunt, since it was flush with sailors from two recently arrived ships, as well as with the whores for whom the sailors were also easy prey. They arrived home afterwards to an empty house and went straight upstairs. Tonight, they would use the blood energy to plot Viviana's downfall.

"How are we to get into her house?" Rufus asked as they sat facing one another on their bed. "We've no key for the front door, and the windows all seem to be barred, from what I could see."

"One of her humans will let us in – or, better still, we can capture one of them, as you did with Elizabeth, and make her take us in."

Rufus looked dubious. "It won't be so easy to do that again. Viviana's bound to be on the alert for us now. And if she's as powerful as Springer said..."

"Yes, she is powerful," replied Serafina, "but every creature has some weakness, and I suspect Viviana's lies in the very reason for her power." With a puzzled frown, Rufus opened his mouth to speak, but Serafina held up a hand to stay him. "Viviana has been a vampire for thirteen hundred years," she explained, "and she's made little effort to retain her humanity, so she's vastly more controlled by her instincts than you or I, or even Anton. She never stirs during daylight hours. She may not even be able to do so any longer. We must attack her during the day, while she sleeps. Of course we'll also be at our weakest then, but we'll have the advantage of surprise and preparation. We don't need to confront her immediately, and if we can manage to keep ourselves hidden from her, she may even believe we've left with Anton."

Far into the night, Rufus and Serafina considered how they might accomplish their plan. The overwhelming difficulty, it seemed to Rufus, lay not just in capturing one of Viviana's minions and inducing him or her to allow them entry to her house, but in preventing her from sensing their presence once they were inside the house, or even close to it.

"I know we've practiced with each other," he told Serafina, "but if she's as powerful as you say, are you sure we can keep ourselves hidden from her at such close quarters?"

"It won't be easy," Serafina admitted, "although her sleep will be very deep. But I don't see what else we can do."

"And how can we prevent her from getting to us through whoever we capture, as she did with Elizabeth? God, Serafina, I wish there was another way."

"So do I, my love, but I think our only hope is to try to take her while she sleeps. We must keep watch on the house, as you did, until one of her humans leaves. I suppose we'll have to bring them back here until daylight – unless you have a better idea."

Rufus shook his head. "We'll need weapons," he said, "and something more than the legendary wooden stakes, I should think. I wonder how easy it would be to purchase a gun?"

"I wouldn't even know how to use a gun," Serafina said. "But I do know how to use a knife, and Viviana has a collection of swords and knives. I saw them when I first woke up in her drawing room. They're in a glass cabinet by the fireplace."

Rufus nodded, biting his lower lip. "I used to practise fencing back in London, so I dare say I can handle a sword reasonably well, or a knife, come to that." Suddenly, the ramifications of their enterprise swept over him like a gigantic wave that knocked him breathless. "Oh, God," he gasped, "what if we fail?"

Serafina reached out to take his hand. Looking into his eyes, she said, "I won't lie to you, Rufus. If we fail, it will almost certainly be the end of us. I doubt if Viviana would let us live after an attempt on her life, even if she could be sure of keeping us in her power."

Rufus nodded again, his face taut with fear, but also determination. "Serafina," he said, clasping her hands in his, "in case—in case we—Serafina, I want you to know that you've brought me more happiness than I ever knew was possible. I didn't know what love was until I met you."

Tears filled Serafina's eyes and began to slide down her cheeks. "It was Anton who saved me from misery and became my protector, but it's you, my darling Rufus, who made me whole again."

At that, Rufus took Serafina in his arms and kissed her, tasting the salt tears on her face. Slowly, between their kisses, they undressed one another and lay down together. Their lovemaking was a sweet and tender expression of everything they felt – of love and desire, but also of their awareness that this might be the last time they would feel such exquisite closeness. Eventually, they fell asleep in one another's arms.

\* \* \* \*

Rufus stared at the high wall and wrought-iron gates from where he and Serafina crouched behind their shield of thorny shrubs. It was their fourth night of vigil, and they'd been there for hours – among the most boring he'd ever spent, he thought, even compared with his enforced sojourn at Aunt Fordyce's Spartan abode. He and Serafina scarcely dared communicate with each other, let alone attempt to draw someone out from the rambling house, in case Viviana should become aware of them. By the time the first light of dawn began to streak the sky with golds and pinks, they had seen no one either enter or exit through the massive gates. They left, deflated and weary, neither of them speaking until they reached home.

They had seen little of Springer since his return, and both were too angry and disappointed with him to seek him out, but went straight to their bed and their deathlike slumber.

They woke to the sound of rain on the window. Rufus got up first, and went to gaze out at the rain-drenched garden below. He didn't relish the thought of spending the night soaking wet as well as bored. When he turned back to Serafina, she was sitting up in bed with a strange, distant look in her eyes.

"Serafina, what's wrong?"

She seemed not to hear him, but climbed out of bed, pulled on her dressing gown and padded across to the door, still staring straight ahead as though in a daze. Or sleepwalking. No, that couldn't be it; she'd been awake when he'd got out of bed. She opened the door and began to walk down the hallway towards Springer's room. Rufus reached out his mind to hers – and encountered nothing but fog. Galvanised by terror, he grabbed his dressing gown and rushed after her, pulling it on as he ran.

"No, Serafina, no! Don't let her win!"

Serafina took no notice. Rufus literally threw himself at her and they fell to the floor in a tangle of limbs and clothing. Rufus heard something clatter onto the wooden floor. It was the ivory paper knife he kept in his bedside cabinet, not a very good weapon, but wielded with vampiric strength...as realisation struck him, Rufus lunged for the knife, grasping it just before Serafina reached it. She bared her teeth with a snarl of fury and fell on him, her hands striving to reach the knife. Rufus gripped her wrists tightly and held her off as well as he could.

"For God's sake, Serafina, it's me! It's Rufus!"

Her only response was a hiss of fury as she shook herself in an attempt to get free. Unable to release his hold on her for fear of what she might do, Rufus resorted to desperate measures. He pulled her towards him by her wrists, and then shoved her hard backwards onto the floor. He heard a thud as her head struck the polished floorboards, and her body went limp. Rufus lowered her gently to the floor and bent over her.

"Serafina, are you all right?"

A low moan answered him, and Rufus scooped her up, carried her to their room and laid her on the bed. To his immense relief, after a few moments she opened her eyes, blinking up at him in confusion.

"Rufus? What happened? Oh, my head hurts!"

Rufus placed another pillow beneath her head. "Hush, darling, you're safe now."

"Safe from what?" A frown of incomprehension creased Serafina's brow, then she gave a gasp and tried to sit up. "It was her, wasn't it? Viviana."

"Yes. I might have known she wouldn't keep her word. I think she was trying to make you attack Anton. You had a knife in your hand, and you were making for his room."

"A knife! How did I get hold of one of those? I certainly don't own one."

Rufus pulled the paper knife from his pocket and set it down on the counterpane. "I don't think you'd have done much damage with it. Thank goodness you weren't anywhere near the kitchen."

There was knock at the door and Springer entered, fully dressed. "What on earth's going on here?" He saw Serafina lying on the bed and hurried towards her, concern on his face. "Serafina, my dear, what's wrong? Are you hurt?"

"Only where Rufus knocked my head on the floor," Serafina told him, her expression deliberately bland.

"He did what?"

Rufus gave him a précis of events.

Springer went to sit beside Serafina and took hold of her

shoulders. "Look at me, Serafina. I want to make sure she's gone."

Serafina stared into his eyes and he returned her gaze steadily. Rufus didn't dare try to find out what he was doing, but after several minutes, Springer released his hold. "There, she's gone now, and I've created a barrier in case she tries her tricks again." He turned to address Rufus as well as Serafina, his voice fraught with anxiety. "Now do you see why we must leave here as soon as we can?"

"I think," said Rufus, "it's all the more reason for us to stay and fight Viviana."

"No!" declared Springer. "Any halfway decent army knows better than to fight against overwhelming odds, and surely you can see now that they are overwhelming."

"That's no reason not to try," Serafina said, sparks of anger glinting in her eyes. "And anyway, if you'd dealt with her when you had a reasonable chance of getting rid of her, we wouldn't be in this mess, would we?"

Springer heaved a sigh. "I can appreciate why you think that, my dear, but things were never quite that simple. Let me try and explain why." He fetched a chair and sat down at the bedside. "Bear in mind that when von Dunkel brought me across, Viviana was already nine hundred years old and I was a new vampire who'd been thrown in at the deep end, so to speak. For a long time after I was brought across, I had no idea she even existed. She was a vast deal cleverer than von Dunkel, for all his university education. Or perhaps it was more animal cunning. At any rate, it was some time before I realised who it was who was setting traps for me. Until then, I'd supposed myself to be the only vampire in existence, at least in that part of the world. I knew I lacked the skills to confront her openly and, as a career soldier, I was already used to moving from place to place. My time with Stefan had been the exception rather than the rule. It seemed only natural to go on the run from her until such time as I felt powerful enough to face her. Discretion is the better part of valour, isn't that what they say?" Springer's lip curled in a self-deprecating smile. "As time went on, however, running became a way of life, and the fact that it enabled me to acquire useful business interests in many different places made it seem not only natural, but sensible as well. It seemed pointless to worry you, my dear, by telling you about something that wasn't your problem. I never dreamed just how tenacious she'd be, or how devious."

No one spoke for several minutes, then Rufus said, "The question is, though, how are we going to deal with Viviana now? Surely you'll agree with us that she must be dealt with, once and for all?"

"No," said Springer. "I'm more sorry than I can tell you about what's happened, and that's why I won't endanger you any further, either of you. There's only one way to deal with Viviana, and that's to kill her. You've already seen some of what she can do, and believe me, that's just the tip of the iceberg. There's nothing we can do without putting ourselves in grave danger, and I refuse to subject you to that. I've already made inquiries, and there's a ship leaving for Australia in two days' time and the three of us will be on it." He stood up, signalling that the discussion was ended.

"No!" cried Rufus and Serafina together.

Serafina glared at Springer. "Anton, don't you dare be so high-handed with us! Rufus and I have already made up our minds. We refuse to spend the rest of our lives fleeing from place to place. We're going to get rid of Viviana, or die in the attempt! If you want to run, you can damned well do it on your own!"

"And you've agreed to this, Rufus?" Springer's voice was calm, but his jaw was set and his hawkish eyes smouldered.

Rufus looked Springer in the face. "I have, yes. We had hoped you'd help us. Your experience would have been invaluable, I'm sure. Since you refuse, however, we'll just have to rely on our own resources. Whichever way you look at it, it's a desperate situation, but Serafina and I are together on this. We can't let Viviana dictate our lives for us."

"Then there's nothing more to say." Springer turned on his heel and left the room.

# CHAPTER THIRTY

As soon as Springer had left, Serafina flung herself into Rufus's arms and burst into tears. "How can he refuse to help us?" she sobbed. "How can he refuse to help *me*? All this time we've been together, and I never knew what a damned coward he is! I hate him, Rufus, I hate him!"

Rufus knew better than to try to reason with her, so he held her until she'd wept out her distress, then fetched a damp cloth from the bathroom and helped her to wipe away her tears.

"That's better," he murmured, stroking her cheek. "Would you like to hunt, or shall we leave it until tomorrow?"

"No, let's do it tonight. If I stay here and do nothing, I'll explode! At least hunting will give me something to focus on."

Serafina set a furious pace as they walked into town. The rain had eased to a misty drizzle that gave the streets a sinister cast, with buildings and lampposts looming at them out of the fog like misshapen giants or monsters. As they approached the Albert Barracks, they caught sight of a man in military uniform some yards ahead of them, his scent informing them he was returning from an assignation with a woman. Serafina and Rufus glanced at each other and began to follow him in earnest, moving at vampiric speed to catch up with him. Serafina took him by the arm and gazed into his eyes. In seconds, he was quiescent, and she led him into the shadows by the barracks wall, signalling for Rufus to join her. Together they shared his blood, leaving him propped up against the wall semi-conscious.

Deep in the shadows, they kissed, licking the last of the soldier's blood from each other's lips.

"I'm still hungry," Serafina murmured, her eyes glowing like the embers of a fire.

Rufus slipped his arm around her waist and they walked back towards Grafton Gully. There, amongst the tombstones that jostled for space with the overgrown grass and weeds, they found a sleeping vagrant and drank from him without so much as rousing him from his stertorous slumber.

They arrived home damp but elated, stripped off their clothes and tumbled onto the bed together.

Serafina ran her tongue around Rufus's lips and down to his neck to one of the veins where fresh blood pulsed.

"Perhaps," she murmured, nipping his skin with her teeth so that he could feel the points of her fangs, "this would be a good time to strengthen our blood link."

Her tongue continued moving down his body, and Rufus felt his own body respond and his fangs begin to emerge.

"And," said Serafina, "perhaps we can find another way to link at the same time." She began to caress him in a way that left him in no doubt of her meaning.

"Oh, yes!" he whispered. "Oh, God, yes!"

They made love purely as vampires, every sense impossibly heightened, every touch a molten pleasure that flowed over and through them and fused them together. In the midst of this excess of delight, Rufus felt Serafina's teeth pierce the vein above his left clavicle. He felt his blood well up, felt the soft pull of her lips as she drew his life force into her. At the same time, he felt his orgasm begin to take him over, and it seemed he might die of sheer ecstasy. Instinctively, he found a vein above Serafina's left breast, bit into it, and became engulfed in the twin raptures of giving and taking pleasure. He heard Serafina cry out, and his own voice join with hers in a sound barely human, the cry of two vampires exulting in a ritual as old as time.

Panting, they clung to one another, unwilling to release themselves from the spell they had wrought. For a long time they lay there, enjoying their closeness, licking the remains of blood from each other with slow, sensuous tongues, basking in the embers of the fire of their passion.

Later, they made love again, their shared blood binding them together until it seemed to Rufus they had truly become one. As he felt the strength of their bond, their minds and bodies working as one, he was certain they could overcome anything, so long as they were together.

\* \* \* \*

"Does it never stop raining here?" Rufus stared in disgust at the rain streaming down the parlour window. "And people say the English weather is bad!"

Serafina came to stand beside him. "Well, at least we won't be snowed in during winter."

Rufus, remembering his childhood at Ravenswood in Cumberland, flashed her a rueful grin. "True enough. Well, if we're going to hunt, I suppose we might as well get it over and done with, but I don't relish sitting in the rain for hours waiting for someone to leave Viviana's house."

"Then why don't we just come back here and practise for when we go to..." Serafina hesitated for a moment as though unwilling to give voice to their mission, "...to kill her?"

"You mean using both our minds together?"

"Yes, and using weapons. We'll need all the powers available to us, and to be able to work closely together, mind and body, if we hope to overcome her."

"But we haven't any weapons with which to practise – unless you count my paper knife."

"Then we'll improvise."

Serafina went to the fireplace and picked up the poker, thrusting with it as though it were a sword.

Rufus laughed. "All right, we'll do that when we get back. Let's get our coats."

As they walked towards town, Rufus recalled the previous night, and how they'd fed together, sharing the pleasure of drinking in blood and warmth and life, and later sharing the pleasure of drinking in each other, and he knew the memory of it would remain with him for as long as he lived, even to the end of time itself.

When they reached Grafton Gully, he and Serafina slipped down the bank and into the cemetery, and before long found what they sought: a vagrant couple curled up together against the bank where they had some small shelter from the rain. By mutual consent, Serafina took the man and Rufus the woman, a poor, bedraggled creature who smelled of gin.

After they had fed, Rufus pulled some coins from his pocket and dropped them into the bosom of the woman's gown. She looked as though she needed a decent meal, though he suspected the money would be used to obtain more gin.

They returned home then, and spent the rest of the night practising with their makeshift weapons until they felt satisfied with their ability to coordinate both movements and minds.

* * * *

The following night was fine, and Rufus and Serafina decided to watch first and hunt later.

"If luck favours us," said Serafina with a predatory smile, "we'll be able to combine the two."

A brisk breeze was tugging wisps of cloud across the sky as they walked to Epsom Avenue, and the full moon hung above the eastern horizon like a huge ball of orange light, washing everything with a subtle golden sheen.

Serafina and Rufus settled into their now familiar hiding place, focusing all their senses on the task at hand. They'd been there for about an hour when they saw the gates begin to open. Serafina took Rufus's hand, and he felt a cool, sharp energy flow between them like an electric charge. As they watched, the figure of a man emerged from the gateway and turned to close and lock the gates. Rufus stifled a gasp of recognition. It was the young Maori he'd seen with Serafina, the one called Tamati. A surge of fury coursed through him. Serafina absorbed it and fed it back to him as a heightening of his senses, so that he could hear the man's heartbeat and the blood flowing in his veins, could smell the warm, musky scent of him, although he was under Viviana's control and it wasn't possible to read his mind yet.

Tamati loped off along Epsom Avenue, unaware of the two shadows slipping though the darkness in his wake. He kept up a good pace, and had soon reached Newton, where he turned into Newtown Road, and then wound his way through several narrower, poorly lit streets where rough, down-at-heel cottages, shops, and the ubiquitous grog shops stood among areas of scrub. The stench was appalling, most likely from open drains or sewage ponds. Raucous noise emanated from the grog shops, and elsewhere dogs barked, babies cried, and people quarrelled and sang and conversed in rough tones. At length, Tamati entered a grog shop. Surmising that he would eventually leave again, Rufus and Serafina remained outside in the shadows. Overhead, the moon, now a butter-coloured disk, progressed across the sky trailing a train of clouds like chiffon draperies. After about half an hour, Tamati emerged from the grog shop in a waft of warmth and smoke and noise and alcohol fumes, and began to retrace his steps.

Rufus and Serafina followed him back along Mount Eden Road as far as the reserve next to the Mount Eden Stockade. They glanced at one another, deciding not to try to intercept him there, since Rufus had already used it with Elizabeth, and it would not do to risk arousing Viviana's suspicions. However, a short way further on, just as Tamati turned into Epsom Avenue, another area of scrub presented a further opportunity. Moving at full speed, they closed on him. As Rufus took hold of him, pinning his arms to his sides, Serafina knocked him unconscious with a blow to his head that carried the full weight of her anger. For a moment, it seemed she might have killed him, but a low groan reassured them. Together they dragged him into the bushes. By the time he was able to stand up again, he was in their power – for the time being at least.

One holding each arm, they marched him the few blocks to their house.

Rufus spoke to Serafina, mind to mind. *What are we going to do if Anton's at home?*

*If we take him to the garden shed,* came Serafina's reply, *it won't matter whether Anton's there or not.*

*But surely he'll know.*

*Oh yes, but that doesn't matter. He knows what we're planning to do – he just doesn't want anything to do with it himself.*

*We'll have to keep Tamati there until tomorrow, since we're planning to go to Viviana's during the day.*

*Serafina shrugged. If we tie him up well, we can keep him until we're ready to use him. And we can gag him too, to keep him quiet.*

*Rufus looked at Serafina. I had no idea you were so ruthless.*

Serafina returned his look, her eyes smouldering. *You forget what he did to me.*

They took Tamati straight out to the garden shed, a damp and musty place that had clearly not been used for some time. A variety of rusting garden implements hung from the walls. Along one side, beneath a dusty and cobweb-shrouded window, ran a bench cluttered with mouldering plant pots, seed boxes and more tools. Taking in its contents at a glance, Rufus ran back to the house to fetch a chair and something with which to bind and gag Tamati, while Serafina held him quiescent by mind control. He still looked groggy, and there was a red swelling on the side of his head where she had struck him. Rufus returned with a chair from the dining room and a couple of damask tablecloths, which he tore into strips, tying them together into longer strips. He sat Tamati down on the chair, realising anew just how handsome he was, with his dark skin and eyes, and his thick, black, curling hair. He looked strong and virile, too. No wonder he was Viviana's favourite. Serafina, unimpressed by his good looks, bound him tightly to the back of the chair with his arms at his sides and his legs tied to the chair legs.

When Tamati regained full consciousness, the first thing he saw was Serafina sitting in front of him on an old wooden crate and staring at him with undisguised loathing. His dark eyes opened wide with surprise, but he showed no fear. "You!" he exclaimed, struggling to loosen his bonds.

"There's no point in trying to free yourself." Serafina's voice was cold and hard. "If you do, I'll knock you out again."

"*You* knocked me out?" said Tamati, staring at her with scorn. "You? A woman?"

Serafina returned his look, and enquired with an arctic smile, "Would you like me to give you a demonstration?"

"Why have you brought me here?" he demanded, ignoring her offer.

"First," said Rufus, "tell us what you were doing in Newton?"

"He was collecting money for Viviana," said Serafina, her lip curling in distaste, "probably from brothels."

Tamati's expression confirmed this.

"How soon is she expecting delivery?" Rufus asked. Tamati said nothing, but directed a look of contempt at him. Rufus shrugged. "Have it your own way." He entered the man's mind to learn that Viviana had expected him back already, and that beneath his bravado, he was as terrified of her as he was enraptured by her.

Serafina spoke to Rufus, but her words were for Tamati's benefit. "Viviana will get her money – and her little pet – when we choose to deliver them. Meanwhile," she turned to Tamati with a predatory smile, "we have a more pressing matter to attend to."

For the first time, Tamati's fear reached his face. "What do you want from me?"

In reply, Serafina stared into his eyes until they went blank. Then she tore open his shirt at the neck. Rufus saw her fangs emerge, and felt his own begin to do likewise. A fierce elation coursed through him as he watched Serafina begin to feed, his mind so melded with hers that he felt every nuance of her experience. As soon as she had finished, Rufus took her place, trusting her to let him know when he'd drunk enough. They mustn't allow Tamati to grow too weak to recover by the time they needed his help with the next stage of their plan.

Their feeding over, Serafina tore off a piece of tablecloth, screwed it into a ball and stuffed it into the unconscious man's mouth, binding it tightly in place. Then, for good measure, they tied him, chair and all, to one sturdy leg of the wooden bench. Together they entered the man's mind and did what they could to prevent Viviana from regaining control of it.

As they walked back to the house, Rufus saw that the sky was beginning to lighten. "I suppose we shouldn't go to sleep," he said, "in case we don't wake again in time."

"You're right. It's important to attack Viviana in the middle of the day, when she'll be most deeply asleep."

"It's a long time to stay awake."

Serafina smiled at him. "Then we'll just have to find some

way to pass the time, won't we?"

# CHAPTER THIRTY-ONE

The sun rode high in an azure sky strewn with puffs of white cloud when Rufus and Serafina left the house, shivering both with fear and excitement. In the little shed, Tamati lolled in his chair, dozing fitfully. Shafts of sunlight shone through the dusty window, catching and gilding the motes of dust dancing in the air. Blinking in the glare, they shook their prisoner awake. Serafina, holding his face so he had no choice but to look into her eyes, soon rendered him quiescent so they could safely remove his gag and bonds and lead him outside.

As they walked along the sunlit street, one on either side of their captive, Rufus began to feel a profound unease that had nothing to do with his and Serafina's mission, nor with his lack of sleep. It was as though something deep within him was crying out for relief, for the comfort of darkness and sleep. He realised it was the daylight itself that was causing his discomfort. It was not that the sunlight was causing him any physical harm, but that his entire being was now attuned to darkness. Just as his vampiric eyes could see clearly in the dark, the daylight was confusing his mind so his vision seemed less defined. The light cascaded over everything so it resembled a blurred kaleidoscope. No wonder he felt disoriented. He could only be grateful the effects were not physical as well.

As they reached Viviana's house, they each took a firm grip on one of Tamati's arms and Serafina released him from her power. At first, he stared at them with surprise and fear in his eyes, then he drew himself up to his full height and looked straight ahead, stony faced and impassive, and opened the gate with steady hands. Rufus could not help admiring his ability to suppress his emotions and deal calmly with the situation at hand. He supposed it came from his warrior ancestry. The Maori had a reputation as fearsome fighters, and he knew from listening to his Uncle Sebastian, who had fought in Crimea, how important discipline and a cool head were in war.

Just as the night revealed its own dark palette to Rufus's sight, so the midday sun imparted an almost surreal quality. The broad expanses of grass seemed to glow like molten glass, and the flowers in their formal beds shone like jewels on black velvet. The darker hued stands of trees lining the walls overlooked all this brilliance like dour and vigilant guardians. Together with the rambling two-storeyed house at the end of the gravel driveway, it was like an English country estate in miniature, but without the human element. Here, no gardeners went about their work in the grounds, no horses whinnied in the stables, no dogs bounded down the driveway to greet them. And no birds sang. Silence lay over the house and its grounds like a shroud. It seemed the very presence of the ancient and powerful vampire had banished all signs of life, as though she exuded some baleful influence that clouded the minds of all who drew near, keeping her stronghold safe from the attentions of the outside world.

Rufus began to be very afraid. Until now, his anger towards Viviana and his love for Serafina had insulated him, but here, in the ominous calm of the vampire's refuge, he was suddenly all too aware of the danger they must face. He felt stifled, unable to breathe, almost unable to move one foot in front of the other.

Then he heard Serafina's voice in his mind, speaking softly, calmly. *Courage, Rufus. She's powerful, but not invulnerable.*

Rufus spoke back to her. *You're right. We have to believe we can defeat her. Together, we will defeat her.*

He took a deep breath and propelled Tamati along the driveway.

When they reached the porch, Tamati drew a key from his trouser pocket and opened the front door. The three of them stepped into the large, high-ceilinged vestibule Rufus had glimpsed previously. Tamati peered about him as though at any moment Viviana might appear to exact punishment. But nothing stirred. The only sound was the heavy ticking of a grandfather clock. The time was twenty-two minutes past noon.

Serafina moved towards a closed door, beckoning Rufus, who still had a firm grasp on Tamati, to follow. She stared around the spacious, opulently furnished drawing room in which she had first woken after her abduction. There was the plush chaise longue with its fat, velvet cushions, the chairs by the fireplace, the rich, oriental rugs on the polished floors. A shudder of fear ran through her, but she quickly suppressed it, taking care to remain withdrawn into herself. No hint of their presence must penetrate the veil of Viviana's torpor.

She turned to Tamati. "Where are the others?"

"I don't know. Perhaps they're sleeping, or out." Tamati's tone was defensive, but he was clearly afraid.

"Look at me," Serafina commanded. Reluctantly, Tamati obeyed. "You know where Viviana sleeps?" Tamati nodded. "Then show us."

Tamati cringed away from her in terror. Rufus gave him a shove and he began to move towards the door.

*Wait!* Rufus spoke into Serafina's mind. *The weapons!*

He strode to the glass-fronted cabinet that held Viviana's weapon collection and wrenched open the locked doors. Selecting a wicked looking stiletto and a bone-handled dagger with a slim, double-edged blade, he returned and offered both blades to Serafina. She chose the stiletto.

"Now," she said to Tamati, who looked as though he wanted to sink through the floorboards, "take us to Viviana."

Visibly trembling at the thought of rousing Viviana from her sleep, Tamati led Serafina and Rufus across the tiled vestibule and up the wide, curving staircase to the balustraded landing overlooking it. Serafina glanced along the passage leading to her former prison, then took a deep breath and looked away again. Tamati led them in the other direction, past a number of closed doors. As they made their silent way, one of the doors opened and Elizabeth appeared. Her eyes grew wide as she saw Rufus and Serafina. As she opened her mouth to speak, Serafina fixed her with a steady gaze. In seconds, the girl was under her control, and Serafina spoke into her mind.

*Don't be afraid, we won't harm you. Find all the others and take them down to the sitting room, and stay there quietly until we tell you otherwise. Do you understand?*

Elizabeth nodded, her seawater eyes empty of expression, and went to do Serafina's bidding.

At the end of the passage, Tamati pointed to a door that,

unlike the others, had an arched lintel like a Gothic window. Rufus realised it must be the entrance to the domed tower.

"She's in there." Tamati's voice was a barely audible, as though he feared Viviana would hear him, even in her death-like sleep.

He made to retreat, but Serafina took a firm grip on his arm and thrust him in front of her and Rufus. Rufus grasped his other arm. Neither he nor Serafina said a word, so withdrawn into themselves, yet so closely linked that they acted as one from an instinct far deeper than thought. Serafina reached past Tamati, slowly and silently turned the brass doorknob and pushed open the heavy door. She placed a forefinger against Tamati's mouth and glared fiercely at him. He nodded, and made no sound as they entered an octagonal room darkened by heavy curtains drawn across the tall windows that took up the whole of one wall.

A glance around the room revealed an elegant oak dressing table and wardrobe, an ornate, tiled fireplace with expensive-looking vases and silver candlesticks adorning its mantelpiece and, opposite this, a massive oak bed with carved bedposts and headboard. On the bed, beneath a crimson quilted-velvet coverlet, lay the unconscious form of Viviana Alexandreu, her chalk-white face seeming almost phosphorescent in the gloom, her hair spread out in waves of night on the snowy pillowcase. Even as she slept, Rufus and Serafina could sense about her an aura of darkness.

Rufus looked at Serafina. Her face was a mask as she sought to control her fear. Together they crept towards the ancient vampire, daggers raised, every sense alert and focused. Released from their hold, Tamati tried to flee, but terror seemed to immobilise him and he sagged against the wall by the open door, his hands clamped over his mouth as though to prevent a scream from bursting forth.

Reaching the bed, Serafina stared down at Viviana's apparently lifeless form. With infinite care she pulled back the bedclothes and lifted her stiletto high above the vampire's breast, all her hatred and loathing pouring out of her and into the blade.

Viviana's eyes snapped open.

Instinctively, Serafina drew back. Viviana sat up, fixing her with eyes like bottomless pits of darkness, and snarled deep in her throat. Serafina stared at her in horror.

Viviana schooled her face into a mockery of a smile. "Why, Serafina," she said in a caricature of seductiveness, apparently oblivious of both Serafina's expression and the stiletto in her hand, "you've returned to me after all. I knew you'd be unable to stay away."

There was a soft thud behind them as Tamati sank to his knees on the floor. In an instant, Viviana was at his side, her eyes like burning coals as she leaned over him.

"My money," she hissed, her voice dripping menace.

Tamati tugged a package from his coat pocket and held it out to her with trembling hands.

Snatching the package, Viviana pulled him to his feet and began to caress him, sliding her hands inside his shirt and over his smooth skin, murmuring, "So pretty, and so strong – for a human. Tell me, Tamati," she purred, rubbing her cheek, catlike, against his, and nipping at his earlobe with her teeth and the tip of her tongue, "have I treated you well?" The young man nodded, beginning to relax beneath her touch. "Yes, my pretty boy, I've given you luxury and pleasure beyond your wildest dreams, have I not?" Tamati nodded again, his eyes fixed on hers in adoration as her hand moved up to caress his cheek and neck. "And this is how you repay me?" Viviana's voice was suddenly like the hiss of a snake about to strike. She thrust the package into his face and then dashed it to the floor. "I should have had this yesterday!"

"But—" Tamati began, his gaze shifting to Rufus and Serafina, his eyes imploring their intercession.

But Viviana had already closed one icy hand hard about his neck and lifted him from the floor as though he were a rag doll. A rattling sound came from his throat and blood and saliva frothed from his lips and dribbled down his chin. His eyes bulged in his head and his hands scrabbled feebly at the fingers that held him fast, his legs jerking like those of a man hanging on a gibbet. Viviana, snarling, shook him like a dog worrying a rabbit. There was a sharp crack and his body went limp. Viviana stared at him for a moment in apparent disappointment. Then she flung him across the room like a child discarding a broken toy. Tamati's body struck the fireplace with a moist crunch and slid down onto the hearth. Blood seeped from his mouth and nose and ears, staining the polished tiles. An oriental porcelain vase, dislodged by the impact of his body, toppled from the mantelpiece and shattered on the hearth beside him, his blood staining its shards dark crimson.

With the air of one having dispensed with minor, but necessary business, Viviana turned to Rufus and Serafina, smoothing her nightgown, seeming unconcerned by the blood now staining its delicate white lawn.

"I do apologise for that distraction. Ah—" she turned to Rufus with a mocking curtsey, "—so this is the delightful

Rufus." She ran her eyes over him in a way that made him feel she could see right through his clothing. "Yes, I can quite see the attraction, though I prefer them a little more rugged, myself." She turned her gaze on Serafina. "How remiss of you, my dear, not to introduce us. Still, it's good to see you've both come to your senses. As I explained to you, Serafina, all this—" She spread her arms wide, as though to encompass the entire estate, "—all this can now be yours, and Rufus's, of course, since he's chosen to join you."

"Oh, yes," Serafina said, her voice harsh with fury. "Ours at a price!"

"But such a small price!" Viviana's voice was almost a purr.

"To betray our kin?" said Rufus. "You call that a small price?"

"Ah, but I'm also your kin, am I not? Besides, consider the benefits: a beautiful home, never to have to hunt in back alleys and feed from the dregs of society – to be safe from human prejudice..."

"To be slaves to a monster!" Serafina retorted, her voice pulsating with disgust and loathing.

"Not slaves." Viviana affected hurt. "No, no, I shall be your protector, and all I ask in return is that you deliver me Anton Springer."

"So you can kill him?" cried Serafina. "I won't do it! Neither of us will! He's worth twenty of you!"

Viviana's features hardened. Her eyes took on a feral cunning. "Why then," she murmured, "as we used to say in the old days, let the games begin. But do you really imagine you can overcome *me*?"

As she spoke, she began to circle them like a wolf eyeing

its prey, her gaze never leaving them for a second. Instinctively, Rufus and Serafina stood back-to-back, weapons at the ready, watching for the slightest opening in Viviana's defences, the faintest flagging of her concentration. Power and malice emanated from her in waves, sickening in their intensity, alien in their nature, even to Rufus and Serafina. It was an effort not to succumb as she sought to batter them into submission.

There came the sound of footsteps on the stairs. Both Rufus and Serafina started in surprise. Viviana snarled like a wild beast, turning towards the sound.

The moment her back was towards them, Serafina and Rufus literally threw themselves upon her, striking at her with their weapons. Viviana shook them off so that Rufus's dagger merely glanced off her right shoulder, ripping the fabric of her nightgown but leaving her flesh unscathed. But Serafina clung to her, driving her stiletto into the vampire's back beneath the shoulder blade, grunting with satisfaction as bright blood soaked through her gown.

Viviana shrieked like a wounded animal and rounded on Serafina, her lips drawn back to expose yellowed fangs. Her eyes blazed with fury. She had become a true predator, driven purely by instinct and the need to kill. They could expect no mercy, no human feeling at all. They were her enemies, and thus her prey. For the first time, Rufus understood how Viviana could have dedicated four centuries to pursuing Springer. He also knew she would never stop until one of them was destroyed. To overcome her, they must cast aside their own humanity, at least for now, and meet her on her own terms. He could only hope they'd be able to return again afterwards.

The ancient vampire had turned so swiftly that she had torn the stiletto from Serafina's hand, leaving it embedded in her back. Now she shook herself like a dog in a vain attempt to dislodge it, and then, apparently deciding to ignore it, launched herself straight at Serafina. Serafina threw herself to one side, but Viviana fell upon her, knocking her to the floor, hands and teeth reaching for her throat.

With a cry, Rufus rushed at her. Viviana threw back one arm to fend him off. Its force knocked the dagger from his grasp, though the blade bit deeply into her hand. She scarcely seemed to notice, returning her attention to Serafina, who was struggling in vain to free herself. Rufus, half-demented with fear and rage, yanked the stiletto from Viviana's back and lifted his arm to stab her once more.

"Stand back, Rufus!" a voice called from the doorway. "This one is mine, I believe."

Incredulous, Rufus turned to see Springer. Immaculately clad as usual, he stood in a shaft of light that shone through the doorway, making his pale hair gleam like mother of pearl. A faint, mocking smile curved his lips, but his eyes were granite shot with fire.

Forgetting Serafina, Viviana leapt up to face Springer with a triumphant snarl. A hiss escaped her lips, as though she had tried to utter his name but was no longer capable of human speech.

"So, Viviana." Springer spread his hands as though offering himself to his enemy. "It seems your long search is at an end."

The sound Viviana uttered was part human, part wild beast.

She flew at Springer, fangs bared, arms stretched out

towards him, her long fingers curved into claws. Just as swiftly, Springer was beyond her reach. For breathless moments they circled one another, Springer always with that mocking smile on his lips. As he doubtless intended, this drove Viviana into a frenzy of vengeful rage. Yet, like the feral creature she now was, she remained focused on her prey. Her eyes never left Springer, watching for the slightest hint of an opening.

So intent was she on her ancient enemy that she failed to notice Serafina swiftly roll beyond her reach and get to her feet. She did not see Rufus rush to Serafina's side, did not sense them as they conducted a rapid mental exchange and then left the room.

Moments later they returned, each bearing a sword whose honed steel blade gleamed in the dim light. Serafina carried a third sword, its blade slender but deadly sharp. Mentally, she called to Springer and threw it to him. Without taking his eyes from Viviana, Springer reached out as the sword arced towards him and caught it. Then Serafina and Rufus ran at Viviana from behind, screaming like savages, their swords raised to strike her. Momentarily distracted by their cries, Viviana's gaze wavered from Springer.

It was only for a fraction of a second, but it was enough.

Springer leapt. His sword flashed, struck, buried itself in Viviana's breast. She sank to her knees clutching at the blade, heedless of the cuts to her hands and the blood welling up to stain the bright steel. Then she raised her arms, her fingers hooking like claws as she sought to grasp at Springer as he stood over her.

"Curse you, Anton Springer!" she rasped through bloody lips.

"No, Viviana, it's your own curse that has turned on you at last. I killed von Dunkel because what he did was evil. Out of sheer malice, he condemned me to an existence I neither sought nor could escape. Merely to feed his own hubris, he imprisoned me forever, and who knows how many others besides. He was a true child of yours, Viviana Alexandreu, and in killing him I did the world a favour."

"Fool!" Viviana gasped through her pain. "In—four hundred—years, you—have—learned—nothing."

"On the contrary," Springer replied. "I've learned that even though I'm a vampire, I can still do some good in the world, or at least refrain from doing evil. I've learned to save lives by controlling the appetites foisted on me by your kin. I've—"

"Spare me—the—sanctimony," Viviana rasped. Her words gurgled in her throat as blood bloomed in her mouth, spilling crimson petals over her ashen skin. The fire in her eyes had dulled. Already they had begun to appear lifeless, even as she struggled against the ending of her long existence. With an effort, she managed to wrest the sword from her breast and fling it from her. She clutched at the wound with both hands, dark, viscous blood flowing between her fingers. She stared at it as though unable to believe what was happening, and then up at Springer. Her bloodstained face was a mask of hatred.

Springer looked down at her, his features impassive. "I'll spare you further pain," he said, "and that's a great deal more than you deserve."

He turned to Serafina. Without a word, she held out her sword to him.

The second Springer's eyes left her, Viviana, with a

supreme effort, dragged herself to her feet. Blood still leaked sluggishly from her chest wound, but it was already beginning to heal. With a grimace of pain, she stooped and caught up Springer's sword. Rufus called out a warning, but by the time it had left his lips, Viviana had launched herself at Springer, wielding the sword as though it were a spear. It caught Springer on his sword arm, drawing blood and knocking his weapon from his hand. With a triumphant shriek, Viviana raised her arm for another attack. Springer leapt back, barely avoiding the ferocious blow she aimed at him. As he stooped to retrieve his sword, Viviana sprang at him, knocking him to the floor, letting her own sword fall as her blood-soaked fingers sought his throat. Locked together they rolled on the floor, Viviana snarling like a crazed animal. She was smaller and lighter than Springer, but her fury seemed to lend her strength. The wound in Springer's arm bled freely, and his breath came in laboured gasps as he sought to keep Viviana's fingers from tightening about his neck.

Serafina shot a look of desperation at Rufus. Both daggers and the swords used by Springer and Viviana still lay on the floor, but it was impossible to reach them without the risk of distracting Springer and putting him in further danger. The only available weapon was the one in Rufus's hands.

Swallowing his fear and revulsion, Rufus raised it in both hands and brought it down with all his strength on Viviana's back. As it bit into her right shoulder, he heard the sharp steel crunch through her shoulder blade and her arm fell limply at her side. With a roar, she sprang up and turned on him, her teeth bared in a snarl that might equally have expressed pain or rage. Rufus drew back a pace to ready his sword for another blow.

But Springer, who had rolled out of harm's way and snatched up his sword as he leapt to his feet, was there before him, striking Viviana a savage blow across the back. The vampire collapsed to the floor, her face writhing in agony, blood pouring from her crushed shoulder and the gash on her back. Rasping sounds came from her blood-caked lips as she tried to speak. But she could only stare, incredulous, as Springer raised his sword above his head.

"No!" cried Rufus, raising his own blade and advancing on Viviana. Both Springer and Serafina turned to stare at him. With an effort, Rufus swallowed the bile that rose in his throat. "I have to do this," he said, "for Serafina, for failing her when she most needed me, and for doubting her love." He turned to Serafina and, like a mediaeval tourney knight to his lady, bowed his head for a moment, saluting her with his sword.

The sound that left Viviana's throat might have been a mocking laugh or a sob. Gritting his teeth, Rufus raised the blade high above his head and brought it down across her throat with all the strength he could summon. Her head rolled back from her body, her eyes staring as though in unbelief. Crimson blood gushed from her neck, describing a brief, vivid arc as Viviana's long life seeped away until it was nothing more than a darkening stain on the thick carpet.

As they watched, the dead vampire's skin shrank back over her bones, sagging into her cheeks and taking on the greyish hue of ash or mould. Then it began to crumble away before their gaze, exposing bones that in moments became bleached and pitted like those of an ancient skeleton.

Rufus felt his breath congeal in his throat. He wanted to

turn away, but could not. His eyes, fixed on the appalling sight, would not close, would not obey his will.

He felt a hand on his shoulder, and Serafina's voice spoke gently to him. "It's over, Rufus. Her insane appetites will never hurt anyone again. You've set us free."

Rufus turned to her, tears carving tracks in his blood-spattered face, his voice catching in his throat. "I did it for you, Serafina. I was a fool for so long, and a coward, too, but your strength and courage showed me what I should be. I know I can't hope to measure up to you and Anton, but—"

Tears filled Serafina's eyes as she reached out to place her finger against his lips. "Rufus, true bravery is doing what's right, even when you're afraid. You have nothing to measure up to."

Springer came to stand before them. For some moments he stared down at the floor, for once seeming uncertain what to say. Then he lifted his head and took a deep breath. "Old habits can come to seem impossible to break, but I finally realised you were right, both of you, and it would have been unconscionable of me to desert you. I beg you to accept my deepest apologies for taking so long to come to my senses. I owe you both a debt of gratitude that I doubt I can ever repay. I can only hope you'll find it in your hearts to forgive my—my weakness. I'm not sure I'll ever forgive myself, but I promise you I'll try to make it up to you, somehow."

Rufus and Serafina said nothing, their hearts too full for words, but Serafina put her arms around Springer and kissed his bloodstained cheek. When she released him, Springer clasped Rufus's hands in his.

"You two go and get some sleep," he said. "I'll deal with things here. It's the least I can do to begin repaying my debt."

Rufus nodded. He tried to speak, but no words would come. Serafina went to him and took his hand.

"Come," she said, "let's go home."

Together, they walked out of the room and down the stairs, and out into the bright day.

## Other Books by Lila Richards

### Restitutions of the Blood

In 1890, when Alex Randall returns from university to his ancestral home of Shillington Hall, he finds his father remarried, less than a year after his mother's death. Dismay turns to anger when a son, Oliver, is born. Convinced the new Lady Randall means to steal his inheritance, Alex flees to London, where he meets and befriends Henri de Saint Clair, a charming, but enigmatic Frenchman. When Alex's friend Charles becomes involved in an illegal duel, and both parties are killed, Alex finds himself on the run from the law, and obliged to leave England. In Paris, he renews his friendship with the still strangely elusive Henri. After a series of misadventures that lead him to the very depths of Parisian society, Henri rescues Alex and restores him to health by means of a mysterious 'restorative' but, before long, Alex's determination to discover the truth about his friend plunges him into a world darker - and more addictive - than anything he could have imagined.

### Vicious Circle

When a listener to The Psychic Connection radio programme is emotionally blackmailed by self-styled spiritual teacher Bob Ferris, resident panellists Joss Cherry and Isabel Sinclair decide to investigate. Meanwhile, the remains of a woman's body are found in a creek-bed in Queensland, Australia. Detective Sergeant Declan Kelly's search for

Richard Forster, the last person to see her alive, leads him to communes in Queensland and New Zealand and the flesh-pots of Auckland's infamous Karangahape Road, until his trail meets that of the Psychic Connection panel. Their investigations culminate in a dramatic confrontation at the disused church where Ferris attempts to implement his bizarre plans to give birth to the New Aeon.

## The Tarot Murders

When a series of bizarre murders based on major trumps of the Tarot rocks the usually staid city of Christchurch, the panel members of radio show The Psychic Connection are drawn into the case when it seems panel member James Myerson may be involved – or even the murderer. Detective Sergeant Declan Kelly (see: Vicious Circle) arrives in Christchurch, on sick leave after being wounded during a stakeout in Queensland, and adds his weight to the Psychic Connection panel's investigation of what the press is calling the Tarot Murders. The murderer's calling card, The Magician, left with each new victim, offers a sinister clue to the killer's identity – if only the panel can solve it in time to prevent the death of one of its own members.

# ABOUT THE AUTHOR

Lila Richards lives in one of the leafy suburbs of Christchurch, New Zealand, with two black cats. She works part-time as a sub-editor and proofreader for the New Zealand Meteorological Service. As well as writing, Lila reads eclectically, sews vintage clothes, and collects things, in particular old movies, owls, Egyptiana, and art deco paraphernalia. From time to time she enters the Middle Ages via the Society for Creative Anachronism (an international mediaeval re-creation group), where she transmogrifies into a ninth-century small-holder's widow living in the west of Ireland, and has attained the rank of Baroness.

www.ingramcontent.com/pod-product-compliance
Lightning Source LLC
Chambersburg PA
CBHW021527250626
47154CB00006BA/2011